Jo Ann Brown has always loved stories with happily-ever-after endings. A former military officer, she is thrilled to have the chance to write stories about people falling in love. She is also a photographer and travels with her husband of more than thirty years to places where she can snap pictures. They have three children and live in Florida. Drop her a note at joannbrownbooks.com.

After thirty-five years as a nurse, **Patricia Davids** hung up her stethoscope to become a full-time writer. She enjoys spending her free time visiting her grandchildren, doing some long-overdue yard work and traveling to research her story locations. She resides in Wichita, Kansas. Pat always enjoys hearing from her readers. You can visit her online at patriciadavids.com.

JO ANN BROWN

An Amish Arrangement

&

PATRICIA DAVIDS

An Amish Noel

LOVE INSPIRED BOOKS

Recycling programs for this product may not exist in your area.

ISBN-13: 978-1-335-47006-5

An Amish Arrangement and An Amish Noel

Copyright © 2018 by Harlequin Books S.A.

The publisher acknowledges the copyright holders of the individual works as follows:

An Amish Arrangement
Copyright © 2017 by Jo Ann Ferguson

An Amish Noel
Copyright © 2015 by Patricia MacDonald

www.Harlequin.com

Printed in U.S.A.

CONTENTS

AN AMISH ARRANGEMENT

Jo Ann Brown

For Leon Barkley, one of my first friends.
Together we learned softball from my dad
and basketball from your brother.
Thanks for your help with my real estate questions
and making this story possible.
A special thank-you to Tina, Melissa and Dina,
who have shared my love for the
Stoltzfus family right from the beginning,
and made each book better.

Then the Lord put forth his hand,
and touched my mouth. And the Lord said
unto me, Behold, I have put my words in thy mouth.
—*Jeremiah* 1:9

Chapter One

Harmony Creek Hollow, New York

The day had started out as Jeremiah Stoltzfus had planned.

It didn't stay that way after a woman dropped into his arms.

For most men, playing the hero for a beautiful woman would have been a dream come true. But most men didn't discover that woman trespassing on a tumbledown farm in northern New York. A farm Jeremiah couldn't wait to call his own.

He'd been invited by the current owner to visit when he reached Harmony Creek. In a couple of days the farm would be his.

At dawn Jeremiah had left his family's home in Paradise Springs, Pennsylvania. He was joining others to build a new Amish settlement near the Vermont border. He'd made arrangements during the past few months, purchasing the farm based on a few photographs sent by his Realtor. After saying goodbye to his *mamm*, brothers and sisters along with their spouses and *kinder* and

knowing it was unlikely he'd see them again for a year, he'd taken a train north to Albany. There, he was met by a van, which drove him the last fifty miles to Harmony Creek Hollow.

The valley edging the creek was set outside the tiny town of Salem. Rolling hills covered with trees and meadows would support dairy farms for the Amish families moving into the area.

The owner of the sixty-acre farm he was buying, Rudy Bamberger, had invited him to stop by before the closing in two days. Jeremiah suspected the old man wanted to size him up first.

Rudy had already asked him a lot of questions through Kitty Vasic, Jeremiah's Realtor. Personal questions that Kitty told Jeremiah he didn't have to answer. However, Jeremiah had no problem with the questions, because the old man had been selling his family's farm. Jeremiah had written a long letter, explaining his background and his plans for the farm and his future. His answers must have satisfied Rudy, because the old man accepted his offer on the farm the next day.

When he'd arrived, Jeremiah had carried his two bags as he crossed the snowy yard past neglected barns. No tracks had been visible. Nothing had gone in or out of the big barn since the last snowstorm. Allowing himself a quick glance at the other outbuildings, which needed, as he'd known, a lot of repairs, he'd walked through the freshly fallen snow to the main house.

The large rambling home had a porch running along the front and the side facing the barn. Through a stand of spruce trees, he could see another house, where a tenant family once would have lived. The few remaining

shutters hung awkwardly at the windows, a sure sign the house was a fixer-upper, too.

He looked forward to beginning—and finishing—the tasks ahead of him as he made the farm viable again. His skills as a woodworker would be useful while renovating the barns and the sap house near the sugar bush farther up the hill.

Climbing onto the porch, he'd set down his bags before he knocked snow off his well-worn work boots. He'd gone directly to the side door. Rudy had told him to use that door when he arrived.

"Don't knock," the most recent letter had instructed him. "My ears don't work like they used to, and I don't want you standing in the cold while you bang and bang. Come in and give a shout."

He'd thrown the door open. "Rudy, are you here?"

A shriek had come from close to the ceiling. He'd looked up to see a ladder wobbling. A dark-haired woman stood at the very top, her arms windmilling.

He leaped into the small room as she fell. After years of being tossed shocks of corn and hay bales, he caught her easily. He jumped out of the way, holding her to him as the ladder crashed to the linoleum floor. His black wool hat tumbled off his head and rolled toward the wall.

"Oh, my!" gasped the woman.

She was, he noted because her face was close to his, very pretty. Her pleated *kapp* was flat unlike the heart-shaped ones his sisters wore. Beneath it, her hair was so black it gleamed with bluish fire in the fading sunlight coming through the door and tall windows. Her brown eyes were large with shock in her warmly tanned face, where a few freckles emphasized her high cheekbones.

She wore a pale pink dress with white and green flowers scattered across it in a subtle pattern. No Amish woman from Paradise Springs would use such fabric. It must be allowed in the new settlement along Harmony Creek. What else would be different here?

But first things first.

"Are you okay?" he asked, not surprised she wasn't the only one who sounded breathless. His heart had slammed against his chest when he saw her teetering. And from the moment he'd looked into her lustrous eyes, taking a deep breath had seemed impossible.

"I'm fine. I had just a little farther to go. Just a little…" Her voice trailed away as the shuddering ladder, which had landed on its side, clattered to the floor.

Jeremiah frowned. There was nothing on the wall to prevent her from falling. He saw the ruined wallpaper and chipped crown molding along with scraps of paper she'd already pulled off were piled on the floor. Why was she tearing off wallpaper in Rudy's house?

"Who are you?" he asked at the same time she did.

"I'm Jeremiah Stoltzfus," he answered. "You are…?"

"Mercy Bamberger." Her face shifted into a polite smile, and he guessed she'd collected her wits that had been scattered by fear. "Thanks for catching me."

"Why are you here?"

Instead of answering, she said, "You can put me down."

Jeremiah was astonished his curiosity about why she was in what would be his house had let him forget—for a second—that he was still cradling her in his arms. He set her on her feet, but caught her by the elbow when she trembled like a slim branch in a thunderstorm.

Hearing uneven thumps upstairs and hoping they

heralded Rudy's arrival, he steered her to the left. There, a staircase was half-hidden behind a partially closed door. Seating her on the bottom step, he picked up his hat as he asked, "Are you all right?"

"I am."

He didn't believe her, because her skin had a gray tint and her voice quivered. He wouldn't push her, because he guessed she was embarrassed by the circumstances. But one question remained: What was Mercy Bamberger doing in his house?

"Bamberger?" he asked aloud. "Like Rudy Bamberger?"

"Yes. Do you know my grandfather?"

Well, that explained who she was and why she was in the house. Glancing up the stairs, his eyes widened when he saw a shadow slip across the top. It was far too small for a grown man and appeared to have four legs.

He watched, saying nothing as he realized the silhouette belonged to a *kind*. A little girl, who looked about seven years old, had braided hair as black as Mercy's. She leaned on metal crutches with cuffs to go around her skinny arms. Her legs were encased in plastic and Velcro from the tops of her black sneakers to her knobby knees. Who was she?

As if he'd asked the question aloud, the little girl cried, "Mommy!" Rushing at a pace that forced his heart into his throat again, because he feared she'd fall, the *kind* flung her arms around Mercy's neck. "Are you okay?"

"I'm fine," Mercy reassured her.

The *kind* glanced at him with a scowl. "I heard the ladder fall and—"

"I'm fine, Sunni." She hugged the little girl. "Jeremiah kept me from getting hurt."

"Who?"

"Jeremiah." Mercy pushed herself to her feet and swung the little girl off the steps. She kept herself between the *kind* and him, showing she didn't trust him though he'd saved her from a broken bone or worse. "He's Jeremiah." Without looking at him, she added, "Jeremiah, this is my daughter, Sunni."

Again he fought not to ask the questions battering at his lips. The *kind* was unquestionably Asian, and her eyes, like Mercy's, glistened like dark brown mud in a sun-washed puddle. She also wore plain clothing with a small print.

Comprehension struck him. Mercy and her daughter weren't Amish. They dressed like the Mennonite women who lived near Paradise Springs. He searched his mind, but couldn't recall if his Realtor had mentioned anything about Rudy living plain. He glanced up at the electric light hanging from the ceiling. Some plain folks used electricity.

Too many questions needed answers.

Right away.

"Hi, Sunni," he said, because he didn't want to upset the little girl or her *mamm* more.

She aimed another frown at him before turning her back on him. When she didn't answer him, Mercy asked the *kind* why she'd been upstairs. He thought she was dismayed the little girl had gone on the stairs by herself until Mercy said, "Be extra careful. Don't forget the floors aren't safe."

"I stayed away from those, Mommy." Sunni raised her left crutch and tapped the floor beside her. "I do that

to check before I go in." Without a pause, she asked, "Can I have a cookie?"

"One," Mercy said with a smile. "Put the bag clip on after you get your cookie."

"Okaaaay," Sunni replied in the same tone Jeremiah had used as a *kind* when his own *mamm* said something he deemed obvious.

He smiled, but again the little girl acted as if he were invisible before she drew her arms from the cuffs on the crutches. Leaning them against the wall, she hurried through a doorway to the right. He guessed it must lead to the kitchen.

His grin vanished as he glanced around the room. Rudy called it his everything room. Hooks on the wall showed where coats, hats and bonnets could be hung. The bare floor was scraped from years of barn boots on it, and the tattered wallpaper was a grubby white. It might once have been a brighter color. The room was furnished with a rickety table and a battered sofa covered with a worn blanket. A desk had a book under one leg to keep it steady on the sloping floor. The interior of the house was in worse condition than the outside. The photographs sent by the Realtor had been misleading.

Had he failed to examine them closely enough in his eagerness to buy the farm and get started on making his dream come true? No, he'd peered at each picture through a magnifying glass to discover every detail. He knew the kitchen cabinets were painted dull brown, and there was electricity in the house. He planned to remove the latter as soon as the papers were signed.

Jeremiah picked up the ladder and raised it against the wall again. Checking it was solidly in place, he looked at Mercy. He was curious why she was peeling

paper off the wall in what would be his house. He could
understand if she wanted to take one of the pictures of
the farm hanging on a fake brick wall behind the desk,
because the farm was her *grossdawdi*'s. In the silence,
the *tick-tock* of a wall clock in the kitchen was loud.

Jeremiah appraised the room again. He intended to
use it for the farm's office, as he guessed Rudy had.
It was one plan among the many he had. His broth-
ers teased him about having to have every detail set in
place before he acted, but trying to find knots in a piece
of wood before he began working on it had kept him
from wasting time when building a piece of furniture.
Being as cautious in his other endeavors seemed wise.

Though he knew, too well, the best of plans could
fall apart. He'd thought his future was set with Emmar-
ita Kramer, but she'd jumped the fence and married an
Englisch guy she'd met at an auction Jeremiah had taken
her to. She never broke the courtship off with Jeremiah,
just left. He should forgive her and forget his shock,
but when he hadn't been able to do either, he'd decided
on a clean start in the new Harmony Creek settlement.

Hearing a throat cleared and knowing Mercy was
trying to get his attention, he turned. She was shorter
than he'd realized. The top of her head barely reached
his shoulder. As she stuck several vagrant strands of
black hair beneath her pleated *kapp*, she regarded him
coolly. She was, he could tell from the set of her taut
lips, as curious about him as her daughter had been.

He had a lot of things he wanted to ask her, too, but
he waited for her to speak first.

She took one step, then another toward him, though
she was at a disadvantage because she had to tilt her
head to meet his eyes. Then, seeing the determination

in them, he wondered if she saw her height as a liability or a way to surprise those who underestimated her.

"You never answered my question," she said.

"Which one?" He couldn't remember what she'd asked him, and he refused to be put on the defensive in what would be his own home.

"The important one. What are you doing here?"

"I came to see Rudy Bamberger." He frowned. "You said he's your *grossdawdi*."

She nodded.

"Then I'm surprised he didn't tell you I'd be coming here today."

"Why?"

He didn't think she was being cagey on purpose. Until now, she'd been straightforward. "He invited me to come and look around."

She shook her head. "I don't understand why."

"Didn't he tell you he's selling me his farm?"

Mercy Bamberger was shocked speechless. Had she hit her head when she'd dropped into Jeremiah Stoltzfus's strong arms after trying to grab another strip of wall-paper? She'd made a mess of this conversation from the get-go.

With the ancient Adirondacks to the west and the gentle Green Mountains to the east, the farm had been a haven for her from the first time she'd come to visit the man she called Grandpa Rudy. It offered the very thing she'd lost and didn't think she'd ever find again. Home. How desperate she'd been for a sanctuary! And how precious it seemed as the promise she'd held within her heart for the past decade was being fulfilled.

She couldn't mess it up. Already she'd made the mis-

take of not keeping a closer eye on Sunni. Her daughter
had been born with a congenital curiosity not dimin-
ished by her physical challenges. Mercy's determination
that the little girl should do anything a regular kid could
allowed Sunni to indulge her quick and inquiring mind.
Telling Sunni not to investigate the rooms upstairs be-
cause the floors were unsafe must have convinced her
to find out how dangerous they were.

Mercy was letting herself get distracted by a hand-
some stranger who appeared to be a few years older than
her twenty-five years. His bright blue eyes that had been
shadowed by his black wool hat identified him as one
of the Amish farmers moving into the hollow. Grandpa
Rudy had told her about the new settlement in one of
his letters. He'd been writing to her every week since
she was eleven years old, the year she'd been adopted
by his son and daughter-in-law and given a chance to
have a new life and the loving family she'd feared she'd
never have again.

She was startled how far up she had to look to meet
Jeremiah's eyes. Few Amish men she'd met had been as
tall as he was. If his ruddy hair hadn't been cut in the
plain style and he wasn't wearing a simple light blue
shirt along with black suspenders and broadfall trou-
sers beneath his black coat, she wouldn't have guessed
this very good-looking man was Amish.

Scolding herself, she recalled how Graham Rapp
was easy on the eyes, too, but he'd broken her heart by
showing how much a "mama's boy" he was by choos-
ing his mother when Mercy refused to be second. She
must not let herself be beguiled by an attractive man
again. Not when so much was on the line with her plans

for the farm and the changes it could make in many young lives.

But the Amish were well-known for their honesty. So why was Jeremiah talking nonsense about Grandpa Rudy selling him the farm?

"I think you're mistaken," she said, hoping her voice didn't quake with the strong emotions rushing through her like lightning in a summer sky. "My grandfather didn't mention anything about selling Come Along Farm."

"Come Along Farm?"

"That's the name he gave the farm when I was little. He urged us to come along and keep up with him while he did chores, so we called it Come Along Farm."

"He didn't tell you he's selling me the farm?"

"No!"

"I'm sorry to take you by surprise," he said gently, "but I'll be closing the day after tomorrow."

"Impossible!" Her voice squeaked, and she took a steadying breath. Sounding as young as Sunni wouldn't help. And she didn't want her raised voice to bring her daughter from the kitchen to investigate. The little girl was upset enough already to have to leave their Mennonite community and Mercy's parents in central New York, and Mercy hadn't missed the glares Sunni had shot at Jeremiah. When she and Graham ended their ill-advised engagement, her daughter had been caught up in the aftermath and no longer trusted men she didn't know. Mercy's attempts to reassure Sunni that the little girl had nothing to do with the breakup hadn't helped.

"It's not impossible. I've got the paperwork in my suitcase on the porch. If you want to see it—"

"I don't have interest in seeing what can't be legit-

imate. It sounds as if someone has played a horrible prank on you, Jeremiah. I'm sorry." She was, because she guessed he'd traveled for hours or days to get there. "But the farm's not for sale."

He opened his mouth to protest, then closed it. Taking a deep breath, he released it. In a calm tone she doubted she could emulate, he said, "There's no sense in arguing. Why don't you get your *grossdawdi*, and we'll settle this?"

"I can't."

"Why not?"

She blinked on sudden tears. "Because he's dead."

When Jeremiah's face became ashen, Mercy wondered if she should tell him to take a seat. It must have been seconds, but it felt like a year before he asked, "Rudy is dead?"

"Yes." She swallowed hard past the lump in her throat.

"When?"

"Last week. It was a massive heart attack. He was buried the day before yesterday." As she spoke, she found it impossible to believe the vital, vigorous man was gone.

Rudy Bamberger had been more than a grandfather to her. He'd been her best friend, the one who had welcomed her into the family after her life had hit bottom. Rudy hadn't been a replacement for *Abuelita*, her beloved grandmother who had raised her when she was called Mercedes in a tiny apartment in the Bronx. *Abuelita* had died two weeks after Mercy's tenth birthday, and everything in Mercy's life had changed, including her name. Yet, Grandpa Rudy had made her feel as if she belonged among the people who were so

different from those she'd known in the city. His love had been unconditional, and she'd returned it.

"I'm sorry," Jeremiah said with sincerity.

She wished he'd been trite instead of genuine, because one thing hadn't changed. He wanted to take away the farm that was her final gift from Grandpa Rudy. How often she'd sat on the old man's lap and talked about taking care of the apple orchard or making maple syrup as he did each spring or what color she would paint the big bedroom! He'd humored her, even when her paint choices went from pink to purple to red and black over the years.

But Jeremiah was saying her grandfather had intended to sell the farm to him.

"But Grandpa Rudy told me the farm would be mine after he passed away."

"Then why would he sign a purchase agreement with me?"

Mercy shook herself from her mental paralysis. She hated admitting she couldn't guess why her grandfather would break his promise to her.

"Mommy, what's wrong?"

Shocked she hadn't noticed Sunni in the kitchen doorway, Mercy put her arm around her daughter's narrow shoulders. "Nothing that can't be fixed," she replied with a smile.

Over the child's head, she shot Jeremiah a frown, warning him not to upset Sunni. She didn't want her daughter to feel as if her world was being taken away from her—again—as it must have when Sunni traveled from Korea to what was supposed to be her forever home. It hadn't been, because her adoptive parents, who'd changed her name from Kim Sun-Hee to Sunni,

couldn't handle having a daughter who wore leg braces. Sunni had been returned to social services as if she were a set of curtains that didn't match the furniture. A disrupted adoption was the name given to it. Or a failed placement. The latter fit better, because it sure felt like a failure for the child involved.

As Mercy had learned herself fifteen years ago when she'd been the one given away by what she'd thought would be her forever family. If the Bambergers hadn't been there to take her in… No, she didn't want to think of that awful time.

Again, she warned herself to focus on the present, not the past. And her and Sunni's future. She had to stop letting her emotions take over. She needed to be logical. Building Come Along Farm into a retreat for city kids would require her to face a lot of bureaucracy on local and state levels. She must be ready to stand up for what she wanted.

"Sunni, if you go and get the book we were reading, I'll meet you in the living room once I'm finished here."

The little girl looked from her to Jeremiah, then nodded. "Okay, Mommy."

Mercy said nothing as Jeremiah watched Sunni hobble away. There was no pity in his expression, and she was grateful. Too many people felt sorry for Sunni, calling her a "poor little thing." Sunni was one of the strongest people Mercy knew and had learned to walk through perseverance and hard work. If only Mercy could help her heal from the emotional wounds she'd suffered, but those would take more time.

As soon as the little girl was out of earshot, Mercy said, "I guess I should see the purchase agreement you say my grandfather signed."

Jeremiah hooked a thumb toward the door. "Give me a minute, and I'll dig out the paperwork I've got."

She considered locking the door, but that wouldn't solve the problem. Instead, she held the door open while he brought in two scuffed duffel bags.

Closing the door, she said nothing while he opened one bag and found a manila envelope. He withdrew a sheaf of pages and sorted through them. In the middle of the stack, he pulled out several and offered them to her.

"Here's everything I got from your *grossdawdi* through my Realtor," he said without a hint of emotion.

Mercy didn't look to discover if compassion had slipped into his gaze. This time, for her. She wanted it no more than Sunni would have. When he handed her the pages, his work-roughened skin brushed against her fingers. Sensation arced between them like electricity, and she jerked her hand away. Being attracted to the man who insisted he was buying her family's farm would be stupid.

If he had the same reaction, she couldn't tell, because she carefully kept her gaze on the papers. She scanned each page, her heart sinking lower and lower. Everything looked aboveboard, and she recognized her grandfather's scrawled signature on the bottom of each page. She didn't stop to decipher every bit of legalese, but grasped enough to know Grandpa Rudy was selling the farm to Jeremiah Stoltzfus.

Just as Jeremiah claimed.

"But my grandfather died," she whispered. "Doesn't that change things?"

"I don't know. This is the first time I've ever bought property." He gave her a lopsided grin that lifted her traitorous heart once more.

Paying it no attention, she returned the papers to him and he put them in his bag. No one could answer the question gnawing at her most. Why would her grandfather promise her the property and then decide to sell it without telling her? She'd often mentioned her plans for the farm. Hadn't he read her letters? Yes, he had, because he'd responded to things in them. But never, she realized with a jolt of dismay, had he written anything about her intention to make Come Along Farm a sanctuary for city youngsters like the one she'd enjoyed when she was a Fresh Air kid years ago, escaping for two amazing weeks each summer from the steam bath of the Bronx.

"I'm not sure what we should do," he said when she remained silent.

"Me, either." For the first time she looked straight into his brilliantly blue eyes. He must realize what she was about to say she meant with all her heart. "However, you need to know I'm not going to relinquish my family's farm to you or anyone else."

"But—"

"We moved in a couple of days ago. We're not giving it up." She crossed her arms over her chest. "It's our *home*."

Chapter Two

Jeremiah had to select his words with care. He didn't know if he'd be allowed to close on the farm as scheduled. He'd never heard of a person dying before property was transferred, because in Paradise Springs most farms were handed down from one generation to the next.

As Mercy said Rudy had meant to do with this farm. He'd changed his mind, but why?

Until he spoke with Kitty Vasic, his Realtor, and got her advice, he didn't know what the outcome of this sticky situation would be. Mercy wasn't going to back down. That much was clear. If their situations were reversed, he suspected he'd be as unwilling to compromise. He *was* unwilling to compromise.

There wasn't room to. Either the farm was going to be his…or it wasn't.

"It's late," he said when he realized Mercy was waiting for him to say something. "I doubt Kitty's office is open. Do you know anyone nearby who has a phone I could use?"

As if in answer to him, a faint ringing came from

beyond the living room. He glanced at Mercy and saw she was as surprised as he was at the unexpected sound.

"Phone!" called Sunni. "I'll get it."

"No! I'll get it." Mercy spun on her heel and ran toward the sound.

Jeremiah followed, too curious to wait. He paid no attention to the large living room as he went after Mercy through what looked like a storage room and then into a bedroom. It was draped in shadows, but a single greenish light glared off to one side.

Mercy grabbed the cordless phone and jabbed at a button. Holding it to her ear, she asked, "Hello?"

The faint buzz of a voice reached him, but he couldn't discern words. His eyes widened when she held the phone out to him.

"It's for you," she said.

"For me?"

"Yes, unless you know another Jeremiah Stoltzfus."

He knew three others in Paradise Springs alone. Taking the phone, he said, "This is Jeremiah Stoltzfus."

"Hi, Jeremiah," replied a strained female voice. "This is Kitty Vasic. I know Rudy invited you to the farm, so I thought I'd catch you there. We need to talk. Rudy Bamberger is dead."

"*Ja*, I know." He glanced toward Mercy, but she'd gone to stand by a window. Talking about this was uncomfortable. For him, the farm and his future were at stake, but she'd lost her *grossdawdi*. He didn't like the idea of losing his opportunity to buy this farm, but he also disliked the idea of taking Mercy's home.

"I've got something tonight I can't get out of," Kitty said. "How about I come over tomorrow afternoon?"

"Tomorrow afternoon should be fine." What else could he say?

"Good. I'll meet you at the farm around one."

He thanked her. Tilting the phone toward the faint light coming through the window, he found the button to end the call. He set it in its holder. It chirped once, and then its glow faded.

"That was my Realtor," Jeremiah said. "She's coming over tomorrow afternoon around one to discuss what happens next."

A soft click sounded in the room before a lamp came on by the side of a bed with a headboard taller than he was. It was carved with a great tree filled with birds and other beasts gathered below it. He realized the lamp must have been connected to a timer.

"I can make myself scarce," Mercy replied.

He shook his head. "Don't. You should be here so you can ask Kitty your questions. In fact, you should contact the Realtor your *grossdawdi* used and have him here."

"I have no idea who that is."

"His name is on the paperwork I signed. Why don't I get it? It might have his phone number. You can call him and get him here, too."

She rubbed her hands together. "Thank you, Jeremiah. You're being nice about this."

"Me? You didn't throw me out on my ear when I barged in."

When she smiled, it was as if another dozen lights had turned on. "I couldn't throw you out after you saved me from my own foolishness."

The pleasant warmth buzzed through him again as his gaze connected with hers. He looked away. Until

he knew what was going to happen with the farm, he needed to keep his distance.

Turning on his heel, he went to where he'd left his bags. He'd get the information she needed and then…

And then what?

Tell her he'd planned to stay here tonight? He couldn't insist Mercy and her little girl find another place tonight. He wasn't sure what, under the circumstances, would happen if he left the property before the disposition of the farm was decided. Possession being nine-tenths of the law…or something like that.

He paused as he saw an overhead photo of the farm. His gaze riveted on the tenant house. It was the answer to tonight's impasse.

Digging among the stack of legal forms, he found the purchase agreement. He paged through it to find Rudy's Realtor's name and contact information. There! He pulled a pencil out of his pocket along with the small notebook that he kept handy to take notes when someone ordered a piece of furniture. Though he planned to concentrate on farming, he knew he'd be doing woodworking on the side until he could get his first crop harvested. His hand tools and small power tools were on their way to Harmony Creek. As he wrote the name and number of Rudy's Realtor, he hoped he wouldn't have to ship those heavy crates back unopened.

He handed the information to Mercy, who nodded her thanks. Returning the papers in the envelope, he dropped it into the open bag. He drew the strings to close it and looked at Mercy. She was as serious as a sinner confessing in front of the *Leit*. Maybe it was for the best she didn't smile again. He was too fascinated by the high arch of her cheekbones and her dark eyes.

"It's getting late," he said. "We're not going to settle this tonight. It makes sense for you and your little girl to stay here. I'll sleep in the tenant house."

Her eyes widened. "That's very kind, Jeremiah, but I'm not sure there's heat in the tenant house."

"I can figure out something." He glanced around the room. "Do you have blankets?"

"There are plenty upstairs. Help yourself." After she'd given him directions to the linen closet and he started for the stairs in the narrow space behind the door, she added, "Be careful. Like I told Sunni, the floors aren't as sturdy as they should be."

"I'll take my cue from her and test the floors before I step on them." He hurried upstairs before his grin popped out and betrayed how pleased he was to have an excuse to see more of the house he hoped would become his.

A pulse of guilt coursed through him, hot and powerful. The farm belonged to Mercy's family, and he'd be upset if someone came along and insisted his brother surrender his claim on the farm where Jeremiah had grown up. But if he walked away, he might not find another farm near Harmony Creek.

Leaving to live elsewhere might be the difference between the new settlement succeeding or failing. A settlement needed about a dozen families to prosper, and a single person not staying as agreed could doom it. He'd made a deal with the other families, and he couldn't break it without trying to stay.

Following Mercy's directions to a linen closet, Jeremiah paused whenever he heard the floor creak beneath him. Each time it wasn't anything more than the sounds made by an old building. He went to the closet beside

the single bathroom on the upper floor and glanced into each room as he passed. Most were empty. Remnants of wallpaper hung in loose strips, and a damp odor filled every breath. Nibbled acorns warned squirrels had invaded. He was sure they were in the attic, too. Once it was warm enough for the squirrels to go outside, he'd check the exterior and block the holes they'd made to get into the house.

If he was here then...

He sighed. "God, You've brought me here. Help me see Your plan and the way for me to be part of this new settlement."

Selecting a couple of wool blankets and guessing there would be plenty of moth holes, he grabbed two more before he went downstairs. He could get by for a single night. If it went as he hoped, by tomorrow night he'd be able to sleep in his own house.

Mercy was waiting in the exact same spot where she'd been when he'd left. Again, guilt tormented him. Part of him wanted to walk away, but he couldn't.

"Did you find enough blankets?" she asked.

"I did."

"They may not be in good condition."

"They're *gut* enough for tonight."

She rubbed her hands together as she had before, and he realized she was as torn as he was. Turning the other cheek was the Mennonites' way, too, but he'd seen how her eyes snapped when she spoke of him keeping her from making a home here for her and her *kind*.

"If it gets too cold," she said, "come back." A hint of a smile played along her lips. "You freezing to death would be a real complication."

When he chuckled, her smile broadened, revealing the gentle person she was.

"Don't worry, Mercy. I'll be fine." He hoped it wasn't a boast. The temperatures had been dropping fast when he came to the house. He headed for the door.

"Do you have anything to eat?" she asked.

Her question stopped him in his tracks. "No."

"Wait here." Mercy rushed into the kitchen. He heard cabinet doors opening and closing as well as drawers being slid in and out; then she returned with a plastic bag filled with odd shapes. "It's peanut butter and jelly and a few slices of the bread I brought with us. Also a couple of cans of orange juice. It's Sunni's favorite, so I always have a bunch on hand."

"It's my favorite, too."

The smile he hadn't guessed he'd see again spread across her face, adding an aura of light to her eyes and skin. "I'm glad!"

That pleasurable something uncurled within him once more as he gazed into her pretty eyes. A man could get lost in those eyes. He looked away. He hadn't come to Harmony Creek to get lost, but to find his dream.

Picking up his duffel bags, he opened one and stuffed the thin blankets inside. He felt like a hobo as he steered his bags and himself out of the house. By the time he'd reached the porch steps, he heard the dead bolt click closed. Mercy wasn't taking any chance he'd have second thoughts and return.

He *would* be there tomorrow, he thought as he trudged through the snow. Because he wasn't ready to give up his dream...when it was within his grasp.

The next morning Mercy surveyed the wall completely stripped of ugly, peeling wallpaper. It'd taken

more effort than she'd expected to get the remaining paper off. Maybe she shouldn't have done more work until she knew for certain what was going to happen with the farm. When the clock on the mantel in the living room had chimed nine o'clock, she'd used the phone in the kitchen and called Darren Paquette, Grandpa Rudy's Realtor. His office was in Glens Falls, more than twenty-five miles away, and she'd been grateful to catch him at his desk.

At least she had been until he told her not to do anything until she heard from him again. When she explained about the meeting that afternoon with Jeremiah and his Realtor, Mr. Paquette warned her to say nothing.

"A real estate transaction is adversarial at best," he'd said, "and this is far from the best situation."

"When can you come here?"

"Tell Kitty Vasic to call me, and we'll discuss it. There's no reason to involve you and Mr. Stoltzfus at this point."

"I'll tell her."

How could he say she and Jeremiah weren't involved in deciding the future of the farm? That was the silliest thing she'd ever heard.

"Are you okay, Mommy?" asked Sunni as she came downstairs.

Mercy smiled at her dear daughter, who looked adorable in her light green dress and with her black braids falling over her shoulders. The little girl was sensitive to everyone's moods, and Mercy didn't want her to get more upset.

"I'm fine, *eolin-i*." The phrase meaning "little one" was one of the few she knew in Korean.

"Is he coming back?"

"Jeremiah?"

"Yeah, him."

She got the broom she'd found in a kitchen closet and began sweeping the wallpaper scraps into a pile. "He's returning this afternoon with a friend of his."

"Is he going to make you sad again?"

Putting aside the broom, Mercy squatted until her eyes were level with her daughter's. "Jeremiah didn't intend to make me sad. But he talked about Grandpa Rudy, and that made me sad."

"Me, too." Her dark eyes glistened with tears. "I miss his water balloons."

"I don't miss that." Mercy forced humor into her voice. "You two made me your favorite target."

"It was fun to be splashed on a hot day."

"It was, wasn't it?" She hugged Sunni, being careful she didn't pull her daughter off balance.

Mercy started to add more, but the door opened. She gasped when Jeremiah walked in. Nobody ever knocked at her grandfather's door, but for the first time, having someone let himself in seemed like an invasion. From where she squatted, it appeared the top of his straw hat brushed the ceiling.

Telling herself not to be frivolous, she made sure Sunni was steady as she came to her own feet. Paper crunched under her sneakers when she turned to him. "I thought you were coming this afternoon."

"It *is* afternoon."

"It is?"

He chuckled. "The hours pass swiftly when there's plenty of work, ain't so?"

Mercy warned herself to relax. His teasing was

aimed at trying to make the situation as comfortable as possible. "There are never enough hours in a day."

"True." He turned to Sunni. "How are you doing today?"

"You aren't going to make my mommy sad again, are you?" her daughter shot back in a tone that warned Jeremiah he'd be sorry if he did that.

Though she wanted to remind Sunni of her manners, Mercy said nothing. How Jeremiah answered could tell her a lot about what he was planning to do next.

Taking off his hat, he held it by the brim. "I'm sorry if I made her sad before." He raised his eyes to meet Mercy's, and she saw his sincerity as he added, "And I don't want to make her or you sad."

"So you say," Sunni retorted, shocking Mercy again. Her daughter wasn't usually rude, but she seemed to have taken an instant dislike to Jeremiah. Should Mercy heed her daughter's instincts…which she now could see had been spot-on where her ex-fiancé had been concerned?

But being rude to someone in their home—or what she hoped would be their home—wasn't acceptable. "Sunni," she interjected in a firm tone, "it's not nice to suggest Jeremiah would do something hurtful on purpose."

As it isn't kind for me to ask why Grandpa Rudy hid how he was selling the farm that he said would be mine. Why? Why would you change your mind without telling me?

"I'm sorry," Sunni said, but her obstinate frown countermanded her words.

"It's okay to ask questions," Jeremiah replied, "but

my *mamm* says you can catch more flies with honey than with vinegar."

"Who wants to catch flies?" The little girl grimaced. "Gross."

Mercy struggled not to laugh as she explained the adage to her daughter. Looking at Jeremiah, she said, "It's past time for Sunni and I to have lunch, and I know how hungry she gets after doing her schoolwork. I'm homeschooling her." Realizing she was babbling, she added, "Have you eaten?"

"I had the last of the peanut butter for breakfast."

"You can join us if you don't mind leftover pizza."

"Leftover pizza sounds like manna from heaven."

Laughing, she said, "I didn't order the manna topping. I hope you like pepperoni."

A slow smile spread over Jeremiah's face, and her heart did a stutter step as his blue eyes shone like a cloudless summer sky. He'd been so serious during their previous discussions. Seeing him smile was like being confronted by a stranger.

He is *a stranger. A stranger who wants your farm.* Telling her heart to behave itself because it'd been so wrong about Graham, she led the way into the kitchen. She'd be a fool to listen to her heart that had believed Graham loved her. Fortunately, she'd realized in time she always would have been a distant second in his affections after his mother.

She'd learned her lesson. Or she should have. Maybe her brain had, but her heart had a lot to learn.

Mercy used the time while she got the pizza out of the ancient refrigerator in the off-white kitchen and began warming it in the oven to regain her equilibrium. She must not be distracted by Jeremiah's beguil-

ing smile when the future of Come Along Farm was at stake. When she got cans of soda—a special treat for Sunni—from the fridge, she listened as Jeremiah tried to engage her daughter in conversation.

Sunni was being cautious, either not replying or giving a single-word answer. It was a reminder, though Mercy didn't need one, of how her daughter had been hurt by Graham's decision to choose someone over them and walk away without a backward look. Too many people had done that to Sunni, and Mercy was determined her daughter wouldn't feel abandoned again.

They were finishing what was a very uncomfortable lunch when a knock came at the door. Mercy watched as the door opened and a woman stuck her head in.

"Anyone home?"

Mercy was on her feet as Jeremiah pushed back his chair. She saw him reach to assist Sunni and shook her head to halt him. Sunni needed to do everything as other kids did. If Jeremiah acted as if he thought Sunni couldn't do something, it would make the little girl dislike him more.

Jeremiah appeared taken aback, but drew aside his hands as Sunni pushed her chair out. When Mercy went to the door, he followed.

"Hi, Kitty," he said before introducing Mercy to his Realtor.

Kitty Vasic was the picture of an elegant, successful businesswoman. She wore a business suit of the brightest pink Mercy had ever seen, and her shoes had spiked heels that must be five inches high. Mercy was fascinated, because she expected the Realtor to topple on each step.

"Mr. Stoltzfus, how nice to meet you in person."

Kitty held out her hand and when he took it, she pumped his hand vigorously. "And you, too, Ms. Bamberger."

"Please call me Mercy," she said at the same time Jeremiah was urging the Realtor to use his given name.

Jeremiah added, "Plain folks don't like to use titles."

"Oh, that's good to know." Kitty smiled. "With you Amish moving into southern Washington County, it's important to learn how to be good neighbors. Don't you agree?"

Mercy considered saying she wasn't Amish, but she didn't want to delay hearing what the Realtor had to say. "We appreciate you coming so we can get this unfortunate situation resolved right away."

Kitty's smile wavered. "Oh, dear! I'm sorry if I led you to believe this could be settled today."

"But I thought—" Jeremiah began.

"Let's talk, and I'll tell you what I do know." She grinned as Sunni appeared in the kitchen doorway. "Well, hello, young lady. You must be a Bamberger because I know Jeremiah doesn't have children."

"Sunni," Mercy said, "this would be a good time for you to finish the story we started last night."

The little girl glanced at Jeremiah's and Kitty's taut faces. Mercy guessed her own expression was as uneasy. With a nod, Sunni went into the dining room, where two overstuffed chairs were set by a fireplace that opened into the kitchen, as well. It needed to be swept because ashes had tumbled onto the floor. Something else for Mercy to add to her lengthy to-do list.

Pushing aside her longing to go with her daughter and forget about these complications, Mercy squared her shoulders. "We can sit in the living room."

Behind her, the *click-click-click* of Kitty's high heels

marked her steps, but Jeremiah's boot falls were surprisingly light for such a tall, muscular man. She shook those thoughts from her head. She couldn't allow herself to become distracted.

She sat in what had been her grandfather's favorite chair by the wide window offering a view of the road through the bare branches of the maple trees. Waiting until the others chose chairs, she gazed at the green tiles on the large fireplace.

"What *can* you tell us, Kitty?" she asked.

"It's unlikely the closing will go on as planned." Kitty shot an apologetic look toward Jeremiah.

His face went as blank as the wall behind him, and his gaze refused to meet hers. The pulse of sympathy surging through her was startling. If he closed on the property, her hopes for Come Along Farm would end. Yet, he had dreams for the property, too. Oh, how she wished there was a solution that could satisfy them both.

When the Realtor spoke again, Mercy focused on her. "We'll need to consult with an attorney," Kitty said, "to determine what New York law says. I've got to admit it's the first time I've been involved with a property transfer where one party died before closing. Mercy, I should have said this before. I'm sorry for your loss."

"Thank you."

"Your grandfather was well respected and well liked. I can't tell you how many times I enjoyed a cup of coffee with him at the Village Diner."

"Did he mention why he decided to sell?" She regretted the question. Talking about private matters when Jeremiah sat a couple of feet away was unsettling.

Kitty reached over and patted her arm. "He was selling it for you and your daughter."

"For us? But he promised…" This time she halted herself before she said too much.

"I don't know what he told you, Mercy, but Rudy mentioned that he wanted you to have a majority of the money. He hoped you'd build a nice home so you'd be close to his assisted-living apartment. He spoke often about you and your daughter and how he looked forward to spending more time with you."

"Why didn't he tell me this?"

Kitty shook her head sadly. "That's something I can't answer. I'm as perplexed as you are. I'm sure he had his reasons, but he never mentioned them to me or Darren." Her eyes narrowed. "Have you spoken with Darren?"

"I called him this morning. He said to tell you to call him."

"I see." Her lips tightened into a straight line, an expression that said as loudly as a shout she was annoyed. "We should wait on discussing this further until Darren can be here, too, to represent Rudy's estate."

"But do *you* think the contract is valid?" Jeremiah asked.

"We should wait—"

"I think Mercy is as anxious as I am to hear your opinion. I understand we can't make decisions without Darren's input, but is the contract valid?"

"From what I've read, the answer is yes and no. In some states, the contract would be invalid upon the death of either party." She glanced from Mercy to him. "But we have leeway in New York. If the heir or heirs are willing, the contract can be completed. However, that is *my* opinion from a quick read on the internet. Until we have an opinion from an attorney, I don't think either of you should assume anything."

Jeremiah turned to Mercy. "You are your *grossdawdi*'s heir, ain't so?"

"One of them, I guess. Rudy is my father's father."

"Is your father alive?" asked Kitty.

She nodded.

"What about his brothers and sisters?"

"My father has six siblings," she replied.

Jeremiah sighed. "Kitty, when my *daed*—my dad—died, everything he had went to my mother. But if she'd died first…"

"The estate would be divided equally among his children." Kitty bit her lower lip, then said, "Unless Rudy left a written and witnessed will that specifies otherwise."

Mercy's heart sank toward her knees as she realized where the conversation was going. If Grandpa Rudy hadn't left a valid will naming her as his heir, the property would belong to her father, her four aunts and her two uncles.

"Do you have names and contact information for your father and his siblings?" asked Kitty.

"I can find them. All but one aunt have telephones."

The Realtor smiled. "I'm glad to hear that. It'll make getting in contact with them much easier. However, paperwork will have to be mailed to them for their signatures. I'm not sure, at this point, whether the signatures will have to be notarized. The probate court will let us know."

"We have to go to court?" asked Jeremiah.

Mercy heard his consternation and understood. It usually wasn't the way of plain folks to deal with courts and lawyers. Matters were settled privately and through prayer, but estate matters were different. She wondered

whom her grandfather had hired to draft his will…if he had one.

She was out of her depth. Ask her about the needs of inner-city kids and the benefits of them enjoying a summer in the country, and she could expound for an hour. Since Sunni's arrival in her life, she'd learned a lot about intercountry adoption and physical therapy and the adventures of the little girl's beloved characters in her favorite books.

But she knew nothing about what would happen with the farm.

"If you agree, Jeremiah," Kitty went on, "I'll share the contract with my agency's lawyer. I'd like him to review it and give us advice to aid us in bringing the contract to a closing." She sighed. "To be honest, this won't be quick. Obtaining an agreement from seven people will take time, and we can't be certain of the outcome."

"Is there another farm for sale in the area?" Jeremiah asked.

"None that I know of. I can make inquiries, if you'd like."

"Ja."

Her eyes cut toward Mercy. "I'll do what I can, Jeremiah, but I can't make promises. Not about this farm or any other."

"I know," he said again.

"And there's one other complication. Your money in escrow may be held by the probate court until there's an agreement among the heirs."

He blanched. "I can't put in another offer until the money is released."

"Yes, though if someone is eager to sell, we might be able to work something out." Kitty sighed. "How-

ever, like I said, I don't know of other farms for sale near Harmony Creek. There's one over by Scotts Lake, seven or eight miles from here."

"Too far for me to be part of this settlement."

"So I figured." She stood.

Mercy clasped her hands on her lap. If the closing went ahead, Jeremiah would own the farm. If the sale had to be approved by Grandpa Rudy's heirs, would Dad and his brothers and sisters decide to sell it to Jeremiah? Two of his siblings would be eager to use their share of the proceeds to invest in their businesses. What about the others? And how many had to say no before Jeremiah couldn't close on the farm? Was it a simple majority or could a single no vote give her the chance to buy the farm herself?

But how? The money she had was already earmarked to fix the house and the buildings to be approved for bringing children to visit. In addition, she needed to buy horses and other farm animals to give the youngsters a true farm experience. Perhaps she could convince her family to let her pay them bit by bit.

She heard Kitty say she'd contact them when she had further information. The *click-click-click* of Kitty's shoes headed toward the door, and Jeremiah went, too, talking with his Realtor.

Mercy didn't move. There had to be a solution to her dilemma, but what?

Unless Rudy left a written and witnessed will that specifies otherwise.

Kitty's words resonated in Mercy's head, and she gasped. What if she found a will? There were many rooms, and she hadn't dared to go into the ones with weak floors. What if she found her grandfather's will

and it proved her assertion he wanted her to have the farm?

She got up and took a single step toward the formal staircase at the front of the house. Pausing, she looked over her shoulder when she heard Jeremiah's deep voice rumbling in the other room. If he knew of her intention to search the house, would he help her or try to halt her? Until she knew for sure, she couldn't let him know what she was doing. She didn't like secrets, but keeping this one might mean the difference between her dreams coming true and their destruction.

Chapter Three

Last night Jeremiah had discovered the tenant house was in worse condition than he'd guessed. It hadn't taken him long to explore it, using his flashlight. A tiny kitchen and a cozy living room filled the first floor. Upstairs were two cramped bedrooms and a bath. Every ceiling had brown water stains, and one wall of the entry hall was pulling away from the house. He'd been able to see light from the rising moon through the crack, and a puddle of slush was piled on the linoleum beside it.

This morning he woke to find the house cold and damp. He'd been grateful for a woodstove in the living room and a few logs stacked nearby. He'd used the rag rug by the stove as a mattress. He'd folded a blanket as a makeshift pillow. He'd told himself, though it wasn't likely it'd be comfortable, he'd endured worse when he'd camped in the woods when he wasn't much older than Sunni.

He'd been wrong.

Every muscle ached, and moving in the icy air seemed to make his bones creak as if he'd aged fifty

years overnight. It was dark, but he guessed it was around 4:00 a.m. It was the time when he usually woke to help with chores before leaving for his woodworking shop.

His tools would be arriving today or tomorrow. He should have waited until he closed on the property before he had the crates trucked up from Paradise Springs. But how could he have imagined the debacle waiting for him in Harmony Creek?

With a groan, he pushed himself up to sit. He grimaced as the frigid air gripped him as the thick blanket fell away. Standing, he went to the stove, which was barely warm. He opened the door and saw the banked embers had burned themselves out.

Jeremiah sent up a prayer of thanks when, after he'd started a new fire in the stove, the air close to the stove warmed quickly. Something worked in the house.

After his quick inspection his first night at the house, he knew not much else did. No water had flowed into the sinks, and flushing the toilet had resulted in strange creaking sounds in the walls as if the pipes were trying to break out. The propane tanks by the back door must be empty, because the kitchen stove had refused to light.

He hoped he would have better results this morning. He opened a door to what might have been a laundry or storage room. A rusty washer lurked beneath shelves covered with dust and droppings. In a closet, he found a lantern but no kerosene.

Brushing the kitchen table off as best he could, he grimaced when it rocked. Were the legs uneven or the floor? That answer and a whole lot more would have to wait until he could see beyond the narrow circle from his flashlight.

He made the same meal he'd eaten last night. A peanut butter and grape jelly sandwich. He thought fondly of the large meal of eggs and sausage and home fries he would have eaten at home. After he said silent grace, he ate standing up. He found a napkin Mercy had added to the bag. He sighed, wondering if it would have been much easier if she'd been rude or snarled like an angry dog. Instead, she'd made sure he had blankets to keep him warm and food to eat.

And she'd been stubborn.

Did she have ideas of her own for the farm? Most likely, as she'd started work on the house. He appreciated that, because he'd spent hours putting together his plans, something his brothers had helped him with while they teased him for trying to look at every possible angle. Taking another bite of the sandwich, he wished his brothers were nearby. He could have used their insight.

A knock startled him. Why would someone come to a house that must have been deserted for years? Setting his sandwich down, he brushed crumbs off his hands and tossed them in the sink before he went to the door.

He opened it and saw a face he recognized. The man who had recruited others to come to Harmony Creek.

"You're Caleb Hartz, ain't so?" Jeremiah asked, remembering how Caleb had spoken at a gathering in Paradise Springs, telling about the fallow farmland on small family farms awaiting anyone who was willing to work hard to improve it.

The man nodded, then swept his too-long blond hair out of his dark green eyes. "*Ja.* I thought I'd stop by this morning to see how you're settling in." His tawny brows lowered. "I assumed you'd be at the main house,

but the woman who answered the door told me I'd find you here."

"Things are a bit complicated." After he invited Caleb into the house, he gave him a quick overview of the situation.

Caleb, who would be one of his neighbors if the sale went through, listened with widening eyes. "I got to know Rudy pretty well. He was a *gut* man. He wouldn't have signed a purchase contract with you if he didn't intend for you to buy the farm."

"Maybe he should have mentioned that to his granddaughter."

Caleb's frown deepened, drawing lines into the thin angles of his face. "It's a puzzle. I've been here a little over a month. Everyone I've talked to—both Amish and *Englisch*—has praised Rudy's honesty. He sold me a battered skid loader I'll need to move hay bales. He didn't make any bones about how much work it would need, and he sold it at a fair price."

"My dealings with him were *gut*, too. I wish I knew why he didn't let Mercy know he was selling the farm."

"I hope you won't have to leave Harmony Creek. We need every family we can convince to join us in order to make this settlement a success."

Jeremiah didn't need that reminder. From the moment he'd expressed interest in joining the Hartz family and the Waglers as well as other founding members of the Harmony Creek colony, he'd been told he must be very sure about his commitment. Each family was vital to the rest.

"I'm not leaving. I'm going to farm here." Saying the words aloud was like taking an oath in the presence of

the Lord, though God was well aware of what was in Jeremiah's heart.

"Aren't you a woodworker by trade?"

"*Ja*, but farming is too much in my blood." He surprised himself by chuckling. "My late *daed* would be shocked because I hated to get out of bed to do chores."

Caleb chuckled. "My *daed* used to threaten to dump cold water on me and my brothers to get us up in the morning."

"Sounds familiar."

"I can ask around and find out if anyone is thinking about selling."

"*Danki*, but I've got to wait and hear what my Realtor learns from her attorney. As my *mamm* has said more than once, there's no need to look for trouble before it finds you."

"Sounds like something my *mamm* would have said, too."

"My brothers believe *mamms* have a special language filled with platitudes for every occasion."

Caleb laughed heartily. "Why is it dark in here?"

"I couldn't find oil for the lantern."

"The house has electricity. Rudy mentioned both houses were wired." With a wave of his hand, he added, "Let's find the fuse box and see if we can get you some light. More important is powering the well pump so you can have water."

Jeremiah followed him into the cellar. As they crossed the dirt floor to where a metal box was affixed to the wall, he wondered why he hadn't considered checking the well pump. Exhaustion could be a reason, because he felt as if he carried the house on his shoulders as he trudged after Caleb.

His neighbor whistled a single note as he popped open the door on the metal box. "A circuit breaker box. Who'd have guessed Rudy had updated his tenant house?" Reaching in, he flipped a switch.

A low rumble came from the far side of the cellar. Jeremiah aimed his flashlight in that direction and saw the well's holding tank. His fatigue fell away as he realized he could have water to brush his teeth once he'd let it run long enough to make sure any rust washed out.

"Danki," he said.

Caleb shrugged. "Glad to help. I'm sure this circuit breaker box isn't the first surprise you're going to find."

Jeremiah was tempted to say the breakers were far from the *first* surprise he'd had since his arrival, but grousing wouldn't get him anywhere. He needed to be patient until Kitty had answers for him. *That* had to be his plan. Wait and see.

A sense of calm settled over him as he realized he had a clear path...for now. He thanked God for helping him see that. He must be patient. Not an easy task when his dream was so close to realization.

Several lights were glaring against the water-stained ceilings when he went upstairs with Caleb. He switched off everything but the fluorescent ceiling light in the kitchen, though he despised its glare.

"Let us know if you need anything before your stuff arrives," Caleb said as he reached for the doorknob. He glanced outside. "Looks like we're in for another big storm." Grimacing at the crack in the wall, he added, "We're living in the barn while we get the house repaired, and our barn is better than this. Feel free to come over if you get tired of shoveling snow out of your house."

"Danki." He knew he wouldn't abandon the house, because that might injure his fragile claim on the farm. "I appreciate it."

"We may be snowed in for a while, because we're one of the last roads plowed by the town. I don't think Rudy sold his sleigh, so if you or anyone at the main house needs something, you can use it."

"Danki." He appreciated Caleb's helpfulness, which made him more determined to be a part of the nascent community. Amish folks assisted one another. Did Mercy feel the same?

"Oh, one other thing I should let you know." Caleb turned the knob. "Wayne Flaud from the settlement north of here in Whitehall is acting as our temporary bishop. If you want me to contact him to get his thoughts on what you should do…"

"Let's see what my Realtor has to say before we bring the bishop into this. I'm sure this will work out for the best. God didn't bring me to Harmony Creek so I could turn around and leave again."

With another nod, Caleb bid him *gute mariye* and let himself out as a burst of cold and a swirl of windblown snow slipped in past him.

Jeremiah guessed Caleb believed his words. Too bad he wasn't so sure himself.

Any hopes spring might have made an early appearance overnight were dashed three days later when Mercy awoke to discover two feet of new snow. She dressed hastily, because the house was cold in the fresh light of dawn.

Peeking past Sunni's door and glad her daughter was asleep with the blankets pulled up to her chin, Mercy

tiptoed down the stairs. They creaked beneath her, and she hoped Sunni wouldn't wake up until Mercy figured out what was wrong with the heat.

Despite herself, she glanced out the window that gave her a view of the trees separating them from the tenant house. She hadn't spoken to Jeremiah since he'd left after the meeting with his Realtor. She'd seen big delivery trucks in the yard the following day and watched him accept delivery of a horse, a buggy and a dozen large wooden crates, which he'd moved into an outbuilding. He'd spent time inside, coming out with pieces of wood, so she guessed he was unpacking what he'd shipped to the farm.

That was a sign Jeremiah intended to stay.

No surprise, but if he thought she'd give up because he was making himself at home, he was in for a big surprise. She'd waited years for an opportunity to host city kids on a farm.

She'd thought her grandfather comprehended her need to pay forward the gifts she'd been given. Instantly, she was contrite. She couldn't fault Grandpa Rudy for his change of heart about what should happen with the farm after he died, but she wished he'd talked to her before signing a deal with Jeremiah.

He was as much an innocent victim of this mess as she was. Of course, if he withdrew his offer, that might make a difference for her aunts and uncles. Would they be more willing to give her time to find funds to set up the farm if they didn't have an available buyer?

Mercy had discussed that with her parents last night. Her father had sympathy for how her plans for the farm might have died along with Rudy, but he'd also emphasized that he'd go along with what his siblings decided.

"I've got to admit," Dad had told her before they'd hung up, "I'd really like to have you and Sunni closer to the rest of the family."

"But there's no place near your house where I could afford to buy land." She'd tried not to sound like a petulant child who hadn't gotten her way.

"If that's what God wants you to do, He'll help you find a way."

She agreed and was sure God had led her to Harmony Creek and the farm. Otherwise, she wouldn't have uprooted Sunni, leaving behind trusted specialists and physical therapists who worked with her daughter.

Now…

Mercy winced as she entered the kitchen and felt the cold wind that had found its way into the house. Opening the cellar door, she heard silence. Why wasn't the furnace running?

A quick check of the fuel tank gauge showed it was half-full. Next, she went to the furnace, which was raised up so high off the floor she had to stand on tiptoe to see the dials. Why wouldn't it start? She tried flipping the emergency switch at the top of the cellar steps.

Nothing.

If possible, it seemed colder when she returned to the kitchen. She needed help. She glanced at the snow sparkling as if stars had fallen along with the flakes. The road twisting through the hollow had vanished. If she called someone, how long would it take them to get to the house?

Her gaze settled on the tenant house. Should she ask Jeremiah to check the furnace? She'd ignored him for three days, but she wasn't sure who else would be able to help them. She didn't want Sunni getting sick from the cold.

Before she could talk herself out of it, Mercy reached for the phone, an old avocado-colored unit she'd found in a drawer. She'd hung it on the wall. The long cord allowed her to walk around the kitchen while she talked. She looked at the faded numbers on the wall beside the phone and dialed the one for the tenant house.

"Hello?" Jeremiah sounded astonished to be answering a phone.

She knew many Amish didn't keep phones in their houses, but had them in the barns or a phone shack shared by multiple families.

"Jeremiah, it is Mercy. Mercy Bamberger." Who else named Mercy would know he was living at the tenant house?

"*Ja. Gute mariye*, Mercy." He sounded awkward and uncertain as he went on. "I hope my work hasn't disturbed you or Sunni. I—"

Not wanting to let the conversation drag along, she said, "I don't think my furnace is working. Will you look at it?"

She could almost see him nod before he told her he'd be over in a few minutes. Thanking him, she hung up.

Starting the coffeemaker, she sighed. If Jeremiah took over the farm, he'd strip the electric wires out of the house. She wondered what it'd be like to live without electricity.

A knock on the door told her Jeremiah was as good as his word. Taking a steadying breath, she opened it. She forced a smile, which she hoped looked more welcoming than it felt.

Knocking snow off his boots, Jeremiah stepped inside. He unwrapped a blue-and-green scarf from around his face and let it hang over his shoulders as he unbut-

toned his black wool coat. Lifting off his hat of the same fabric, he placed it on the counter near the door.

Her heart beat a bit too fast when she stood close to him again. She'd thought of him as a problem, but with him an arm's length away, she couldn't help noticing, as if for the first time, his strong jaw and the intelligence in his compelling blue eyes. As he pulled off worn work gloves, she stared at the nicks on his knuckles and stain on his fingertips. He was a man accustomed to hard work.

Graham, her former fiancé, popped into her mind. A fastidious man, his hands always looked as if he'd just had a manicure. She'd been surprised to discover he had his nails done when he took his mother to the beauty shop. When he'd told her it made Mrs. Rapp happy, Mercy had, at first, seen it as a sign of him caring deeply about others. She hadn't guessed he'd cared more about his mother than he'd ever care for her.

"Thanks for coming over," Mercy said, holding out her hand for Jeremiah's coat.

He handed it to her, and waves of cold washed over her. It must be more frigid outside than in the house. Maybe the furnace hadn't gone out too long ago and fixing it would be easy.

"What have you done so far?" he asked, combing his fingers through his reddish hair.

"I checked the fuel oil tank." She set his coat over a kitchen chair. "There's oil in the tank, so I don't know what's wrong."

"Let me look at it."

"Thanks!" She motioned toward the cellar door. "It's down there. I'm hoping it's something simple."

"Something simple is about the extent of my skills

at fixing furnaces." He gave her a grin. "Just in case, do you have the name of the person who did furnace servicing for Rudy? It's probably the same company that delivers oil."

"I probably can find it. He kept that sort of stuff in his desk." As coffee finished dripping into the clear pot, she asked, "Do you want a cup?"

"I'll have one when I'm done." Without another word, he went to the cellar door and opened it. His work boots, which were as battered as his gloves, thumped on each step.

Mercy heard Jeremiah pull on the chain to the bare bulb near the furnace. Hurrying into the room with Grandpa Rudy's desk, she grabbed a black shawl from a peg. She threw it over her shoulders, holding it close with fingers as clumsy as a collection of icicles.

The desk was heaped with papers and envelopes her grandfather must have tossed there in the days before he died. For a moment Mercy had to blink back tears. Throughout the mess of the past days, one thing hadn't changed. She missed Grandpa Rudy, the very person she wanted to turn to now.

Mercy found a receipt from the oil company and was relieved to see it had an emergency service number at the top. Putting it in the pocket of her black apron, she hurried into the kitchen to be ready to call the oil company if Jeremiah couldn't fix the furnace.

She paused when she heard uneven steps on the stairs to the second floor. Sunni was coming down the stairs without her crutches. Mercy frowned. Her daughter had promised to use them on the stairs. Worse, the little girl had wrapped herself in a blanket that threatened to trip her.

"Sunni, you need to be careful," she chided gently.

"I was afraid of turning into an ice cube if I waited a second longer," the little girl said. "Why's it so cold, Mommy?"

"Something's wrong with the heat."

Before Mercy could say more, assertive footsteps came from the cellar steps. She turned to see Jeremiah in the doorway.

Sunni mumbled something under her breath and scowled at Jeremiah.

His gaze followed Sunni when her daughter walked into the living room, her pose beneath the blanket one of disdain. He arched his brows at Mercy.

"Were you able to see what's wrong with the furnace?" Mercy asked.

"Nothing's wrong with it." He wiped his hands on a filthy cloth he must have found in the cellar. "Your fuel oil tank is empty."

"But I checked the tank before I called you. The gauge said it was half-full."

"The gauge is broken. The tank is completely dry."

"I never considered the gauge might be wrong."

"No reason you should."

"You did." She pushed away from the stairs and flinched when the door gave a threatening creak. One disaster at a time. Reaching under her shawl, she pulled the receipt out of her pocket. "I'll call the oil company's emergency number and see if they can deliver some oil."

He glanced out the window. "They won't be able to get in until the road is plowed."

As if on cue, the rumble of a big truck could be heard coming toward the house. She saw the huge wing of the plow as it pushed snow in large, thick chunks into the yard. She shuddered, thinking of the heavy work of

clearing the driveway. Her car was stored in the rickety garage, and the old-style door opened straight out, so she was going to have to clear a large area there, too.

Mercy made the call to the oil company, who assured her they'd be there before nightfall. Apparently, she wasn't the only one needing service on the cold day.

"You can't stay here with Sunni," Jeremiah said after she hung up. "The house is going to get colder and colder. The tenant house is a bit better, but you'll get so chilled going over there, it probably won't make much difference. Isn't there a fireplace in the living room?"

"Yes."

"Did Rudy use it?"

When she nodded and Jeremiah offered to start a fire, she was relieved. She found a box of matches in the kitchen junk drawer and followed him into the living room, where he checked the fireplace, looking up at the top of the firebox where the damper opened into the chimney. He drew back, wiping soot from his trousers.

While Sunni watched from the couch, as silent as she was whenever Jeremiah was near, he quickly arranged slabs of wood in the fireplace. Mercy handed him the matches and went to sit with her daughter.

He struck one match and held it to the small bits of paper he'd stuck among the wood. Small flames rose, and Mercy resisted the yearning to hold out her half-frozen hands, knowing there wouldn't be much heat yet. She needed to wait until the fire caught on the dried wood.

Suddenly, Jeremiah jumped to his feet and staggered. Thick smoke chased him toward the middle of the room.

"Get out!" he yelled.

Chapter Four

Mercy grabbed Sunni and ran toward the living room door, but paused when she heard a window slide open with the rattle of glass behind her. Jeremiah waved the smoke from the hearth out the window. Snow fell into the house, but he ignored it as he coughed. She put Sunni down and ran into the kitchen. She filled a bucket with water.

He threw the water on the hearth, where it sizzled. He stirred the ashes, making sure the fire was completely out. Then he took the glass of water she offered him. He drained it in one gulp and coughed a couple more times.

"I told you to get out," he said. "With this dried-out wallpaper, the fire could have spread fast."

"Why would I leave you here?" she asked, annoyed he treated her as if she were Sunni's age. "Once I heard you open the window, I knew the smoke would be sucked out."

"Maybe I was planning to jump out the window. Did you consider that?"

"No."

He gave her a wry grin. "Neither did I. Once I could see through the smoke, I was able to see the fire was dying out." He raised a single finger when she started to speak. "But you and Sunni should have gotten out of the house."

"To freeze in the snow?"

He sighed as fresh air poured into the room, dispersing the smoke. "I thought you said your *grossdawdi* used the fireplace."

"He did." Mercy took the glass from him.

"Recently?"

She shrugged. "I don't know. I almost always visited during the summer vacation."

"I suspect debris in the chimney has piled up over time. After it's cleaned out, there shouldn't be a problem." He grimaced. "But right now you need heat."

"I can turn on the oven and open the door."

"Gas or electric?"

"Electric. Why?"

"I don't want you to have to deal with gas fumes." He gestured toward the kitchen. "You two go into the kitchen. Shut the doors and roll up towels and put them at the bottom. That should keep the heat in as much as possible."

"How about the fireplace between the kitchen and dining room? There are ashes on the hearth." She glanced at the smoke stains on the ceiling. "Do you think it'd be safe to try to light that one?"

"Let me check." He followed her and Sunni into the kitchen.

He knelt by the hearth as she turned on the oven and opened the door, hoping the old stove was up to heating the kitchen. Unlike the one in the living room,

the kitchen fireplace was utilitarian. No fancy tiles. Just plain brick turned dark after decades of use. He reached in to check the damper. Paying no attention to the ashes, he stretched out on his back and peered into the chimney.

"It looks open." Jeremiah got up and knocked ashes off his pants. "Let me try a small fire. Got anything else to burn?"

She grabbed a handful of newspaper from the pile left by her *grossdawdi*. "How about this?"

"It'll burn long enough to see if the smoke goes up the chimney or not."

He cheered and Mercy smiled, giving Sunni's shoulders a squeeze, when the thin wisp of smoke was drawn up the chimney. Going into the living room, she realized there were only a couple of pieces of wood left. She took them into the kitchen and handed them to Jeremiah.

"You keep the fire going, and I'll get more wood," she said.

"Mercy, I can do that. It's cold outside." He started to stand.

She put her hand on his shoulder, the motion automatic. But her response to the strong sinews was anything but. Jerking her hand back, she wanted to shake it to stop her skin from tingling.

Somehow she was able to say, "No, you watch the fire. I'll be right back."

Racing to the door, she flung it open. She pulled on her boots before she stepped into the deep snow on the porch. Quickly closing the door, she wasn't fast enough to avoid seeing Sunni's dismay that Mercy had left her with Jeremiah.

Mercy took a steadying breath as her fingers contin-

ued to quiver from the memory of Jeremiah's shoulder beneath them. Had she lost her mind? It was a big mistake to be attracted to him. Even if he didn't want her farm, she was still reeling from a broken engagement. On top of that, her daughter didn't like him.

She hurried to the split wood that had been stored on the porch to dry. She gathered pieces in her apron and turned to go inside.

She stopped as she looked across the snowy yard. It was broken by a single set of footprints. Jeremiah's.

No, she was wrong. There were other footprints. She recognized the tiny, scampering ones of a squirrel intent on finding where it had hidden its stash of acorns. A line near the pine trees separating the big house from the tenant house looked as if they belonged to deer. They would be having as difficult a time as squirrels in the deep snow. Once the house was warm, she needed to spread hay for the deer and strew a few handfuls of the birdseed she'd seen in a cupboard. Grandpa Rudy always had made sure his bird feeders were kept full, despite the concern of bears helping themselves to the seed.

All God's creatures need to eat, and we are His hands to take care of His creation.

How many times had she heard Grandpa Rudy say that? Oh, how she missed him!

A gust of wind swirled snow into her face, and Mercy hurried inside. As she let the wood roll onto the floor beside the hearth, Jeremiah smiled at her.

"Perfect timing," he said. "I was about to go out and make sure you hadn't frozen into a chunk of ice."

"My mommy is doing the best she can!" asserted

Sunni, jutting out her tiny chin. She flounced into the dining room and hid behind a book.

Mercy started to apologize to Jeremiah for Sunni's behavior.

He motioned aside her words. "She's cold, and she's scared. I should have thought before I spoke."

"You know it doesn't have anything to do with what you said." She wouldn't sugarcoat Sunni's antipathy to him. "I'm sorry she's being bratty to you." *And I know I should be honest why, but I can't when I'm too embarrassed by what happened with Graham.*

"She's a kid. I've got enough nieces and nephews to know when they get something in their head, it's not easy to get it out."

"Do you have a lot of them?"

"More all the time, thanks to my brothers and sisters." Standing, hc looked at the fire crackling contentedly on the hearth. Already warmth was pushing aside the cold. "Keep feeding it wood, and it won't go out." He hesitated, then said, "I should get going."

She asked before she could halt herself, "So how many brothers do you have?"

Jeremiah wondered why Mercy was extending the conversation when it had seemed, moments ago, she couldn't wait until he left.

"Six. Three older and three younger," he said. "And two sisters. Add in their spouses and kids, and we have a full table when everyone comes together." He couldn't halt his smile. "*Mamm* is never happier than when everyone is sitting around the table together. Do you have brothers or sisters?"

"Now, but I was an only child when I lived in the Bronx."

"I can't imagine being an only." *Or living in a big city.* "I've always been surrounded by siblings, which most of the time I appreciated."

She nodded. "I know what you mean. I've learned how siblings can be your best friends, but also they know exactly how to annoy you best."

"So your family used to live in New York City? I didn't realize Mennonites lived there."

"I wasn't Mennonite then." Before he could ask what she meant, she said, "I need to make Sunni breakfast. I promised her pancakes. Would you like some, too?"

"I had some toast when I woke up, but that was several hours ago, so I'd be grateful for a second breakfast. I've got a long day ahead of me."

"Unpacking more of those big crates?" Color rose up Mercy's cheeks, and he guessed she'd blurted out the question before thinking.

"*Ja.* I had my woodworking tools sent up from Paradise Springs before I realized..." He wasn't surprised when she went to collect the makings for breakfast. Why did she act ashamed? The situation they were in wasn't her fault. She was as much a victim of misunderstandings as he was. He hurried on to fill the abrupt silence. "I want to make sure nothing got broken between Pennsylvania and here."

"That makes sense." She took a bowl out of a glass-front hutch built into the wall opposite the fireplace. She put flour and eggs and other ingredients in the bowl and she mixed them together.

She closed the oven door and hefted a cast-iron pan

out of the drawer beneath it. After heating the pan, she poured pancake batter into it.

Sunni peeked in. The frown she gave Jeremiah didn't need translation. She wished he'd go away and stay away.

Lord, help me find a way to let this kind *know I'm not her enemy. Or her* mamm*'s.*

The little girl had to be aware of the tension between Mercy and him. Sunni was old enough to understand there was a problem, but couldn't grasp the intricacies of estate law. *He* didn't get it, either, though Kitty had explained it to him. It was too bad they couldn't help each other, but his plans for the farm and Mercy's were different.

When Mercy put pancakes on a plate and set it on the kitchen table, Sunni asked, "Can I eat in the dining room?"

Mercy hesitated; then she nodded. The little girl poured herself a glass of orange juice, picked up her plate and carried her breakfast into the other room.

"I'm sorry," Mercy said as she returned to the stove.

"It won't help to force her to spend time with me," he replied.

"True." She set a stack of lightly browned pancakes in front of him. The edges of the pancakes were crisp, just as he liked them. As he started to say that, she interrupted him. "I need to explain why she's acting like this."

"Okay."

She faced the stove. "I was in a relationship that didn't work out, and she was upset when Graham and I went our separate ways after I realized I would always play second fiddle to his mother."

"*Danki*. I was beginning to think it was personal." He couldn't help being curious about how serious she and her Graham had been. He hoped not as serious as he'd been about Emmarita before she left her Amish life behind. He hoped Mercy didn't have as many regrets as he did.

"It's not. The move has upset her more than I'd guessed it would."

"And the possibility you won't be staying here isn't helping." He smothered the sting of Emmarita's betrayal by concentrating on the problem he and Mercy shared.

"Not a bit."

"Have you heard anything from your family?" he asked after he paused to say a silent grace. He picked up his fork so he didn't have to look at her as he waited for her answer.

"Nothing definitive. Dad said they're planning a conference call to discuss the farm." She put a cup of fragrant *kaffi* next to his plate before going to the stove to make her own breakfast. "Everyone will want to share his or her opinion."

Jeremiah waited until she brought a plate with four pancakes to the table. She pushed two more onto his plate before she set hers down. After getting herself *kaffi* and offering him juice, which he passed on because it would taste sour after the syrup, she pulled out her chair and sat. She bowed her head, and he said nothing while she thanked the Lord for the meal.

Could she be thanking God for Jeremiah's company? Maybe she was grateful to have endured another day with him. Was she just being more polite than her daughter? Possibly, because she must want to move ahead with the farm. For the first time, he won-

dered if he was being shortsighted trying to stay, but what else could he do? Until his funds were released from escrow, he couldn't purchase another farm. His sole choice might be to return to Paradise Springs, and he wasn't ready to start over at square one.

Not yet.

Jeremiah looked for a safe topic to disrupt the silence. "You said you learned about siblings. It sounds as if you eventually had some."

"I had two brothers and a sister after I was adopted."

"Adopted?" He was glad she seemed focused on her food so she didn't see the astonishment on his face. No doubt she heard it in his voice.

"When I was eleven. That was after my *Abuelita*—my grandmother—died. She'd been raising me."

"What happened to your parents?"

She chased the syrup around her plate with a piece of pancake, but didn't lift it to her mouth. "A car accident when I was two years old. They were on their way to the hospital for the birth of their second child when they were struck by another car. *Abuelita* told me the police said they died instantly. She said I needed to be grateful they never felt any pain before they went to heaven, but I couldn't be when I was a little girl who couldn't understand why God wanted to take my mama and papa and my unborn sister away."

"Mercy, I'm so sorry." He hated the sight of tears seeping into her eyes. How many had she cried through the years as she mourned those she could barely remember?

"Thank you." She dabbed a knuckle at her eye and squared her shoulders. "*Abuelita* took me in and became more like my mother than my grandmother. Everything

I know of my parents is from what she told me and from the picture of them on their wedding day. I don't know what happened to that photo. To be honest, Jeremiah, it seems like someone else's past. Once I was adopted by the Bambergers, my life began anew."

"Certainly you haven't forgotten the first eleven years of your life?"

"No, but I took Grandpa Rudy's advice. He urged me to treasure the memories of those who had left me behind. I have many precious ones of *Abuelita*, and I can re-create every detail of that photo. I can even recall the name of the studio where it was taken. Lincoln Photography on Fordham Road. I remember it because I thought President Lincoln had taken their picture."

"I doubt your parents would have appreciated you thinking they were that old." He chuckled. "Kids always think their parents are ancient. Sunni probably thinks you're older than the hills."

"Thanks." A grin transformed her face, and he knew he would gladly sit and look at it for hours at a time.

Shaking his head, he warned himself not to be silly. He was the only one of his siblings not married or getting ready to marry, but now was the worst time to get involved with anyone. Most especially with the woman who held the key to his future in her slender hands.

Not Mercy, his conscience argued, *but her family.*

Jeremiah pushed his plate away enough so he could fold his arms on the table. "I was nearly grown when my *daed* died, but it wasn't easy to lose him."

"No matter what anyone says, there's no good time to lose someone we love."

She didn't seem surprised that he turned the conversation to such a sad subject. In fact, she seemed grateful

he was listening and wasn't trying to relieve her pain with more jests.

Quietly, she added, "Knowing they're bound for a better place is supposed to ease the loss, but it's sad to think of not seeing them for a very long time."

"A *very* long time, I hope."

She nodded, then took a sip of her orange juice. "I should have finished that before I began the pancakes." Without a pause, she went on. "Jeremiah, I know you're as eager as I am to hear from my father and his siblings. We've got to be patient."

"I'm trying."

"Me, too." She put down her glass. "It sounds as if your family lives close together."

"Except for my oldest sister, everyone lives within a mile of where we grew up."

"Not my father's family. Shortly after they were married, my parents joined others who wanted to start a new church in western New York. That's what they told me anyhow."

"You don't believe it?"

"I'm sure they're being honest, but I think it's strange my dad's siblings moved away from Harmony Creek, and they're scattered from New York to California. I think that was one of the reasons Grandpa Rudy was glad to have me come every year. The rest of the family's visits were infrequent."

"Which explains," he said slowly, pondering the ramifications, "why nobody thought it odd Rudy was leaving the farm to you. It sounds as if none of the rest of them wanted it."

"Let's hope they still feel that way." She paused when Sunni came into the kitchen. After Mercy made more

pancakes for her daughter, the little girl rushed away to the dining room as if she feared Jeremiah was infectious with a horrible disease.

He waved aside Mercy's embarrassed apology as she added another serving of pancakes to his plate. "Kids are kids. She'll accept me when she's ready."

"I pray so." As she handed him the syrup bottle, she said, "Dad hopes to get back to me in the next few days, though nothing is settled until everyone agrees. I can't imagine any of them coming here." She glanced out the window at the sparkling snow. "But then I can't imagine why they left this beautiful hollow in the first place."

"Some people need to get out from under their family's shadow, whether it's the shadow of success or failure."

"Is that why you came here?" She put her fingers to her lips. "I'm sorry, Jeremiah. I shouldn't have asked you such a personal question."

"Why not? I've been asking you personal questions."

"I want you to know I wasn't asking why in the hope of discovering something that would give me an upper hand in claiming the farm."

He put his hand on her arm and wasn't surprised to find it trembling. What startled him was how swiftly he was suffused with warmth as if summer had arrived and flooded the house with sunshine. Knowing he should pull away, he didn't. He liked the sensation of her soft skin beneath his fingertips.

"That's not why I asked about your past, either. Mercy, we can't let this situation make us too competitive or too bitter."

"I know, but…"

He lifted his hand from her arm as she tensed be-

neath his fingers. "The truth of why I came here is because I wanted to start over. The woman I thought I'd marry decided to marry someone else."

"I'm sorry."

He believed her. She felt everything so deeply, and he hoped she couldn't tell he wasn't being completely honest when he said, "*Danki*, but Emmarita is in the past. I want to look to the future, so I came to Harmony Creek. Here I can be part of the building of a new settlement. It's exciting to think the steps I'm taking could lead to a place that will provide homes for Amish families for generations to come."

She didn't reply, so he pushed back his chair. With a swift prayer of gratitude for the meal, he stood.

"If you'll excuse me," he said, "I need to see if there are usable tarps in the big barn. It looks like more snow, and the roof on the barn where my tools arc has more holes than an old pair of sneakers."

"Thanks for your help, Jeremiah."

"*Danki* for breakfast."

When again she remained silent, he put his hat and coat on and turned up his collar before he opened the door. A cold blast of wind sucked him out onto the porch.

He looked across the yard toward the barns. *Lord, I could use your help in seeing the way I should go. I'm here to help make this settlement a success. How can I without this farm?*

It was possible in the coming months, after they had houses fit to live in, one of the other families might be able to offer him a place to stay. He could return to making furniture, though it would take time to establish the business, and he'd have to discover what he needed to

do to open a woodworking shop in New York. Selling many of his tools in order to raise money for the farm had seemed like a *gut* choice before he found the situation was far more complicated than he'd imagined.

He did a quick inventory in his mind. He had enough tools to do simple projects. Eventually, he could buy new tools to make furniture, which would boost his profits.

But could he set aside his dream of farming? And how could he ask Mercy to put aside hers so he could have the future he wanted along Harmony Creek? He was no closer to the answer than he'd been the moment he saw her in the house.

No, he was further away because his attraction to her was sure to complicate the situation unless he was careful.

Very, very, very careful.

Chapter Five

Mercy made certain the ladder was secure against the wall before she tore off the final pieces of hideous wallpaper after lunch later that week. She was glad to toss aside the tea rose pattern and watch it flit onto the pile of scraps she'd made. If she'd had to look at the ugly wallpaper much longer, she would have had nightmares about the disgusting pink roses for a full week.

She laughed as she climbed off the ladder. Once she swept up the strips, she'd never have to see it again.

Pausing as she stepped onto the smooth wood floors, she imagined how the walls would look with a fresh coat of paint. The dark woodwork would complement it. With the variety of oak furniture in the room and forest green tiles edging the fireplace opening, the room would look inviting. She wasn't sure why her grandfather hadn't changed it years ago.

Her feeling of accomplishment faded. Was it silly to do all this work? If the farm wasn't going to be hers, she was wasting her time redoing the house to make it a home for her and Sunni.

She wasn't going to sit around and wait to hear from

Dad. If they agreed to let her somehow buy the farm, she'd regret the time lost. She'd already sent a copy of the approval she'd gotten as a foster parent before Sunni was placed with her as well as other forms to county and state offices to begin the approval process for turning the farm into a summer camp for underprivileged city children.

Though it was difficult to think about warm weather when it was snowing—again!—and drifts were rising over the bottom of the porch railing. It was getting so deep Sunni didn't want to go outside. And it was cold! Even with a full tank of fuel oil, the house couldn't shake its chill. No wonder Sunni had made a tent out of blankets in the dining room to give herself a warm cocoon where she could read and color.

Chafing her cold hands, Mercy decided to do something to keep her warm, too. Not sweeping up the damp wallpaper strips. She'd turn her attention to finding the will Grandpa Rudy must have left somewhere in the house.

Two hours later she was running out of places to look on the first floor. She'd gone through the stacks of papers, mail and unread newspapers on her grandfather's desk. She'd checked every cubbyhole and drawer, including the "secret" one he'd shown her when she turned thirteen. He kept nothing in it more secret than his stash of root beer candies.

She resisted stopping to read the papers her grandfather had kept. Later...

Going to the back stairs she preferred rather than the grander front staircase, Mercy went up. The floors over the kitchen were sturdier than at the other end of the house.

Where should she begin? Where would Grandpa Rudy have put such an important document?

Mercy gnawed on her lower lip as she looked along the upper hallway. He'd told her so often that he'd made a will. Or that he was going to. If he had, wouldn't he have kept a copy somewhere in the house?

Both attorneys in nearby Salem had told her that they hadn't helped him draft a will. Why would Grandpa Rudy have been so specific about leaving her instructions on what to do after his death if he hadn't left a will somewhere? Maybe he hadn't gotten around to putting his thoughts on paper.

No, she didn't want to believe that.

Had Grandpa Rudy taken his business elsewhere? He liked to travel throughout the county as well as in the nearby hills of Vermont. His old truck had a half million miles on the odometer, proof he had friends far and wide throughout the area. Should she contact other law offices in the area?

The idea gave her a headache, because it probably would be a waste of time. Not that she didn't have time to waste. Talking to her parents last night had been as discouraging as the search for the will. Her father's siblings disagreed about what to do with the farm.

"There's no hurry," Dad had said. "Let them take the time they need to consider everything. Rushing them will annoy everyone, and making such an important decision hastily is sure to give us a reason to be sorry later."

Mercy wasn't sure if her parents were among the ones who would be irked if she pressed for an answer. She'd gently reminded them how vital it was to start the licensing procedures for the farm before she could

open it to children. When her mother had expressed surprise, saying she thought Mercy's foster care license would suffice, Mercy bit back her irritation. Several times before she'd left, she'd outlined for her parents what she needed to do in preparation to make Come Along Farm possible.

"I keep my important papers in my room," Mercy said aloud, smothered by the silence. "Maybe Grandpa Rudy did, too."

Pushing on the door she hadn't opened since the funeral, she started to step into her grandfather's room, then froze in the doorway. Everything about the room was a reminder of him. At the foot of the bed was the bright red-and-green afghan he'd made when he decided learning to crochet would keep his mind sharp. Two more afghans, one black-and-white and the other a gaudy yellow, were draped over an upholstered chair whose springs were gone. The seat dropped to the floor.

A low, long dresser between the room's two windows was covered with photographs. When she'd first come to the farm, the pictures had been on a table downstairs. She'd pestered Grandpa Rudy to identify each person and tell her how they were related to her until on one visit, she discovered he'd moved them upstairs. Though he'd never complained, she guessed he'd gotten tired of sharing the same stories over and over.

She stepped back. She couldn't go in and touch his things. Not yet. Not when the pain of losing him was so fresh.

Tomorrow, she promised herself. Tomorrow she would come back if she hadn't found a will in the house. In the meantime she could look in the other rooms where the floors were solid. Perhaps up in the

attic, though she shuddered at the idea of the spider-webs in the stairwell.

"Knock, knock," came a shout from the first floor.

Even with the voice distorted by the narrow stair-case, she couldn't mistake it for another or ignore how her heart began to beat a bit faster.

Jeremiah!

Since the breakfast they'd shared the day the heat went out, she'd seen him at a distance and waved when he noticed her outside. He hadn't come to the house, though she'd heard the sound of hammering, and she guessed he was doing work on the tenant house.

Hurrying down the stairs, Mercy caught sight of Sunni slipping into the kitchen. Jeremiah either hadn't noticed her or was pretending he hadn't.

Jeremiah had taken off his black felt hat, leaving his reddish-brown hair tousled. Her fingers tingled at the thought of brushing those strands into place.

He turned to her, and her breath caught. The cold wind had burnished his face, emphasizing the strong planes that realigned when he gave her a cautious smile.

Regret slashed her. In other circumstances she and Jeremiah might have become friends, but the future of the farm remained a chasm between them. She had no idea how to cross it.

And is being friends all you aspire to become with him?

She paid no attention to the soft voice from deep within her. Instantly, she wondered if doing that was a mistake, because she hadn't heeded what it whispered when she was seeing Graham. Maybe if she'd listened then…

Jeremiah spoke, freeing her from her uneasy thoughts.

"I wanted to let you know, Mercy, I've got some cattle being delivered in a couple of days."

"Cows? Here? Now?"

His face became grave. "You don't have to remind me, Mercy, how foolish I was to make these plans before the farm was officially mine. If your family decides not to sell to me, I'll have the animals removed and sold. I wanted you to know so you weren't surprised when the livestock truck backs up the drive."

"Thank you. I appreciate you letting me know." She hated how they spoke as polite strangers who intended to remain that.

"I didn't want you to think I was going behind your back."

"That never crossed my mind," she said, bowled over by his words. She'd met very few Amish people, but the ones she'd met lived a life of faith and truth.

"Gut." His smile returned. "We've got to stop thinking the other one believes we have ulterior motives for everything we do or say."

"How do we do that?"

"By accepting whatever happens with the farm is God's will."

Mercy couldn't return his easy grin. God's will? Had it been God's will that her first placement had been disrupted by jealousy? Why would God allow her to fall for Graham so he could make her feel as if she was a second choice?

"Are you okay?" Jeremiah asked, his ruddy brows lowering.

"Fine. Or as fine as I can be, under the circumstances." That was the truth, and she wasn't going to

spill why she couldn't accept God's will as easily as Jeremiah seemed to.

He scanned her face, puzzled and looking for answers. She wasn't going to share the details of her time in foster care when it'd seemed as if God had abandoned her. She'd told Graham about that, and he'd been shocked at first. Later, he'd acted as if her failed adoption was somehow all her fault.

Only much later had she realized he was repeating exactly what his mother had said. The woman had always been quick to point out what she saw as Mercy's shortcomings. Everything that went wrong, even rain on a day when they'd planned to go to an outdoor concert, was, in his mother's eyes, Mercy's fault. It made no sense, but Mercy would have endured it if Graham had—just once—stood up for her.

He hadn't.

Not once. He quickly agreed with Mrs. Rapp, no matter how ridiculous the older woman's opinions were.

If Graham had been willing to get out from under his mother's thumb, Mercy might not have rushed to Harmony Creek before she realized Grandpa Rudy had put the farm up for sale.

Her best friend, Erika, had warned Mercy to consider Graham's proposal very, very carefully before agreeing. "If it's a choice between what his mother wants and what you want," Erika had told her more than once, "you're going to lose every time."

"But I love him," Mercy had argued, "and he loves me."

"I'm sure you're right, but he'll always side with his mother. Be careful."

She hadn't been. She'd given her heart totally, believing if she loved Graham enough, he'd change.

He hadn't. When the tough decision had to be made of where they'd live, he'd listened to Mrs. Rapp instead of doing what was best for his future wife and stepdaughter. His assumption Mercy was wrong for not understanding his mother's needs were most important hammered the final nail in their relationship's coffin, killing hopes she'd had of a future with him.

He hadn't come to say goodbye after she'd left a message on his phone that she and Sunni were moving to Harmony Creek. He'd never returned her call, making her feel like a fool.

One thing she knew for certain. She wasn't going to be a fool for a man ever again, no matter how handsome or nice he was.

Jeremiah couldn't help being curious what Mercy was thinking. Her face was clouded with strong emotions, which he hoped had nothing to do with the arrival of the cows he'd planned to be the beginning of the farm's dairy herd. Every instinct urged him to ask her how he could help. Even more, he yearned to pull her into his arms and offer her comfort for whatever was hurting her.

He couldn't do either.

Not letting the frustrated sigh sift past his lips, he waited for Mercy to say something.

When she did, he wasn't surprised it was a lame excuse to end their conversation. His frown returned when she mentioned going into Salem to pick up groceries.

"The roads aren't plowed yet," he said.

"Oh."

Her face was so dejected he hurried to say, "You could take the sleigh."

"Sleigh?"

He nodded. "There's one in the big barn. It's half-hidden under a blanket, but other than being covered with dust, it looks in *gut* condition. The runners may have some rust. If they do, I can sand it off, and you'll be on your way as soon as we hook up Hero to the sleigh."

"Your horse's name is Hero? Isn't that an odd name for an Amish horse?"

"It's the name he had when I bought him, and he's been my hero more than once when he got me home during a storm." He grinned. "He's very even-tempered, so you shouldn't have any problem with him."

She backed away slowly. "Thanks, but I'll make up something out of whatever is in the kitchen."

He was baffled again, but comprehension burst through him like a shooting star on a summer evening. "You don't know how to drive a horse, ain't so?"

"I never have." She glanced out the window toward where her car sat beneath deep snow. "I've been able to depend on my car to get me where I need to go."

"But you want to live on a farm with horses."

"For the children to ride."

Spying her daughter, who was peeking through the kitchen doorway, clearly eavesdropping, he acted as if he hadn't seen the *kind*. He didn't want to send her scurrying away again. "Wouldn't those *kinder* enjoy rides in a wagon, too?"

She folded her arms but laughed. "Jeremiah Stoltzfus, has anyone ever told you that once you get an idea in your head you hold on to it like a snapping turtle?"

"I'd like to think I have more sense than a turtle that

won't let go even to eat." He hooked a thumb toward the door. "Might as well get started with your lessons."

"Not now."

"Why not? I've got the time, and today isn't going to be the only day you'll need the sleigh before the snow melts."

Again, she paused. Was she looking for an excuse he'd have to accept?

He realized how much he'd misconstrued her silence when she said, "I can't go outside to take driving lessons and leave Sunni alone in the house."

"Bring her along. I'll teach her, too."

"She's only seven years old."

With a laugh, he said, "I was younger than she is the first time the reins were placed in my hands." He looked straight at Sunni. "Do you want to try?" He cut his eyes to Mercy. "What do you say?"

He wasn't sure if he or Mercy was more shocked when Sunni stepped into the room and asked, "Can we, Mommy?"

Chapter Six

Mercy wanted to say no to driving lessons, but how could she when Sunni was opening up to Jeremiah for the first time? Though he might not be in their lives for long, it was good to see her daughter begin to trust another man.

But was Mercy ready to trust another man?

You're agreeing to learning to drive a sleigh, not accepting an offer to go on a date with him. That little voice was becoming more annoying, but it also was correct. *He's trying to make you less dependent on him during these storms.*

She was shocked the thought irritated her more. Poor Jeremiah! It seemed she could find an ulterior motive in whatever he did. Not his ulterior motive, but hers.

"Mommy, can we drive the sleigh?" asked Sunni, warning Mercy she'd been lost in her self-recriminating thoughts too long.

"All right." She didn't get a chance to add more before her daughter let out a cheer and began singing "Jingle Bells."

Jeremiah was grinning as broadly. "Let me get Hero

hooked up to the sleigh. It may take fifteen minutes or more because I need to get the sleigh out of the barn."

"It'll give me time to make up a thermos of hot cocoa and get us bundled up," she said, excitement bursting through her. Hadn't she come to the farm to try new things? Learning to drive the sleigh would be a great place to start.

"Jingle bells, jingle bells, jingle all the way," sang Sunni at the top of her lungs as she spun about like a flat-footed ballerina.

With a wink, Jeremiah put on his hat and left. He called back that he'd pull the sleigh up to the door.

Mercy worked around her jubilant daughter and delighted in Sunni's joy. She hadn't seen her daughter so elated since before Grandpa Rudy's funeral. And Mercy was happy, too. The idea of speeding over the snow in a sleigh was exciting.

She was about to wrap a scarf around Sunni's neck when her daughter pulled away and ran to the door.

Mercy wasn't surprised to see the sleigh looked as if it'd been hit by an avalanche and buried under boulders. The paint was scraped off the dented side, but the runners were straight, and Jeremiah's horse was pulling it without too much effort.

"Ready?" she asked Sunni as she reached for her own scarf and the thermos and trio of cups.

Sunni threw open the door, then halted. "Where are the jingle bells?"

"All I could find," Jeremiah said, "was this harness."

Sunni whirled. "But, Mommy, the song is 'Jingle Bells.' We have to have jingle bells."

Before Mercy could reply, the little girl whirled and

ran up the stairs at a dangerous speed for a child wearing two leg braces.

Mercy steeled herself, praying she wouldn't hear the dreadful thump that meant Sunni had fallen on the steps.

"Are you okay?" asked Jeremiah from right behind her.

She turned to discover he'd come up on the porch. "She shouldn't go so fast up the stairs."

"Words every *mamm* has said for as long as there have been stairs. We all take a few tumbles in life and are not much the worse for it, ain't so?"

"Certainly." She appreciated how he acted as if Sunni was like every other child.

"Why does she wear those braces…if you don't mind me asking?"

"I don't." She smiled. "But I don't know. We've gotten as many different opinions as we've had doctors for her. Most recently her pediatric orthopedist said we should worry less about what caused the weakness in her legs and concentrate on helping her walk better."

"And run."

Her smile broadened. "She's learned that well."

When Sunni came down the stairs at the same pace she'd gone up, both Jeremiah and Mercy jumped forward as the little girl stumbled three steps from the bottom. Between them, they caught her and set her on her feet.

"I know, I know," Sunni said before anyone could speak. "I need to go more slowly and use my crutches, but we have jingle bells." As she began singing the song again, she held up her right hand and shook it.

Jeremiah's eyes grew wide at the sound of bells jangling.

Taking the toy from Sunni, Mercy held it out to him. It was a wooden half circle into which was set a half dozen tiny metal bells.

"What is it?" he asked beneath the little girl's enthusiastic singing.

Mercy answered as softly, "A toy. Kids use them to make music in school. We got it as a therapy tool for Sunni last year. It helped strengthen her grip." Showing him how fingers wrapped around the wooden handle while the bells were shaken, she smiled. "I didn't realize she still had it."

Jeremiah raised his voice to include the little girl. "We've got our jingle bells and our cocoa, so let's go."

Mercy watched as he went outside. Sunni followed, and he swung her up onto the sleigh's bench. He sat beside her. They looked back in a silent urging for Mercy to hurry up.

She did and laughed as she hadn't in longer than she could remember when Jeremiah reached to assist her into the battered sleigh. At his touch, even through his thick gloves and hers, the day suddenly had seemed warmer.

When she sat beside him, he unlashed the reins from the dash and showed her how to hold them. He told her to loop the reins up between her pinkie and the next finger, grip them in her fist and let them go out between her thumb and first finger.

"That gives you the most control," he said, adjusting her hands slightly. "Hero is well trained, so call his name, and he'll go."

"And to stop him?"

"A simple 'whoa.' You don't have to tug on the reins. He'll stop right away." Again, he aligned her fingers. "There you go. Whenever you're ready."

She made the mistake of looking at him to ask another question. His face was so near to hers their misted breaths mingled in the cold air. As her gaze locked with his lustrous blue eyes, she knew she should look away before he got the wrong idea.

Or the right one.

Even that thought couldn't convince her eyes to turn from his handsome face. As close as they sat, she could see the faint shadow of whiskers along his jaw. Her fingers tingled, teasing her to tear off her gloves and stroke that firm line. She caught a motion from the corner of her eye. His hand was rising to cup her cheek. She leaned toward it, eager to feel him against her.

"Jingle bells! Jingle bells!" sang Sunni abruptly.

The cheerful song brought Mercy to her senses. Jeremiah, too, she guessed, because he quickly slanted away from her and urged her to give the command to go.

She did, and the horse moved at a walk toward the road. Her thoughts sped far faster as she pondered what would have happened if Sunni's innocent singing hadn't intruded. Trying to convince herself it was better she didn't know, she wondered when she'd started being dishonest with herself.

"Hold that board right there," Jeremiah urged Sunni, who kept a suspicious eye on the hammer and nail he was positioning. It was the first board for the roof of a chicken coop. After finishing his barn chores, including milking and feeding the calves delivered earlier in the week, he'd wanted time outdoors.

He smiled at Sunni. The little girl didn't trust him completely, but she didn't scurry in the opposite direction when he approached as she had before they drove the sleigh along the twisting creek that slept beneath a sheet of ice. When, during her midmorning break from her schoolwork, she'd come to watch him building the chicken coop, a simple box with a door and shelves for the hens to lay on, he'd pretended as if nothing significant had happened. Maybe if he acted as if she'd sought him out right from the beginning, he wouldn't send her fleeing again. He kept up a steady narration of everything he did, and Sunni had inched closer and closer.

Then she began asking questions, barely giving him time to answer before she fired another one—or two—at him. She asked about the coop and the chickens that would live inside. She wanted to know what color he planned to paint it and what he intended to name the chickens. He answered questions about what the chickens would eat and where they would sleep and when the rooster would crow.

Asking her to balance the board might threaten the status quo, but Jeremiah kept reminding himself with God's help, anything was possible. Even persuading a *kind* he didn't mean her ill will. He was curious if Sunni's skittishness was for the same reason as Mercy's.

What do you know about women? he asked himself. He'd believed Emmarita when she said she was coming back. He hadn't guessed she was seeing her *Englischer* at the same time Jeremiah was escorting her home from youth events. She'd jumped the fence, and unlike two of his brothers' wives who had done the same, she hadn't returned...though he'd waited several months to make sure. When he heard she'd married her *Englischer*, he

knew he needed to put the past behind him. He listened to the hopes of having a farm of his own, the hopes God had put inside him. It was easier to heed that portion of his heart when he closed off the part filled with pain at Emmarita's betrayal.

Focusing on his work, Jeremiah made sure Sunni's fingers weren't close to where he was hammering. She'd become silent, but the fact she was standing there seemed like a precious victory.

"Mommy!" Sunni suddenly shouted and released the plank.

Jeremiah grasped the board to keep it from swinging out and striking the *kind*. His heart hitched, and he knew he couldn't blame his heart's reaction totally on fright for the little girl.

His gaze riveted on Mercy as she walked toward them. Her cheeks were burnished by the cold to the same shade as her lips, which appeared delightfully kissable. The image of his hands framing her face while he sampled her mouth was so real he lowered his eyes and swung the hammer, barely missing the nail and his thumb in his work glove. He set down the hammer, knowing, when he was that distracted, he might not miss next time.

"What are you making?" Mercy's tone hinted that she hadn't noticed how distracted he was by her.

He wasn't sure if that was *gut* or annoying.

"It's a chicken choop," Sunni answered.

"A chicken *coop*," he corrected with a smile.

"But…" Mercy looked hastily away, but not fast enough because he saw her cheeks redden more.

He wasn't going to pretend not to understand. She'd agreed on the day he taught her to drive not to look for

secret intentions behind every word or deed. He wished she'd trust him.

Though he wanted to ask why she always painted him with such negative intentions, he said, "Mercy, didn't your *daed* tell you it may be several weeks before he gets an answer from his siblings?"

"He did."

"But you are working to fix up the main house. Sunni was telling me that you're painting the living room." He saw *mamm* and daughter exchange a glance, but couldn't guess what it meant. He hoped nothing. "Like you, I don't want to wait until everything is decided. If I do and they sell me the farm, I must not be so far behind on fixing up the place I can't get a decent crop in the fields or have a place to put it when it's harvested."

"I know." She raised her eyes to meet his, and he realized he'd misjudged her reaction. She wasn't angry. She was frustrated her family hadn't made their decision. "I'm sorry this is dragging on."

Stepping around the coop so it wasn't between them, he put his hands on Mercy's shoulders. "It's not your fault."

"Thanks for saying that, but every time the phone rings, I hope it's my father with news." She grimaced. "I'm tempted to silence it and let the answering machine get the calls. That way, I'd only have to check once a day."

"Why don't you?"

Her eyes brightened. "I think I will. I'm tired of being on a ladder and having to rush down to answer it. In case it's Dad." A smile played at the corners of her mouth. "I almost tipped over the paint can yesterday. If I had, Sunni and I would be green now."

"It wouldn't be a bad color on you two," he replied in mock seriousness. "And we could use a bit more green with this snow."

The little girl giggled, and Jeremiah let his lips tilt up in a grin.

"I'll leave that to the leaves," Mercy said.

Groaning at her pun, he felt the tension dissolve around them. They might have different goals for the farm, but they were stuck in limbo together while her family debated.

"Why don't we keep doing what we've been doing?" he asked. "Any fixes we do will benefit whoever gets the farm."

"That makes sense."

"And we don't have to walk around on eggshells."

"Eggshells?" asked Sunni, looking around as if she expected to see a pile waiting to be picked up. "Where are they?"

Again, he and Mercy chuckled, and Sunni joined in.

Jeremiah rested one hand on the top of the coop. "Whether you or I or someone else ends up with the farm, me building a simple chicken coop won't make any difference. It seems strange to live on a farm without chickens."

"You can't be thinking of putting them out here now," Mercy said, wrapping her arms around herself as a frigid gust rocked the trees beyond the barn.

He shook his head. "Ordering chicks was another thing I did before I left Paradise Springs. They'll be shipped once the weather warms up. By fall, they should be providing eggs." He gave her a wry grin. "Sorry they won't be laying in time for Easter."

"Don't worry," Mercy said. "We'll have eggs to dye for Easter."

Sunni looked relieved, but grimaced when Mercy reminded her schoolwork waited in the house.

As her daughter went inside, Mercy asked, "Do Amish kids dye eggs for Easter?"

"Some do. My *mamm* hid plastic eggs filled with jelly beans for us to find."

"I assume you have church services on Easter."

"*Ja.* Good Friday is a fast day until noon, so we can spend the morning in prayer. On Easter, we rejoice together."

"Mennonites consider it a time to be with family, and we have services on Friday and Sunday." She patted her hands together and glanced toward the house. "I should make sure Sunni is doing her schoolwork."

Gut sense told him to let her go, but he didn't want to let the moment end. "You've got a lot of questions about Amish folks."

"If I stay here, I'm going to have Amish neighbors."

He almost said if she ended up with the farm, the settlement could be in jeopardy. He needed to stay and help it grow. There wasn't any reason to repeat what had been said already. They knew what was at stake, so why belabor it?

"Why don't you come with me to a service?" he asked. "This Sunday is a church Sunday. I think you'll get plenty of answers to your questions there."

"I didn't know your services were open to outsiders."

"They are, but few non-Amish are willing to sit on hard, backless benches for three hours to listen to sermons in High German."

"I don't understand that language."

"Visitors have someone to translate for them. I think you'd find it interesting, Mercy." *Please, God, let her say* ja. He didn't want to consider why it was suddenly so important to him that she agree, but it was.

"Thank you, Jeremiah. We'll come." Her smile banished the cold around him...and inside him.

When she walked away, he was glad she hadn't expected him to say something else. He wasn't sure what he would have said, but he was certain anything he blurted out would reveal the farm was no longer the main reason he was glad he'd come to Harmony Creek.

She was.

Chapter Seven

Jeremiah whistled one of his favorite hymns as he put the finishing touches on the chicken coop. He laughed at the sign tacked over the door.

Welkoom Hoom.

Sunni had brought it out to him right after breakfast. She'd proudly announced she'd painted it for his Amish chickens so they'd feel right at home in the coop.

It had taken every bit of restraint to keep from grinning. Not only were the words different from any he knew in *Englisch* or *Deitsch*, the everyday language of the Amish, but most of the letters had drips of green paint beneath them. He wondered if Mercy knew what her daughter had been doing.

He knew the little girl was fascinated with the idea of chickens and gathering eggs, because she'd talked of nothing else while he put the sign in place. As much as he wanted the farm to become a part of the new Amish community, he hated the idea of Sunni not having her chance to help with the new chicks.

With each passing day, the situation was becoming more of a potential disaster, no matter which one of

them ended up with the farm. Did Mercy's *onkels* and *aentis* and *daed* realize that? He doubted it. Would it do any *gut* to ask Mercy to discuss it with them?

But did he want them to announce their decision if it cost him the farm?

He no longer knew.

You know, God, he prayed, *what is to come and why. Help us to walk the path You have prepared for us, even if our hearts are broken.*

He flinched. No matter what choice the Bambergers made, his heart was going to be hurt because if he took possession of the farm, Mercy's heart—and Sunni's— would be shattered. For the first time he began to wonder if he should walk away. He could have Kitty find him another place. It might take too much time and risk the success of the settlement, but how could he stand by and watch Mercy hurt?

Help me, God, to trust You have a way to resolve the unresolvable.

When Mercy heard a knock at the door that afternoon, she made sure her kerchief was in place before she answered it. She didn't want to meet one of her neighbors for the first time with her head not properly covered, because she knew Amish women always wore what they called prayer *kapps* or a kerchief like hers. Dust and spiderwebs didn't count as a proper covering, though she guessed there were plenty on the off-white kerchief.

A pulse of excitement caught her off guard as she wondered if Jeremiah stood on the other side of the door. What was she thinking? He'd been very kind to teach her to drive the sleigh so she could get to the village after a snowfall.

But he wanted her grandfather's farm, and if the family's decision went against her, he would do everything he could to buy it. Nothing had changed.

No, that wasn't true.

A few things had changed. She couldn't see Jeremiah as a rival trying to ruin her plans. Instead, her heart seemed to glow whenever he was around.

Throwing open the door, she was unprepared for the surge of disappointment when she realized it wasn't Jeremiah. She'd been silly to think he'd come to the front door and knock. He always walked in.

A woman, whose face was half-hidden by a garish purple and yellow crocheted scarf covering her mouth and nose, stood on the porch. From the top of her striped stocking cap to the tip of her boots topped by a ring of fake fur, she looked ready to go sledding on the hills beyond the barn.

The woman pulled aside her scarf to reveal the lower half of her face. "Are you Mercy Bamberger?"

"I am." Mercy motioned for the woman to come in.

Even if the woman was there to try to sell her something she didn't want, Mercy wasn't going to leave her out on the porch in the biting wind.

When the blonde woman set a briefcase on the floor and began to unzip her thick parka, Mercy asked, "What can I do for you?"

"I'm Whitney Albright with Washington County Children's Services." She opened a pocket on the side of the briefcase and pulled out a simple business card.

Mercy took it and glanced at it. The card confirmed what Whitney had said.

"I'd like to talk with you if you've got time," Whitney said.

"Certainly. Let's go into the living room."

Curiosity accompanied Mercy into the room, which was comfortably warm in the afternoon sunshine. She couldn't help being curious about whether Whitney thought of how the glass in the windows rattled whenever a strong gust struck the house. Motioning for the woman to take a seat on the couch, where the cold air seeping around the sills wouldn't reach her, Mercy took a chair facing the sofa.

"I'm sorry to come unannounced," Whitney said as she sat and set her briefcase on her knees. "I did try to call. Several times yesterday. But while I got your answering machine, I didn't want to leave a message before I had a chance to talk to you. When I tried again this morning and got the machine again, I thought maybe I'd drive over and take a chance on catching you at home."

Mercy explained how she'd turned off the phone's ringer so she wasn't interrupted while she was painting. Without giving the other woman a chance to reply, she hurried on. "If this is about my daughter not being signed up to go to public school, I made arrangements to homeschool her for the rest of this year. I plan to have her go to the Son-Rise Charter School next fall."

Whitney held up her hands and shook her head. "This isn't about your daughter, Mercy, though I'll tell you I did stop at the school in Salem to find someone who knew you. They explained to me the arrangements you'd made for Sunni. You know you can get special needs services through the public school system, though she's going to the charter school, I assume."

"Yes, because we had that arrangement with our school district where we lived."

"If anyone tells you differently, call me and I'll talk

to them." She smiled, but it was cool and without humor. "Some superintendents look for ways to cut costs. Not that we've had such a problem with the Salem school district, but we like to make sure none crop up."

"I appreciate that." Curious why the woman was visiting, Mercy asked if Whitney would like something hot to drink.

"That would be nice. Coffee or tea or whatever you have."

"I have green tea."

"Perfect."

Rising, Mercy went into the kitchen and put the kettle on. She glanced into the dining room and saw Sunni curled up in a chair, sound asleep. The little girl had had nightmares last night. It was good she could catch up on her sleep today, especially until Mercy discovered why a social worker had come to the house.

Whitney took an appreciative sip of the tea, but waited until Mercy was sitting again before she opened her briefcase and pulled out a laptop. "As I said, I'm not here to speak to you about Sunni. However, I'm here *because* of your daughter." The social worker looked abashed as she added, "I guess I should have told you right from the get-go I was forwarded a copy of your files and I've read them."

"I know files are shared among social workers."

"Good." Whitney relaxed a bit as she pushed the button to activate her computer. Raising her head, she wore what Mercy called a social worker's *I hope you can get me out of a jam* face.

The first time she'd seen it was when she was in the system herself. She'd forgotten about it until another social worker spoke to her about taking in Sunni on an

emergency placement. Seeing it again whetted her curiosity and her trepidation.

"You are," Whitney said, "in a somewhat unique position of having exactly the experience we need."

Mercy felt her jaw drop. Another child? Here? She thought of all she'd had to do in order to be approved as a foster parent before Sunni was placed with her. There had been more paperwork and home visits and counseling when she applied to adopt her daughter. Enough to kill off a whole forest was what Dad had said with a laugh.

Glancing around the half-painted room that opened onto another where wallpaper was peeling off a wall and the floor sloping enough to send Mercy chasing after a nail when it fell and rolled away, she looked at the social worker. Was this a joke?

"I know this is unexpected," Whitney said, "and it may not be perfect timing, but I rarely find the time is perfect when a child's placement has been disrupted and we need to find a temporary placement."

"Oh, I'm so sorry to hear about a placement falling apart."

"I know you are."

Mercy wondered exactly how much the social worker knew about her story and Sunni's. How many files had Whitney perused before she came to Harmony Creek? No doubt, there were thick files outlining how she and Sunni had come to be part of the Bamberger family.

At the thought of her family, Mercy stiffened. What was she thinking? She needed to tell Whitney, while she understood the gravity of the situation, now was the worst time for her to consider having another child placed with her family. Even a temporary one. No, most

especially a temporary one, because Sunni didn't need to deal with more change.

"I know you're not ready," Whitney said in her calm voice.

Mercy bit back a laugh. "Look around you. Come Along Farm is weeks away from being ready for me to apply for approval."

"But you are a licensed foster parent?"

"I am."

"Parker, a nine-year-old boy, needs a placement." The blonde leaned forward, lowering her computer's top and putting her elbows on it. "He's a unique case because we don't get many failed international adoptions in this county. In fact, he might be the second one in sixty years. Mercy, you know how it is to be an outsider in a closed community, and your daughter was born in Korea as Parker was."

"Why does he need a placement?"

"His prospective adoptive parents can't deal with his many severe food allergies. You're raising a special needs child, so I can't imagine a better place for this boy while we look for another adoptive family than with you and Sunni."

Wanting to groan that Whitney was expecting too much of her and her daughter, Mercy said nothing. Instead, she prayed. *Lord, You don't have to tell me this is crazy. I know that, and I also know Your hand brought Whitney here. Come Along Farm is supposed to be a haven for children. How can I turn away the first one You present to me?*

A sensation of calm draped over her as she held out her hand. "Can I see his placement report?"

"It's on the computer." Whitney pressed several keys

and then turned it so Mercy could read the report that wasn't so different from the one she'd been given with Sunni's other paperwork. It was from the Korean adoption agency and translated into sometimes confusing English. The information was sparse and included his age, gender, a couple of paragraphs outlining what his Korean caretakers had observed about him, and weight and height.

"His name in Korea was Park Jae-Eun, I see," Mercy said.

"The Kentons changed it to Parker Kenton, wanting to keep part of his Korean name as part of his new name." The social worker smiled sadly. "It'll be easier for him in the States, I suppose, but his Korean name means talent and mercy."

"Mercy?"

Whitney nodded. "When I was looking for foster families with Korean-born children in the county, I saw your name, which was why I requested your file."

"He has several food allergies," Mercy said after finishing the two-page report from Korea, "but I don't see anything here."

"They apparently weren't discovered until he was here. He had no problem with Korean food, but Americans eat a wider variety of products."

Wondering why Parker's new family hadn't changed their own diets to accommodate the boy, Mercy looked at the list of Parker's allergies. Peanuts and shellfish were the first of nearly a dozen items, but it wouldn't be difficult to work around his allergies.

"Am I wrong," Whitney asked, "to think you make a lot of your meals from scratch? Parker seems to have extra trouble with prepared foods."

The social worker had an uncanny ability to guess

what Mercy was thinking, or more likely, Whitney was very good at her job and had prepared herself for questions and concerns Mercy might have.

"I don't make as much from scratch as I normally would, because we don't have anything canned in the cellar." Second thoughts filled her. Sunni needed her during this difficult time, and bringing a second child into their family would curtail the time she had to work on the house. She couldn't reduce the time she spent teaching Sunni, and a nine-year-old would require homeschooling, too. So much paperwork needed to be filed, and...

"You'll want to see this." Whitney held out a small photo.

Mercy looked at it and knew her protests and logical thinking were useless. The moment she saw the proud expression on the boy's face that announced he didn't need anyone's help, she recognized a kindred spirit. Especially when she noticed how his taut shoulders revealed he was trying to hide his pain of being unwanted from the camera.

Oh, how easily she remembered those feelings! And the photographs taken against an office wall while people looked on with pitying smiles. Mercy had been older than the boy the first time she'd been subjected to the humiliation of knowing she was nobody's child. When *Abuelita* had died, Mercy's sole parent had become the state government, an indifferent guardian at best. She'd been snatched from *Abuelita*'s apartment so quickly she hadn't had time to pack the photo of her parents, her most precious possession, before being bundled up and put in a car with strangers. She'd been told her personal belongings would follow. One box had...but the photo hadn't been in it. Her other box had vanished.

A chance question when she'd asked if she would be going to her Fresh Air family had saved her from what probably would have been a life in the system. A caring social worker—Mercy couldn't remember her name—had contacted the family who'd welcomed her for the previous three summers to their farm in northern New York. But the family's agreement to take her on a trial basis hadn't been the salvation she'd expected. She hadn't been able to wait to return to the family she'd thought of constantly while she was away from it. But the fun times she'd enjoyed each summer with the two daughters had become intolerable misery when the older daughter had become wildly jealous of Mercy and the attention she'd garnered in the very conservative community.

The placement had fallen apart, and she'd found herself in a car with the social worker who'd brought her north. Returned to the city, she'd been placed with a family who used the stipend from five foster kids to help pay for their own expenses. She'd remained there, virtually ignored, for the longest four months of her life.

Then adults she hadn't known came to the house. She'd realized they were social workers, and they'd given her no warning other than she needed to pack her personal items. The other kids in the house had been told the same. Though none of them had much, they'd delayed as long as they could over the task while they'd spent time speculating about what was about to happen to them. The older children had been resigned to being put with another family in another school district, but Mercy had been terrified.

Her fear had grown when the other children were dropped off to meet other social workers so they could be introduced to their new foster families, but she'd

been driven out of the city. Nobody had told her where she was going until they'd left the city behind.

She'd been taken to meet Frieda and Kevin Bamberger, a Mennonite couple whose biological children were much older than she was. When she'd reached their comfortable home, she hadn't had high hopes. At the time it'd been another change she didn't have any say in.

But she'd been welcomed as if she'd been a part of their family her whole life. A portion of her bedtime prayers every night still included her gratitude for the two people who had stepped up to be her parents.

She had a chance to help a young child who was caught in the same trap. The Bambergers had welcomed her into their home and their hearts, giving her a new name and a new identity, though there was a remnant of Mercedes Ramirez hidden deep within her, and a family as precious to her as the one she'd shared with *Abuelita*.

"All right," Mercy whispered as she stared into the boy's face.

"All right?" repeated Whitney, astonished by Mercy's sudden about-face. "Does that mean you're willing to take Parker on a temporary basis? It could be a month or two before we find him something permanent. In the meantime, the county will provide you with an epinephrine injector in case he goes into anaphylaxis. Instructions for its use are right on the box, and you need to get familiar with them right away so you don't have to stop to read them if he has an allergy attack. Are you ready to deal with that?"

There wasn't a single doubt in her heart, though her head was blaring warnings like a fire siren. "Yes, we'll take him."

Chapter Eight

"Heard anything about what's going to happen with the farm?"

Jeremiah glanced at Caleb, who was helping him set up his woodworking equipment. For now it was a makeshift workshop, but it was in one of the sturdier outbuildings. They'd set up a portable gas generator outside to power the equipment. His neighbor had worked with him, as well, in closing up the holes in the tenant house wall so it no longer snowed indoors. In exchange, Jeremiah intended to make a few pieces for his friend's house. He'd already sketched out a large kitchen table and the benches and chairs to go with it.

"Nothing," Jeremiah said as he shifted a heavy saw a few inches to the left so there was enough space to walk past it. "I guess they're still making up their minds."

"No news is no news, ain't so?"

He grinned at his friend, who was stretched out beneath a table saw. "That's not exactly how I've heard it."

"But it's true. No news means nothing's been decided."

"You're right." Jeremiah leaned against a stack of

planks as his gaze swept the workshop as if he'd entered it for the first time. He'd found the weathered boards in a small barn and brought them to his workshop. If he needed one for a project while Mercy's family discussed the farm, he'd check with her. Using Rudy's bulk tank in the barn to hold milk was one thing, but it'd be completely different to take the valuable wood without permission.

Wiping his hands on a stained cloth, Jeremiah looked out the dusty window beside him. His brows lowered at a surprising sight. He hadn't heard the late-model silver car pull into the driveway. Did Mercy have a friend visiting?

As if he'd asked the question aloud, Caleb paused in examining the underside of a piece of equipment he'd been oiling and came slowly to his feet. "What's so interesting?"

"I didn't know we had company."

Neither man spoke as a blonde *Englisch* woman came out of the house and got into the car. There was a jaunty bounce in her step.

"She sure looks happy," Caleb said. "That bolt is not turning as smoothly as it should. Want to check it?"

"Sure." Jeremiah didn't move from beside the window. "Do you know her?"

Caleb stepped closer to the window and peered out. The car was close enough so he could get a *gut* view of the woman's face before she turned to look over her shoulder while she backed the car out.

"I've never seen her before," Caleb said. "I've met some of the *Englisch* farmers in the area, but not too many of the women. My sister said the *Englisch* women are friendly when she's gone to the store." He paused for

a single heartbeat. "You seem very interested, Jeremiah. But please don't go jumping the fence after some *Englischer*. We need you to help build our settlement. We're six families since the Bowmans moved in yesterday."

Jeremiah nodded and assured Caleb that he was committed to the Harmony Creek settlement. He waited for the pain those words about jumping the fence always created. It came, but not as before. The memory of Emmarita's leaving without saying goodbye was no longer agonizing. However, Caleb's words were a reminder of what Jeremiah had tried to ignore.

Mercy was Mennonite. Getting more involved with her and her daughter would be silly. He had to ignore how his heart beat faster whenever he thought of Mercy's black hair and eyes the color of freshly overturned earth.

Had his thoughts shown on his face? Or had he revealed the truth in other ways?

Caleb gave him a sympathetic glance. "Staying separate from the world is tougher some times than others, ain't so?"

Jeremiah must have given his friend an answer, but once it'd left his lips, he couldn't recall what it was. That Caleb gave him a companionable slap on the shoulder when he left—exactly as one of Jeremiah's brothers would have—was the proof that he'd soothed his friend's concerns.

Lingering in his shop, Jeremiah knew Caleb was worried about Jeremiah falling for a woman who should be off-limits to him. His neighbor also held the weight of the settlement's success on his broad shoulders. Adding more concern to Caleb's already overflowing plate was one of the last things Jeremiah wanted to do.

Either he or Mercy was going to be leaving the farm. Every way he looked at it, there was no future beyond friendship for them. He needed to keep that in mind.

Always.

Jeremiah's resolve lasted exactly as long as it took him to walk over to the main house.

Mercy turned from the stove as he came in. The aroma of chocolate swept through the kitchen. It wasn't as enticing as Mercy, who had a dab of flour on one cheek and a line of chocolate beneath her other eye.

Don't think of her as enticing, he warned himself, but not being honest with himself was foolish.

"I assume the other person looks worse," he said with a wink at Sunni, whose dark braid was dusted with flour.

"What?" asked Mercy.

"You look as if someone gave you a black eye."

She glanced in the mirror over the sink where Rudy must have shaved. When she gasped and reached for a washcloth to clean her face, he and Sunni laughed. Sunni giggled harder when Mercy washed the flour out of her braid.

"Call me when the cake's ready to frost," Sunni said once the last of the white was out of her hair.

"I will. You know I depend of my best spatula cleaner." Mercy bent to kiss the top of her daughter's head.

Jeremiah couldn't keep from imagining how those lips would feel against him. He composed his expression when Sunni left the room and Mercy faced him.

Her easy smile disappeared. "I'm glad you came over, Jeremiah. I need to talk to you about something important, so you're not surprised."

"You sound like I did when I told you the cows were being delivered. Are you having something delivered, too?"

His attempt at levity fell flat because she nodded.

"Did you see the car in the yard earlier?" she asked as she motioned for him to sit at the table.

"*Ja.* I assumed you had a friend visiting."

"Not a friend. Not yet anyhow. The woman who came here is Whitney Albright, and she's a social worker with the county."

"Oh." He wasn't sure what else to say. Had Whitney come for something to do with Sunni? But wasn't the little girl's adoption final? There shouldn't be a reason for a social worker to come to the house, unless…

Was Mercy already going ahead with her plans to get approval for Come Along Farm? Had her *daed* given her some hint to what his siblings had agreed to? She would have told him, wouldn't she?

"Whitney wanted to ask if I'd be willing to take in another child temporarily," Mercy said in not much more than a whisper.

"Are you going to?" He tried to ignore the cascade of relief as he realized, for now, she didn't know more about the future of the farm than he did.

No ulterior motives, he chided himself. She'd concurred, and he hadn't seen a sign of her reneging. He was judging her unfairly.

She wiped her hands on a towel. "As long as I've got room, I'll never turn away a child who needs a home."

When he chuckled, she frowned and asked what was so funny.

"You stating the obvious," he replied. "You want Rudy's farm so you can fill it with *kinder* every sum-

mer. It's not a big step to imagining you trying to fill this whole house with youngsters year-round."

"Not a whole houseful. Just one little nine-year-old boy who needs a home because his placement failed."

"His what failed?"

"Failed placement is a term social workers use for when a child is placed in a home with either foster parents or prospective adoptive parents and then the child needs to be removed."

"And saying it failed means the parents don't want the *kind* any longer?" He shook his head in disgust. "What were they thinking? A kid isn't something to return to the store because it's not a great fit."

Pulling out a chair, she sat facing him. "I agree, but sometimes it's for the best. If the match isn't a good one, it can be worse on the youngster than being moved somewhere else." She slid a photo toward him. "This is the boy."

Jeremiah didn't want to look. Getting more caught up in her life and her plans would complicate their already complicated situation. As he saw the determination in her eyes, he was curious why one boy she'd never met was so important to her.

He reached for the photo.

Breathe!

Such a simple order shouldn't be difficult to follow, but Mercy found it hard to draw in a breath and release it as she waited for Jeremiah's reaction to Parker's picture.

When Jeremiah smiled, she relaxed, astonished how taut her shoulders had become.

"He looks like a normal nine-year-old." Jeremiah tapped the photo. "You can tell he doesn't want to sit

still for someone to snap his picture. But why did Whitney choose you? Don't take this the wrong way, but I would have thought the state would wait until a decision is made about the farm."

Standing, she got a cloth to clean off the table. "I'm a licensed foster parent, and I've taken in other children on an emergency basis until a permanent foster home could be found."

"There must be other foster families in the area."

"There are, but Whitney liked the idea of Parker being with a family who already has an Asian child."

"Parker? That's his name?"

"Yes."

"It sounds very grown-up for a kid."

"I know. It's the name his adoptive parents gave him, but it won't be legally his name until he's adopted. Until then, he's legally Park Jae-Eun."

"That's a mouthful."

"And Jeremiah isn't?"

He smiled. "I never said it wasn't."

"I wanted to let you know there's going to be another child in the house," she said.

"Why would you take on the responsibility of another *kind* when everything about the farm is up in the air?"

"Because I know how painful a failed adoption is for a youngster."

"Sunni had a failed adoption?"

"Yes. They happen more often than you'd expect." She drew in a deep breath and released it through tight lips. "The couple who were going to adopt Sunni didn't want a daughter who depends on braces."

He flinched.

"Why are you startled?" she asked.

"Amish families consider a *kind* with physical or mental challenges a gift from God who will bring a very special love to everyone."

"Do you give them physical therapy and such?"

"Of course. We may not have doctors among us, but we appreciate and admire the work they do to keep us healthy." When Jeremiah came to his feet, he said, "Be careful, Mercy. I admire your intentions, but..."

He didn't add more as he left the house.

She was not sure what he could have said. He was right. She needed to be careful with her heart. With the boy and with Jeremiah, who could break it easily.

Chapter Nine

On Sunday morning Jeremiah had Hero hitched to the buggy and ready to go a little before eight. They were going only a quarter of a mile, but a cold wind would make walking difficult. He hadn't hurried because they had the leisure of starting out later than he was accustomed to in Pennsylvania.

He shivered, pulling his coat's collar up to cover his nape. Slapping his hands together for what little warmth he could find, he was pleased when the door opened and Mercy and Sunni came out.

He wasn't surprised when Mercy picked up her daughter and half ran toward the buggy. Both were hidden beneath heavy coats, hats, mittens and scarves.

With a nodded greeting because his teeth were chattering too hard to speak, he handed Sunni and Mercy into the buggy. He jumped in on the passenger side, pushing Sunni over with a laugh toward Mercy, who had to slide into the driver's position.

"I thought you'd want to drive." He held the reins out to her.

When she didn't hesitate to take them, he motioned

for her to turn the buggy with care in the shoveled area of the yard. He trusted Hero to know what to do, even if Mercy wasn't sure.

"My toes are getting warm!" Sunni stared at a metal box on the buggy's floor.

"That small heater probably won't warm much more than your toes," he said. "The bishop permits their use because of the cold, cold weather in northern New York."

"The bishop is the one who makes the rules?" Mercy looked along the twisting road, then called to Hero to go.

"The *Leit* will meet to discuss and create the *Ordnung* for our district, or we will once we have enough families to be a true district. We need about a dozen."

"What's that?" Sunni asked.

"*Leit* means our people." Jeremiah was pleased the little girl was curious about Amish ways, too. "The *Ordnung* are the unwritten rules we live by. They deal with everything from how we wear our clothes to what equipment we can use. Each item is discussed, prayed about and voted on. Our bishop helps us stick to it by defining certain aspects of life that haven't been specifically discussed. Like using small heaters in our buggies. Eventually, we'll meet to decide."

"I vote for having them," Mercy said with a laugh. "It's nice to know, even if my fingers freeze off, my toes will be safe. That is, assuming we get next door in one piece."

As they drove from sunshine to the cooler shade where thick pine trees edged the road, Jeremiah said, "You're doing *gut* with driving."

"My mommy can do anything." Sunni's tone stated

he was a *dummkopf* for not already knowing that. "When I'm having trouble with my spelling, she tells me to try. She says you can't know what you can do until you try. Right, Mommy?"

Mercy didn't shift her gaze from the ruts that could catch a buggy wheel. "That's right, *eolin-i.*"

"That means 'little one' in Korean," Sunni said.

"You speak Korean?" He looked at Mercy, astonished.

"A few words. I learned them from my beautiful daughter before she forgot most of her Korean as she learned English." She winked at Sunni. "I know a lot of Korean baby talk and a couple of songs. That's about it."

Smiling, Sunni began to sing a children's hymn whose tune he recognized. When she finished the first verse, she said, "That's how Koreans sing it, Jeremiah."

"Do you know more?"

He leaned back against the seat and listened to the little girl's chirping voice singing every verse of the Korean hymn. He couldn't remember the last time he'd felt so at ease, not determined to rush off to do the next thing. It was unexpected, and he decided to enjoy the moment.

He wasn't sure when another like this one would come again.

The drive went too quickly for Mercy. She was anxious not to make a mistake and embarrass herself and Jeremiah. What if their Amish neighbors weren't pleased he'd invited her? In the weeks she'd been living on the farm, she hadn't done more than wave to her neighbors. She knew they were as busy as she was

with trying to make homes out of the mostly abandoned buildings on the farms in the hollow.

Jeremiah had told her Caleb and his sister were living in one section of their main barn while they fixed up the house, which would have fallen in a few years if they hadn't come to rescue it. So she wasn't surprised when, exchanging places with Sunni and taking the reins as Hero pulled the buggy onto a farm lane, he drove to where other buggies were parked near a barn in desperate need of paint.

Stepping out, Mercy made sure Sunni was holding her hand. A boy led Hero toward the lower portion of the barn, and Jeremiah motioned at a door on the upper level that was up a sloping concrete apron.

"Usually," he said, "we gather outside and enter in a certain order, but it's too cold for little ones and the oldsters to stay out a second longer than necessary."

"And everyone else in between," she managed to get past her teeth, which were clenched so they didn't clatter together.

Mercy didn't say anything as they entered the barn. Ropes had been hung from side to side, and bright quilts hooked to them with clothespins. It was an ingenious way to make individual rooms out of the large space. However, the center of the space was open and filled with simple benches. A dozen benches faced the other dozen, and she guessed the women sat on one side and the men on the other. It was the same in the church she attended.

About thirty people milled around, and she was amazed they made up only six Amish families. She'd known Amish parents had many children and multiple generations lived beneath a single roof, but she was

overwhelmed by the number of members attending the service. Especially when she realized most of the people were around her own age. That made sense, because it would be the young people seeking a new life by Harmony Creek.

She couldn't fail to notice the shy glances in their direction. She realized a few of the prayer coverings were quite similar to hers while the organdy on other women's heads was heart-shaped. The women must come from different church districts, maybe different states.

When a tall blonde walked toward them, Jeremiah grinned.

Mercy was shocked at the pulse of something unpleasant racing through her as the lovely woman approached. It couldn't be... No, it was impossible she was jealous of how the blonde returned Jeremiah's smile so warmly. There couldn't be any future for Mercy and Jeremiah other than as friends. She should be happy for him that a beautiful Amish woman was pleased to see him.

Lord, please keep my heart from making another mistake. I don't know if it can survive shattering again.

Jeremiah turned to her, and she schooled her face into the best imitation she could of a calm expression. His brows lowered. He was puzzled by her reaction.

So was she!

"This is Caleb's sister Miriam," he said. "She was a teacher in her old community, so I asked her to translate for you. Miriam, these are the Bambergers. Mercy and Sunni."

"We're so glad you've decided to join us for worship today." Miriam's voice was like a song, each word a pleasant note, but Mercy had noticed a flash of discom-

fort in her eyes when Jeremiah mentioned she'd been a teacher. Maybe she missed that job.

Mercy dampened her curiosity, knowing she couldn't pose such a personal question to someone she'd just met. Instead, she said, "Thank you. I hope I can follow along."

Miriam gave her a warm smile. "If you need help, squeeze my hand, and I'll translate or explain." She glanced at Sunni and away. "The other *kinder* are over there on the far side of the room. They're waiting for you."

Her daughter didn't need a second invitation. She crossed the space in her rolling step. Two girls close to her age met her about halfway, talking over each other in their excitement to meet her.

When it was time for the service to start, Sunni sat on one side of Mercy and Miriam on the other. Mercy tried not to stare at the massive man sitting in the first row. His gray beard reached to the center of his chest, and his deep-set eyes had an intensity that awed her.

"Is that Abraham, Mommy?" asked Sunni in a stage whisper.

Miriam had overheard Sunni's question. Her answer was serious, though Mercy saw her eyes twinkling. "That's Wayne Flaud. He's our acting bishop."

"He looks like the picture of Abraham in Mommy's Bible."

Hushing her daughter, Mercy hoped the bishop hadn't heard her daughter's comments. If he had, he didn't react as the *Leit* stood for the first hymn.

It was sung, as Jeremiah had warned her, at a very slow pace, taking two or three times longer to sing than it would have during a Mennonite service. She bowed

her head and joined in the silent prayer, grateful for this opportunity to discover more about Jeremiah's world. She hoped it would help her understand him better, because he was becoming a bigger and bigger part of her and her daughter's lives.

The afternoon sun had warmed the air considerably by the time Jeremiah drove the buggy toward Rudy's farm. Sunni was asleep, her head on Mercy's lap, exhausted from playing outside with the other *kinder* after the communal luncheon in the barn.

"What did you think of the service, Mercy?" Jeremiah asked. "Other than how uncomfortable the benches are?"

"Was I that obvious?"

He rushed to answer as he struggled to keep from laughing at her shocked and humiliated expression. "No, you weren't obvious. It's the complaint we often hear when someone who isn't Amish attends our services."

"I've got to say I missed the comfortable pews I'm accustomed to. The way you sang the hymns was amazing. The man who started each line—"

"The *vorsinger* is what he's called."

"He kept everyone together, so nobody got too far ahead or too far behind."

He turned the buggy into Rudy's drive. Drawing back on the reins, he stared at the black car parked there. A tall, balding man was stepping out. "You've got company, Mercy."

He felt her flinch. "It's Alfred, my father's oldest brother." She hesitated, then said, "I think."

"You think?"

"I haven't seen him in ten years. He lives in California, and he only comes for funerals." She sighed. "Though he didn't come for his father's."

"Was there bad blood between them?"

"My uncle doesn't get along well with anyone in the family. He thinks nobody is ever right except him."

His brows rose in astonishment. Mercy spoke her mind and was determined to take over her *grossdawdi*'s farm, but on other subjects, she tried to look for a solution that worked for everyone involved.

Her *onkel* glanced from her to Jeremiah and Sunni, his frown deepening with each passing second, while they got out of the buggy. The little girl must have sensed the tension because she didn't say a word.

Jeremiah saw a flood of questions in the older man's expression, but her *onkel* asked, "Why is the door locked?"

Mercy took Sunni's hand before walking between the snowbanks to where her *onkel* had gone up onto the porch. She gave the cantankerous man a kiss on the cheek.

"Why didn't you let me know you were coming, Uncle Alfred?" she asked as she pulled the key out of her purse.

Instead of answering her question, he tapped his toe impatiently. Color faded from Mercy's face.

Jeremiah struggled not to frown when he realized her *onkel* saw her as a *kind*, no older or more responsible than Sunni.

"I'm tearing down wallpaper and painting," she answered, but her voice quavered, "and I didn't want someone to walk in and trip over the mess."

"You shouldn't be doing anything to the house until its future is decided."

"Dad knows I'm working on the house, and he agreed anything I do will increase the property's value."

Onkel Alfred waved aside her words. "You shouldn't lock the door. This door was never locked while my father and mother lived here."

Doubting she'd get anywhere with her *onkel*, who wasn't interested in what she had to say, Jeremiah stepped past Mercy. He opened the door and led the way into the house. He waited for the explosion he guessed would come when her *onkel* saw the changes she'd made.

Alfred began to list everything he thought Mercy was doing wrong. She seemed to shrink within herself, and Jeremiah respected how she didn't fire protests to defend herself.

Just as an Amish woman would do, whispered his own thoughts. Silencing them, he was shocked when a small hand slid into his.

He looked at Sunni's troubled face.

"I don't like that loud man," she whispered.

"He's your grandfather's brother."

"Still don't like him."

He gave her a quick smile. He didn't like Alfred Bamberger, either, though he'd barely spent two minutes in his company. Any man who bullied Mercy and acted as if he knew everything and she knew nothing wasn't, in Jeremiah's estimation, worth getting better acquainted with.

"Mercy, have you forgotten your manners?" demanded her *onkel*, gesturing with his head toward Jeremiah.

Her cheeks became red, but she said calmly, "Uncle Alfred, I know my parents have told you about my daughter, Sunni."

The little girl greeted him with a tentative smile.

Alfred ignored her. "And who's he?"

"This is Jeremiah Stoltzfus," Mercy said, putting her arm around Sunni's shoulders. "Jeremiah, this is—"

"Are you the one who intended to buy the farm from Rudy?" asked the older man.

Jeremiah's first reaction was to laugh at the man's hypocrisy, but he hid it, because he wasn't really amused by how Alfred Bamberger dismissed Mercy. "I am."

"You're Amish, aren't you?"

"I am." He wondered if the man was always this rude. If so, he could understand why Alfred didn't get along with his siblings.

"What did you intend to do with the farm?"

"Farm it," he said in the same clipped tone the older man used. "I've got ten dairy cows in the barn. I'd arranged for their purchase before I came here, because Rudy said it was okay."

Alfred rubbed his eyes with his thumb and finger before sighing. "That sounds like my father." He grimaced. "Father hated the idea the farm might be subdivided and sold as house lots." Again, his gaze drilled Jeremiah. "He was so eager to keep the land as a farm he would have agreed to any deal."

"The price we agreed upon was fair." He wouldn't pretend not to understand what the other man was implying.

"That's yet to be seen. On behalf of my brothers and sisters, I've come to get an appraisal done on the property. An honest appraisal, not what Rudy believed

it was worth to someone who said he planned to work the land."

Jeremiah didn't wince, not outwardly, as Alfred's words slashed through his tattered hopes. That the family might demand more in exchange for selling the farm wasn't something he'd considered. He and Rudy had negotiated in *gut* faith, and the Realtors involved must have agreed it was a fair deal.

Hadn't they?

"Dad didn't mention you'd be coming," Mercy said in the same deferential tone.

"He doesn't know, but he'll be grateful when he has the facts from someone who is truly part of the family, which you aren't, Mercy."

Jeremiah looked at her in horror. How could Alfred throw in her face she hadn't been born a Bamberger? That was beyond cruel.

But Mercy motioned for him to say nothing.

Her *onkel* asked a couple more questions and walked into the living room. When they didn't follow, he bellowed Mercy's name.

Jeremiah grasped her arm as she stepped forward to follow. "He shouldn't speak to you so," he hissed, fighting to control his outrage.

"It's okay, Jeremiah." She patted his cheek gently and smiled. "I'm used to him, and it's nothing personal."

"Nothing personal? He said—"

"He's said the same thing to my sisters-in-law and my cousins' spouses. He doesn't consider anyone a true part of the family except him and his siblings, and those siblings reluctantly." Her smile broadened. "He'd prefer he was an only child."

"But—"

"Thank you, Jeremiah." She glanced at the door to the living room when her *onkel* shouted again. "But let me handle this."

She was gone before Jeremiah could agree, which was for the best, because for the next hour Alfred interrogated Mercy and him on every facet of the farm. That they could answer his questions seemed to irritate him. The man had come to the house with a chip on his shoulder. Whenever he could, Jeremiah deflected questions fired at Mercy by answering them or turning the conversation to the land rather than the house.

Alfred left with a warning not to change another thing before the appraisal. "I'm sure the family has other plans for this property than a silly summer camp."

Jeremiah bit his lip when he saw tears blossom in Mercy's eyes. Arguing with her *onkel* could make the situation worse. When the older man shot a rancorous glance in his direction, Jeremiah knew the warning was aimed at him, as well.

When the door shut behind Alfred Bamberger, Sunni rushed to throw her arms around Mercy.

"I don't like him, Mommy," the little girl said, hiding her face in Mercy's apron. "He didn't speak to me. Not even when I said hi."

Jeremiah squatted by the *kind*. "Sunni, some people are so angry inside they can't be anything but angry on the outside. It doesn't have anything to do with you."

"That's right," Mercy said. "Uncle Alfred isn't a happy person." Helping her daughter out of her coat, she added, "I think I'll make hot chocolate for us. Do you like that idea?"

With a cheer, Sunni hugged her *mamm*, but with ex-

citement this time. The *kind* ran into the kitchen to select the cups they'd use for the treat.

Jeremiah came to his feet as Mercy asked, "You'll stay, won't you?"

"I need to get Hero in, but then I'll come back." Putting his hands on her shoulders, he knew he might be foolish, but he couldn't let her bear the burden of her *onkel's* threats alone. "Mercy, you can't be certain anyone else in your family will listen to what he plans."

She sighed again. "I know Uncle Alfred. That he's talking about subdividing the land to build houses means that's what he wants to do."

"It would probably bring the greatest return to your *daed* and his siblings, but only if they sell each lot themselves. A building contractor might offer less than I did because a builder would need to make a big profit in return for his investment."

She looked out the window at rolling hills set against purplish mountains reaching up into the clouds. "I can't imagine these hills covered with houses."

"Don't worry."

"How can you say that?" she asked, looking up at him.

"Because I trust in God's plan for my life."

"I wish I could, too."

At the regret in her voice, he longed to draw her into his arms and hold her until her fears vanished. It would be a mistake because he could be jeopardizing everything he was working so hard for.

Chapter Ten

After her *onkel*'s visit and his determination to squeeze every possible penny out of the property, Jeremiah wasn't sure if either of them would end up with the farm. He didn't say that to Mercy, but he guessed, by the way she evaded his eyes, she'd had similar thoughts as she threw herself into preparations for Parker Kenton's arrival, the foster *kind* being placed with her.

She and Sunni ignored her *onkel*'s edict and painted one bedroom a fresh blue for the boy. A bed was found in another room and cleaned. After a new mattress was delivered at the beginning of the week, she topped the bed with a duvet decorated with circus animals. Rudy's black-and-white afghan was draped over the footboard.

Jeremiah was asked over and over for his opinion of the room. "Because you're a boy," Sunni said each time.

Everything in the bedroom was ready by a chilly Tuesday afternoon when a silver car rolled to a stop in the yard. When the driver got out, Jeremiah recognized her as the social worker who'd come to speak with Mercy. She glanced at where he stood with Mercy and

Sunni, but said nothing. She went to the passenger side and opened the door.

No one emerged.

The woman—her name was Whitney, ain't so?—bent and spoke quietly.

Sunni cut her eyes to Mercy, who was looking at the car with anticipation and anxiety.

Patting the little girl's shoulder, Jeremiah guessed Mercy was considering the changes another *kind* could make in their lives. Including his. The thought was a sure sign he was too involved with the Bambergers.

A boy oozed out of the car. The first word that came to Jeremiah's mind was sullen. The *kind* stared at the ground and didn't acknowledge them.

Parker was short for his age and skinny. He wore a new winter coat with blue jeans and stylish sneakers. His previous foster family must have provided for him well, though they weren't able to continue caring for him. When he pulled off his knit cap, his fine black hair danced with static electricity.

He glowered and licked his fingertips before running them over his hair. Most of the strands settled, but others stood up like insane cowlicks.

Whitney put her hand on his shoulder, but he shook it off. He walked to where Jeremiah stood with Mercy and Sunni on the front porch. He didn't say a word.

Mercy opened the door and ushered everyone through the elegant front entry and into the living room.

Whitney undid her coat and motioned for Parker to do the same. He balled up his coat and threw it on a chair. The social worker started to reprimand him, but Mercy shook her head gently.

Arching her pale brows, Whitney said, "This is

Mercy and her daughter, Sunni. Sunni was born in Korea as you were."

"Who cares about stupid Korea?" muttered the boy. His voice held the hint of an accent.

"And I'm Jeremiah Stoltzfus." He offered his hand to the boy as if Parker were a grown man.

For a second, the *kind*'s indifference cracked. He eyed Jeremiah up and down. He seemed to gather his defenses around himself and scorned Jeremiah's hand. "Why are you wearing a clown hat?"

Because of the *kind*'s accent, Jeremiah thought he said *crown hat*. He realized his mistake when Mercy replied.

"Jeremiah isn't a clown. He's Amish. Amish men wear black hats like that in the winter, Parker."

"My name isn't Parker."

Whitney's voice took on a stern edge. "We've talked about that, and you agreed, for now, you're going to stick with Parker."

The *kind* subsided, but crossed his arms over his chest and stood with his chin raised in defiance.

If the boy wanted another name, Jeremiah knew what it should be. Trouble. The boy was going to be trouble. Jeremiah hoped Mercy was prepared.

He wasn't sure he was.

Mercy was so proud of her daughter. Despite Parker's disdain for everything Sunni said and how often he called her silly or stupid, the little girl persisted. No doubt, Sunni remembered her own rough transition into what became her permanent family. Mercy certainly recalled her own, and she knew exactly how Parker was feeling.

Unwanted. Worthless. Determined to show the world he wasn't either.

"This is for you." Sunni placed a bright blue teddy bear in Parker's hand. Her smile wavered when he didn't say anything. "It's nice to have a special friend when you're somewhere new. Blueberry has been a good friend to me, and I hope he'll be a good friend to you."

Mercy didn't catch what Parker replied under his breath. She guessed she'd be better off not knowing.

Parker tossed the bear on the bed and then picked up his suitcase. It nearly knocked him off his feet. Jeremiah slipped a surreptitious hand under one side to help guide it onto the bed. Parker shook his head when Whitney said it was time to go downstairs, but came along reluctantly upon the social worker's insistence.

Whitney stayed for several hours, then got ready to leave to allow the family to begin to adjust to each other.

When Mercy started to make supper, she asked Jeremiah if he'd like to stay.

He heard her nervous tone, and he agreed. With two *kinder*, including one who protested over anything anyone said to him, she could use another adult there.

"I'll set the table," he said as she took hamburger and potatoes out of the refrigerator. "And keep the kids away from the stove."

"They're upstairs. Sunni knows if she wants fries, she needs to stay away while I cook them."

"She's a known quantity. The other one isn't." He paused by the table. "Where do you want these papers Whitney left with you?"

"Would you mind putting them on the desk?"

"Be glad to." He began to gather them up. His eyes

widened as he noticed the name on several of them. Mercedes R. Bamberger.

"Is your name really Mercedes?" he asked. "Like the fancy car?"

"Jeff and Pat have a Mercedes," said Parker, puffing out his chest and striding into the kitchen as if he owned the place. Jeremiah knew Jeff and Pat were the couple who were supposed to have adopted the boy. "Do you have one?"

"No, I've got that dented Ford out there." Mercy shot Jeremiah a glance, and he stepped between the boy and the stove.

The boy looked at Jeremiah, who said, "No car for me. But I've got a horse named Hero and a buggy."

Rolling his eyes, Parker opened cabinet doors and peered inside.

"So your name is really Mercedes?" Jeremiah asked.

She plucked the page out of his hand. "Yes, my name is Mercedes. It's Spanish for mercies, and it's the name I was given when I was born. The Bambergers asked if they could call me Mercy. I agreed, because I was getting a new life, so why not a new name?" She smiled coolly. "Especially when they didn't pronounce it as *Abuelita* did."

"I always wanted a shorter name like my brothers have. I liked my *daed*'s name. Paul. Nice and simple." He rubbed his chin. "*Mamm* always said I should emulate the prophet Jeremiah and stand up and speak of the Lord."

"I didn't think the Amish evangelize."

"We don't. Or I should say, most of us don't. She meant I should proclaim God is *gut*."

"This place is ugly," Parker announced from the far corner of the kitchen.

"If you think it's ugly now," she said as she began cutting the potatoes into short lengths, "you should have seen it when I moved in here."

Mercy didn't smile when she saw the child's shock. He'd expected to annoy her with another of his insults, but she'd been a foster kid. She knew the games and the rules. Dislike everything. Push and push to see how much you could get away with.

And Parker had been yanked out of the familiar world he'd known and brought across the Pacific to a strange culture. The family that was supposed to be his forever had failed him, leaving him to be tossed into the system. Now he found himself in a plain home. That was enough to make the boy's head spin...and her heart ache.

"Can we watch TV?" the boy asked.

"We don't have one." She scraped more potatoes, figuring she'd need more than twice as many as she used when she made French fries for her and Sunni. A hardworking man and a growing boy had hearty appetites.

"How do you play video games if you don't have a TV?" His eyes widened. "Do you have a handheld?"

"No."

"Then you play on the computer."

Mercy shook her head, but Sunni, who came into the kitchen, replied, "We don't have a computer or whatever a handheld is."

Parker stared at them as if they'd crawled out of a woodchuck hole and announced they'd been hibernating. "What do you *do*?"

"Read and color," Sunni said.

"Take care of the animals and pray," Jeremiah added.

"Teach Sunni and cook." Mercy motioned to the stove.

"Build a chicken coop." Sunni giggled and glanced at Jeremiah.

"Drive the buggy," he said with a laugh, "and teach Mercy how to drive the sleigh."

Before Mercy could think of something to add to the list, Parker threw his short arms up in the air, grumbled something and stamped away. She heard his footsteps on the stairs and overhead. She looked from the heating oil to the ceiling.

"What is it?" asked Jeremiah.

"Could you do me a favor? There's the door by Parker's room that leads into the section of the house with weak floors. I meant to lock it before he arrived."

"I'll get it."

"Be careful."

His reddish brows rose. "By that, I assume the door has to be locked from the bad side."

"Yes." She flashed him a sympathetic smile. "I've looked for the key, but I haven't found it." *Among other things, like my grandfather's will*, she wanted to say, but kept that to herself. She wasn't comfortable with Jeremiah knowing she hadn't given up the search. "Just turn the latch on the dead bolt." As he turned to go, she repeated, "Be careful."

"I'll do my best."

"I'm sure you always do."

He paused and looked at her. The kitchen seemed to telescope, the distance between them vanishing. Everything vanished, except them. A connection, invisible and powerful, matched every breath she took to his.

She wasn't sure how long they would have stood—frozen inside a splendid moment in time—if the hot oil on the stove hadn't snapped. She turned to the stove, and Jeremiah rushed away.

Steadying her breath and her heart that seemed to be beating at fast-forward, she tried to focus on cutting the fries. She patted the potatoes dry, because she didn't want the oil to splatter.

When she heard footsteps behind her, she saw her daughter standing in the doorway but not in the kitchen.

Sunni clamped her arms over her narrow chest. "He says he's not coming down for dinner."

Mercy didn't need to ask who *he* was. "Did you ask him nice?"

"Of course." Her daughter seemed insulted at the question. "But he won't open his door."

"Did he tell you why?" Infecting Sunni with Mercy's worries that the boy might try to run away would make the situation more tense.

"No! He said bad words."

Mercy turned off the burner and sent up a quick prayer of thanks the boy was still in the house. Holding out her hand, she said, "Come with me."

She didn't want Sunni to get more upset, but she wouldn't leave her daughter in the kitchen with the hot oil on the stove. When she heard Jeremiah on the front stairs, she asked him to keep an eye on the stove. He nodded, though curiosity burned in his eyes. Again, she felt the pull of the unseen contact between them. She broke it, knowing she had to find out why Parker was refusing to come and have his supper.

He must be hungry. Whitney said she'd offered to stop to get burgers, but the boy had refused. Climbing

the stairs, she went to the room between Sunni's and Grandpa Rudy's.

"Parker?"

"That's not my name!" came back a snarl.

"All right, whatever your name is." Mercy kept her voice even. "It's time for supper."

"I'm not hungry."

"Yes, you are. Have you ever had French fries before?"

"Of course!" A hint of vacillation sifted into his retort.

"Homemade ones?"

For several seconds there was no answer. The door opened slowly, enough for Parker to slip through.

As he started to close it behind him, Mercy put out her hand and kept the door from shutting. He glared at her, and she met it without comment. Finally, he lowered his eyes and stepped aside.

She pushed open the door and gasped.

The room looked as if it'd been ransacked. The drawers were pulled from the dresser. The bed had been torn apart, and the pictures on the wall—at least the ones Parker could reach—were ripped down and tossed in a corner.

Sunni gave a soft cry of dismay and picked up the blue teddy bear she'd given Parker. Tears filled her eyes when she touched the stuffing peeking out of where the bear's ears had been.

"Why?" she asked.

"It's a stupid bear, and you're stupid for liking it. Only a cripple would like something like a stupid bear." Parker crossed his arms and raised his chin, daring them to try to make him apologize.

It was at that point Mercy knew this placement was going to be harder than she'd guessed.

A lot harder.

Jeremiah had come up the stairs after making sure nothing would burn on the stove. He didn't hesitate to step into the room as Sunni ran and threw herself in Mercy's arms. He turned to the boy, who regarded them with contempt. Parker also had, Jeremiah noticed, steeled himself as if he expected to be punished harshly for what he'd done and said.

It was *gut* the *kind* understood he shouldn't have destroyed the room and the gifts Mercy and Sunni had given him. Teaching the boy to respect those who wanted to help him would be easier if Parker knew the difference between right and wrong.

Mercy started to step forward, but Jeremiah put his hand on her arm. Warmth exploded from her skin to his. For a split second, he wanted to step out into the hall with her and forget the angry boy and the hurt little girl. Just for a moment. A single moment while he gazed into Mercy's pretty eyes. If he bent forward, would she shy away from his lips?

Knowing he was being imprudent, especially when the *kinder* needed them, he said in a near whisper, "Let me, Mercy."

"Jeremiah, this isn't your problem." Her voice was as hushed as his while Parker's gaze moved from one of them to the other as if trying to read their lips.

"I know, but I can take him off your hands while you clean up this mess."

"He should help, so—"

"Look at him." He cut his eyes to the boy. "Every-

thing about him says he's waiting for a fight or to be punished."

"I don't want to fight with him. I know he's scared."

"So let me give him something to take his mind off his fears."

For a moment, Jeremiah thought Mercy wouldn't trust him. She glanced between the boy and him.

"I'm not going to take him out behind the woodshed," he said quietly. "That wouldn't help anything."

"I know."

"Mercy, let me help. Can you hold dinner for about an hour?"

Indecision raced across her face, but then she nodded.

Thrilled by her trust in him, Jeremiah made sure his face remained stern as he turned to the boy. "Come with me."

"I don't want to."

"I didn't ask if you wanted to. I asked you to come with me." He kept his voice steady, wondering if *Daed* had struggled, as Jeremiah was now, when he'd needed to punish one of them.

Maybe he shouldn't have volunteered to help. He didn't know a lot about kids, other than when he spent time with his nieces and nephews. But there wasn't time for second thoughts. He'd offered, and the boy needed to learn actions had consequences, whether *gut* or bad.

Jeremiah herded the boy down the stairs. He thought Parker would argue again when told to put on his coat, hat and mittens along with his boots. The boy was reluctant but he complied and rushed out the door when Jeremiah opened it.

"Whoa, there." Jeremiah caught Parker by the hood

on his coat as the *kind* started to jump into a snow-bank. "If you get wet, you'll be cold by the time we finish the chores."

"Chores? What are chores?"

Surprised a nine-year-old didn't know the term, Jeremiah held the coat as Parker strained against him. "Chores are what we do to earn our keep here."

"The county is paying for me."

"And how long do you think they'll do that? A man can't depend on someone else to pay his way. Don't you want a *gut* and exciting job when you grow up?"

The boy stopped trying to pull away. Frowning, Parker said, "Sure."

"What do you want to do?"

"Be an astronaut or a fireman or maybe a police-man."

Jeremiah ignored his yearning to grin. "Those are important jobs, and they have one thing in common. They will require you to work hard to learn everything you need to know to do the job. Ever think of being a cowboy?"

"Yeah," the boy drawled, clearly suspicious.

"Here's your chance."

"Huh?"

Pretending he hadn't heard Parker's question, Jeremiah kept a hand on the boy's shoulder as they walked toward the barn. Jeremiah acted as if he didn't have a care in the world, but kept snatching glances at the *kind*'s face when they entered the barn where the cows waited to be milked.

"It smells in here," the boy said.

"It does, doesn't it?" He saw Parker's shock that Jeremiah wasn't insulted by his blunt words. "But give it

a chance. Once you get used to the smell, it's kind of a nice stink."

"You're crazy!"

Jeremiah smiled. The sooner the boy learned he couldn't get a rise out of Jeremiah, the sooner Parker might start listening to him. Really listening.

"Okay," Jeremiah said, trying to sound more certain than he felt, "I'm going to milk the cows, and you're going to clean up." He pointed at the gutter behind the cows and then handed the boy a short-handled shovel. "Pick it up and put it on that pile over there." He pointed toward a stained spot on the concrete floor near the door leading into the barnyard. "It can stay there for tonight. We'll move it outside tomorrow when it's warmer."

"You want me to shovel that—?"

"Manure? *Ja*, I do."

"That's child abuse."

"Not even close." He grinned at the boy. "Once I know you can handle that, I'll let you help me milk the cows."

"I don't want to milk old, stinky cows."

"Well, that's *gut*, because these cows are neither old nor stinky."

Again the *kind* stared at him as if Parker feared Jeremiah had lost his mind.

"B-b-but…" The boy sputtered on the single word.

"You said you wanted to be a cowboy, ain't so?"

"I did, but cowboys ride horses."

"Which need to be cleaned up after, too."

"Really?"

"*Ja*, really." Smiling, Jeremiah said, "You'd better get started."

He left the boy staring at the shovel and went to get

the milking equipment out of the storage room. When he returned, Parker was poking at the gutters behind the cows. Jeremiah didn't glance at him when he heard a clang as Parker started to work.

The battle wasn't over, but Parker was willing to listen to him. Maybe Jeremiah had helped Mercy tonight. He hoped so. It felt astounding, he realized, to be on the same side for once. He prayed it wouldn't be the one and only time.

Chapter Eleven

Sunni was paging through a picture book in the living room the following week, so Mercy kept Parker in the kitchen while she washed the dinner dishes. He complained about not having TV, and he couldn't seem to find anything to do. Sleet tapped at the window, and she could scarcely make out the shape of the barn on the far side of the yard.

"Can you see where Jeremiah is?" asked Parker as he set a cup of cocoa on the table.

Mercy wasn't sure what had happened in the barn the night of Parker's arrival, but whatever Jeremiah had said or done had made a huge impression on the boy. At the same time Parker looked for any chance to spend time with Jeremiah, he resisted every request she spoke, and he treated Sunni badly, making nasty comments to her over and over or stepping into her way when she was trying to navigate the stairs.

She recognized the pattern she'd seen in other foster kids. They'd shared stories about how they disrupted a placement on purpose. Even then, she'd understood what they hadn't said. When they had no control over

their lives, being pulled from one foster home to another and maybe sent home to live with one parent for a while before being dropped back into the system, they'd decided to grab what control they could. They were determined to make sure the placement didn't work, pushing their foster parents to the edge and past it with their antics. One girl she'd shared a room with for a couple of nights had put it succinctly, "I got rid of them before they got rid of me."

However, he hung on every word Jeremiah spoke. She wondered if Parker had been close to a father figure in Korea. According to the reports Whitney had left for Mercy, Parker hadn't transferred that respect to Mr. Kenton.

Yet the child admired Jeremiah and hopped to obey any request he made. She should be grateful the boy heeded one of them. Asking Jeremiah to step in made her uncomfortable because each time was a reminder that sometime, hopefully in the near future, one of them would have the farm and the other must leave.

But she knew it was more than that. She looked forward to every time Jeremiah came to the house or she ran into him in the yard. He'd had dinner and supper with them every day since Parker's arrival, and he'd lingered into the evening. His calm presence stopped arguments between the two children before they got heated.

"No, I don't see him," Mercy replied when the boy repeated the question. Louder this time. "He's smart enough not to work outside in a storm."

"Is he your boyfriend?"

"No." She ignored the regret that erupted in her at the simple answer.

"Why not?"

"He's Amish, and we're not." It was the easiest explanation to give the boy.

How could she explain to a nine-year-old about the feelings she didn't understand herself? The very thought of spending time with Jeremiah made her smile. When his hand brushed hers, even inadvertently, her heart thumped like hail on a roof. His kindness with the children touched her soul, for she couldn't help thinking of how Graham hadn't even wanted to discuss having a family. While Jeremiah spent time with Sunni and Parker, making them want to like him, Graham had barely tolerated her daughter.

But there was something else, something indefinable that drew her to him like a child to a cookie jar.

"You aren't Amish?" Parker asked, again interrupting her thoughts. "You wear a funny hat, too."

"It's my prayer covering." She put the last pot on the drainer and reached to let the water out of the sink. "The Bible asks women to cover their heads when they pray. As I pray throughout the day, I don't have to worry about my head being uncovered when I do."

"If you're not Amish, what are you?" He paused for a moment, then asked, "What's Amish?"

Mercy gave him a very brief answer, knowing, as a child who'd never encountered plain people, he wouldn't be able to handle too much information at once.

"Hey!" he shouted in the middle of her explanation. "There's Jeremiah." He rushed to the window that gave him the best view of the barn. "What's he doing?"

Mercy walked to stand behind him. Wiping her hands on a towel, she peered through the storm that didn't seem in a hurry to abate.

Across the yard, Jeremiah was bending over a trac-

tor parked by the barn. She'd been surprised when he drove it out of the barn until he explained he didn't plan to use it in the fields. Instead, he wanted to use the tractor's engine as a power source.

"It looks as if he's fixing the stationary engine that runs the milking machines in the barn," she said.

Parker wore an unexpected smile. "I like helping with milking. It's fun, but I wish Jeremiah had different cows."

"What kind of cows?"

"His cows give white milk. I like chocolate milk."

She drew her bottom lip between her teeth so she didn't laugh.

"Don't you?" the boy demanded.

"Certainly I like chocolate milk."

"So why doesn't he get chocolate milk cows?"

"You'll have to check with him." Putting the towel on the counter by the sink, she said, "You can ask him tonight."

"I will!"

As the boy went to the table to finish his hot cocoa, Mercy remained by the window. She watched Jeremiah's easy, economical motions as he got the tractor's engine running. When he came inside, she'd make sure she had something warm for him to drink. She couldn't wait to tell him about chocolate milk cows.

It had been the longest conversation she'd had with Parker without him copping an attitude on her. She hoped it would be the first of many.

When Parker appeared in the barn, looking furtively over his shoulder, Jeremiah guessed the boy had snuck out of the house. He considered sending Parker back,

but Mercy would know to look first in the barn if she wanted to find the boy.

She was having a rough time with her foster *kind*. Was Parker missing his adoptive *mamm* so much he was determined not to let Mercy get close? Or was he mad at the whole world? Jeremiah tried to put himself in the *kind*'s shoes. To be yanked out of what he thought was his forever home was enough to give the boy a reason to distrust everyone.

"I didn't expect you to come out in the storm," Jeremiah said as he bent to clean a cow's udder before he attached the portable milking machine.

"You're doing your chores, so I'm here to do mine." He picked up the shovel, no longer skittish around the cows. "Besides, it's boring being stuck in the house. All they want to do is read or rip off wallpaper."

With a nod, Jeremiah wished Parker would show Mercy some respect. He couldn't force the boy to do so. All he could do was be a *gut* role model for how a man treated a woman.

"Mercy said there are cows that give chocolate milk," Parker said a few minutes later. "How come you don't have one?"

"Because I like strawberry milk better." Without batting an eye, he pointed to a ruddy Jersey cow munching hay and ignoring them. "So that's why I have a strawberry cow."

Jeremiah fought not to laugh as Parker stared in astonishment. He'd been a lot younger than the boy when his own *daed* told him the same silly story about red cows giving strawberry milk. Most likely, he'd worn the same expression of disbelief and childish yearning to believe the story was true.

"You're kidding," Parker said.

"No. The milk these cows give can be made into chocolate milk and strawberry milk and cheese and other things."

Understanding dawned on the boy's face. "So cows are pretty important."

"Ja."

"And milking them is important?"

"Very important. They depend on us to care for them, and in return they give us milk to use." He emptied the milker into a pail to carry it to the dairy tank. "We must heed what God told Adam and Eve in the Garden of Eden."

"God?"

"Ja. God told them: *Be fruitful, and multiply, and replenish the earth, and subdue it: and have dominion over the fish of the sea, and over the fowl of the air, and over every living thing that moveth upon the earth.* That means we need to take care of the animals and birds and fish that can't take care of themselves."

"Like cows?"

Jeremiah nodded. "Something every cowboy needs to know. You're well on your way to becoming one if you want."

Parker grinned. "Do I get a hat?"

Whipping off his black wool hat, Jeremiah set it on the boy's head. "There you go."

"This isn't a cowboy hat." He pulled it off with a disgusted frown.

"The very first cowboys wore hats very much like this one."

"Really?"

"Really."

The boy set the hat back on his head, paying no attention to how it dropped onto his nose. "Let's do the milking."

"Said just like a cowboy."

When Parker grinned, Jeremiah's heart swelled with happiness. He'd been curious how his brothers could welcome *kinder* into their lives, though they weren't the *kinder*'s biological *daeds*. They loved the youngsters as much as the *bopplin* born within their marriages. Admiring them, he'd wondered if he could open his heart so wide. He was beginning to believe he could.

Wide enough to let one naughty boy, one very opinionated little girl and one lovely woman into it.

If the situation with the farm was resolved... He might as well wish for stars to dance around the sun at noon.

But with You, all things are possible. That's what Jesus taught, and what I believe. All things are possible, including finding a way out of the mess of who owns this farm. Even falling in love with the one woman standing in the way of me achieving that dream.

Jeremiah began to whistle as he carried the milk can to the dairy tank, happier than he'd been in longer than he could recall.

He was startled when he returned to clean the next cow and saw Mercy and Sunni walking into the barn.

Sunni rushed to him. "Can I help, too?"

He smiled. "Of course you can. The more hands to help the faster the job goes, but you need to ask your *mamm.*"

"Can I help, too?" Sunni asked.

Jeremiah grinned at the little girl's excitement to have a chance to spend time with him and Parker. After

putting up with her foster brother's pranks and scathing comments, it was the first time since the boy's arrival she'd asked to do something when Parker was involved.

"Certainly, *eolin-i*," Mercy said, ruffling her daughter's hair.

Parker stared at her. "I know what that means. It's Korean."

"I'm glad you remember your Korean." She gave him the warm smile that lit up the recesses of Jeremiah's heart, even when aimed at someone else. "Maybe you can teach Sunni the language. She wasn't much more than a baby when she came here, so she's lost most of what she knew."

The boy's lip curled, and Jeremiah knew he was about to say something rude. Before Parker could speak, Jeremiah said quietly, "A *gut* cowboy always helps those around him. He knows he may have to depend on others while tending the cows, so he lets others know they can depend on him."

Parker looked at him, wide-eyed, then nodded. "I'll try."

"Thank you," Mercy said. "Maybe you could help me learn, too."

"You want me to teach *you*? But you're a grown-up."

"I'm a baby when it comes to learning Korean."

The boy stared hastily at his boots, and Jeremiah would have gladly given Parker a penny—or a dollar—for his thoughts. Was Parker regretting his lack of respect toward Mercy when she treated him kindly? Or were her gentle ways tearing down the walls the boy had raised to protect himself from more hurt? Either way, Jeremiah hoped Parker realized how blessed he was to be in Mercy's care.

"Jeremiah!" Sunni's excited cry rang through the barn. She was by the calf stall. The newest calves, four of

them, had been delivered yesterday from the auction barn in Cambridge, about ten miles south. They bawled whenever he entered the barn, hoping to get his attention and something to eat.

Squatting next to Sunni, he smiled when she gazed up at him in awe.

"Look!" Her grin was almost too wide for her face. "He's sucking my fingers!"

"*She*'s hoping for milk, and she thinks your fingers might have some because they don't look much different to her than the cow's teats."

"You can't tell a girl cow," Parker taunted, "from a boy cow. You're a stupid girl."

"Enough," Jeremiah said quietly, and the boy subsided. "You were saying, Sunni?"

Her nose wrinkled, but she hurried to ask, "When does one of the cows come over to feed them?"

"The calves don't get to drink the milk from the cows. We do."

"That's not fair! She's a baby cow. She should have first dibs."

Leaning one arm on the top of the stall, Jeremiah said, "It might not sound fair to you, but what I feed the calves provides more nutrition than cow milk. They'll grow stronger much faster with milk replacer." He motioned for Parker to join them. "Would you two like to feed them?"

Sunni cheered loudly enough so the calves jerked, staring at her with the whites of their eyes showing. Instantly, she began cooing as she tried to get them to come to her.

Parker was less enthusiastic. "You want both of us to feed them?"

"I'll help you," Jeremiah said, pretending he'd misunderstood that Parker didn't want to share the task with his foster sister.

"I don't need…" He shuffled his feet. "If you show me how to do it, I can handle baby cows."

"I'm sure you can. You, too, Sunni. That's why I asked you." Straightening, he said, "C'mon. I'll show you how I mix up the milk replacer, and we'll fill the bottles."

Within minutes the youngsters were holding the large bottles with both hands as the calves drained them so fast the milk replacer dribbled out of the sides of their mouths. Mercy took over the task of cleaning the udders before Jeremiah hooked on the milker. They worked in easy harmony as if they'd done the tasks together a hundred times before.

Mercy paused to check the *kinder* and help refill the bottles so the other two calves could have their turns. "Are you having fun?"

Jeremiah hoped Parker would reply, but Sunni did. She nodded with a grin that revealed her loose tooth. It was her first one, and the little girl was excited about it.

Jeremiah kept hoping that while they finished the milking and other chores, Parker would say something nice to Mercy.

Nothing.

When Mercy sent the *kinder* to the house through the early evening sunshine, Parker refused to go. A single glance from Jeremiah changed the boy's mind, and he stalked out, his tightly fisted hands jammed into his coat pockets.

"Give him time," Mercy said as she wrapped a scarf around her neck.

Jeremiah reached for the light switch. "I'm trying,

but how much time does he need to realize you're the best thing that could happen to him now?"

"Were you always grateful for what adults did for you? Surely you weren't that well behaved."

Closing the door behind them, he sighed as the cold scraped across his face. "I can't remember the last time I felt like a naughty kid. Not even when I was a scholar."

"That's no surprise. Were you the good boy, the one your teacher could expect to be quiet and study hard?"

"*Ja.* Sadly, I was also the one my parents seldom had to scold, though I was surrounded by siblings who enjoyed pranks and jests."

"Not sadly. It's a credit to you that you were working hard for what you wanted, even when you were a child."

"What about you? Were you the *gut* little girl?"

He was surprised when she faltered a moment before saying, "Eventually."

Wanting to kick himself for forgetting she'd endured the same uncertainty and temporary homes Parker did, he wished he could see her face better in the dim light. "I'm sorry. I shouldn't have asked that, Mercy."

"Why not? Having a wonderful childhood with siblings and two parents who were always there for you isn't anything to be ashamed of. It's something to celebrate." She looked past him to the *kinder* who were almost to the house. "It's what I'd hoped to offer Sunni here. A permanent home she knew would always be there for her." Before he could reply, she waved aside his answer. "Enough of the dreary. Let's enjoy spending time with the children."

He caught her gloved hand in his own. "And each other."

"Yes, and with each other." She smiled and squeezed

his fingers as they swung their hands between them on the short walk to the barn.

Again, Jeremiah's contentment was short-lived.

Sunni suddenly ran toward them. "Mommy! Mommy! We saw kittens. Can we bring them inside?"

"If you can find them," Mercy said with a chuckle.

Ten minutes later two dejected *kinder* gave up the search. The kittens seemed to have disappeared.

"Barn cats are very, very skilled at hiding," Mercy said to console them. "I used to play hide-and-seek with the kittens in the hayloft." She laughed. "They always won."

As she continued to tell the *kinder* about when she visited her *grossdawdi*, Jeremiah kept going toward the porch. But he couldn't walk away from the truth.

Mercy's connection to the farm was real and deep. Far deeper than his own.

Lord, if You've brought me here, I know You have a reason. And I also know Your reason can't be to bring Mercy unhappiness. Look at her!

He watched as she spoke with the *kinder*. Parker was acting as if he didn't need to listen, but he was as Mercy gave them ideas on how to lure the kittens to them tomorrow with fresh milk and calm voices and no quick motions.

She's a warmhearted woman, Lord, and she's eager to do whatever she can to help anyone else, even a young boy who challenges her at every turn and other kinder *she's never met. I don't know what path You have given her to walk, but please don't let it be filled with more hurt.*

And please don't let me cause that hurt.

Chapter Twelve

Jeremiah ran his hand along the planed log. Its smooth surface would make an excellent mantel. With a few imperfections left by the growth of the tree that once had stood on the farm, the log would be the exact complement to a fieldstone fireplace. Two days ago an *Englischer* renovating a house on the road between Salem and the Vermont border had stopped by, saying he'd heard Jeremiah was a woodworker. When Jeremiah had shown him the log, the man had been skeptical...until today. After seeing the work Jeremiah had done, he'd agreed to come back tomorrow so he could get the log and have it put in place right away.

A few other commissions like that one would add to the funds Jeremiah would need to move forward with his plans to buy a farm, whether it was Rudy's or another.

The thought jolted him as he was about to pick up another piece of wood. It was the first time he'd admitted to himself that there might be alternatives if Mercy's family decided not to accept the contract he'd signed.

He hadn't spoken with his Realtor in two weeks. Maybe Kitty had learned about a nearby farm for sale.

He grimaced. If there was a farm available along Harmony Creek, he would have heard about it from Caleb or one of his other neighbors.

Could he walk away after giving his word he'd help with the settlement? Maybe one of the other families would agree to let him live with them until he found a place of his own. Mercy might be willing to rent him some of her fields to use as pasture and planting.

And he'd be able to see her and the *kinder*.

"You've gotten in too deep, Stoltzfus," he muttered to himself as he hefted the log and laid it against the wall where it would be out of the way.

The door to his workshop opened, and his heart started doing a jig in his chest at the thought of Mercy stepping out of his thoughts and into his shop.

When Parker's head appeared around the edge, Jeremiah tried to ignore the flush of disappointment. He was glad to see the boy, but...

"Can I come in?" Parker asked.

"No touching the equipment," he said.

"You tell me that every time I come in." The boy pouted.

"And you still have five fingers on each hand." He winked at Parker to soften his words. "Let's keep it that way."

Parker picked up a piece of pine and pulled out a barely sharp kitchen knife. Running it down the side of the wood, he smiled. "See? I'm careful."

"I see, but you'd do better with a whittling knife than that one." He didn't ask if Mercy had given the boy permission to take it. He knew she hadn't.

"Where can I get one?"

"We can check the hardware store in the village, but first I need to see you can be trusted with it."

"I can. I can be trusted with anything."

Jeremiah simply arched his brows, and the boy got the message. No amount of bragging was allowed in the workshop.

"Can I ask you something?" Parker lowered the knife and wood onto his lap.

"What?"

"Will you help me change my name?"

He wasn't surprised. Parker had mentioned doing that several times since his arrival. "To what?"

"I haven't decided yet. Not my Korean name. Nobody can pronounce it."

"I understand," Jeremiah said, thinking of how Mercy had said the same thing about her birth name.

"I want something other than Parker. It's a dumb name." He grimaced. "Those dumb people stuck it on me."

He frowned at the boy. "You shouldn't call the Kentons *dumm*."

"But they are. They waited and waited for a kid of their own, and then they couldn't wait to get rid of me. That's pretty dumb."

"Even so, you shouldn't call any adult *dumm*." Thinking of the names Parker had used to upset Sunni, he added quickly, "Or any *kind*, either."

"But it's okay to say Parker is a dumb name? I— Ouch!" He stared in horror at the thin red slice on his index finger. The line widened as blood ran from the cut.

Without a word as the knife clattered to the floor,

Jeremiah grabbed the *kind*'s wrist. He ignored Parker's shrieks as he thrust the cut finger into a bucket of cold water he kept nearby for such emergencies. Deftly, he dabbed an antibacterial cream from his first-aid kit on the wound and bound it.

"There you go."

Tears ran down Parker's face, but he regarded his bandaged finger with as much curiosity as if it belonged to someone else. "Will I have a scar?" He raised his eyes, which sparkled with abrupt excitement. "Like the ones you have?"

Jeremiah looked at his fingers, which showcased the long hours of hard, hands-on work he'd done since he was younger than Parker. All his knuckles, including his thumbs, bore scars, and his left palm showed where a fishhook had become embedded in it when he'd been showing off for his older brothers and their friends. Each mark told a story and evoked a memory, some *gut*, some not so *gut*, especially when he'd needed stitches on his right forefinger after being bitten by a dog shortly after he'd turned ten.

"If you end up with a scar," he said as he gathered the supplies and put them in the first-aid box, "it won't be like mine, but yours will be there to remind you to be careful as mine do."

"Will girls like my scar like Mercy does yours?"

Shocked to feel heat rising up his face, Jeremiah kept his head bent so the *kind* didn't see his reaction. "I don't think Mercy cares about my scars one way or the other."

"Sure she does." Parker climbed onto the chunk of wood, but didn't reach for his knife. "I've seen her touching them. A lot. I think she likes them. A lot."

The boy was right, Jeremiah knew. About Mercy

touching him when she wanted to make a point or to console him or to make a connection. He treasured each memory of her fingers against him, but he tried not to think of them too often. For all he knew, she might have another man in her life. Someone more important to her than he was. She seldom spoke of her life in central New York. Thinking of how she rushed to the mailbox as soon as the postal carrier drove past, he wondered—not for the first time—if she was eager to hear from someone special.

But he wasn't about to discuss his feelings for Mercy with a nine-year-old.

As he put the box on its shelf, he said, "You should tell God how grateful you are the injury isn't worse. Asking for healing wouldn't be a bad idea, either."

"You're always talking about God. Do you really believe in him?"

"*Ja.*"

"Oh." The boy picked up the piece of wood he'd dropped and rolled it between his fingers. Staring off into the distance, he asked, "Aren't you going to ask me if I believe in God?"

"I figured you'd tell me if you wanted me to know."

The *kind* didn't answer quickly.

Jeremiah gave the boy time to think while he walked over to the plow he'd brought inside. He'd cleaned off the rust but needed to straighten it. The plow would be ready for him—or whoever owned the farm by the time the snow melted—to work in the fields. If he was going to be able to complete the purchase of the farm, he must buy workhorses or mules. He'd need six on a team to work on the slopes, which were far steeper than in Paradise Springs.

"I'd like to believe in God," Parker said at last. "Mercy said you Amish live as you do because you want to be close to God."

"The apostle Paul wrote in Romans 12:2: *And be not conformed to this world: but be ye transformed by the renewing of your mind, that ye may prove what is that good, and acceptable, and perfect, will of God.* That's what our ministers preach and how we try to live."

"Did the Possible Paul—"

"*Apostle* Paul." He couldn't halt his grin. "An apostle is someone who teaches us about being *gut* Christians."

"Paul, huh?" The little boy started to add more, but the sound of a car pulling into the yard intruded.

Hearing a groan from Parker, Jeremiah knew it must be Whitney's. She was scheduled to come by today for a visit to check on how Parker was fitting in.

"Let's go." Jeremiah motioned with his head toward the door.

He thought Parker might protest, but the boy walked toward the door. Every inch of the *kind* announced he wanted to go anywhere but into the house to meet with Whitney and answer her questions. Jeremiah secretly shared the boy's dislike of someone poking and prodding into his life, but the social worker needed to be sure the placement was a *gut* one for all involved.

Jeremiah's steps faltered as he was following the boy outside. This meeting could be Mercy's chance to hand the troubled *kind* over to someone else, but he couldn't imagine she would. He'd seen the pain in her eyes whenever she mentioned Parker leaving for a permanent placement. The kid might challenge her endlessly, but she wasn't ready to give up the battle to reach him.

"Hey!" called Whitney when Parker tried to sneak past her unseen.

The boy stopped, his hands behind him and his head lowered. He didn't return the greeting.

Instead, Jeremiah did as he walked toward the silver car.

With a smile, Whitney said, "Hi, Jeremiah! Has our boy been spending time with you?"

"Ja." He crooked a finger toward Parker, who reluctantly edged forward. "You'll probably want to see this right away."

The social worker's smile faded when she saw the boy's bandaged finger. "What happened to you, young man?"

Again, Parker was silent.

Whitney's gaze shot toward Jeremiah, and he realized she was waiting for an answer.

"Parker learned a *gut* lesson about using the right tool for the job," Jeremiah replied calmly. "It's a cut."

"Does he need stitches?"

Shaking his head, he said, "No. It bled a lot, but it'll heal quickly. It's not much more than a long paper cut. He can show you in the house, and I'm sure Mercy will rebandage it for him."

"I'll do that." She flashed a quick smile at the boy. "Go and let Mercy know I'm here."

Parker took off running as best he could through the piles of snow.

Once he was out of earshot, Whitney turned to Jeremiah. He told her how Parker had hurt himself.

"He won't make the same mistake again," he finished.

"Because he won't have access to knives?"

"No, because I'm going to show him the correct way to whittle once I know he's willing to be cautious."

"I don't know," she drawled.

"This is a farm, and boys on farms learn how to whittle and use a knife as a proper tool. If he's going to be here for a while, he needs to know what the other boys do, or he'll experiment on his own. Who knows how he could hurt himself if he did that?"

Whitney nodded slowly. "I see. Does that mean you intend to remain around to teach him how to use a knife?"

He shook his head. "I honestly can't answer that. Not until Mercy's family decides what they want done with the farm."

"You know starting a children's summer camp is Mercy's dream, don't you?" Whitney asked, flashing a guilty glance at the house as if revealing an unspeakable secret.

"I know. She wants to help *kinder* enjoy getting away from the summer heat in the city."

"No, Jeremiah, it's more than that. Mercy knows her life would have been very different if she hadn't been a Fresh Air kid. She wouldn't have known the family who took her in before the Bambergers became her foster parents and then her adoptive parents. Come Along Farm is her way to repay an immeasurable debt." Whitney looked at the house again and sighed. "Will it be enough for her?"

"I don't know," he replied.

"I don't know, either, but I do know there aren't too many women her age who would have agreed to look after a very angry, very hurt, very destructive and hateful child as she has."

"Parker is a challenge, but he's not hateful." Jeremiah thought of how the *kind* was changing…slightly.

"Parker? You don't have any idea whom I'm talking about, do you?"

"No. I thought we were talking about the boy."

"No, I'm talking about Sunni."

He couldn't hide his shock. "Sunni was destructive and hateful?"

"Yes."

"But she's such a *gut* kid."

"Now." Whitney ran her fingers lightly over the handle of her briefcase. "I've probably already said too much. If you want to know more, you'll need to ask Mercy. I wanted *you* to know, other than Sunni and the rest of her family—and I'm not too sure about her family—nothing is more important to Mercy than paying back the compassion and love she was given after her grandmother died with a bigger dose of compassion and love. Please remember that."

"I will." What else could he say as Whitney walked toward the house?

Everything and everyone kept reminding him Mercy didn't want the farm for herself. She wanted it for others.

Lord, am I being selfish to believe the farm is the only way I can help this settlement to grow and succeed? How can I stand in her way if I care for her?

And he more than cared for her, he knew. He was in danger of falling in love with her. He found it difficult to imagine a day without her being a part of it. Her smile was the last thing he thought of before falling asleep and the first thing he envisioned in the hour before dawn. The brush of her fingers set off fireworks

along his skin, and the thought of kissing her left him breathless.

So how could he stand in the way of her making her dreams come true? *How, Lord?*

He turned to walk toward the barns, not sure he was ready for the answer to that question.

Mercy wasn't surprised when Jeremiah offered to help her do dishes after supper. She guessed he was curious how the meeting with Whitney had gone. She eased his concerns by telling him the social worker had been impressed with how quickly he explained what had happened to Parker's finger and why and how Jeremiah intended to prevent such things from occurring again.

"She seems very taken with you, Jeremiah," she said with a chuckle.

"I'm a very taking guy." He grimaced. "Is that even a thing?"

"Who knows? Thank you for being so up-front about Parker's injury. Once Whitney saw it was exactly as you described, she was satisfied."

"And Parker ended up with, as he described them, very cool bandages."

"Don't tell him that I bought those strips with cartoon characters for Sunni. He won't be happy then."

"I'd hoped they'd be getting along better by now."

She shrugged. "I've got to admit having him treating her badly has strengthened her." A faint smile tugged at her lips. "I suspect, in spite of my best efforts, I've babied her a bit because of her physical challenges. Parker cuts her no slack."

"That's a nice way of saying he's rude to her."

"But not to you." She smiled. "I don't know what you're doing, Jeremiah, but whatever it is, don't stop."

"I'm not planning to. By the way, I intend to start tapping the maple trees in the sugar bush tomorrow. If it's not too cold, why don't you and the *kinder* join me? I could use extra hands, and I think they'll find it fascinating. I did when I first saw sap coming out of a tree when I was a kid."

"That sounds like fun."

"It should be." He chuckled. "Do you know what Parker asked me earlier today?"

She gave a half laugh. "I don't want to try to guess. Knowing him, it could have been anything."

"He asked me if I believed in God."

Putting another stack of dirty dishes into the sink, she said, "I assume you told him you do."

"*Ja*, but I don't think he was looking for such a simple answer. He's trying to figure out why we live as we do in Harmony Creek." He picked up another plate to dry. "For a child who's so quick to anger, he can be deeply introspective when presented with a new idea. It's too bad apparently nobody has ever spoken to him about such things before he came here."

"I plan to take him to the closest Mennonite church with me on Sunday. It's about thirty miles from here." She hesitated, then asked, "Would you like to come with us?"

"You came to Sunday services with me, so I guess I should return the favor."

She faced him. "I should warn you that boys Parker's age sit with the men."

"That should make for an interesting morning, ain't so?"

Her breath grew swift as her gaze was caught by his.

Strong emotions glistened in his eyes that burned a fiery blue. His fingers curved along her cheek, the warmth of his palm caressing her skin. As he stepped closer to her, he gently tilted her face toward him.

He was going to kiss her! Every nerve went on alert, and she was aware of him as she'd never been, the scent of the soap he used, the rough texture of his arms beneath her fingertips, the way his hair fell forward over his eyes as he bent to bring her lips to his.

A loud cry came from the mudroom, and Mercy yanked herself away from him. Shoving the dishrag that had been dripping unnoticed on the floor into Jeremiah's hands, she ran to referee the latest argument between the two children. She sent Sunni to the dining room and Parker into the living room, telling them to cool off.

From behind her as she stood in the middle of the empty room, she heard Jeremiah say, "*Ja*, I think it's going to be very interesting at church." He went into the kitchen.

She was about to follow, then paused. The moment between them was gone, and she would be wise not to let it happen again. She wasn't sure she could step away without kissing him next time.

Chapter Thirteen

Mercy wasn't sure who was more excited when the next day dawned with a cloudless sky and temperatures that should rise above freezing by midday. The kids were thrilled when they heard Jeremiah's invitation to help him with tapping the maple trees. She was just as excited, praying she'd have the chance to discover if he'd truly intended to kiss her.

She had to insist the children eat a hearty breakfast. They wanted to rush out and get to work right away. She also made them show her what they were wearing. She told Parker to zip his coat and wrap a scarf around his neck. When Sunni protested wearing her snow pants, Mercy refused to let her daughter draw her into an argument. If she didn't wear them, she wasn't going.

Seeing a hastily hidden smirk on Parker's face, Mercy wanted to ask what he'd said to persuade Sunni to go out without proper clothing. She didn't. Later, when she had a chance to speak to her daughter alone, she'd find out. Why Sunni listened to him when he said such things was a mystery to Mercy, but her own sib-

lings were so much older than she was, so they hadn't shared growing up years with her.

Mercy found a new problem when they went outside. The snow was melting, and walking through the high piles was as difficult as slogging through knee-deep mud. Watching Sunni, she wasn't sure the little girl could trudge up the hill and into the woods.

"Who wants a ride?" asked Jeremiah as he appeared around the house with an ancient toboggan topped with buckets and spiles to use to tap the trees.

The toboggan's front was scraped as if it'd hit bushes or caromed off a tree. No cushions eased the hard seats, but he connected a new nylon rope to it.

Not waiting for an answer to his question, he bowed. "Young ladies first."

His words earned a giggle from Sunni as she climbed on, and a mouthed "Thank you" from Mercy. She was grateful for how he didn't act as if Sunni was incapable.

At first, Parker was going to ride, but he changed his mind when Jeremiah asked him to help carry the battery-operated drill he'd use to make the holes for the sap. Jeremiah grabbed two handfuls of buckets off the toboggan, leaving plenty of room for Sunni.

When Mercy urged Jeremiah and Parker to go ahead, the boy followed him toward the clump of trees halfway up the hill behind the barn. She pulled Sunni on the toboggan, following the path Jeremiah and Parker had made. It was a beautiful day, cold but the sunshine glistened on the unbroken snow. She pointed to animal tracks and had Sunni guess which animal might have made them. Crows sang their raucous songs as they wheeled overhead, and Sunni giggled with delight at the ride through the snow.

"Just like when we went in the sleigh, Mommy!" she called out.

"Except I'm playing the horse's part."

That brought more laughter from her daughter, and Mercy's footsteps grew lighter, even as the wet snow tried to hold her back.

Jeremiah paused and let Mercy catch up. "Do you want me to take the toboggan?"

"No, I'm fine."

"That you are." He gave her a wink that made her heart dance with delight.

He went to a tree and walked around it. Looking up at the sky, he shifted partway around again. "Okay, here's the southeast side of the tree."

"Is that important?" Parker asked.

"It is. The southeast side gets sunshine first in the late winter." He held out his hand for the drill. "Stay back."

Sunni clambered off the toboggan so she could watch as the drill whirred, sending pieces of wood flying in every direction. Her eyes were wide as she leaned closer.

Mercy put her hands on her daughter's shoulders, drawing her back slightly. She didn't want the little girl hit by the debris.

Picking up a thin twig, Jeremiah showed Parker how to clean the shavings out of the hole. "This way, they won't get in the sap." He hammered a spile into the tree.

"Will the tree be okay?" Sunni asked with sudden concern. "You're not hurting it, are you?"

"It'll be fine." Jeremiah gave her a gentle smile. "We won't be greedy, so the tree will have plenty of sap to carry up its branches to grow leaves. This is a grown-

up tree." He pointed to the trunk at chest height. "Once a tree is ten inches around at this height, it can share its sap with us."

He showed Mercy how to place the bucket on the hook built into the tap so it would catch the drippings. He warned her to be careful the bucket's handle wasn't in the way. When the first drop fell with a ping into the bucket, Mercy was as enthralled as the children. While Jeremiah helped Sunni set the metal "roof" over the bucket, he explained the folded piece would prevent windblown leaves and other debris from falling into the sap. Some would find their way into the bucket, but not as much as if the bucket was left open.

"It looks like it's wearing a hat," Sunni said with a grin.

Motioning for them to follow, Jeremiah began drilling another hole in the tree. He did three in the smaller trees and four in the massive ones. Each of the others had their tasks. Mercy waited while Parker cleared the hole, leaving tiny specks of wood on the snow at his feet. She and Sunni set the bucket and cover in place.

They fell into an easy rhythm as they moved from one tree to the next. After drilling holes in twenty-five trees, Jeremiah called a halt.

"If we do more," he said, "I won't have time to collect the sap, make the syrup and milk the cows." He ruffled the top of Parker's hat, leaving it askew. "Even with my *gut* assistant here."

The boy grinned. "Can I help make syrup, too?"

"*Ja.* I'll need everyone to pitch in." He stepped aside to let Parker clear out the hole. "Wait a moment, Mercy, before you put the bucket on. Do you *kinder* want to try a sample of the sap?"

This time, Parker went first. He bent and stuck out his tongue beneath the hole exactly as Jeremiah instructed. The boy waited and waited, then frowned at Jeremiah, as if he thought the man was playing a trick on him.

"You've got to be patient," Jeremiah said with a laugh. "Sap comes out one drip at a time, and it's pretty chilly, so it's moving slowly."

"Let her try." He pointed to Sunni and stepped back, disgruntled.

"All right. Sunni, you want to have a taste?"

Mercy smiled as Sunni stepped forward to take her turn. She stood as Parker had. Silence, except for the rustle of birds in the higher branches, settled on them as she waited with her tongue poised near the hole. When she yelped in excitement, Mercy knew a drop had finally emerged.

"It's sweet!" Sunni's face glowed with happiness.

"Wait till you taste how sweet the syrup will be." Jeremiah turned to Parker as Mercy gave her daughter a hug. "You want to try again?"

"Yeah." His surly tone surprised Mercy because he hadn't used it with Jeremiah since the day of his arrival. He stepped forward, elbowing Sunni aside. As she fell into the snow, he ordered, "Get out of my way, cripple!"

Hearing Mercy's dismayed gasp, Jeremiah grabbed the boy by his shoulders and pulled him away from the tree. Anger blared through Jeremiah, and he wasn't sure he could quiet it. Mercy's face was as pale as the snow as she lifted her daughter to her feet, and fat tears showered Sunni's cheeks. He wasn't sure if she was physically hurt or wounded by the cruel words.

"Mercy, will you and Sunni finish putting the bucket on there? We'll meet you at the house." Without another word, Jeremiah walked away, tugging Parker with him.

The boy started to speak several times as they went toward the tenant house. Each time, Jeremiah cut him off sharply.

Steering him inside, Jeremiah motioned for Parker to take a seat at the kitchen table. He half expected the boy to make a snide remark about the state of the house, but Parker stared at the floor.

"Why would you say something horrible to Sunni?" Jeremiah asked, not wanting to beat around the bush.

"I dunno," he muttered.

"I think you do. You treat Sunni and Mercy as if they're manure on the bottom of your boots."

The boy clamped his lips closed.

Knowing he needed to take another tack, Jeremiah forced his voice to be calm. The boy wasn't going to respond to anger. Parker would get defensive and close up.

Quietly, Jeremiah sighed.

The boy looked up, startled.

"Parker, I thought you wanted to be here working with me."

"I do." The boy bumped his toe against an uneven floorboard and again didn't meet Jeremiah's gaze.

"I can't work with someone who says bad things to other people."

"People say bad things to me."

He sat on a chair beside the *kind*'s. "I'm sorry to hear that, Parker. People used to say bad things about me, too."

"You?" The boy's head jerked up, revealing his shock. It made him look younger than his nine years

and vulnerable. "But everyone says what a nice guy you are. When we went to the hardware store last week, I heard a man say he wouldn't be as willing as you are to wait to get what he'd signed papers for." Puzzlement threaded his brow. "What papers?"

Not wanting to be distracted from the issue at hand, Jeremiah said, "Business stuff. Nothing important now." He was astonished to realize how true his words were. As much as he wanted to own the farm, at that moment his whole attention was on the *kind*.

"What did they say about you?" Parker asked.

"I was too short. I was too chubby. I was stupid because I had a hard time alphabetizing my spelling words."

The boy's nose wrinkled. "I hate alphabetizing my spelling words, too."

"I couldn't see the point of doing it when I could be in the barn working with the cows or whittling. The cows and that stick of wood didn't care if I knew which word should come first." He leaned toward Parker. "And they didn't care what anyone else said about me. They didn't care about anything other than I did my chores and took care of them. So that's what I did."

"Me, too."

"But as much as you and I are alike, there's one way we're different. I try never to say anything hurtful to someone else. Jesus asked us to treat everyone else the way we want to be treated."

"That's what I'm doing."

Jeremiah caught and held the boy's gaze. "Do you really want Sunni to say such nasty things to you?"

Parker's shoulders sagged. "No."

"Then why do you say them to her?"

"Sometimes I get mad."

"I know how that is."

The boy stiffened. "Do you? Sometimes I get so mad I want to hit someone."

"I know."

He frowned. "I thought Amish guys didn't fight."

"We shouldn't, but once, when I was about your age, I thought about hitting the bully who said bad things about me. I didn't."

"Why not?"

"Because I knew I was loved the way I was."

Parker shook his head. "Good for you. Nobody wants me."

"No? Mercy opened her home to you. Sunni includes you in everything she does. Don't you realize she thinks you're someone special? Haven't you noticed how she was eager to help in the barn because you were helping there?"

He shrugged, not wanting to be swayed by Jeremiah's words. "Maybe she thought she was missing out on something."

"Maybe she did, but she didn't realize it until you showed her how much fun chores can be. She never was interested before you came here."

Tears bubbled out of the boy's eyes, and Jeremiah had to resist his immediate impulse to put his arms around Parker and comfort him. The *kind* needed to realize his mistakes and decide to change.

"I'm sorry, Jeremiah. Don't hate me, too."

"I don't hate you. Nobody on the farm hates you."

"Sunni does." He wiped his nose with his arm. "She has to. I hate me."

"If she hated you, she wouldn't want to spend time with you. And she does."

Parker dashed away more tears. "She's a silly little girl."

"Maybe, but that silly little girl doesn't hate you. I don't hate you, and Mercy doesn't." He put a hand on the boy's shoulder. "Let me tell you one more very important thing. God loves you."

"How do you know that?"

"Because His son told us so." He gave the boy a gentle smile. "He loves all his *kinder*, including when we make mistakes. I've made plenty." The image of Emmarita's face flashed through his mind, but he easily ignored it. "God chose for me to be exactly like I am, so He must love what I am. Just as he loves you. Believe it." He tapped Parker's chest. "Right here, believe it. Next time you feel angry, give that anger over to God. He doesn't mind, and He'll ease the pain in your heart."

"He will?"

"Ja." Coming to his feet, Jeremiah said, "I think you know what you need to do."

"Apologize to Sunni?" He got up. "Will you come with me?"

"Of course."

A few minutes later Jeremiah stood beside the boy while Parker asked Sunni to forgive him. When the little girl did with a sincerity Jeremiah found endearing, he saw gratitude in Mercy's eyes. He put his arms around all of them, pulling them into a hug. Feeling Mercy's soft hand on his back, he knew he'd lost the battle to stop himself from loving her.

That made everything more difficult, and he needed to figure out what to do about it. But right now he was going to enjoy holding her—and the *kinder*—close.

Chapter Fourteen

The interior of the church could have belonged to the one Mercy had attended with her parents in central New York. Plain, whitewashed walls and simple benches. A trio of windows on either side of the pews had no stained glass like other churches in the village.

Adjusting her prayer covering, she walked with Sunni to a bench on the women's side. She glanced at where Parker sat next to Jeremiah. The boy's legs swung as he waited for the service to start. When Jeremiah bent to whisper something in his ear, Parker gave him a big grin.

How she wished she could get such a response from the boy, but he refused to trust her. She kept telling herself not to take it personally. He didn't trust any woman as far as she could see, and he had good cause. Not only had he been abandoned by his mother in Korea, left at a grocery store according to his records, but Pat Kenton had let him love her and then turned her back on him, as well.

Someday, sometime in the future when Parker was old enough to understand, she hoped she could tell him

how much she empathized with his fear of loving again. Mrs. Kenton had chosen her other life over her son's, as Graham had chosen his mother over Mercy...and her Fresh Air family had chosen their older daughter's lies over Mercy's and their younger daughter's protestations of truth.

Life wasn't fair, but it was good.

She wasn't sure who'd said that first, but she believed it with every ounce of her being. If Parker would let her closer, she might be able to convince him she knew his sense of betrayal. Maybe someday...but not today because he'd ignored Sunni and her, talking only to Jeremiah in the car. Even so, she longed to see the boy smile at something she said or did with as much joy as he did when he was with Jeremiah.

Jeremiah... Did he suspect she'd invited him to the Mennonite service hoping he'd feel comfortable enough that he'd consider putting aside his Amish life to join the Mennonites? It wouldn't be so different for him.

Except he wouldn't be part of the new community on the banks of Harmony Creek.

Praying about what to do so they could have a future together hadn't brought her any answers. Few people joined the Amish, and fewer stayed. The dedication to community and to a life separate from the rest of the world was too much for most people who hadn't been raised in it.

As well, there was the issue of Come Along Farm. Opening a summer camp for children probably wouldn't fit with the Amish ideas of staying separate. She glanced at Sunni, who was looking everywhere but at Parker on the other side of the aisle. From Whitney, she'd learned Amish might adopt, but it was usually an internal mat-

ter. A baby born to an Amish girl who couldn't rear it
would be given to another family.

*But if I can't become Amish and he won't become
Mennonite, there's no future for us.*

That thought echoed through Mercy's head as she
listened to the service but kept glancing over to where
Parker sat beside Jeremiah. When the boy yawned, Jer-
emiah put his arm around the child and leaned Parker
against him. She smiled gently before Sunni nestled
against her. Pushing her worries from her mind, she
gave herself over to the peace filling the sanctuary.

Mercy was smiling when, after the service, she led
Sunni to where Jeremiah and Parker were waiting by
her car. Urging them to get in out of the windy day, she
slid behind the wheel. She turned the key to start the
car and twisted the dial so the heat would fill the space.
Other cars were backing up and pulling out of the park-
ing lot, so she waited.

After turning to check both children wore their seat
belts, she asked the question that weighed so heavily
on her mind. "So what did you think of the service,
Jeremiah?"

"The harmony when you sing the hymns is pretty.
Four-part harmony, ain't so?"

"Yes, and we sing the hymns at a quicker tempo than
you do. I hope that didn't trip you up."

"I was able to keep up." He gave her a smile, which
did delightful things to her middle.

"You know that's not what I meant."

"Maybe I did. Maybe I didn't." He winked at the
children.

Sunni began to giggle, but Parker looked baffled as

if he couldn't figure out why someone would find the conversation amusing.

"I've made up my mind," he said abruptly.

"About what?" Mercy asked.

"My name."

"Is that so?" she asked, careful to make her voice sound calm. "What other name have you decided on? Or do you want to keep the one you've got?"

"Not Parker." His nose wrinkled. "I sound like someone working in a parking lot."

Jeremiah chuckled. "I had the same thought when I first heard it."

The boy remained serious. "I thought about Jerry because it's like your name, Jeremiah, but you might think Mercy is scolding you when I do something wrong."

Again, Jeremiah laughed, but Mercy could see how deeply touched he was by the child's desire to be connected to him. Her eyes were awash in tears she didn't want to let fall because the boy might think she was upset.

"So tell us your name!" Sunni leaned toward him, excited.

"I want to be Paul." He looked at Jeremiah. "I remember hearing you say the day I arrived Paul was your dad's name. That's right, ain't so? And, if I'm Paul, you won't get confused when Mercy's talking to us."

When Jeremiah nodded, Mercy realized he was so overcome with emotion he was unable to speak. Not only was the boy picking up his way of speaking, but Parker had also chosen a name that meant so much to Jeremiah.

Clearing his throat, Jeremiah said, "You're right.

Paul was my *daed*'s name, and I think he would have been happy to share it with you."

"All right. Call me Paul." Without a pause, he asked what was for lunch.

"Would you like to stop somewhere to eat?" Mercy was no longer surprised by Parker's— No, she needed to remember to call him Paul and let Whitney know about the change once she was sure the boy wouldn't pick a different name tomorrow. She was not surprised by Paul's focus on his next meal. The boy seemed endlessly hungry. "There's a nice diner between here and the farm. Grandpa Rudy used to take me there once or twice each summer when I visited him. You'll get so much to eat you'll feel like a stuffed turkey at Thanksgiving."

That brought cheers of excitement from the back seat. When she glanced at Jeremiah, he smiled.

"How could I say no when I'm outnumbered?" he asked with a chuckle.

She backed the car out, determined to enjoy the day and the company the Lord had given her.

Jeremiah wasn't surprised when Mercy walked beside him as the *kinder* raced toward the diner's door.

Slanting her head toward him, she murmured, "You do realize the importance of the name he picked, right? It's his way of telling you he wants to be a family with you."

"It's pretty overwhelming."

"It is, isn't it?" She squeezed his arm and smiled. "You've worked wonders with him, and he knows that, though he can't—or won't—say it. Are you truly okay with him using your father's name?"

He nodded, and unabashed tears gleamed in his eyes. "My *daed* used to say that he wanted a dozen *kinder*. He and *Mamm* were blessed with the nine of us, but it feels now as if he's one more kid closer to his goal."

When she gave him a lovely smile, he wasn't sure how the day could get better. He thought about taking her hand, but they'd reached the door where Sunni and *Paul* were waiting impatiently. He opened the door and ushered them inside.

The diner was long and narrow. A single line of booths edged the windows overlooking the parking lot. Cutting the building down the middle was a curved counter. The stools were repaired with black electrical tape. However, everything was sparkling clean.

When Mercy led the way to the booth she called her favorite, he followed the *kinder*. He couldn't fail to notice the glances in their directions. They were the only plain folk in the diner.

A waitress in a simple white shirt and black pants beneath her red-checkered apron took their orders. Fortunately, the menu for *kinder* was limited, so Sunni and Paul selected quickly. Chicken nuggets for Sunni and spaghetti for Paul. After checking that none of the boy's allergies would be triggered by what he'd ordered, Mercy asked for an open-faced hot turkey sandwich. Glad the others had ordered first, Jeremiah debated between two favorites and settled on chicken Parmesan.

The servings were as huge as Mercy recalled and as delicious. The children wasted no time cleaning their plates, their eyes continuously shifting toward the pie trolley on top of the gray counter.

When the waitress came to remove their plates, she

asked if they wanted dessert. The enthusiastic response came from Jeremiah as well as the children.

The waitress smiled. "Just so you know, we get our pies from an Amish woman."

"Do you have *snitz* pie?" he asked.

"We do."

"Then two adult-size servings and two kid-size ones. Two cups of *kaffi*—coffee—and two glasses of milk."

"Chocolate?" interjected Paul.

She nodded. "Chocolate it'll be."

As she walked away, Sunni asked, "What is *snitz*?"

"Wait and see." He winked at Mercy as the kids wiggled with anticipation.

The waitress returned with their drinks before going to the counter to cut four slices of pie. She smiled as she set the plates on the table.

Paul wrinkled his nose as he looked at the dark brown filling in his serving. "What is it?"

"Is it chocolate?" asked Sunni, peering at her slice from every direction.

"It's *snitz* pie." Jeremiah grinned. "If you don't want it, I'll eat it." He held out his hand. "I never pass up a piece of *snitz* pie, especially my *mamm*'s. Ask anyone, and they'll tell you Wanda Lapp makes the best *snitz* pie in Lancaster County. Maybe the whole world."

"Why isn't her name Wanda Stoltzfus?" asked Sunni, ever the one to try to nail down every detail.

"Because she got remarried after my *daed* died."

"My father is dead, too." The little girl's lower lip began to tremble. "And my mommy." Her gaze darted to Mercy. "Not this mommy, my before mommy."

"My whole family is dead," stated Paul, not to be outdone. As he began to tell an outrageous tale that

sounded as if it'd come from a television show too violent for a child his age, he must have seen the adults weren't buying his story. "It's true!"

"But it's not *gut* conversation for the dinner table." Jeremiah caught the boy's eyes and tilted his head toward where Mercy and Sunni sat. "The ladies, you know. They don't like rough talk like cowmen use. That's very important, ain't so?"

Mercy picked up her cup of coffee and took a sip so the boy didn't see her lips twitching with a smile. When Paul agreed with Jeremiah, she guessed the child had no idea what Jeremiah meant, but he wasn't going to let anyone see that.

"But what is it?" persisted Paul.

Mercy decided Jeremiah had teased the children long enough. "Apple pie."

Paul shook his head. "It looks strange."

"Because it's made with dried apples." She looked at the boy, who was clearly torn between standing firm so he didn't look as if he was giving in to her and his obvious longing to give in to the temptation to try the pie.

"It tastes like apple butter."

"Yummy!" announced Sunni and dove into her dessert.

Not to be outdone, Paul broke off the tiniest piece with his fork and stared at it. "It's polite to eat what's put in front of me," he said, obviously repeating something he'd heard at his previous home.

Mercy exchanged a glance with Jeremiah as she wondered how many times Paul's prospective mother had uttered those words. Her sorrow at what the boy had experienced vanished when Paul's eyes lit up as he tasted the pie.

"Can we have seconds?" he asked as he jabbed his fork into the pie for another bite.

They laughed, and Mercy savored the chance to look at each of them as they all smiled at the same time. It hadn't happened often. She hoped it would more often from this point forward.

"Mommy! Stop! Now!"

When Sunni screamed, Mercy looked in the rearview mirror and saw her daughter's terror. They'd just driven out of the diner's parking lot.

Jeremiah swung around. "Mercy, pull over!"

She twisted the wheel. The car behind her honked in annoyance, but she ignored it as she jammed the shifting lever into Park. As their car rocked to an abrupt stop, she jumped out at the same time Jeremiah did.

He tore open the door on his side and leaned over Paul, who was straining to breathe. The boy's lips were already turning blue, and his face was swollen with hives.

Grabbing her purse, she pulled out the epinephrine injector she'd been carrying since Paul joined their family. She ran around the car, pushed Jeremiah aside and flipped the top off the injector. She gripped it tightly before grabbing the fleshy part of the boy's thigh. She pressed the injector against his pants. Hearing a click, she counted off ten seconds.

"We passed an urgent care just before we pulled into the diner," Jeremiah said.

"Can you drive a car?"

He nodded. "But I haven't in a while."

"Get in and drive." She climbed between the two children, keeping her eyes on the wheezing boy. "Go!"

Jeremiah jumped behind the wheel and jammed the shift into Drive. They were thrown back against the seats as the tires squealed when he rammed the gas pedal to the floor.

"You're going to be okay," she said as she brushed Paul's bangs from his brow that was covered with cold sweat.

She heard Jeremiah praying and added her own prayers that they'd reach the urgent care quickly and as another car blared its horn at them—without an accident.

Hours later, when Mercy sat across from Jeremiah at the kitchen table having a calming cup of tea while he drank coffee, she strained her ears to listen for footsteps upstairs. The children had been worn out by the day's exciting events.

"A single piece of candy with a single peanut in it." Mercy shook her head. "He didn't realize he'd grabbed one with a peanut from the bowl by the cash register. Not until it was in his mouth."

"But he's all right."

"I'd like to say my nerves are all right, too."

Jeremiah laughed quietly. "Maybe yours are. I think mine will calm down in a month or so. You were *wunderbaar*, Mercy. You didn't stop to think. You did what you had to do."

"You would have done the same."

"I'd like to think so, but I was shocked when his condition was getting more dire by the second."

Letting her shoulders sag and wincing at the ache from holding them taut for so long, she said, "Thank God it turned out all right."

"*Ja*, we must most definitely thank God. He was with us, protecting us."

"Especially when you were driving." She allowed herself a smile. "I didn't realize your previous driving experience was as a race driver."

Again, he chuckled. "Just so you know, I was praying as fast as I was driving." He sipped his coffee. His hands remained unsteady.

Just like hers. *Thank You, God, for watching over Paul today and guiding us to get help for him.*

"I hope you enjoyed the Mennonite service," Mercy said, needing to talk about something other than Paul's close brush with death.

"It was interesting. Like an Amish one, but yet not like it." He gave her a weary smile. "And I don't mean just the pace of the singing."

"If you'd like to come with us again, you're welcome." Wishing she could come out and ask him what she really wanted to know—would he ever consider becoming a Mennonite?—she couldn't. If he said no, then that ended any hopes for them to have a future together.

You're getting ahead of yourself, her conscience whispered. *He hasn't said anything about the future other than his plans for the farm. Can't you see what comes first?*

Pain twisted in her stomach. Jeremiah had been honest about the fact his dreams were his number one priority. If Graham had been so forthcoming, it would have saved them a lot of hurt.

"*Danki*," he replied, "but I may be doing some traveling."

"Really?"

"Caleb mentioned that he may need me to help him

find other families for the settlement." He didn't add more, but she understood what he wasn't saying. If it wasn't God's will for him to have the farm, recruiting others to come to the Harmony Creek settlement might be the best way for him to help it thrive.

"When would you be leaving?"

"Most likely soon. Once spring comes, there won't be time for anything but fieldwork and chores." He gave her a weak smile. "Caleb suggested I go to central New York. Actually not far from where your family lives."

"You should stop in and see them if you do."

His brows lowered. "You don't think I'd try to influence them into selling me the farm?"

"I thought we weren't going to look for hidden motives." She didn't say the words harshly, because the thought had slipped through her mind, as well. "My parents would be glad to offer you a place to stay because you're my friend."

Did she see him flinch at *friend*? Or was she hoping he had? Could he feel about her as she did about him?

Her hopes he might faded when he asked, "Would there be anyone else you'd like me to take a message to? Did you leave someone special behind in central New York?"

She snorted. "How many men do you know who'd be willing to date a woman with a child, especially one with special medical needs? I could count them on the number of hairs on a bald man's head!"

"My brother Daniel married his wife, who was responsible for a *kind* with Down syndrome and her *grossmammi* Ella, who has Alzheimer's."

"Maybe so, but he's one of a kind."

He folded his arms on the table and shook his head.

"Actually not. When my brothers—and sisters—have fallen in love, they haven't cared about the complications of *kinder*. Our family has grown very quickly in the past couple of years with additions, *bopplin* and older kids."

"Then your whole family is one of a kind. Most men I've met head in the other direction once they find out I have a child."

"Two."

"But for how long?" She raised her eyes toward the ceiling where the children should be asleep.

"What do you mean?"

"How long will Paul be here? There are so many reasons he could leave, some having to do with the social services. Others to…"

When her voice faded, he put his hand over her fingers on the table. "Others having to do with who ends up owning the farm? Is that what you were going to say?"

"I'm sorry, Jeremiah." She gazed at his hand on hers, confused. On one hand, she thrilled in his touch. On the other, she struggled to trust him. She knew he wasn't Graham, but her heart bore the scars of that betrayal.

"Mercy, you must realize if your family decides to sell me the farm, I'm not planning on throwing you and the kids out ten seconds later."

"I know, but you've got your plans for the farm." She slid her hand out from beneath his. Thinking clearly when his rough palm burnished her fingers was impossible.

Standing, she went to where she could look at the first stars poking through the crisp winter night. When Jeremiah moved behind her, he didn't touch her, but she

was as much aware of his breathing as hers. In the silence she could hear his heartbeat matching her own. If she leaned back, even an inch, her head would be against him.

"Mercy, will you look at me?" His voice was no more than a whisper, but she could hear sorrow in it. "Tell me what you're thinking."

Facing him, she stared at the top button on his shirt. Meeting his gaze when she was so unsettled might be foolish.

"Why is it taking so long?" Not giving him a chance to answer, she added, "You've got to be asking that yourself."

"Some people need time to make an important decision. My family teases me because sometimes I'm the last one to make up my mind, but I've got to look at the decision from every angle so I know I've made the right one."

In spite of herself, she raised her eyes toward his. "Did it take you a long time to decide to buy this farm?"

"It took me a long time to realize I was happier farming than doing anything else. I immediately started looking for a *gut* place to go because I knew there weren't any farms I could afford near Paradise Springs. I wasn't sure where I'd go until Caleb talked to me about Harmony Creek. Coming here seemed the perfect answer."

"Until you got here and found us."

He arched his brows, and she saw a hint of his smile before it swiftly vanished. "I don't blame you."

"You should, you know."

"No, I shouldn't. For a reason neither of us can guess, God brought us together like this. He knows the future.

We can't do anything but believe His reasons are for our *gut*, and if we continue forward toward what He has planned for us, we'll know His blessings."

"So we wait."

He shrugged, and his smile reappeared. "I don't see any alternative."

"I know." She clasped her hands behind her so she didn't reach out to throw her arms around him and beg him to hold her. "And every day we don't hear is another day Paul can stay here." She allowed herself a faint grin. "Not that any day is easy with him."

"Eventually, he'll realize what a blessing you and Sunni are for him." He went toward the door.

Had her face betrayed her longing to be in his arms? "And you. He wants your respect more than anything else now."

"Learning to respect you and Sunni would go a long way toward earning that."

"But he'd have to share you with us, and he's made it clear he doesn't want to."

He sighed and pulled his coat off the peg by the door. "He's a confused *kind*."

"I agree."

"So what can I do to help?" He reached for his scarf.

"Keep doing whatever you've been doing. I can see so many changes in him when he's with you. He listens to you."

"Sometimes."

"Which is a lot more than he listens to me. I know he craves action. That's one of the reasons he likes doing chores with you. Painting doesn't interest him."

He put his hand on the doorknob, but didn't turn it.

"I'll be collecting sap and starting the evaporator to make syrup in the morning. Paul can help me."

"That should definitely keep him busy."

"Oh, I'll find lots for him to do." His eyes twinkled and then grew serious again. "He truly is blessed to have you care about him so much. Just as I am." He bent and kissed her cheek. "Sleep well, Mercy."

He was gone before she could reply. Raising her fingers to the place where his lips had grazed her face, she stared at the closed door.

He'd kissed her.

True, it'd been as chaste as a kiss he'd give the children, but he'd kissed her.

She wished she knew what it meant.

Chapter Fifteen

"Cool! Hey, Sunni! Come and see this."

Shocked by Paul's eager invitation to Sunni, whom he didn't want hanging around him, and not sure what the boy was up to, Mercy jumped up from where she was mending yet another rip in the knees of Paul's trousers. She ran to where the cellar door was open.

He stood a couple of steps below her on the stairs and looked at her with an excited grin. "Why didn't you tell me you were putting a pool in the cellar? This is the coolest house ever!"

"Pool?" She edged past him. She halted when she heard the unmistakable sound of moving water. In fact, if she hadn't known better, she would have guessed there was a waterfall in the cellar.

"How big is it? I wanna see." The boy reached for the switch to turn on the lights.

She grabbed his wrist, not wanting to risk him getting a shock.

"Go!" she cried. "Get Jeremiah. Tell him we've got a flooded basement." Looking over her shoulder, she repeated her order.

As Paul started to go, there was a pop. Lights went out, leaving the house in a dusky twilight, and Sunni squealed from upstairs.

Mercy went up and into the kitchen. She grabbed a flashlight from the junk drawer. When she sprayed the light, she saw the water was halfway up the stairs. High enough to have flooded the electrical box and shorted it out. Boxes and other items bobbed on the rising water. She was tempted to try to snag them, but didn't want to fall into the filthy water topped by what looked like an oil slick.

It seemed forever before Paul returned with Jeremiah. When she heard Jeremiah calling, she wanted to sag with relief.

Instead, she shouted, "In the cellar!"

He hurried toward her and whistled. "I thought Paul was exaggerating. There really is a swimming pool here."

"It's rising fast."

"The snow is melting quickly, and the ground is frozen, so the water must have found its way through the foundation." He paused. "Sounds like it's pouring in over behind the fuel tank." As he started up the stairs, he said, "Let me get the generator from my workshop. We'll hook it to a pump. Rudy must have one around here."

"I'll look for it after I open the bulkhead."

"*Gut* idea. That'll give the water an exit out of the cellar."

Warning both children to stay away from the cellar steps, Mercy didn't pause to grab a coat. She stuck her feet into boots and rushed out into the evening dusk. Glancing at the workshop where Jeremiah was unplug-

ging the generator as fast as he could, she ran through the slushy snow and deep puddles beginning to ice over again. The cold should stop the flood.

She put her foot against one side of the double doors and pulled the other. It moved with the protest of rusty hinges. She groaned when she saw another door at the base of the stairs. Water was seeping out, reaching the top of the first step even as she watched in shock.

Hurrying to where Jeremiah pushed the generator across the yard while he balanced hoses over his shoulder, she told him about the door. "If we open it, we'll get washed away."

"Look for a pump while I get the generator ready to go. You know what one looks like?"

She nodded and ran toward the garage. Her grandfather had kept a small pump on a shelf when she was a kid. Was it still there?

Finding it, her next question was if it worked. There was no way to find out without hooking it up. She handed it to Jeremiah. He deftly connected the pump to hoses and then to the generator. Yanking on the starter cord, he bent to push open one of the cellar windows. He shoved one hose inside, then started the pump.

Water whooshed out, spraying them. He switched off the pump, grabbed the hose that had showered them with dirty water and tossed it in the direction of the road. When he restarted the pump, water erupted in a geyser again, but fell harmlessly into a snowbank.

Once assured the pump was working, Mercy followed Jeremiah into the house. He told her he had enough gasoline to keep the generator running for the next twenty-four hours.

"By then, the weather will probably have turned cold

again." He sighed. "I hope so, because if it stays this warm, the sap will run too fast and won't be *gut* for syrup."

Throughout the evening, Jeremiah checked on the level of the water in the cellar. It didn't begin to lower until it was time for the children to go to bed, unhappy they'd had cold sandwiches for supper.

"Now you know how it is to live like the Amish do," Jeremiah said with a chuckle as they started up the stairs.

He got peeved looks in return, but, by the time they went upstairs, he'd brought kerosene lanterns from the tenant house and barn. Mercy helped Sunni and Paul brush their teeth, making sure they skimped on water. Until the well pump was running again, they had to conserve what was in the tank. Paul perked up, glad to skip his bath.

Mercy was relieved when Sunni and Paul went to sleep quickly. She'd piled her grandfather's crocheted afghans on top of their beds, hoping to keep them warm until morning. If it was too cold when she went upstairs, she'd carry them into her bed, where they would keep each other from freezing.

When she came into the living room, she sat on the sofa where she'd been working what seemed like days ago. A kerosene lamp gave off more light than she'd expected. She picked up Paul's pants. She'd gotten the patch sewn on one knee and needed to finish one on the other knee.

"I don't know how he can rip out the knees of his trousers when there's a couple of feet of snow on the ground," she said wryly.

Jeremiah closed the woodworking supply catalog

he'd been looking at and set it on the table beside the other end of the sofa. "The boy has a rare talent for such things."

"Another week is almost over." Her needle darted in and out of the denim, jabbing with her frustration as she added, "And nothing has changed."

"I don't want to talk about the farm and your family tonight."

"Neither do I, but the delay in getting an answer has been much on my mind, especially with the flooded cellar."

He gave her a cockeyed grin. "Me, too. That's why I don't want to talk about it. Why don't we talk about something we haven't talked about?"

"What's that?"

"Rudy." He shifted so he could look at her, leaving himself mostly in silhouette. "I never met the man, though everyone tells me about him. Everyone but you."

She frowned. "I talk about my grandfather all the time."

"Bits and pieces. Tell me about the Rudy you knew."

For a moment she was silent. Not because she wasn't sure what to tell him. She wasn't sure what to tell him *first*. So many memories were layered on top of each other, images as clear in her mind as the photo of her parents in *Abuelita*'s apartment.

How could she explain to Jeremiah how important Grandpa Rudy had been to her? Not once had he made her feel like she was different from his other grandchildren. He didn't care she'd had other parents before the Bambergers. She was his granddaughter, and that was all that mattered.

"He loved to laugh," she said. "Apparently, he was

a prankster his whole life. Any tin can could contain a fake snake. Any glass could be a dribble one, and I quickly learned to look before I sat. He really loved whoopie cushions."

"He sounds like fun."

"He was, and what he liked was for someone to play a trick on him. I spent hours before each visit trying to come up with something to surprise him and make him laugh."

"And did you?"

"I don't know if I ever surprised him, but he always laughed. He found much joy in everything. He considered everything he could see and hear and touch a gift from God, and he was thankful every day of his life." Lowering her mending to her lap, she gazed out the window toward the dark backyard. "He grew rows of rhubarb behind the house, though he was allergic to it. Touching it gave him hives, but he made sure the rhubarb grew every year and invited the neighbors to pick it."

"Why?"

"Because his wife loved rhubarb, and he'd loved her. She died quite young, so I never met her." She blinked back sudden tears. "I don't think I'd ever been so proud than when he told me, though I looked like my mother, I reminded him of his late wife." She felt her cheeks heat. "I'm sorry. I know you Amish think pride is wrong."

"I think there are exceptions to everything, even *hochmut*. It sounds as if that compliment was one." He reached across the cushion between them and took her hand. "*Danki* for sharing your love for Rudy with me, Mercy. I've known from the beginning how important the farm is to you, but I thought it was only because of

your hope of helping *kinder*. I see you want the farm to be a tribute to your *grossdawdi*, who helped you find the family you thought you'd lost."

"I never thought of it that way."

When he didn't reply immediately, she realized he was giving her the chance to consider his words. And she did. Was building the farm into something special important because it symbolized what she'd found after losing everything and everyone important to her?

He shifted again, closer to her. She could see his intense expression. She dampened her lips, and his eyes followed the motion. Quickly, she looked down.

His fingers beneath her chin brought her face up. She shivered as a powerful warmth sliced through her, radiating from where his fingertips touched her. When he tilted her mouth toward his, she wondered why she was fighting what she yearned for. His face, which was rough with a day's growth of whiskers, brushed against her when he lightly kissed her right cheek.

Her breath caught. Was another chaste kiss all he wanted? It was so sweet, but when he moved to kiss her other cheek, she caught his face between her palms. His eyes burned like the heart of a fire, sparks glinting through their shadowed depths.

"Kiss me," she whispered softly.

"I am kissing you."

"Kiss my lips."

"I want that more than you can know, *liebling*."

The gentleness of his lips mesmerized her, and she deepened the kiss. When he started to lift his mouth away, she steered it back to hers.

With a chuckle, he pulled her closer as he captured her lips again. His kiss was a delicious confirmation

of the feelings she'd prayed he shared with her. She shouldn't be falling in love with him, not when he wanted to take her farm from her, but she wouldn't lie to herself or to him. Being in his arms was what she wanted right now and for the rest of...

She drew back. When he arched a brow at her, she realized he knew the course of her thoughts. Were they similar to his own?

Then she realized she didn't care. Sliding her hands up to his shoulders, she leaned forward once more. This time when he kissed her, thoughts of pulling away vanished. For one special moment, the past and the future didn't exist. Only now. The worries would return, but for now she wanted to relish his kisses.

"Danki," Jeremiah said when Mercy slid another slice of French toast onto his plate. She'd started the gas stove with a match, enabling her to make them a warm breakfast.

"You're welcome."

That was the longest sentence she'd spoken to him since Paul had insisted Jeremiah join the rest of them for breakfast. Mercy was quiet, not teasing either Sunni or Paul. Was she thinking, as he was, of the kisses they'd shared last night? She hadn't met his eyes since he came in.

He understood too well. Sleep had been elusive last night. Lying awake, he'd stared at the water-stained ceiling in the tenant house. The shadows of bare branches had rocked in the moonlight as wind groaned beneath the eaves. He'd fallen asleep a couple of times, but something jerked him awake. Finally, he realized he wanted to avoid dreaming about having Mercy in his arms.

It couldn't happen again. Well, it easily could, but he needed to make sure it didn't. Their kiss hadn't changed anything. They remained rivals for the farm, and, more important, she wasn't Amish.

If she was willing to try...

He didn't allow the thought to form. He'd seen others try, drawn by what they saw as a bucolic life. Few of them lasted more than a couple of months. Though he had no doubts Mercy could do whatever she put her mind to, her yearning to build Come Along Farm and help city kids wouldn't fit into an Amish life.

Would they?

He honestly didn't know how strict the *Ordnung* would be for the settlement because they hadn't begun discussing it yet. So far, each family was living by the rules established in their home district, and that served them well.

"Can I have more?" Paul held his syrupy plate up for another piece, too.

"You've got a hollow leg," Jeremiah said with a chuckle.

The joke fell flat when nobody else laughed.

Though he knew the French toast must be delicious, it tasted like sawdust in his mouth. He ate and then waited while the *kinder* went into the other room to do their schoolwork.

"Finished?" Mercy asked as she reached for his plate. She was stacking the dishes by the sink, planning to wash them once the electricity was on and the well pump was working again.

"Ja." He needed to build a solar setup to power the well pump so he didn't have to be dependent on the grid. He could have his younger brother come up and put a

couple panels on the roof. But first he needed to check if the rafters could support the weight.

Telling Mercy why he was going up in the attic, he took the flashlight from the drawer and left the kitchen. Her urging to be careful with the weak floors sounded automatic. She said the same words each time one of the *kinder* went upstairs alone.

Floorboards creaked as Jeremiah crossed the second floor to get to the attic door. When he opened it, he heard water dripping. He wasn't surprised there were holes in the roof. Everything about the house needed repairs.

He switched on the flashlight and aimed it at the rafters. He didn't need to test the rafters with a nail to see if there was dry rot. Several of them were bowing and one was broken. It'd dropped across the attic, crushing boxes stored there.

A scan of the boxes showed him that the contents had probably been ruined before the rafter collapsed. He calculated what the cost of replacing the broken rafter would be. Once it was in place, the other rafters should straighten. The roof could then support two solar panels.

As he started toward the stairs, the flashlight's beam flickered on a box set off by itself. It was on its side, and he guessed it had been pushed aside when the rafter broke. He froze as the light showcased the words: *Personal items of Mercedes Ramirez.*

He picked up the box, shifting it carefully so he didn't break anything in it. Or anything else, he realized when he heard the tinkle of broken glass.

Closing the attic door behind him, he took care as he crossed the creaking second floor. He rushed into the kitchen.

Mercy looked over her shoulder, and her eyes widened. "What do you have there?"

"Something you've been looking for."

She put the measuring cup she held on the counter. When he set the box on the table, he turned it so she could see the words.

She gasped and pressed her fingers to her lips. "Mercedes Ramirez? This box has to be from before I was adopted."

"My guess is it's from when you first were put into the state's care."

"How do you figure that?"

He answered her question with a question. "Remember what you said last night?"

Her flush deepened, and he knew she was blushing at the thought of what had been said with words *and* kisses.

Tapping her cheek, he said, "This is charming." He didn't give her a chance to reply as he went on, "I remember how you said Rudy told you that while you resembled your *grossmammi* in temperament, you looked like your *mamm*."

"He mentioned that several times through the years."

"Don't you see what it means, Mercy? Rudy saw your *mamm*, and the only way he could have done that was by seeing the photo of your parents. The one you remember from when you were a kid." He patted the box. "It could be in here. Can I open it?"

She nodded, her teeth clamped on her lower lip.

Unfolding the flaps, he lifted out the topmost item. A stuffed rabbit made like a crazy quilt in the brightest colors he could imagine.

Mercy took it carefully. "I remember this. *Abuelita*

made it for me for my fifth birthday." She touched the ears, which once had been a brilliant white and now were a sad and stained brown. "What's it doing here?"

"I don't know." He picked up a *kind*'s heavily embroidered dress. "Do you recognize this?"

"Yes," she whispered. "*Abuelita* made matching ones for me and her for a block party when I was six or seven. She said it would give her practice for when she made my *Quinceañera* gown when I turned fifteen."

"What kind of gown?"

Running her fingers along the flowers and birds stitched into the small dress, she said, "It's a Hispanic custom for a girl's fifteenth birthday. There's a big party, and she dresses like a princess in the fanciest dress you can imagine. Of course, I never had a *Quinceañera* because, by the time I was fifteen, I was living a Mennonite life."

He dug a couple of damp picture books out of the box, but they fell apart in his hands. With care, he reached for the final item in the box. It was surrounded by shards of glass. He lifted it out and discovered it was a picture encased in a cheap metal frame. The glass that once had been inserted in it was broken.

Handing it to Mercy, he said nothing.

She stared at the picture that was black with mold. Half of it had been gnawed away. Whoever or whatever was depicted in it had become an indistinct blur.

"Maybe it's not the right picture," Jeremiah said softly. "Maybe we can find the picture of your parents somewhere else upstairs."

"It's the right one." She cradled the ruined picture as if it were a *boppli*. "Look! You can make out the word

'Lincoln' on the bottom. Lincoln Photography is where the picture was taken."

"I'm sorry, Mercy. I wish we could have found it before damp and mice got to it."

Lowering the frame to her lap, she touched her chest right over her heart. "I keep my birth parents right here. Nothing's ever changed about that."

When tears flooded along her cheeks, he started to apologize.

"Thank you, Jeremiah," she said. "You've cleared up a mystery that's bothered me for years."

"I wonder why it was here."

"I don't know, but knowing the picture wasn't thrown away is a weight off my heart." She reached up and ran her fingers along his jaw.

When she guided his mouth to hers, he could think of a dozen different reasons he shouldn't kiss her. He could think of only one reason why he should. He loved her. Later he would think of the complications. Now he savored the sweet caress of her lips.

Chapter Sixteen

Jeremiah drew in a deep breath of the moist air in the sap house the next morning. The small outbuilding was barely large enough for the evaporator, the stack of wood that heated it and shelves where he'd put empty bottles and his tools. It took several hours every other day to cook the sap into syrup because he was making small batches. The sap needed to go past water's boiling point by ten degrees before it started to cook into golden maple syrup. Once it did, he filled bottles and set them on a shelf to cool.

Bending, he checked the fire under the evaporator. He shoved a couple more pieces of split wood in so the heat stayed steady. If he stayed on the farm, he would like to tap more trees. He could buy a gas-powered evaporator and make enough syrup to sell at the farmer's market in Salem. Several of the other families were already planning to set up tables once spring came, selling everything from freshly made bread to goat milk soap to eggs and dried herbs.

If Mercy's family decided to sell him the farm. If

they didn't increase the price beyond what he could afford. If he was able to make a success of the property.

Why was it easier to think about the farm than Mercy's eager response to his kisses? Each time the memories tried to assert themselves, he silenced them. They were a reminder of how witless he was. He'd known right from the beginning Mercy was Mennonite. She'd invited him to her church and hadn't hid how much she hoped he'd consider being baptized as a Mennonite. The picture of her family, though it'd been ruined, was another indication she was definitely *Englisch*.

God, how have I failed to see I'm making the same mistake again? Show me a way to fix this without ruining everything.

He snorted. What made him think God was going to bail him out of this predicament? Jeremiah had gone in with his eyes open, but should have kept his heart closed. He had to find the words to tell Mercy though she was *wunderbaar* in his arms, he was committed to helping the Amish community.

For what purpose? That vexing voice was back, demanding he be honest with himself. *What purpose do you have for building a home in Harmony Creek if you're not going to share it with the woman you love?*

"Jeremiah?"

He looked up, startled to discover Sunni standing in the sap house's doorway. He'd been so lost in his thoughts he hadn't heard the door open.

The little girl was bundled up in her winter coat and snow pants and boots. Her steps were stiff as she came in. Her motions reminded him instantly of Mercy's when she was nervous.

He wanted to put the *kind* at ease, but he couldn't

when he didn't know why Sunni was there. Apparently alone, because she closed the door behind her.

"Hi, Sunni!" he said with a smile.

The little girl was adorable in her winter clothes that left only her nose and dark eyes visible between her scarf and the hood of her coat. She looked as round as she was tall. When she pulled her scarf off, she wore the most somber expression he'd ever seen on her young face.

"Are you okay?" he asked.

She nodded as she edged around the evaporator, gazing up at the steam rising into the vent and outside.

"Do you want something?" A stupid question. She wouldn't have taken the long walk from the house unless she had a reason.

He pulled a bench from beneath the shelves and motioned for her to take a seat.

She did as she loosened her coat and pulled off her mittens, shoving them into her pockets.

"Is the syrup done?" she asked.

"Another fifteen minutes should do it." He squatted in front of her. "Sunni, you look like a gal with something on your mind. Why don't you spit it out?"

Opening her mouth, she hastily closed it.

"Sometimes," he said, "the most difficult words are the first ones. Push them out, and the others will follow."

Sunni swallowed hard. "Do you like my mommy?"

"*Ja*. Your *mamm* is a nice person. I think everyone around here likes her."

The little girl shifted to perch on the very edge of the bench. "I don't mean that kind of like. I mean do you *like* her?"

"Ah…" He understood what the child was asking, but he also knew whatever he said might be repeated to Mercy once Sunni returned to the farmhouse. "I think that topic should be discussed by your *mamm* and me. Don't you think so?"

Sunni slowly nodded.

"Gut." He came to his feet. "Do you want to stay until the syrup is ready?"

"Will you promise me one thing?" she asked instead of answering his question.

"Amish don't make promises. We trust our word is as *gut* as a promise."

She stared at him, baffled. Her lips moved as she repeated his words as she tried to make sense of them. The moment when she got the meaning was obvious because the lines threading her forehead vanished.

"All right. I believe you," she said.

"Danki." He was amused by her stern composure. It wouldn't have been out of place for a bishop. "What did you want to ask me?"

"Please don't hurt my mommy."

He flinched at the words the *kind* spoke with a yearning from the little girl's heart. "That's the last thing I'd ever want to do, Sunni. Your *mamm* is a kind and generous woman, and I admire how hard she works."

"I know Mommy is kind, but I don't want you to hurt her."

"How do you think I'd hurt her? By buying the farm?"

Sunni shook her head. "Not that. I don't want you to hurt her like Graham did. He said he loved her and asked her to marry him. I'd hoped she'd say no, but she said yes, and then he made her cry and cry when he al-

ways did what his mother wanted. Not just once, but a lot of times because his mother didn't like Mommy. That old lady was mean to Mommy and to me."

He realized the little girl was speaking of Mercy's former boyfriend. No, Graham actually had been her fiancé. Had he missed that fact, or had she failed to mention it? Not that it mattered. From Sunni's sorrowful words, it was clear whatever had been between Mercy and Graham was over. All that remained was a little girl determined to protect her *mamm*.

He folded Sunni's small hands between his much larger ones and held her gaze. "I don't ever intend to hurt your *mamm*. I don't want to see her cry, either."

She regarded him dubiously. "Graham said that, too. More than once I heard him say that, but then Mommy cried over and over again for months. She tried to make it work because she thinks I need a daddy."

"What do you think?"

Again, the little girl took time to ponder before she answered. He wondered if she'd always been such a deep-thinking *kind*, or if her experiences in leaving Korea and coming to a new family only to have them discard her had made her question every aspect of everything around her. In so many ways, she seemed too old for such a young *kind*.

"I thought our family was perfect. Me and Mommy and Grandma and Grandpa and the rest of the family."

"Especially Grandpa Rudy?"

"Uh-huh." Sunni's eyes grew luminous with tears, and he realized he'd never given thought to how the old man's death had affected this little girl. "When Mommy told me she was going to marry Graham and he'd be my new daddy, I tried to be happy, but I didn't like him."

"For the same reason you didn't like me at first?"

"No, I didn't like him. I didn't know then how someone could be so mean and make my mommy cry. I know that now."

Jeremiah sought words to soothe the *kind*'s pain, but anything he could come up with seemed trite. He wondered if Mercy knew how badly her broken engagement had both relieved and hurt her daughter.

Sunni didn't seem to notice he hadn't answered. "But then Paul came along, and he's part of our family." Her mouth twisted. "Lots of the time, I don't like him, especially when he says bad things about me or Mommy, but I could get used to him being my brother." She sighed. "So many people come and go. I think that's what makes Mommy sad. It makes me sad, too, when people can't stay." Again, she sounded far older than her few years, but her voice cracked when she added, "Especially people like you, Jeremiah."

She jumped to her feet and left the sap house, the door slamming in her wake.

He wanted to give chase, but he couldn't leave the evaporator. Or maybe that was an excuse, because what could he have said to the little girl?

He stared at the evaporator as an unexpected thought burst into his head. Should he leave the Amish before being baptized? Could he? Until he'd met Mercy, he'd never considered he'd ever make such a choice.

He laughed at the irony. When Emmarita had jumped the fence, he'd assumed it'd been a rash decision made to please her *Englischer*. Maybe it had been, but as he wrestled with the choice himself, he suspected she hadn't left her family and friends behind easily.

Or him.

It's long past time to forgive her. The whisper of his conscience seemed loud in the quiet. He forgave her as he comprehended what Emmarita had faced as she made her decision to leave. He knew, as he hadn't before, the choice hadn't been easy for her.

But Emmarita had made her choice. He now must, too.

Mercy picked her way through the icy patches on her way to the mailbox. She'd be so glad when spring arrived, and the last of the snow was gone. An electrician had fixed the circuit breaker box and gotten the furnace started so they had light and heat in the house. Even so, the generator sat nearby, ready to pump out water if it seeped into the cellar again. The next time she spoke with her father, she would ask him if he knew of a way to seal the rock foundation to keep water out.

She opened the metal mailbox that still had Rudy's name on the side. Pulling out the stack of mail inside, she smiled when she saw a folded copy of the latest edition of *The Budget*. She looked at the index on the left side, and her smile broadened when she saw a listing for the Mennonite church they used to attend. Sunni enjoyed hearing news from there because sometimes her friends' names were mentioned by the correspondent. When Paul was at his worst and made fun of the names or what her friends were doing, Sunni ignored him.

That was the only time.

With a sigh, Mercy closed the box. She'd hoped by now the two children would have gotten over their obvious distaste for each other. Should she say something to Whitney? Disrupting Paul with another placement wouldn't help him, but Mercy didn't like her daugh-

ter being the target of his cruel teasing. Sunni was too young to understand why Paul was acting out, and Mercy was running out of ideas for how to bridge the gap between the two of them.

Riffling through the envelopes, she halted and stared at the return address on the bottommost one. Tucking the newspaper under her arm and the rest of the mail in her coat pocket, she ran up the slushy driveway. Mud splashed on the hem of her coat and her dress as she sped across the yard, hitting many of the puddles hidden beneath the grass that had been matted by the winter's heavy snow.

Pausing at the door of Jeremiah's shop, she peered inside. It was empty. Where was he? His buggy was in the yard, and it was too early to start the milking.

Mercy heard a thud, then a crack. He must be splitting wood on the far side of the house for use in making the last of the maple syrup. He mentioned at breakfast the wood box was empty. As she rounded the porch, she saw him with his ax raised before he brought it down in a quick, smooth arc. The blade cut into the chunk of wood on top of a stump. Two pieces of wood tumbled to the ground.

As he bent to pick them up, he must have seen her, because he halted and called a greeting.

She didn't slow until she reached where he stood. Her face must have revealed her thoughts, because he asked what was wrong. She tried to answer, but had to take a moment to regain her breath. He waited with more patience than she would have if their situations were reversed.

Holding out the letter, she said, "It's from my family's

lawyer." Her voice cracked in spite of her efforts to hide her trepidation.

"What does it say?"

"I don't know. It's addressed to you."

When he set aside the ax, leaning it against the wood-pile, he took the envelope. He pulled off one work glove, then the other before he took a knife out of his pocket and slit the top of the envelope open.

She held her breath as he drew out a single sheet of paper. She couldn't guess if such a short missive was good news for her or bad.

He read it fast, then read it again.

"What does it say?" she asked as he had.

He swallowed hard. "Your family has come to a consensus about the future of the farm."

"They've decided to sell it to you, haven't they?" She didn't know why she'd bothered to make it a question. His hesitation had told her the truth.

"I think maybe, but I'm not sure with the fancy lawyer language. Why don't you read it and tell me what you think?"

She took the letter and had to puzzle through the meaning of a couple of the long, elaborate sentences. The beginning of one seemed to contradict its ending, but she understood enough to know why the letter had been addressed to him. Her father and his siblings intended to honor the purchase contract Jeremiah had signed.

"Congratulations, Jeremiah," she said as she returned the letter. She wished she could show more enthusiasm, but how could she when she was numb? "It's okay. You can celebrate if you want."

"How can I celebrate when I know what this decision means to you and the summer camp you wanted

to have for city *kinder*?" He folded the letter and put it in the envelope.

"You're going to make your dream of having your own farm come true, Jeremiah. I'm happy for you." She blinked on hot tears. "Despite what I may look like, I'm happy for you."

"You look lovely."

"I wasn't fishing for a compliment."

"I know, but I wanted to give you one I should have said long ago." When she didn't answer, he asked, "What will you do?"

"I want to build a summer camp for city kids." Her gaze swept the place that soon wouldn't be her home. "It'll have to be somewhere else. I owe a great debt to the people who run the Fresh Air program. It's my mission. I know you may not understand because Amish don't do mission work."

"Some do."

"Not many."

He sighed. "You're right. Not many do."

"You probably want to tell Caleb you'll be staying here." She took a step back. "I need to check on the kids." Her breath caught sharply. "Paul!"

"Won't Whitney let him stay with you?"

"I don't know." Her voice broke as she added, "I don't know about anything." She raised her chin. "Congratulations, Jeremiah. I know Grandpa Rudy would be thrilled to know the plans he made with you are going to work out."

Turning on her heel, she raced around the side of the house. She heard Jeremiah call after her, but she didn't slow. She wasn't sure how much longer she could pretend she was okay with her best chance to make her dream come true being dashed.

Chapter Seventeen

Putting the last dish in the cupboard, Mercy draped the damp dish towel over the rod hanging off a cabinet. She glanced at the clock. She'd finished exactly two minutes before Whitney was supposed to arrive. Yesterday, after the letter came from the family's lawyer, Mercy had called the social worker and explained what had happened.

"Don't worry, Mercy," she'd said. "Things can be worked out in situations like this."

Mercy had prayed Whitney was right. She'd planned on talking to the social worker on her next visit about when Paul would be free to be adopted. She wanted to get her name at the top of the list of potential adoptive parents.

The crunch of tires on frozen mud in the driveway announced the social worker was punctual as always. Opening the side door, Mercy motioned for Whitney to hurry in. The day was as cold as if the thaw had never happened.

A motion in the yard caught her eyes. Jeremiah strode toward the house, and she was relieved he was

going to be with her when she spoke to Whitney about Paul's future.

"Brrr," said the blonde as she unzipped her coat. "I don't think this winter is ever going to end."

"It seems that way."

"Hi, Jeremiah. Good to see you again." She pulled off her coat and looked around. "Where are the children?"

"Upstairs." Mercy took a step toward the staircase. "I can get them."

"No!" The social worker's voice was startlingly sharp. "I need to speak to you without the children first."

Mercy motioned for them to come into the kitchen. What was bothering Whitney? The blonde was usually calm, even when Paul snarled at her.

Jeremiah's brows lowered, a sure sign he was puzzled by Whitney's odd behavior, too. He sat at the head of the table, but didn't say anything.

"Want coffee, Whitney?" she asked, reaching for the pot.

"No, thank you." Putting her briefcase on the chair, Whitney stood behind it. "I think what I have to say is best said quickly."

"What's wrong?" She couldn't keep from glancing at Jeremiah, who was watching the social worker.

"The Kentons have been in contact with us for the past two weeks. Their social worker has spent time with them. She believes they're sincere in wanting their son returned to them."

Mercy stared at Whitney, sure she'd heard her wrong. Somehow, she pushed out a question. "They want him back?"

"Yes."

"Can they do that?" Mercy answered her own question before the social worker could. "I mean, I know they can ask, but why are you agreeing?"

"Parker—"

Jeremiah said with quiet dignity, "He calls himself Paul now."

"I know, but the Kentons still want to call him Parker." Whitney sighed. "I'll let them know again that he prefers the other name. Mercy, Jeremiah, I know you're attached to the boy, but he was with the Kentons for more than six months, and, though they were overwhelmed and needed a break, they've put together a support network they—and we—think will make the placement a success."

"Does he have input into the decision?" Jeremiah asked.

"He's a child." She cut her eyes to Mercy. "You know children aren't in any position to judge what's best for them in the long run."

Mercy lowered herself to a chair and clasped her hands in her lap. "I know the hurt jerking a child around can create. I had two placements before I came to the Bambergers, and I was a very angry child who didn't trust anyone." She stared at the table crisscrossed with nicks and gouges, the sign of long use. "If it hadn't been for Grandpa Rudy, I don't know if I ever would have trusted again."

When Jeremiah's hand covered hers, she knew he was offering what comfort he could.

"I understand," Whitney said as she looked from Mercy to Jeremiah.

"So do I," Mercy replied with a sigh.

Jeremiah erupted from his chair. "And that's it? You aren't going to give us time to say goodbye?"

"Of course you'll have time." Whitney sighed. "I'm not heartless, but I've got to think what's best for him."

"Staying here is best for him." Jeremiah's scowl deepened.

Mercy put her hand on Jeremiah's arm. She'd never seen him so furious and knew he was fighting to keep his temper under control. "Getting angry won't help."

"So you're going to let him go?" He snapped his fingers. "Just like that?"

"Please don't make it harder," she said.

"I don't know how it could be." Hurt blazed in his eyes as they locked with Mercy's. "Why can't he stay here with Mercy so she can adopt him?"

"We have a two-parent family who wants him," Whitney replied. "Our first choice for a child is always to have two parents."

"But they didn't want him, and Mercy does."

Knowing it was Jeremiah's grief speaking, Mercy interjected, "Whitney, will you excuse us?"

"I'll wait in the living room." She glanced at her watch. "I can give you twenty minutes. No more."

Once the social worker left the kitchen, Jeremiah came around the table so he stood beside Mercy. "I love that boy. I don't want to lose him."

"I know. I love him, too, but he has a chance for a home with two parents who love him."

"Two parents who tossed him aside like an unwanted puppy."

Wondering how she could reach through his hurt to help him understand, she knew the only way was to be

honest. "Jeremiah, I don't like this any more than you do, but—"

"What if they decide they don't want him again?" He flung out his hands. "Will they throw him away again?"

"We have to pray they won't."

His shoulders dropped, and she knew she'd finally gotten him to understand. Paul's life, like theirs, was in God's hand. They had to trust God would watch over the boy.

Going to the base of the stairs, she shouted for the children. She frowned when she got no response. Paul… She'd just gotten used to calling him that, and now she had to remember to address him as Parker. He might refuse to answer her, but Sunni always came when Mercy called.

"Are you up here?" she tried again.

She heard Whitney coming from the living room and Jeremiah from the kitchen, but she ran up the stairs. Why weren't the children answering?

Jeremiah exchanged a glance with Whitney as Mercy's voice drifted to them. Before he could speak, Mercy rushed down the stairs. Her face was a sick shade.

"What's wrong?" he asked.

"Sunni and Parker have disappeared." She looked at the shocked social worker. "They aren't here."

"Let me find them," he said. "They couldn't have gone far."

"If they heard us…" Whitney choked out.

Shoving his black hat on his head, he ran out of the house. Ten minutes later he'd searched the outbuildings and the tenant house. Fruitlessly.

Mercy was waiting on the porch when he returned to the house. "Whitney wants to call the police."

"Not yet," he said. "I'll get our neighbors to help find them."

The social worker opened the door. "No, Jeremiah. The boy is my responsibility. We have to call the police before he runs away too far."

"We don't know if they've run away. They may have slipped out before you got here. I'm going to check with the neighbors. Someone must have seen them."

Whitney started to protest, but Mercy silenced her by touching her arm.

"Let Jeremiah try. Give him an hour."

"Two," he insisted. "That's enough time to check every place along the creek."

"Give him two hours," Mercy pleaded. "If the kids see policemen, they may hide instead of coming out of wherever they are."

"An hour. No longer, and it's against my better judgment." Whitney wrapped her arms around herself. "I'm risking my job on this."

"We know, and we appreciate it." Mercy kept talking to the blonde as she steered Whitney into the house. Looking back before she closed the door, she mouthed, "Find them. Fast."

Jeremiah loped along the drive and toward Caleb's farm. As the word spread through the hollow, more and more people joined the hunt for the *kinder.* He asked everyone to check their own outbuildings and then the woods on both sides of the creek. He hoped Sunni and Paul hadn't tried to cross it because the ice was no longer thick enough to hold them.

Time sped past too fast. Ever conscious of how little

time they had to search so many acres and buildings, his hope the youngsters could be found before the police were called began to fade. Leaving Caleb to direct the search as the hour elapsed, Jeremiah hurried to where Mercy and the social worker waited.

Whitney was on her cell phone as he came in. When Mercy looked at him, he shook his head, sick at heart for failing her. She'd trusted him, and he'd let her down. He thought of what Sunni had told him about Mercy's ex-fiancé not being there for her. He hadn't wanted to do the same.

She offered him a cup of cocoa, and he took it gratefully. His toes felt like a quintet of frozen blocks of ice in each of his boots. As he raised the cup to his lips, a motion outside caught his eye.

Smoke coming from the sap house? He hadn't left a fire in there after he finished the latest batch of maple syrup.

"Mercy, I think I know where they are."

"Where?" asked both women at the same time.

He pointed out the window toward the sap house. Setting down his untasted cocoa, he grabbed Mercy's coat and thrust it into her hands. She was pulling it on as she followed him out of the house. Behind them, Whitney yelled for them to wait up. They kept going.

The ice sent Mercy skidding into him. He grabbed her hand as they climbed the hill to the small building.

When he threw open the door, heat struck his face. He stepped inside and called, "*Komm* out! I know you're in here."

Sunni peeked around the side of the evaporator. "Jeremiah!" Looking back, she motioned. "It's okay, Paul. Jeremiah will make it okay."

* * *

Mercy saw the pain on Jeremiah's face and knew he wished desperately Sunni was right. She stepped into the sap house, but halted Whitney from pushing past her.

"Let us talk to them," she said, "while you call the police and let them know the kids have been found."

For a second she thought the social worker would insist, but then Whitney nodded. "I'll meet you at the house in ten minutes."

"It may take a bit longer."

"I can't give you more time, Mercy. We're already late meeting the Kentons."

Nodding, Mercy headed for the far end of the sap house. She doubted her feet touched the floor more than twice as she bounded forward to sweep the children into her arms. Sunni clung to her, and Parker did, too. When Jeremiah put his arms around them, they stood in silence for the length of two heartbeats.

Sunni and Parker began explaining how they'd started a fire beneath the evaporator to stay warm.

"While we waited for that woman to go away." Parker shivered.

Mercy put her arm around him and gave him a comforting squeeze, knowing he wasn't cold, but scared. When Jeremiah drew the boy away and bent so his eyes were even with Parker's, she draped her arms over her daughter, clasping her hands in front of Sunni.

"If we hid, that lady couldn't take Paul away," her daughter said.

"Whitney wants the best for him," Jeremiah said.

"We're the best for him." Her daughter looked up at her. "Isn't that right, Mommy?"

"She wants to take me back to people who don't want me," the little boy insisted. "I don't want to go!"

"Would you try spending a weekend with the Kentons?" Mercy asked.

The boy and the man wore identical expressions of dismay, but understanding lit Jeremiah's eyes and he nodded.

"Just a weekend?" Parker asked, suspiciously.

"Yes, for now. Maybe it won't be as bad as you think it'll be."

"Maybe."

"You know you won't be going alone," she said softly as she reached out to take the boy's right hand. "God will be with you whether you are here or somewhere else."

"I know." He looked at Jeremiah, who took his other hand. "I can lay my bad feelings at His feet, and He'll sweep them away with His toes."

Mercy didn't try to restrain her smile. "That's right. You're a smart boy to figure that out."

"I didn't figure it out. Jeremiah told me."

Jeremiah winked at him. "I'm glad you listened. I need to go and let the searchers know the kids have been found. I'll meet you at the house, okay? I'll be back as fast as I can."

Mercy nodded, knowing he hoped Parker would be there when he returned. She smiled. She wasn't sure how, but she'd find a way to persuade Whitney to wait.

Her concerns were needless because when she and the children entered the house, Whitney took her aside and said the Kentons had called and arranged to meet Parker the next afternoon.

"So he can stay here until then?" Mercy asked.

"If you make sure he's here when I come back."

"I'll do my best. I won't let either of them out of my sight until then."

Parker stared, openmouthed, when Whitney said he could stay overnight. He stammered out his thanks as Sunni squealed with excitement.

"Why are you sounding like a pig?" Parker asked. "Is it because you look like one?"

"Mommy!" cried Sunni. "Tell him I'm not a pig."

Knowing the kids' temporary truce was broken, Mercy herded them into the kitchen and sat them at the table once Whitney left. But she couldn't keep from smiling as they bickered. Even that annoying sound was precious while she spent these last hours with Parker.

Somehow, she managed to keep her tears hidden and her voice cheerful while they had supper and she tucked the children into bed. She kissed their freshly washed faces and wished them pleasant dreams. As she went down the stairs, she heard hushed voices and footsteps. She looked back to discover Sunni sneaking into Parker's room. She suspected when she checked later, she'd find them curled together like the litter of kittens in the barn.

Jeremiah was waiting at the bottom of the stairs. Crooking a finger, he walked into the living room. She caught up with him and put her arms around him, leaning her face against his strong back.

"Thank you," she whispered. "Thank you for finding them."

Facing her, he said, "I've been thinking, Mercy. Whitney said a two-parent family is always the best choice for a *kind*. Do you know Sunni believes you

agreed to marry Graham because you wanted her to have a *daed*?"

"No." Shock raced through her. "I didn't know she knew that."

"So you were marrying him to give her a *daed*?"

"It's embarrassing to admit, but it's partly true. I did think I loved Graham."

He took her hands and led her to the sofa. Sitting beside her, he asked, "You *thought* you loved him?"

"Yes, until I realized what love really is. You taught me that."

"As you've taught me." He brushed his lips against hers. "I need to ask you something. Would you consider staying here on the farm as my wife?"

"So we can try to adopt Parker if things don't work out with the Kentons?"

"In part, but I'm asking because I love you and I can't endure the thought of losing you." He smoothed loose strands from her face. "I thought I couldn't hurt worse than when the woman I loved jumped the fence and married an *Englischer*. But the idea of being without you is torture. Marry me, Mercy."

"Does that mean you're willing to become a Mennonite?"

"I'd hoped you would consider being baptized Amish, Mercy. You've seen how we live, and you seem comfortable with it."

She wasn't surprised at his request. And he was right. During the days when they were without electricity, she'd learned to manage the household and keep them fed. "I want to tell you yes, but I told God I'd repay the kindnesses done to me when I was little. Won't that be impossible if I became Amish?"

"I don't know, but I can present your idea for Come Along Farm to our bishop."

"But what about your plans for the farm?"

"We're two smart people. I'm sure we can figure out a way to make both our dreams come true on this farm."

"Assuming the bishop is okay with it?"

"*Ja.* I must get his opinion if it's permissible for an Amish woman to oversee a summer camp."

"Do you think he'll agree?" she asked as her heart danced within her.

"I don't know Wayne well enough to be sure, but I know he'll listen and pray for guidance."

"I have information I'd put together earlier, if you want to give it to him."

"Let's pray there will be an easy way to resolve this. If Wayne says he's okay with your plans for a summer program, we can—"

Her finger against his lips halted him. "One problem at a time, Jeremiah."

"I don't consider getting you to agree to marry me a problem." Folding her hands between his, he asked, "If we can work this out, will you marry me?"

She gave him her answer with a kiss that told him far better than words how much she loved him and wanted to be his wife.

Chapter Eighteen

The candles had been blown out, and the chocolate cake was gone except for a few crumbs on the platter. Outside the cozy kitchen, a chilly October wind whistled at the eaves.

As Mercy looked around the kitchen, she had to smile. The house didn't look different, but in the past months, it had gone through as many changes as she had. Wayne Flaud had been hesitant about Mercy being baptized. He refused to start baptism classes with her until she lived a full Amish life for six months.

She'd agreed and, with Jeremiah's assistance as well as her neighbors', complied. She attended baptism classes with the bishop, a process that took longer than usual because of the distances involved. Instead of meeting weekly with him, they met twice a month when he came to join the *Leit* for services.

And last month, at her final session with the bishop, whom she discovered wasn't as rigid and imposing as his appearance had suggested, Wayne had told her after hours of prayer and long correspondence with other bishops, he couldn't see how it would be a problem

for her to bring in Fresh Air kids for two weeks each summer. It was, he told her, no different from Amish families who took in *Englischers* in a farm-stay bed-and-breakfast for them to discover what an Amish farm was like. She'd wanted to throw her arms around him and hug him, but she'd simply said, "*Danki*, Wayne."

Mercy yawned as Jeremiah entered the kitchen. She wouldn't ever get tired of looking at the sparkle of happiness in his eyes when his gaze shifted to her.

Picking up the last of the dishes, she put them in the sink. "Next time I'm not going to plan a wedding the day after you throw a birthday party for me."

"I'd rather hoped you wouldn't ever be planning another wedding." He gave her one of the scintillating smiles she adored.

"Sunni will marry someday."

He chuckled. "Let me enjoy her being a *kind* before I think of her marrying and making me a *grossdawdi*. Now admit it. You had a *wunderbaar* time at the party."

"I enjoyed every moment of it, but the idea of another huge party tomorrow is overwhelming."

"Be grateful you're here instead of the tenant house." Jeremiah slid his arm around her waist, but kept his other hand behind his back. Was he hiding something? "I think every corner is covered with food to be served tomorrow. *Mamm* and my sisters-in-law cooked as if there were forty families here instead of seven. I don't know if they've left me a place to sleep."

"Most of my relatives will be coming in the morning. They kindly found places to stay in the villages around here, so the house won't be filled to capacity before the ceremony begins." Her eyes widened as she recalled the service would be in High German, a language she was

struggling to learn. She recognized more words every church Sunday. "Jeremiah, did you ask—?"

He tapped her nose. "All my siblings, except Isaiah who, as an ordained minister, will be helping with the service, and their spouses have offered to translate portions of the ceremony not in English as well as the songs."

"My family will know most of them, I'm sure." She smiled. "I've already warned them not to harmonize and to sing really, really, really slow."

"Look what I found!" called an excited voice from the stairs.

Sunni and the boy they again called Paul ran into the kitchen, sliding to a stop inches from Mercy. Jeremiah smiled at them. Sunni would become his daughter after tomorrow. Paul would be their son as soon as the adoption paperwork was completed in the coming weeks.

It was as if Paul had been with them his whole life. When he'd returned to the Kentons for the planned visit, Whitney returned with him only a few hours later.

"The Kentons changed their minds yet again," the social worker had said with an outraged frown. "I can assure you they won't have another chance. As you said, Mercy, jerking a child around is cruel."

Paul shoved an envelope into Mercy's hand.

"What's that?" she asked.

He shrugged. "I found it in the back of the top drawer in my dresser when I was trying to find clean socks." The boy's room continued to look as if a gale swept through it twice a day. "It's got your name on it."

Mercy gasped when she recognized Grandpa Rudy's handwriting on the envelope. Could it be the will she'd searched in vain for? She hoped not, because that could

complicate Jeremiah's ownership of the farm he'd closed on four months ago.

Pulling out the single sheet with quivering fingers, she read aloud:

"My dear Mercy,
"I hope you and your darling daughter have found the perfect home for yourselves with the proceeds from the farm. I know you wanted the farm to make a camp for city children, but my farm needs too much work for you and Sunni to handle alone.

"I have enclosed a copy of the deed for fifteen acres across the road from the farm. It's big enough for you to build a house, a barn and riding area for your summer kids."

"Fifteen acres?" Jeremiah glanced at the surprisingly flat fields edged by Harmony Creek. "Why didn't we see your *grossdawdi*'s name as a neighboring landowner on the deed for this property when I closed on this farm?"

"I don't know." She continued reading.

"Ask Jeremiah Stoltzfus for his help. He seems like a good man, for my farm and for you."

She smiled at Jeremiah, who was shaking his head in amazement.

"I never guessed," he said, "why he asked me so many questions before he agreed to sell me the farm. Your *grossdawdi* was a matchmaker, Mercy."

"He knew a good thing when he saw it." She gave

him a quick kiss before continuing to read Grandpa Rudy's letter.

"The land has been held in trust for you. Make your difference, Mercy, in other lives. But remember you don't carry a debt for how your life has turned out. You may think you are beholden to us for you being a part of the family. You aren't. You weren't an obligation. You were a blessing, a gift to all of us."

It was signed "your loving grandpa."

She pressed the letter to her heart as she whispered, "I love you, too, Grandpa Rudy." Raising her eyes to Jeremiah's, she said, "We have Wayne's approval, and we can have Come Along Farm and your farm. What an amazing birthday gift!"

"Would you like another?" Sunni asked. "It's time, Jeremiah."

"Time for what?" Mercy saw the ill-concealed grins on the children's—no, she needed to use her *Deitsch*— the *kinder*'s faces.

Jeremiah took her hand and sat her at the table. "Before anything else, I want to tell you I've solved another mystery for you. When I spoke with your parents during their visit here last month, they were as surprised as you were to learn the box of possessions from *Abuelita*'s apartment ended up in Rudy's attic. They did know about the box, because your social worker mentioned it. Apparently, your parents were in the middle of a move because your *daed* was changing jobs around the time you came to them. Your *mamm* assumes they gave your social worker this address to make sure the box

was safely delivered." He drew his hand from behind his back and handed her a manila envelope. "Open it."

The envelope wasn't thick, so there couldn't be anything more than a page or two inside. Was it something to do with Paul's adoption? No, Whitney had said they'd filled out all the necessary forms, though there would be more to sign the day Paul's adoption became final.

"Open it!" Sunni urged.

"Open it!" shouted Paul, and the two *kinder* began to repeat the words over and over.

Mercy did and reached inside. She pulled out a single slick piece of paper. It was blank, so she turned it over.

"Oh, my!" she whispered as she stared at the photograph. The woman's face matched the shape of hers, and the man's eyes crinkled as hers did when she smiled. Her parents! It was the photo she'd last seen whole the day *Abuelita* died. "But how…?" She couldn't finish the question because words refused to push past the thick lump in her throat.

Jeremiah sat beside her and leaned her head against his shoulder so they looked at the picture together. "I found an address on the framed photograph. I wrote to the photography studio and asked if they were still in business. I heard from the wife of the man who'd taken that picture. He's passed away, and their son is running the business. They searched the old files and found the negative for the picture of your parents. I had them make you a new print."

"Look!" She motioned for the children to come closer. "These are your grandparents. Gilberto and Amada Ramirez. They—" She sat up straight. "But I'm Amish since I was baptized last month, and the Amish don't like photographs."

He gave her a gentle smile. "We don't like photos taken of us. Your parents weren't Amish, so there's no problem with you having it."

"Danki," she whispered as she wept.

"Are you sad, Mommy?" asked Sunni.

"We want you to be happy," Paul quickly added.

"I'm happy. Happier than I've ever been." She hugged each of them.

Jeremiah said, "I wanted your family to be as complete as possible on our wedding day."

Holding the picture over her heart, she put her other arm around Paul and Sunni. As Jeremiah drew them closer, she said, "You've given me what I wanted my whole life. A family that's all my own."

"And my own, too," he said.

"And my own," repeated the *kinder* together.

They all laughed in the moment before Jeremiah captured her lips that would be his for the rest of their lives.

* * * * *

AN AMISH NOEL

Patricia Davids

This book is dedicated with love and hugs
to my granddaughter Shantel.
Merry Christmas, honey.
PS: Don't forget to do your chores.

If thou, Lord, shouldest mark iniquities,
O Lord, who shall stand?
But there is forgiveness with thee,
that thou mayest be feared.
I wait for the Lord, my soul doth wait,
and in his word do I hope.

—Psalms 130:3–5

Chapter One

"He's not going to try and cross the river. No one is that stupid." Luke Bowman drew back on the reins of the draft horses pulling the large bobsled. The massive gray Percherons stopped, but they tossed their shaggy heads, making the harness bells jingle. They were eager to finish the task and head home. Their snorts sent duel puffs of white mist into the cold November air. Luke watched in disbelief as a snowmobile with two riders continued to barrel toward the frozen river winding through the snow-covered valley below his father's cornfield.

Noah, Luke's youngest brother, leaned on his ax handle as he stood behind the driver's seat. "I remember when you did it on Jim Morgan's snowmobile. More than once. That looks like the same machine."

It did look like the same machine, but Luke doubted it was his *Englisch* friend aboard. More than likely it was Jim's younger brother Brian riding into trouble. "We never crossed this early in the year. The ice isn't thick enough. It won't hold them."

Noah pulled his scarf up to cover his face. "This cold

snap has been bitter even for late November. Maybe the ice is thicker than you think."

Luke didn't mind the cold. His stint in prison made him cherish every moment he could spend out in the open. "It would have to be this cold a lot longer to freeze running water."

He and Noah had come out to gather a load of firewood from the stand of trees along the river. Four inches of fresh snow from the night before made easy pulling for the team. The sled was three-quarters full of logs lashed together, and the men were on their way home.

Luke watched the snowmobilers a second longer, then he turned the horses toward the river. Noah almost lost his balance on the flat sled at the unexpected move and had to grab hold of the seatback to keep from falling off. "What are you doing?"

"We're gonna pull those fools out of the water unless they drown before we reach them."

The red-and-white machine didn't stop. It hit the river's edge at a fast clip and traveled a full fifty feet out onto the ice before the front end broke through, spilling the riders. Luke shouted at the team and slapped the reins, sending the horses into a fast trot across the snow-covered field, knowing he might be too late. If the riders were dragged under the ice by the current, they would drown.

One of the snowmobile riders had been thrown clear of the open water. He lay sprawled facedown on the ice. The second rider was desperately trying to claw his way out of the river but the edge of the ice kept breaking in front of him. The snowmobile teetered precariously, half in and half out of the water as it hung by the rear tread.

"Whoa, fellas." Luke drew the horses to a stop at

the riverbank. He saw the first rider trying to stand. It was a young boy.

"Help! Somebody help us!"

Luke shouted to the boy struggling to get to the other rider. "Lie down! Spread your weight out on the ice!"

Tossing the lines to Noah, Luke jumped off the sled. From the toolbox under the seat, he grabbed his ax along with a coil of rope and started toward the river.

The boy was following Luke's orders. He lay down and wiggled toward the rider in the water. He grasped his buddy, but Luke saw he was too small to pull the bigger boy to safety.

Luke quickly tied a loop around his waist as Noah joined him at the river's edge. "I should go. I'm smaller."

Luke considered it for a second then shook his head. "I'd rather drown than face *Mamm* and tell her I let you get killed. Take a hitch around that tree so you can pull me back if I go through. The current is strong in this curve."

"Don't make *me* tell *Mamm* I let *you* drown."

"I'll do my best. Hang on, boys, I'm coming!" Luke hacked a long branch from a nearby tree and stepped out on the ice. The thick layer of fresh snow made it hard to see where he was putting his feet. He used the branch to feel his way, making sure the ice was solid until he got near the two boys. At that point, he lay down and edged toward them. The cold bit through his pants and gloves as he crab-scuttled along.

"Hurry!" the little one shouted, looking over his shoulder.

Luke recognized him. "Alvin Swartzentruber, are you okay?"

"Help me, Luke." The fourteen-year-old stayed sprawled on the ice, holding on to the other rider.

Every time Luke thought he could move faster, the ice cracked with a sickening sound beneath him. Would it hold? He couldn't help the boys if he went through, too. Finally, he worked his way to within a few feet of them and stopped, not wanting to add his weight to their precarious spot. "I thought you had better sense than this, Alvin."

"I reckon I didn't today."

"I reckon not. Who you got with you?"

"It's Roy. Hurry, Luke, I can't hold him."

"You can. I'm almost there. Roy, can you hear me?" Roy was Alvin's older brother. Luke knew them well. He knew their sister, Emma, even better, or he had once. They didn't speak to each other these days.

"Help." Roy's voice was barely audible through his chattering teeth. His lips were tinged with blue and his eyes were wild with fear.

Luke was close enough to reach them with the branch. He slid the end past Alvin. "Hang on to this, Roy, and let go of your brother."

He was afraid the bigger boy would pull the smaller one in if he went under.

Roy grasped the limb with first one hand and then the other. "I—I got it."

Luke needed room to pull Roy free. "Alvin, roll away from the hole and go to my brother. Stay on your hands and knees until you get close to the shore. Follow my trail. The ice was strong enough to hold me—it should hold you."

With the younger boy headed to safety, Luke inched closer to Roy. He heard the ice beneath him groan.

I'm not ready to meet you, Lord, but if this is the rea-son You got me out of prison and put me here today, at least help me save this boy first. Don't give Emma one more reason to hate me.

He forced his thoughts away from Emma and the heartache he had caused her. "Roy, I'm gonna slip a loop of rope over you. You're gonna have to get it under your arms. Can you do that?"

"I think so."

"Goot." Luke worked the rope off over his head and shoulders and prepared to lay the loop over Roy.

"Is… Alvin…safe?"

Luke glanced back. The boy was climbing the bank to where Noah stood with the rope snubbed around a tree. "He's fine. You will be, too, in a minute."

"I can't…hold on. Can't…feel…my hands." Roy started to sink.

"Don't give up."

The boy's head went under. Luke made a grab for him, plunging his hands into the frigid water.

Emma looked up in relief when she heard a horse and buggy come into the yard. Rising from her quilting frame, she crossed to the window. Her father should've been back an hour ago. She was anxious to hear what his doctor had told him about the fatigue he couldn't shake.

Her father, Zachariah Swartzentruber, had always been a big man. He stood six feet tall, but she hadn't noticed until this moment how his clothes seemed to hang on his frame now or how bent he was becoming. He moved slowly, as if his actions were painful or dif-ficult as he got out of the buggy. She hoped the English

doctor had discovered what was wrong and prescribed some medicine to make her father better.

She held open the door as he came up the walk. "How was your trip, *Daed*?"

"It was a long way. The traffic gets worse every time I must go into town. The foolish *Englisch* rush past without a care in their big cars."

Their little Amish community of Bowmans Crossing was more than five miles off the state highway. Even so, the traffic in the area was increasing, as were the accidents involving buggies and cars.

She waited until her father took a seat at the kitchen table. "What did the doctor have to say?"

"Is there any *kaffi*?"

"*Ja*, I made a pot about an hour ago." Going to the stove, she pulled a brown mug from the shelf overhead and filled it to the brim with the strong brew from her coffeepot.

"*Danki.*" He accepted the cup from her hand and stirred in a heaping spoonful of sugar. He sat staring into the liquid, stirring slowly.

Fear crept into Emma's heart. It wasn't like her father to be so quiet. Something was wrong. "What did the doctor have to say, *Daed*?"

Her father took a sip of coffee. "This is *goot*. You always could make good *kaffi*. Not like your mother. Her *kaffi* was always weak as dishwater."

Emma swallowed hard. It was unusual for her father to speak about his deceased wife. The Amish rarely talked about loved ones who had passed on. Her worry spiked, but she knew better than to keep pressing him. When he was ready, he would tell her what the doctor had discovered.

She poured herself a cup and carried it to the table. "*Mamm* was a frugal woman. She could stretch a nickel into a dime and give you two cents change."

A tiny smiled lifted the corner of his lip. "That she could. I think sometimes she used the same grounds for three days in a row."

"I like my coffee stout. I would rather save on other things."

He looked at her then. "You need a new dress. I would not have you looking so shabby."

The front of her everyday dress was stained and the cuffs were getting thin, but it had at least another year of use before it went into the rag bag. "I can't wear a good dress to do laundry and scrub floors. This one will do for a little longer. My other workday dress is not so worn, and I have a nice Sunday dress. I don't need anything else."

"If a fella was to come courting, you'd want to look nice. We can afford the material."

They couldn't, but that wasn't the point. She saw her father had something serious on his mind. "No one is coming to court me. What's wrong, *Daed*?"

"Wayne Hochstetler intends to ask you out."

She sat back in surprise. "Wayne? How do you know this?"

Wayne was a widower and the eldest son of their neighbor to the west. He and his family belonged to a different church group, one that was more conservative, but Wayne was known as a stalwart member of the Amish faith and a good farmer. His father was the bishop of their church district.

"I spoke with his father. Wayne is looking for a wife. He has a young daughter who needs a mother."

"I hope he finds one, but what makes you think I would be interested in going out with him?"

"Because it's time you married. It's past time. You will be thirty soon. That is old enough to be settled."

"I'm barely twenty-five, *Daed*."

"That is still plenty old enough. I want you to seriously consider Wayne as a husband. His father and I are good friends. This would make us happy."

"I thought marriage was a question of who would make *me* happy." She once believed Luke Bowman was that man, but she had been mistaken. Sadly mistaken.

"Love can grow from friendship and mutual respect. If there is someone else, *dochder*, please tell me now."

"I have enough to do taking care of you and the boys. There isn't anyone I'm interested in."

"*Goot*, then you will consider Wayne?"

"Not until you give me a better reason than my age and your friendship with his father. What's this about? Why this sudden interest in seeing me married off? I have plenty of time to meet the right man and fall in love."

He sighed heavily. "You may have the time, but I do not. The news from the doctor was not *goot*, but it was what I have been expecting."

Her heart pounded painfully, stealing her breath. "You are frightening me. What did he say?"

"I have inherited the same disease that took my father when you were but a small child. My kidneys are failing. The doctor thinks I have a year, maybe two, before it is my time to stand before God and be judged."

She stared at him in disbelief. "Is the doctor sure? Can't there be some mistake? I know you've been ill, but you'll get better. You can see another doctor."

He reached across the table and took her hand in his. "I knew this was coming when I started having the same type of pain that wore down my father. I can only pray that God has chosen to spare my sons."

"And me? Can this disease come to me and my children?"

"You forget. You are my stepdaughter. I married your mother when you were only a babe. Your father died in a farming accident. This disease I inherited cannot come to you."

It was true. She always forgot that Zachariah wasn't her real father. "You have been a father to me in every sense of the word save that one small thing. I could not love you more if we were bound by blood."

"You are a true child of my heart, Emma, but I won't be able to care for you and the boys for much longer. I need to know someone will look after the lot of you when I'm gone. It falls to you now. The boys are too young."

"I don't have to be married to take care of my brothers. You know I will always do that. The church will help us."

"Wayne has a prosperous farm. Combined with my land, it will be more than enough. You will not be dependent on the charity of others. Do not mistake me—there's nothing wrong with accepting charity when you need it, but it is much better not to need it. I'm not afraid to face death but I am afraid of leaving you and your brothers without a secure future. Can you understand that?"

"*Ja*, I do. I can't believe this is happening." She didn't want to believe it. Not her big strong father. There had to be some mistake.

"I'm sorry to burden you with this news, but in one sense, it is a blessing. Few men are given the chance

to know when their end is coming. I have time to pre-pare. You will have time to prepare as well. You must find someone to care for you when I cannot. Wayne is a *goot* man. A fine farmer. I hope you will consider him."

Emma arose and carried her mug to the kitchen sink. Setting it carefully on the counter, she stared out the window. How could she refuse Zachariah's request? She couldn't. Everything she had, everything she be-lieved in, was due to the kindness and love of the man who had chosen to become her father.

"Where are the boys?" he asked.

She stared out the kitchen window at the snow-cov-ered farm looking pristine and sparkling as the clouds parted and sunshine chased away the gloomy afternoon. God's beautiful white blanket covered the holes in the barn roof and disguised the junk her father piled up along the sides of the sheds. No one could see how the henhouse roof sagged or how badly it needed to be re-placed. "They took a load of firewood to Jim Morgan's place. They should have been back by now."

"You know how they like to look at Jim's toys. Maybe he is giving them a ride on his motorcycle again."

"I hope not." She hated that her brothers were fascinated with *Englisch* vehicles. She disliked that Jim and his brother encouraged them, but her family needed the money Jim was willing to pay for the wood the boys cut and hauled.

Her poor brothers. They would be heartbroken when they learned this news about their father. She wanted to ease the pain for them, but she didn't know how. Tears pricked the back of her eyes. She brushed them away. "I wish they would come home. I know you want to share this news with them, sad though it is."

"I will tell them, but not yet. Not today."

She turned to face him. "Why wait?"

He stirred his coffee without looking at her. "Christmas is coming. You know how excited Alvin is about his school Christmas program. I don't want to ruin that for him. This news can wait until after the New Year. A month or two won't make any difference. Perhaps by then they will have the news of your coming marriage to cheer them up and make them feel secure."

"I see your point." Except that meant she would have to carry the burden of this information alone.

"I hear someone coming. Is it the boys?"

The sound of hoofbeats reached her. She glanced out the window and her traitorous heart gave the same funny little flip it always did when she caught sight of Luke Bowman. He drew his buggy to a stop in front of the house.

Luke. The man she had once hoped to marry. The same man who had made it painfully clear that he didn't care about her at all. The memory of their parting years ago still had the power to bring tears to her eyes.

Jim Morgan had been the one who told her Luke was leaving that night. She had packed a bag and rushed to find him before it was too late. At the bus station, she had gripped his arm, willing him to see how much she cared.

"I love you, Luke. More than my own life. More than my family. I'll go anywhere as long as I can be with you. You need me as much as I need you. I know you love me."

He brushed her hand aside. His face was blank as he stared at the ground. "You don't get it, Emma. I don't need you. I don't want you tagging after me. Stay here. Live a simple life. Be happy with some farmer and have six kids of your own."

"I don't want to stay without you. I love you. Please, let me come with you."

"Why would I? You've become a nuisance. I don't love you, Emma. I never did." He turned away and started to board the bus as her heart broke into tiny pieces. On the steps, he paused. "Forget about me. Find someone else."

He took a seat by the window and left her weeping at the bus station. He never looked back. She knew because she had watched until the bus was gone from sight.

She had meant nothing to him, while he had meant everything to her.

But not anymore.

It was a blessing that he had rejected her offer to go out into the world with him. Nineteen, lovestruck and foolishly naive, she hadn't understood the powerful hold his growing drug use had on him then. She thought her prayers and her love could change him, save him from himself, but she had been wrong. Luke had been caught in a downward spiral that brought shame and heartache to her and to his family. He had disappeared into the city where he went from using drugs to selling them until he was arrested. It had taken time in prison to free him from his addiction.

Emma blew out a deep breath as she watched Luke get out of his buggy. She'd gotten over her feelings for him ages ago. Now, he was simply someone she chose to avoid. In the year and a half that he had been back among the Amish, she'd managed never to be alone with him.

Pushing her painful memories and broken dreams into the deep recesses of her heart, she dumped her coffee down the drain. "Luke Bowman is here."

"Luke? I wonder what he wants."

Chapter Two

"Are you going to come in with me?" Still seated in Luke's buggy, young Alvin gazed fearfully at the house.

"*Ja*, I'll come in." Luke knew exactly how the boy felt. He'd been in the same position more than once in his life—having to face the consequence of his foolhardiness. The boy had learned a hard lesson today. Older brothers did not always know best.

Luke stood in the cold air waiting for the boy to get out. His hands still ached, but at least he had the feeling back in them now. His buggy horse whinnied to Zachariah's horse hitched at the rail in front of the house. The black gelding nickered back. Flecks of foam on the animal proved the horse had covered more than a few miles recently. Why hadn't he been put away? It was bad for a sweaty horse to be left standing in the cold. Zachariah knew that. Maybe he was leaving again soon.

"She's gonna be mad." Alvin scooted a shade closer to the open door but didn't get out.

Luke knew whom the boy meant. "She'll be thankful that you're safe. Trust me."

"For a little bit. Then she's gonna be mad. You don't

know what my *shveshtah* is like when she gets her feathers ruffled."

"Actually, I do know what your sister is like when she's angry."

Luke didn't bother trying to explain ancient history to the worried boy with him, but he still recalled the tongue lashings Emma had given him when she'd discovered he and Jim were experimenting with drugs. His life would have been a lot better if he'd taken her scolding to heart, but he hadn't. He'd let the drugs pull him deeper and deeper into trouble until he ended up in prison. Like most fools, he'd had to learn his lesson the hard way. Even now, he worried that he might fall back into his old ways without the threat of prison hanging over his head.

Alvin finally got out of the buggy. Luke followed him up the porch steps. At the door, Alvin drew a deep breath and turned the doorknob. Luke followed him in. Emma and Zachariah were waiting for them in the clean and cheery kitchen. The room had wide-plank pine floors. A blue checkered cloth covered the long table in the center of the room. A star quilt in bright shades of red and white covered a quilting frame in front of the far window. The mouthwatering smell of roasting meat and vegetables came from the oven. A pan of rolls sat rising on the stovetop. Emma had always been a good cook.

Luke took his black hat off. Alvin pulled his off, too, and stood at Luke's side, staring at the floor. From his own experiences, Luke knew Alvin wouldn't be able to sink through it and disappear no matter how hard he wished he could. He put a hand on the boy's shoul-

der and nodded to Alvin's family. "Afternoon, Emma, Zachariah."

"*Goot* to see you, Luke. What brings you here with my youngest in tow? Has he been up to some mischief?"

"Alvin, where is Roy?" Emma didn't bother to acknowledge Luke. He was used to it, but it still hurt when she pointedly ignored him.

"There was a sort of accident," Alvin muttered.

"What kind of accident?" Zachariah rose unsteadily to his feet. Emma stood beside him wide-eyed. She pressed a hand to her chest.

"Roy is okay," Luke added quickly to reassure them. He pushed Alvin forward. "You had best tell them everything from the beginning."

Alvin nodded, took a deep breath and looked at his sister. "We took the wood to Jim Morgan's house like you told us to do, Emma. We unloaded it and stacked it in his shed. When we were done, Jim let us sit on his snowmobile. The red-and-white one that goes so fast. You've seen it, haven't you?"

"And?" Emma prompted, the concern in her eyes giving way to speculation.

"Jim went inside to get our money, and his brother Brian showed Roy how to start the snowmobile. Brian let us take it for a little ride. Just a short one. We were coming right back. It was loads of fun. Then…"

Her eyes narrowed to slits. She propped her hands on her hips. "Then what?"

"Roy drove it out on the river," Luke continued when it was clear that Alvin was out of courage. "The machine broke through the ice. Alvin was thrown clear, but Roy was dumped in the water. Fortunately, Noah and I saw the whole thing. We fished Roy out and got him

back to my folks' place. *Mamm* and Rebecca thought it best that he stay in bed for a day or so to make sure he recovers and doesn't come down with pneumonia."

Rebecca was married to Luke's oldest brother. She was Emma's cousin and had worked as a lay nurse in the community before she married Samuel. Luke knew Emma would trust her judgment over anyone else on the subject of her brother's health.

Zachariah sat down. "Sounds like my boy took more than a little dunking."

Luke turned his hat in his hands. "He was in the water for a good bit."

"He got swept under the ice, but Luke saved him," Alvin said, looking up with admiration in his eyes.

Uncomfortable with the praise, Luke ruffled the boy's blond hair. "God helped a little. He kept me from falling through the ice, too."

"I know how treacherous the river ice is this time of year. You risked your life to save my son. *Danki.*" Zachariah rose to his feet again and held his hand out.

Luke accepted the man's thanks and shook his hand. "Anyone would have done the same."

Emma rubbed a hand across her forehead. "So Roy has ruined a machine that costs hundreds if not thousands of dollars. How are we going to pay for it? Does your brother possess a single grain of common sense? What came over him to try and ride a snowmobile? And you just went along with him as if it were okay. I honestly don't know what to do with you, Alvin."

"Told you," the boy whispered under his breath. He stared at the floor again.

Luke was hard-pressed not to smile. "I managed to get a rope on the snowmobile and pull it off the river

after Roy was safe. It will take some work, but it will run again."

"You went back out on the ice? You risked your life to retrieve a stupid machine? What is wrong with you, Luke Bowman?" Emma's eyes snapped with fury.

Taken aback by her anger, he gaped at her. She had no idea how attractive she was with her cheeks flushed with color and her hands propped on her shapely hips. Her dress was a deep blue, the same shade as her eyes, and her white *kapp* accented the fiery red of her hair. She was a fine figure of a woman now. Not at all like the skinny girl that he'd dated back when he was nineteen. They had both changed, but he remembered the sweet taste of her lips as if it were yesterday.

"What were you thinking?" Emma demanded.

Luke fastened his gaze on the floor. Best not to think about the times he had kissed those pert lips. "I was thinking it would be a shame to let a fine machine fall into a watery grave. Jim is a good friend of mine."

"You are unbelievable!" Emma stormed out of the room and up the stairs. The sound of a door slamming overhead reverberated through the house.

Zachariah swung his gaze to Luke. "Forgive Emma's temper. She has had a trying day."

"Having Emma mad at me is nothing new. I'll live." Luke quelled his desire to follow her and make amends. It wouldn't do any good, anyway. She could barely stay in the same room with him, let alone listen to his apology.

Zachariah laid a hand on Alvin's shoulder. "I'm glad you are safe. I give God thanks for His mercy. Are you well enough to go take care of my horse?"

"Sure."

"Danki, sohn."

When the boy left the room, Zachariah gestured toward the chairs at the table. "Please, sit down, Luke."

"I didn't plan to stay."

"Humor an old man. Sit for a spell."

"You're not so old, Zachariah." Against his better judgment, Luke took a seat. He knew having him around made Emma uncomfortable. If he heard her coming downstairs, he'd leave.

Zachariah leaned back in his chair. "I feel as if I am a hundred today. How is your family?"

"Everyone is fine. I don't know if Emma told you, but Samuel and Rebecca are expecting a child in May." Luke's oldest brother had married Zachariah's niece a year ago. Rebecca and Emma had remained close friends.

"She mentioned it the other day. That is *goot*. A blessing to be sure. Is your father's business keeping all your brothers busy?"

Luke's father owned a woodworking shop. Luke and his four brothers as well as several other carpenters from the area made furniture for a high-end furniture dealer in Cincinnati. "We've been busy, but *Daed* plans to close for a month after Christmas and take *Mamm* down to Pinecrest, Florida, for a few weeks. They haven't had a vacation in years. *Mamm* says she can't take the cold the way she used to. She wants to visit the Amish settlement by the sea."

"I understand how she feels. I have often wanted to go there myself. Luke, I wanted to talk to you because you're a fellow who knows his way around machinery. I've collected a fair number of items that need some restoration work before they can be resold."

Luke smiled. "You collect junk, Zachariah."

The older man chuckled and gave Luke a wry smile. "*Ja*, I do. But not all of it is junk. Some of it just needs a little elbow grease and a knowing hand to set it to rights. I've heard you keep your father's equipment in tiptop shape."

Luke grimaced inwardly. He did now, but he hadn't always been so diligent. An accident in which his oldest brother had been seriously injured made Luke realize how he had failed his family yet again. Now, he took every step of his work seriously. "I try to keep things in working order."

Zachariah leaned forward. "I want to get my new hardware store open the Monday after Christmas. It's almost finished. After that, I want to get this place in order over the winter. I want it ready for a farm sale in the spring. It's time to get rid of it all."

"That's a tall order." Zachariah owned numerous sheds and buildings crammed to the rafters with all manner of stuff. Clearing it out would be a monumental task.

"I know it's a tall order. That's why I'm looking for help. My boys and I can't do it alone. Roy likes machinery and hardware. He has a gift for it. That's why I want the hardware store finished. He'll run it one day, but he doesn't have the skill to get all of my broken-down machinery working. I'd like to hire you to help me for the next few months."

"I already have a job."

"Surely your father could spare you a few days a week. That's all I'm asking for. A few days a week to look over what I have and see what can be repaired and fix it if you can."

"I think Emma would rather you ask someone else."

"Your breakup was a long time ago. It's water under the bridge to her."

Zachariah might see it that way, but Luke wasn't so sure Emma did. "I don't think it would be a good idea."

Zachariah stared down at his hands for a long moment. When he looked up, Luke saw desperation in his eyes. "I've been remiss in not putting money aside for Emma's dowry. Time just went by too fast. What I get from the sale of my machinery will go to her. She'll marry soon. I don't want her going to a new husband empty-handed. I wouldn't ask you if it wasn't important. What do you say? Can you give me a hand?"

Emma was getting married? Luke shouldn't have been surprised, but he was. Emma was old enough and a fine woman, but it still came as something of a shock. It was hard to imagine her as someone's wife, but she deserved happiness. He wanted her to be happy.

Would helping secure her dowry make up in some small way for his treatment of her in the past? If so, then maybe he could finally put away that guilt.

Tears streamed down Emma's face as she leaned against her bedroom door. She didn't even like Luke anymore. So why did the thought of him risking his life for a chunk of metal turn her blood ice-cold?

He had risked his life to save Roy, too, and she hadn't bothered to thank him.

His bravery she could admire, but she couldn't bear his foolhardiness. He hadn't changed. He would always be the same reckless man who broke her heart.

Rubbing her eyes with both hands, she faced the sad truth. She still went soft inside when Luke smiled

at her. For some unknown reason, he still had a hold on her heart.

Until she remembered how irresponsible he was. Why couldn't she get over this silly schoolgirl infatuation with him?

Sure, he was a fine-looking man with broad shoulders, slender hips and blond hair that curled just enough to make a girl want to comb it into order with her fingers. There were plenty of nice-looking men in her community, but none of them affected her the way Luke did. Her feelings didn't change the fact that he had gone to prison for dealing drugs after he left the Amish.

It was wrong of her to hold any man's past against him, but she couldn't forget the way he had brushed aside her tender heart when she offered to give up everything and leave with him that night so many years ago. She'd learned a bitter lesson. Luke didn't care about anyone but himself.

She thought she loved him then, but it hadn't been true love. It had been a foolish teenage crush. He had been right to reject her. Now, she knew better than to believe he cared.

Scrubbing her cheeks vigorously to erase the past and the traces of her tears, Emma paced the confines of her small bedroom and struggled to regain her composure. It wasn't just Luke. It was everything. Her father's illness, his desire for her to marry quickly, finding out her brother was ten times more foolhardy than she believed possible—it all added up to a burden too big to carry alone. Luke Bowman's arrival today was simply the straw that broke the camel's back.

And she was a weak camel to begin with. She sat

down on the edge of her bed, wishing she could start the day all over again and have it turn out differently.

A gentle tap at her door proved that wasn't going to happen. "Emma?"

"Come in."

Her father peeked around the door. "Are you all right?"

"*Nee*, I'm not. How can I be after your sad news today?"

He entered the room and sat down on the chair against the far wall. Leaning forward, he braced his elbows on his knees. "You will be fine. You are so much like your mother. She was a strong woman, too."

He was wrong. Emma wasn't strong, but he was being brave in the face of his illness. She could do no less. She would pretend to be brave. For him. "What are we going to do with Roy? He's gone too far this time. He could have been killed. Alvin could have been killed. I think you should tell them how ill you are. Maybe that will shock them into behaving."

"They will learn of it soon enough. Let them be boys for a few more weeks. Perhaps Roy's dunking in the river has taught him a lesson."

At sixteen, Roy was in his *rumspringa*, the years between childhood and adulthood when Amish youth were free to experience the outside world before they were baptized. Once an Amish man or woman chose to be baptized, they embraced the strict rules of the Amish faith, rejecting the outside world forever. If they chose to remain a part of the English world before baptism, they would be able to do so without being shunned by her church group, although not all Amish churches were so open-minded.

Emma had left her *rumspringa* behind at twenty and joined the faithful that same year. She knew Luke had yet to make that decision. He had been living Amish for a year and a half, ever since his release from prison, but he hadn't taken his vows. At twenty-five, his family and the congregation would soon begin pressuring him to make a choice. He couldn't stay on the fence forever. It was time to declare his intentions. Was he going to be *Englisch* or Amish?

She forced herself to stop thinking about him. "I pray you are right and Roy has learned his lesson, but he is hardheaded."

"Like I was. There's an old Amish proverb my father was fond of using. 'Experience is a hard teacher. She gives the test first, then the lesson afterward.'"

"At least Alvin may not follow him so willingly in the future." Alvin was a sensitive boy and not prone to troublemaking unless Roy put him up to it.

"Alvin looks up to Roy as only a younger brother can. It will take more than this incident to tarnish Roy's image in Alvin's eyes."

Her father was probably right. "Did you look up to your older brother in such a fashion?"

Zachariah chuckled. "Your hair would turn gray if you knew half the things my brother, William, and I pulled when we were their ages."

She giggled, amazed she could smile after all that she had learned. "You should go and visit him." Her uncle and his wife along with her father's sister had remained in Missouri when her father moved to Ohio twenty years ago. He had been to visit them only once in all that time.

"Before it's too late, you mean? Don't look so sad.

You're right. I should go. Perhaps I will after the New Year. Until then, I have a lot to do here."

Besides farming, her father had always planned to open a hardware business that catered to a few of his Amish neighbors with things like lanterns, nuts, bolts and his prized key-cutting machine that was powered by an ancient diesel generator. Only the shell of the building had been completed. The rest of the things he had collected over the years were junk in her eyes, but occasionally someone needed a part for a broken bailer and Zachariah Swartzentruber was the man to see. He had five bailers in various stages of rust sitting in a long shed he'd built to house them. He never came home from market day empty-handed.

Tears pricked her eyes again. What would she do without him? The doctor had to be wrong. "The boys and I will help with whatever you need."

"I know you will. I want to get my store finished and stocked by Christmas. I have loads of things just waiting to be put out on shelves."

His store was a room he'd built off the side of the house. The roof was on and the walls were framed, but that was all. His shelves were nothing more than long boards stored in the shed alongside the rusting bailers. "Roy and Alvin can help you finish the store."

"I need more help than they can give me. My hands are getting weak, and I can't swing a hammer the way I once did. I need a man's help."

"You're not going to ask Wayne Hochstetler, are you?" The idea of seeing him daily while the work was completed was troubling. What if she didn't like him enough to walk out with him? How could she face him

day after day knowing he was sizing her up to be his wife?

"*Nee*, for if Wayne has his mind on courting you, he might not be any use to me. A lovesick fellow often makes a poor worker."

"Then there are a number of young men who should suit your needs nicely. How much will this cost?"

He rose and cupped her cheek with his hand. "Don't worry your head about it, daughter. Buy the material for a new dress, and let me worry about the money."

"All right." She smiled for him.

"That's my girl." He started to leave the room.

"I'll put an ad for a hired man in the newspaper tomorrow."

"No need. I've already hired someone. He starts on Monday."

Her heart dropped like a rock and she closed her eyes. *Please, please, please, don't let it be him.*

"Who did you hire, *Daed*?"

Chapter Three

"I don't feel so *goot*. I don't think I'm ready to go home."

Luke suppressed a smile at Roy's downcast expression as he sat on the edge of the boy's bed the following morning. Roy looked less like a drowned rat today and more like a fella ready to get up to mischief as soon as Rebecca let him out of bed. Both of them knew better than to make that move without her permission. Luke's sister-in-law was a force to be reckoned with. She and Emma were cut from the same cloth.

Why hadn't Rebecca mentioned that Emma was seeing someone? While most Amish sweethearts kept their relationship a tightly guarded secret from the community until the banns were read a few weeks before the wedding, family members usually knew what was going on when a couple became serious. Zachariah's announcement yesterday had hit Luke like a ton of bricks, although he wasn't sure why.

That was a lie. He knew why. Emma held a place in his heart that no other woman had been able to fill.

She should marry. Wasn't that why he had stepped

aside all those years ago? Because he wanted her to be happy? He wanted her to build a life in the Amish community where they had grown up. Emma belonged here. She embraced the Amish way of life. It was something he had never been able to do.

All through the rough times when he was on drugs and then behind bars, he imagined Emma living a contented life. He was able to find comfort in that. It had soothed the pain of knowing how poorly he'd treated her. His words that night had been cruel, but they had been for her own good. He knew how much her family was going to need her. He had learned her mother didn't have long to live, but he had been forbidden to tell anyone, even Emma.

Roy plucked at the covers. "I think I should stay here another day or two."

"You're fine. You're just afraid of what your *daed* is gonna do."

"Not *daed*. Emma. She has a way of looking at you that makes you feel two inches tall."

"I've seen that look. Your *daed* didn't seem well when I saw him yesterday."

"He's been feeling poorly for a spell, but he saw the doctor yesterday. I'm sure he'll be better soon."

"Until then, I reckon that means he needs you and your brother's help more than ever with the farm chores."

Roy glanced from beneath his lashes at Luke. "Was he mad at Alvin?"

"A bit. Emma more so."

"There's no surprise." Roy rolled his eyes, forcing Luke to hide another grin.

"Mostly they're thankful both you boys survived. It was a dumb stunt."

Roy scowled. "Micah and I watched you ride a snowmobile up and down that river a few years ago."

"It was a dumb stunt when I did it, too. Micah who?"

"Micah Yoder. We thought it looked like mighty *goot* fun. He would have enjoyed it."

"I'm sure he would until he ended up in the water. Not so much fun then, was it? It could easily have been your brother lying here in your place. Or worse. You know that, don't you?"

A stoic expression settled on Roy's face. "*Ja.* I know."

Luke waited a few moments to let that thought soak in. "Your father mentioned he wants to get some of his equipment ready to sell in the spring. He asked for my help to repair some of his machinery. He offered to hire me for a couple of months."

Roy's face split into a wide grin as he scooted up in bed and leaned against the headboard. "Are you gonna take the job? That would be *wunderbar.*"

"I'm glad you like the idea." Luke still didn't know what had come over him. He never should have accepted Zachariah's offer. He hadn't even spoken to his own father yet.

"I have so many things to ask you, Luke. You know everything about life in the city and about the things an Amish guy needs to do if he wants to live English. You can teach me that stuff, can't you? I'm a quick learner."

A chuckle made Luke look over his shoulder. His brother Samuel stood in the doorway. Samuel's face still bore the faint scars of the burns he had suffered when their gasoline generator exploded. Luke's carelessness had contributed to the accident. He knew Samuel had

forgiven him, but he had a hard time forgiving himself. His one consolation was that Samuel's need for a nurse after the accident had brought Rebecca into their lives. Samuel considered Rebecca's love well worth the pain he had suffered.

Samuel advanced into the room. "Luke can teach you how to get into trouble anywhere, Roy. Amish or *Englisch* trouble, it doesn't matter to him. I'd avoid his company if I were you."

"He sure saved my hide yesterday."

"And the lesson learned from this?" Luke prompted.

"Don't take a snowmobile out on the river no matter how thick the ice looks."

Luke shook his head. He recognized a restless spirit in Roy. It was the same restlessness that had filled him at that age. "The lesson is to stay off snowmobiles and all *Englisch* machines."

Roy cast him a sheepish look. "I doubt I'll get the chance to ride one again since I almost ruined Mr. Morgan's."

Luke thumped his finger into Roy's chest. "It serves you right. Just so you know, Jim Morgan came by to collect his machine. His brother isn't going to be riding for a while, either. Jim wasn't happy to hear Brian let you boys ride off without adult supervision."

Samuel chuckled again. "That is the pot calling the kettle black. You and Jim were always up to no good when the adults weren't looking. He's the one who taught you to drive a car when you didn't have a license."

Luke frowned at his brother. "You're not helping, Samuel."

His brother laughed again. "*Daed* wants to see you downstairs."

Luke nodded and rose to his feet. "Okay. I'll check on you later, Roy. Stay in bed or Rebecca will have your head on a platter and mine, too."

Luke followed Samuel out of the spare bedroom. In the hallway, Samuel gave him a sidelong glance. "You took a job working for Zachariah? You're joking, right?"

"I don't know what happened. I opened my mouth to refuse, but that wasn't what came out. I agreed to a part-time job for a few months. Maybe more."

"What were you thinking? Did sticking your head under the ice freeze your pea-size brain?"

"Maybe so." Until recently, Samuel's teasing would have made Luke fighting mad, but these days the brothers had come to understand and respect each other.

"There's no maybe about it. Then again, it will get you out from under my feet."

"Sammy, you'll come crawling to find me the second that finicky planer jams again, begging me to fix it."

"On bended knee. You're the only one who can coax that machine to do its job. Zachariah might have made a smart move getting you to help him."

Working for Zachariah was a bad idea for so many reasons. Number one—Emma would hate having him around.

Number two—he already had a job working for his father in the family's woodworking and gift shop. He wasn't sure his father could spare him.

Number three—Emma would hate having him around.

His parents were sitting at the kitchen table when he came downstairs. The fact that his mother wasn't offer-

ing him food proved it was going to be a serious talk. His father folded his hands in front of him. "What is this about you taking another job?"

Luke looked back and forth between them. "How did you find out?"

"Rebecca spoke to Emma this morning."

Luke shoved his hands in the pockets of his pants. The Amish might not use telephones, but that didn't stop news from spreading like wildfire. "Zachariah talked me into a part-time job working for him. It was a mistake. I'll tell him I've changed my mind or that you can't spare me."

"What sort of job is it?" his mother asked.

"He wants help finishing his hardware store before Christmas. It would be mostly simple carpentry, stocking shelves and taking inventory. I don't think the man knows half of what he has stashed away."

Samuel rubbed a hand over his new beard, the one he'd started growing after his marriage, and scratched at his chin. "Luke, you suggested that we add a hardware section to our gift shop. I've been seriously considering it. Won't Zachariah be in competition with us?"

Luke's father snorted. "In all the years I've known him, Zachariah Swartzentruber has rarely finished a project he started. He won't become our competition. I doubt he'll ever complete his store."

"Isaac, that is unkind," his mother said with a sharp-eyed scowl at her mate. "Our neighbor has asked Luke for help. What do you think, Samuel? Can we spare Luke for a few weeks? Don't forget, your father and I will be gone to Florida for a month after Christmas."

Samuel fixed his gaze on Luke. "Will you have to notify your parole officer that you have a new job? Work-

ing and living here was one of the conditions of your early release, wasn't it?"

It wasn't common knowledge that he was still on parole. Only a few people outside the immediate family knew. His parents didn't like to discuss anything to do with his time in prison. He had caused them enough embarrassment in the community. He was surprised his brother mentioned it in front of them. "I'm not moving, and it would be in addition to my work here, so it shouldn't make a difference."

Samuel propped his hands on his hips. "If a neighbor needs help, we must give it. We can spare you, Luke. We're caught up on our Christmas orders for both the gift shop and the woodshop. Unless we get more than a few rush orders, Timothy, Noah and I can handle your work. As long as you can make any equipment repairs we need."

"You don't have to pick up my slack. I'll tell Zachariah I can't do it."

"How is Emma?" his mother asked with a look of innocence.

Suspicious at the abrupt change of topic, Luke shrugged. "Fine as far as I know. Ask Rebecca. She'll know more than I do."

"Won't it be hard for Emma to have you at her home? The two of you were close once. She was broken-hearted when you left."

His father shook his head. "That was a long time ago, *mudder*. They were *kinder*."

Luke avoided his mother's sharp gaze. He and Emma hadn't been children, but they had been too young to know what love was. He tried for an offhand tone. "I'm sure Emma couldn't care less if I work with her father or not."

"You are right about that." A cold voice he recognized came from behind him.

He spun around to see Emma and Rebecca standing in the doorway to the living room. They must have come in through the back door, for both women wore their traveling bonnets and cloaks. Emma had a fixed smile pasted on her face. Rebecca shook her head and glared at him.

His mother rose to her feet. "Emma, how nice to see you. If this arrangement is all right with you, then it's okay with us. Luke can work for your father."

Great. Now he was stuck with the job. Maybe it was for the best. Maybe if he and Emma spent some time together they could put the past to rest and start over. He wasn't expecting friendship, but he hoped for something more civil than the icy stare he was getting at the moment.

"How is Roy?" Rebecca asked, pulling off her bonnet.

"Goot," Samuel said. "He's been a better patient than I was."

She laughed. "That wouldn't take much. Come, Emma, I'll show you up to his room. He was very blessed that Luke was able to reach him under the ice and pull him out. I hope he knows that."

Emma pulled off her bonnet, too, and dropped her gaze to her hands. "I haven't thanked you for saving his life, Luke."

"You're welcome." He'd dive in a freezing river again if she would just smile at him—say she forgave him.

She didn't. She left the room and followed Rebecca upstairs.

* * *

"You can't still be mad at him after all these years."

"I don't know what you mean." Emma avoided eye contact with her cousin.

"I saw the look you gave Luke. If your eyes were a frying pan and Luke was an egg, he'd be burned to a crisp."

"You're being silly. He's right. I couldn't care less about what he does or where he goes." And that was exactly how she would behave from now on. She wasn't about to be known as a weak-willed old maid carrying a torch for someone who didn't love her.

"I'm beginning to think you care more about Luke than you're letting on." Rebecca paused to knock on a door halfway down the hall.

"Come in." Roy's muffled voice smote Emma's conscience. She should be worrying about him, not about what Rebecca or anyone else thought of her relationship with Luke.

Emma pushed open the door. Her brother was sitting up in bed with a checkerboard on his legs. Noah, the youngest Bowman son, was sitting beside his bed on a chair. He looked up and smiled. "You have fine timing. He was about to beat me."

"For the third straight game," Roy added.

Emma marched up to the bed and propped her hands on her hips. "For someone who cheated death, you look pretty good to me."

He sank back against the pillows. "I'm still shook up, *shveshtah*."

"I hope you are. Your foolishness could have put you in an early grave."

Rebecca came to her side, her arms crossed over her chest. "He looks a lot better than he did yesterday."

Emma bent to capture his face between her hands. She planted a kiss on his forehead, which he promptly wiped away. "He looks *wunderbar*. Can I take him home?"

"Maybe. I need to examine him first. Hold your arms straight out to your sides, Roy."

He did. She nodded and made a small sound of approval. "Does that hurt?"

"Nee."

"Goot. Open wide and stick out your tongue, but keep your arms up." He did and she bent closer to examine him. "Now, flap your arms up and down."

He shot her a quizzical look, but did as she asked.

Rebecca glanced at Emma, but couldn't keep a straight face. "Does he look like a baby bird getting ready to fly the coop?"

Emma nodded. "He does."

"Then I think he's ready to be released." Rebecca took a step back as Roy glared at her. Noah started laughing and almost fell off his chair.

"Ha! Ha! Very funny, cousin." Roy tossed his covers back, sending the checkers flying.

"That's a good one, Rebecca." Noah slapped his thigh and kept laughing. "I'm gonna call him Birdie Roy from now on. A fella needs a nickname for sure. Birdie Roy. Tweet, tweet."

Roy fumed at Noah. "I'm going to get dressed. Where are my clothes?"

"Mamm washed them. I'll fetch them for you unless you've got a hankering to go sit on the clothesline for a spell. Tweet, tweet." Noah left the room, still chuckling.

"Now look what you did. I'll never hear the end of this." Roy folded his arms over his chest.

"See you later, little cousin." Laughing, too, Rebecca waved and left the room.

Emma gave her brother a quick hug. "I'm so glad you're all right. Forgive our teasing."

"I guess I have to. But if Noah keeps this up, he's gonna get a snowball in the face the next time he steps outside."

"Vengeance is not our way," Emma chided. Roy was still such a child. He would need to grow up so fast once their father was gone. It hurt to think of the pain he would soon go through when he learned the news. Maybe her father was right. Maybe the boys deserved this one last happy Christmas. She would do that for them.

"I'll put a handful of snow down his back if it will make you feel better," Luke offered from the doorway. "That's not vengeance, it's brotherly love." He came into the room with a bundle of clothes in his hands. "*Mamm* sent me up with these."

Emma's heart did its funny skip, but she quickly ignored the sensation. "*Danki*, Luke. As soon as he is dressed, I'll take him off your hands. My buggy is outside."

She left the room so her brother could have some privacy. Luke followed her into the hall and stopped close beside her. Too close. She could see the gray flecks in his blue eyes when she looked into his face. The soap he used accentuated his own unique masculine scent. It must be one of Rebecca's. She made a number of

herb-infused bars that smelled delightful. Emma was sure she hadn't smelled this one before. She breathed in deeply, not wanting to exhale.

How foolish was that? As soon as she decided she wasn't going to care what Luke did, she couldn't stop thinking about him.

"Tell your father that I'll be over first thing Monday morning."

"All right."

He hesitated, then said, "I don't want to make things uncomfortable for you, Emma. Are you sure you are okay with this?"

He looked truly concerned about her. How was she supposed to answer him?

"Luke, it doesn't matter to me if you work for my father. So long as you keep true to the teachings of our faith."

His eyes went from warm to frosty in a heartbeat. "You mean stay away from drugs."

If he was angry with her, so much the better. "You know what I mean. Our faith has many rules, and you like bending the rules."

"What if I say that I've changed? Would you believe me?"

"I would pray fervently that is true."

"Not exactly what I wanted to hear."

She crossed her arms tightly over her chest. "It's the best I can do."

"Then maybe I should tell your father I've changed my mind." He pulled back. A shadow slipped across his eyes.

Was it pain? Had she hurt him? That was never her intention. "I'm sorry."

"Don't be. It's best to get our feelings out in the open. I'll speak to your father tomorrow."

This wasn't about her feelings. It was about her father and what he needed. "*Nee*, Luke. *Daed* can use the help. He's not been well. You would be doing him a great favor if you came to work for him."

"There are a lot of fellows he could hire to help."

"But you understand machines. You will know what can be fixed and what is junk fit only for scrap. At least he'll make a little money off that."

"And making money is important, isn't it? Of course it is. What woman wants to go into a marriage empty-handed?"

She drew back in shock. "Marriage? Who said anything about marriage?"

"Zachariah mentioned it in passing."

Her cheeks burned with humiliation. Was her father trying to force her hand by spreading the story that she was about to wed? She pressed her lips together. "He shouldn't have said anything. Nothing is decided."

"I understand. Amish couples like to keep things secret. Don't worry. I won't say anything."

"Danki." But she was going to have plenty to say to her father.

Luke's gaze softened. "Whoever he is, Emma, he's a fortunate man."

His eyes pulled at her heartstrings, making her long to move into his arms and rest her head on his shoulder the way she once had. She licked her suddenly dry lips.

Roy came out of the bedroom. "I'm ready."

Emma tore her gaze away from Luke. "I have to go."

She followed her brother down the hall. At the stairwell, she glanced back and saw Luke was still watching her. Was it a trick of the light, or did she see regret in his eyes?

Chapter Four

On Saturday afternoon, Emma traveled to the home of her friend, Lillian Keim. Lillian was the teacher at Alvin's school, but the two women had been friends since the cradle. It had been Lillian who listened to Emma pour out her grief when Luke left. Lillian's family had moved away not long afterward, leaving Emma to tell her friend how well she was recovering through letters. It was easier to bend the truth in writing. Then, two years ago, Lillian, her parents, her brother and her new little sister had returned to Bowmans Crossing so that Lillian could take the teacher's post that had opened up. Emma was delighted to find they picked up their friendship right where they left off.

As Emma stopped her horse in front of Lillian's house, she recognized her cousin Rebecca's buggy tied to the hitching rail. The three of them were the planning committee for the school's Christmas program.

"Hello," Emma called as she entered the house.

"We're in the living room," Lillian called back.

Emma crossed the kitchen and turned the corner to see Rebecca and Rebecca's mother, Ina Fisher, sitting

on the sofa with cups of tea in their hands. Lillian sat in a chair facing them. She gestured toward another chair beside her. "Come and sit here. I was just telling Rebecca and your *aenti* your news. I hope you don't mind."

"What news? Hello *Aenti* Ina. I wasn't expecting you to join us. How are you?" Emma approached the couch and kissed her aunt on the cheek.

Ina gave a long-suffering sigh. "Not bad for a woman my age. You young people don't want to hear about my arthritis or my sciatic pain."

Rebecca winked, and Emma knew she had to say something. "I'm so sorry you are suffering, *Aenti*. I must say, you bear up remarkably well. I don't know how you manage."

Apparently mollified, her aunt smiled a little. "*Danki*, child. I try."

Emma sat in the chair next to Lillian. "Were you talking about Roy's escapade? He's fine, although I fear he may not have learned his lesson."

"Lillian told us that Luke Bowman is working for your father. That must be odd for you." Ina took a sip of her tea, but her sharp eyes never left Emma's face.

"I don't find it odd at all. Why should I?" Emma kept her face carefully blank. Ina was well-known as a gossip in the community. Emma didn't want to fuel new speculation about Luke and herself.

Ina shrugged. "No reason, other than I do wonder if he will be a bad influence on Roy."

Rebecca gave her mother a speaking glance. "Luke is not a bad influence on anyone. Shame on you for implying otherwise."

Ina pressed a hand to her heart. "I didn't mean to speak ill of him. Gracious, no."

"I thought not." Rebecca sipped her tea, but her frown remained.

"I was merely thinking that Roy is the age when he would find Luke's prior life exciting."

Lillian shook her head. "Prison can hardly be considered exciting."

"Not to us, of course," Ina conceded.

"Not to Roy, either," Emma stated firmly, but she wondered if she spoke the truth. No matter how hard she tried to keep Roy from straying, she wasn't sure she could. As Luke had at his age, her brother seemed determined to live an English life.

Rebecca set her teacup in the saucer on the small table in front of her. "We're here to plan the Christmas program, not to gossip about my husband's brother."

Lillian giggled. "Where's the fun in that? If you will step outside, we'll be happy to talk about you instead."

Emma chuckled. "I hope the art of gossip isn't a lesson you are teaching our *kinder* at school."

"I'm afraid it is a lesson learned more readily at home than at school." Rebecca gave her mother a pointed look.

Ina put her teacup down, too. "Let us hear your ideas for the program this year, Lillian. This Thursday is the first of December, so we need to get moving."

Lillian opened a notebook she had sitting on her lap. "My thought was to tell the Christmas story from the shepherds' point of view. They were, after all, the first to hear the good news of our Savior's birth. Emma, I'm sure Alvin told you I want him to sing a solo. He has a remarkably beautiful voice. He's not keen on the idea. I hope you can encourage him to do it. I don't want to force him."

"He does sing well," Ina admitted. "What song did you have in mind for him?"

"'The First Noel.'"

Rebecca clasped her hands together. "It's a lovely Christmas song and one of my favorites."

"Will the other children have a chance to sing, too?" Emma asked. Alvin wouldn't want to be the only one.

Lillian leaned forward. "Oh, absolutely. Since we are telling the story of the shepherds, we could start with the hymn 'While Shepherds Watched Their Flocks.' I will have one of the fourth-grade girls be the angel that appears to them. How many shepherds do you think I should have?"

Rebecca shrugged. "It doesn't say how many there were in the Bible. I think four or five would be a good number."

"I agree. Then I will have the first-and second-grade girls be the host of angels. Eight of them in all. We'll also need to choose someone to play Joseph and Mary. Who would like to help with the costumes?" Lillian glanced hopefully around the room.

"I can," Emma said.

"What about scenery or sets?" Rebecca asked.

Lillian folded her notebook closed. "Timothy Bowman has expressed an interest in helping with that."

Ina frowned. "He doesn't have a child in school."

"His niece, Hannah, is a new student with us this year." Lillian smoothed her skirt, keeping her eyes downcast.

Emma caught Rebecca's eye. Was Timothy interested in courting their friend? Rebecca's expression said she had no idea.

The sound of the front door opening was followed

by childish laughter. Lillian's little sister came hurrying into the room. "Lilly, I got a Christmas present for you, but I can't tell you what it is."

Emma smiled at the girl. Born with dwarfism, Amanda was three years old and a happy, active child. Many Amish families had members who were little people. Lillian's family was thankful that Amanda had none of the health problems that often accompanied the disorder.

Lillian's mother, Marietta Keim, came into the room and greeted everyone. She leaned down to her daughter. "Amanda, your sister has visitors. You shouldn't interrupt."

"I'm sorry, but I had to tell her about her present."

Lillian pulled her close. "I'm so glad you did. I shall be on pins and needles the entire month wondering what it is."

Marietta held out her hand. "Come help me gather the eggs, Amanda."

"Okay." She rushed to her mother's side, and they both went out.

The women spent the next half hour working on the details of the program. After Rebecca and her mother left, Lillian crossed her arms and stared at Emma. "Well?"

"Well, what?"

"Luke Bowman working for your father. That can't be good."

"It doesn't matter to me what Luke does or where he works."

"It used to matter a lot. You can't take up with him again, Emma."

"Who said I was?"

"He'll break your heart again. Men like him always do."

There were no other men like Luke Bowman. He was one of a kind.

She rose from her chair and went to stare out the window. "I'm not getting involved with him. He's not interested in me. He's been home over a year. If he wanted to walk out with me, he would have asked ages ago, and I would have turned him down. My father is pushing me to wed someone else."

Lillian sat bolt upright. "What? Who? Why?"

"Wayne Hochstetler. Because it's time I married. I'm not getting any younger."

"We are barely twenty-five. We're not old maids. Not yet."

"I don't want to be an old maid, and neither do you."

"That's where you're wrong. I intend to remain single, but we are talking about you. Are you walking out with Wayne?"

"Not yet. This is something his father and my father cooked up between them, but apparently Wayne is on the lookout for a wife."

Lillian sat back. "He would be with such a young daughter to raise. It might be a good match, Emma. He's a steady fellow, hardworking and not bad looking. He has a nice farm. You would have a ready-made family."

Emma couldn't come up with a thing against him except he wasn't Luke. "If you think it's such a good deal, why don't *you* marry him?"

"I told you. I'm going to be single and teach school all my days. I love it."

She rose and went to stand at Emma's side. Slipping an arm across Emma's shoulders, Lillian drew her close. "We have been friends a long time. I remember how

upset you were when Luke left and didn't take you with him. I thank God he had that much sense, but I could cheerfully horsewhip him for the pain he caused you."

"I didn't know you were such a violent person."

"Okay, I wouldn't horsewhip a bug, but I could send Luke Bowman to stand in the corner for the rest of his life."

Emma managed a smile. "I can see you have the makings of a great teacher. Please don't worry about me. I'm okay. Having Luke work for my father has stirred up old memories, but that's all they are. Memories. I live in the here and now. He can't hurt me."

"I pray you are right."

Emma prayed that she was, too.

Sunday was the off Sunday when there wasn't a church meeting. The Amish had church every other week. Luke's family remained at home that day. His father led a quiet morning of prayer and Bible reading. Luke tried to keep his mind on the words his father spoke, but his thoughts kept drifting to Emma and the look on her face before she left with Roy. There had been something in her eyes when she gazed at him. Was it possible that she still cared after the way he'd treated her?

He should have found a gentler way to break it off between them. He had known that she loved him. He had loved her, too, although he never told her that. His feelings for Emma had frightened the wits out of him. Marriage would have tied him to the Amish life forever. She never understood his need to be free from his family's expectations and from everything Amish

that had stifled him. Drugs had given him the feeling of freedom he craved, but only for a while.

If he had allowed her to come with him, it would have ruined her life. Leaving her behind was the only good thing he'd ever done for her. Did she understand that?

It didn't seem likely, but there had been something in the way she looked at him that gave him hope.

Hope for what?

What was it that he wanted from her? To rekindle their teenage romance? He was too old and too jaded to think that was possible.

Forgiveness? He craved that, but he didn't expect it. How could he when he had never explained why he left her.

Did he hope for a new friendship with her? Maybe.

None of it mattered if he wasn't staying in Bowmans Crossing. The closer the time came for him to make a decision about staying the less certain he became of what he was going to do. From the moment he got out of jail, he had been struggling to fit in, to find where he belonged. Once his parole was up, he would be truly free. Free to leave. Free to stay. Which did he want?

His whole life he had rebelled against the strict and narrow Amish world he'd been born into. He'd never felt as if he were a part of it. Only sweet Emma had made it bearable. Her shy smiles, her adorable laugh, those tender stolen kisses. Oh yes, Emma had tempted him to stay, but her love hadn't been enough.

Luke had grown to envy his *Englisch* friend, Jim Morgan. It had seemed that Jim and his buddies had a million choices. They had money to spend, cars to take them anywhere they wanted to go. There had been par-

ties, loud music, fun and later there had been drugs, too. The Amish singings and picnics Emma wanted to attend seemed dull as dirt in comparison.

Always a risk taker, Luke dove headfirst into a lifestyle that had seemed too good to be true. And it was.

The occasional party drugs hadn't been enough after a while. He sought escape more often, and one of Jim's buddies supplied what he needed. Although Luke had believed he could quit whenever he wanted, he hadn't been able to do so. In the end, he rejected Emma's love, lost the respect of his family and his self-respect, too.

And he had no one to blame but himself.

Now, the Lord had led him full circle. He was back at the same crossroads. Stay or go? Which would be best for his family? Their unwavering support and love had given his life new meaning, but did he belong here?

If only he could be sure he wouldn't fail them again.

At noon, his mother prepared a light meal, and afterward Luke walked down to the riverbank behind the house. The water was frozen a few feet out from the shore, but it was open in a winding path down the center of the river. A flock of mallard ducks flew up from the open water, circled and landed farther downstream, quacking their displeasure at being disturbed. He tossed a stick into the water and watched it drift away.

"What is troubling you, *brudder*?"

He recognized Joshua's voice and turned to see all four of his brothers walking down to join him. "I'm not troubled."

Joshua stopped a few feet away and folded his arms. "I've heard that before. I didn't buy it then and I'm not buying it now."

"What gives?" Noah asked. At twenty, he was the

youngest of the Bowman sons and the least Amish looking with his short brown hair, English clothes and blue ball cap. He was taking advantage of his *rumspringa* to enjoy some non-Amish activities, but Luke knew Noah had every intention of joining the faith in a few years.

"Are you thinking of leaving us again?" Trust Samuel to get straight to the point.

"We all want you to stay," Timothy added quietly. "I hope you know that."

Luke nodded, unable to speak until he swallowed the lump in his throat. "I know you want me here."

Samuel laid a hand on Luke's shoulder. "But?"

"But I wish I knew for certain that I could stay."

Joshua tipped his hat back. "Luke, no one but you can make that decision. Why do you think you should leave?"

Joshua had believed he could convince Luke to return to the family. He had tracked Luke down and found him selling drugs to support his habit. Shame and guilt kept Luke from accepting Joshua's help. Unfortunately, they both were swept up in a drug raid, and his innocent brother had been sent to prison, too. Amazingly, Joshua didn't harbor any ill will toward him.

Luke stared at the ground. "I should leave because I'm a drug addict and a convict. How many Amish fellows can say that?"

"Ex-addict. Ex-convict," Samuel said sternly.

Luke glanced at him. "Am I? Therein lies my dilemma. I'm not using drugs now. I don't want to go back to prison, and failing a drug test would put me there in a heartbeat. I'm straight now, but once prison isn't hanging over my head, will I give in and start using again?"

Samuel shook him by the shoulders. "You won't."

Luke pulled away from his brother. "You don't know that because I don't know that."

The fear of falling back into that life hovered over him every day. He wasn't strong. He'd failed before. He could fail again. Why was he so different from his siblings? Looking into their faces, he knew they didn't understand his fears. How could they? They were all so sure of their place in life.

Forcing a smile, he hooked a thumb toward the house. "Why don't I beat you at a game of checkers, Samuel? That always makes me feel better."

Noah shoved his hands in the pockets of his jacket. "*Daed* has already challenged him. You'll have to wait and play the winner."

"Go on, then. I'll be up in a minute."

His brothers walked reluctantly up the hill. He threw one more stick in the water and followed. As he entered the back garden gate, he saw Joshua's wife, Mary, sitting on a bench. She had her eyes closed and her face raised to the afternoon sun. Several of the gourd bird-houses he had painted added color to the winter landscape. "I know how you're feeling, Luke."

"I doubt that." He took a seat beside her.

"You feel lost. Others seem to know exactly what they want out of life and you still don't know what you're seeking. For two cents, you'd put a boat on the river, get in it and drift away until you reached the sea or sank." She opened her eyes and looked at him. "Am I close?"

"Amazingly so."

"I was like you before I had Hannah."

Luke knew some of her story. Mary had left the Amish as a young girl, ended up with a man who used

and then abandoned her when he found out she was pregnant. Alone and on the streets, she was taken in by a drug dealer named Dunbar, who planned to sell her baby when it was born. She gave birth alone and managed to hide Hannah from him in an Amish buggy, leaving a note with her child that she would come back for her.

What she hadn't known was the buggy belonged to two teenage Amish boys who panicked when they discovered the baby. They left her on the doorstep of the nearest Amish farm. It was only thanks to Miriam Kauffman, an ex-Amish nurse, and Sheriff Nick Bradley that Mary was eventually reunited with her baby, and the drug dealer was sent to prison. Nick and Miriam married and adopted Mary. When Hannah was five, Joshua rescued the mother and child during a tornado and soon fell in love with them both. Once again, it had been Luke's weakness that almost ruined everything for them.

"You are a stronger person than I am, Mary. You've seen how weak I can be. You suffered because of it."

"God gave me someone to make me strong. He gave me Hannah. He will give you the strength you need if you trust Him."

"I don't know that I believe that. I have the feeling that I'm out here on my own. I think He's washed His hands of me. I don't know why you haven't."

"Because Joshua loves you."

"I don't understand that, either. He tried to help me and I pulled him down with me. He spent time in prison because of me. I gave the man who hated you information about you in exchange for drugs when I was in prison."

"You didn't know Kevin Dunbar's intentions. He used you."

"He kidnapped Hannah and could have killed her because of me."

"God, in His great mercy, spared my child. You told the authorities where Dunbar was going once you knew what had happened. Nick got my little girl back because of your help. You were part of God's plan all along, Luke. Don't doubt that."

"I'd feel better about being part of the solution if I hadn't caused the problem. I don't deserve another chance to mess up someone's life." If he stayed, it would happen. To Mary or to Hannah or God forbid to Emma. He would fail them when they needed him most. In his heart of hearts, he knew it.

Mary sighed softly. "I've never told anyone in the family this other than my husband, but I tried to kill myself when I lost Hannah the first time. It was hard to believe God could forgive me for such an act. The truth is God forgave me long before I made that terrible decision. He sent His only Son to die on a cross to save me from my sin. God forgives all of us. I was the one who couldn't forgive myself until I realized that God had sent Joshua to love me in spite of everything. Your sins will be forgiven if you accept the truth of our Savior's sacrifice for you, Luke. Until you accept that and forgive yourself, you won't find happiness here or anywhere."

"It's easier said than done, Mary."

"You're right. It is. But it's possible. Now let's go in. I'm getting cold and your mother was making some hot cocoa." She rose to her feet.

Luke stared at her in amazement. "I hope my brother

knows how blessed he is to have found a woman like you, Mary."

She grinned. "I tell him often, so he's not likely to forget."

Luke chuckled. He could hear Emma saying something like that. Emma was a strong woman, too. If only he could undo his past mistakes and make her love him again.

No, he was a fool if he tried to hold on to that hope, but to his dismay, it wouldn't die.

Chapter Five

Luke spent Monday morning prowling through Zachariah's sheds and barn, taking stock of what equipment the man had squirreled away. He found eight chain saws, none of which worked, and a half dozen two-man saws that only needed sharpening; six bailers in various stages of rust; three silage blowers; eighteen carriage wheels; twelve sets of harnesses; four plows; four harrows; fifty-five assorted sizes of horseshoes and a busted corn binder. As he went through, over and around the piles, he made notes in a small spiral notebook. Roy worked with him, but Alvin had school and wouldn't be home until after three o'clock.

Zachariah came out to check on their progress occasionally, but for the most part, he puttered in the half-built hardware store. Luke gained the impression that it was hard for Zachariah to see his holdings being assessed by someone with an eye to selling them. He didn't see hide nor hair of Emma. Was she avoiding him?

Stupid question. Of course she was.

Where they could, Luke and Roy moved Zachariah's

hoard to lay it out for better access and to inventory the cardboard boxes and wooden crates filled with gears, bearings, nails and assorted small tools. They were both covered with dust and grease within a few hours.

"I count twenty-three oil lamps complete with shades and wicks in these boxes. Looks like only one shade is cracked." Luke replaced the last lid and moved to tally the rope and tackle hanging on pegs nearby.

"What are these?" Roy asked, pulling a tarp away from a stack of silver-and-blue metal panels in the hayloft of Zachariah's largest barn. Luke suspected the horses' and cattle's need for hay was the only reason this part of the barn hadn't been overtaken yet.

Luke stopped counting the pulleys and puzzled over Roy's find for second. "I think they're solar panels."

"The kind that make electricity?"

"*Ja.* I wonder how your *daed* came by them. I always thought they were expensive to buy."

"He probably traded for them. That's what *Daed* does. He trades for stuff. He rarely buys anything. Could these be used to charge up my cell phone?"

"I'm sure it could, but I don't know how to make it work."

Roy flipped the cover back over the solar array. "I thought you were gonna tell me to get rid of my phone. That's what Emma would say."

"I know a lot of guys your age carry them. You aren't baptized yet, so you don't have to abide by the church rules."

"Emma says I need to. She is always harping about how hard it will be to give up my *Englisch* things later. She says it's better to give them up now before I get attached to them."

"She might have a point. You shouldn't be too hard on your sister. She means well."

"I know. It's just that she tries to be our mother. She's not."

"She's been taking care of you and Alvin since you were little. You can't blame her for wanting to see that you turn out right."

"How I turn out is going to be my decision, not hers."

The boy had a point. No amount of his mother's prayers or pleading had kept Luke home when he was ready to leave. "Once she gets married, she won't have as much time to fuss at you."

Roy's eyebrows shot up. "Emma is getting married?"

"Your *daed* mentioned as much. I figured you knew."

"I thought my sister would be an old maid forever."

"So you don't know who she has been seeing?" Was that odd, or was Roy simply too caught up in his own life to see what was happening under his nose? Luke was ashamed to admit that he had been like that at Roy's age.

"*Nee.* Wow. Who will take care of Alvin?"

"I reckon you and your father can manage."

"I'll be leaving. I mean, one of these days I'm gonna live in the city. That's where all the excitement is."

Luke tensed. "What kind of excitement?"

"Lights, movie theaters, televisions, bars, girls that dress fancy. Micah and I talked a lot about the things we'd see there."

Relaxing a bit, Luke was relieved that Roy hadn't mentioned drugs. "None of it is free. How would you pay for a place with lights and a television?"

"I'll get a job."

"It's not as easy as it sounds." Without the simple ba-

sics such as a driver's license and social security card, and with only an eighth-grade education, a decent job was almost impossible to come by. To his deep regret, Luke had chosen the wrong way to make money.

"Is that why you came back, because you couldn't find work?" Roy asked.

Luke hesitated, but decided to tell Roy the truth. Maybe it would keep him from making the same kind of mistakes. "Living here is a condition of my parole. You knew I went to prison, didn't you?"

Roy shrugged. "Sure. Everyone knows. I think it's cool."

Luke rounded on the boy. "It wasn't cool! I spent a year of my life locked in a cage with men you never want to meet. I made stupid decisions, and people got hurt. I paid the price for that. A lot like your ride on the snowmobile. Only there wasn't anyone standing by to haul my soggy behind to shore. I pulled my brother Joshua into trouble with me, and it was only by the grace of God that we survived."

Roy backed away from Luke's anger. "I'm sorry."

Luke sucked in a deep breath and blew it out, letting his anger flow away with it. "I'm the one who is sorry. Forgive me."

Roy rubbed his hands on his pant legs. "It must have been hard, but it's over now."

"It's not over. I'm not in jail, but I'm still on parole until the end of my sentence. That means I have to report to an *Englisch* parole officer every month. If I don't do what they tell me, I can be sent back to prison."

"I didn't know that."

Another month and then he would truly be a free man. A man able to live his life as he saw fit without

reporting to anyone. Without this great shadow hanging over his head.

"You have to understand that the *Englisch* world is much more than lights and movies, Roy. It has a very dark side. You need to think long and hard about what you're leaving, and why you're leaving. If you decide to live *Englisch*, you need to be prepared."

"That's why I'm glad you're here. Where did you stay when you first left?"

Luke cringed at the memory. "In a crummy old motel a few blocks north of the bus station in Cincinnati called the Gray Cat. I had heard that a bunch of ex-Amish kids were staying there. I didn't have a clue about life off the farm let alone how to survive in a dangerous slum. The management charged way too much for those run-down rooms."

The owner had also had unscrupulous contacts eager to employ the underage and unsuspecting youths who desperately needed jobs when their money ran out or was stolen.

"The Gray Cat. That is the kind of stuff I want to learn. I knew you'd help me get out of here."

"Then you are doomed to be disappointed because I'm not going to help you leave. You don't know half the dangers that are out there."

"I'm not staying here. I'll be bored out of my skull for the rest of my life."

"How do you charge your cell phone, anyway?" Luke asked to change the subject. He could see he wasn't getting through to the boy.

Roy looked disappointed, but said, "I have three batteries that I rotate. Fannie Erb has a phone charger that runs off a car battery. Alvin stops by there on his way

to school, leaves one with her and picks it up on his way home. If he forgets or school isn't on, I go to Brian Morgan's place. He lets me use his charger for a small price. Well, he used to. I'm not sure he will after I wrecked the snowmobile. If we could get a solar panel running, I know a lot of fellas from our neighboring church group who would pay to use it."

"From Bishop Hochstetler's church? I thought they didn't permit any phones at all. Not even a community phone booth."

"They don't, but some kids have them, anyway. They sure don't want to get caught with one. Bishop Hochstetler had the parents of one kid shunned after he was caught with a phone. The bishop claimed they hadn't raised their son properly."

"Was this your friend Micah?"

Roy nodded. "I was the one who got the phone for him. He gave it up after that. He didn't want his folks punished for the things he did."

"I can understand that."

Every Amish congregation decided on the *Ordnung* for their church. Some were much more conservative than others and their bishops held great sway over the members. Bishop Hochstetler's group was one of the strictest. His church members lived without indoor plumbing or running water. Their children weren't allowed a *rumspringa*, but were all expected to join the church when they came of age. Members were even forbidden to use reflectors on their buggies, including the orange slow-moving vehicle triangle that adorned the back of every buggy in Luke's congregation. Luke didn't agree with their way of thinking, but he respected the people who adhered to the old ways so staunchly.

"Did Micah stop seeing you because of his parents' shunning?"

"*Nee*, not because of that."

Luke was shocked by the sadness in Roy's voice.

Outside, the clanging of a bell signaled the noon meal was ready. Roy started for the ladder. "Emma doesn't like us to keep her waiting. Come on."

Luke stayed rooted to the spot. He'd known this moment was coming, but that didn't make it any easier. He would have to share a meal with Emma and her family. He would have to sit across from her and pretend she didn't set his head spinning like a top. He'd have to pretend it didn't matter that she was thinking about marrying.

Who was the fellow? He was dying to know.

Emma had her emotions well in hand by the time she rang the dinner bell. Luke's presence was nothing more than a minor annoyance. Nothing of their past relationship remained. She wanted to make sure he got the message in case he thought otherwise.

After everyone had washed up and taken their place at the table, she carried the platter of meat loaf and turnips from the oven and placed it in front of her father. She took her place opposite Luke, folded her hands demurely and prayed silently.

Her father cleared his throat to signal the prayer was ended and reached for the dish Emma had put on the table. "Meat loaf and boiled turnips. My favorite. I hope you like them, Luke."

Emma stifled a small grin. Luke didn't like meat loaf, and he hated turnips.

"I do. It's one of my favorite meals, too," Luke said.

Her glance flew to his face. He was grinning at her with a twinkle in his eye. "I'm surprised that you remembered, Emma."

Of course he would find a way to put her on the spot. He knew exactly what she had done, but she could hardly claim she remembered he disliked them. She raised her chin a notch. "I didn't. It was a pure coincidence."

"A happy one for me, it seems." He loaded his plate and passed the platter to Roy.

Emma fumed silently as the meal continued, but a covert glance at Luke proved he hadn't touched his turnips and was only picking at his meat loaf. She took pity on him and fetched the half dozen leftover dinner rolls from the day before. She offered him the plate and he took three.

"What do you think of my collection, Luke?" her father asked.

"You have a good amount of salvageable equipment. It's going to take some time to get the bulk of it in running order."

"How much time do you reckon?"

"Six months, maybe. Truthfully, it would be better to wait until warmer weather to work on it."

"I reckon you're right about that." Disappointment clouded her father's expression.

"I think you should concentrate on getting your hardware store finished," Luke added quickly. "A lot of the small things like the horseshoes and nails can be sold in your store without waiting for a farm sale. The chain saws and handsaws will likely sell, too. This time of year, everyone needs firewood. Does the log splitter work?"

Roy shook his head. "We've been splitting our wood by hand for the past two years."

"That's too bad, but once your store is enclosed and can be heated, repairing things like the log splitter and other small equipment will be much easier."

"That will be our plan, then," Zachariah announced. "Starting this afternoon, we'll get busy finishing the walls."

Luke buttered his roll. "Where did the solar panels in the hayloft come from?"

Zachariah scratched his chin. "Let me think. I remember now. I traded a green-broke horse to an *Englisch* fella over by Berlin. It was a poor trade on my part. I thought I could resell them for more, but most folks want them installed and guaranteed. I intended to read up on it but never got around to it. I still have that book somewhere."

"If you find it, I'd like to see it."

Her father looked her way. "Any idea where it might be, Emma?"

"It's in the bookcase in the living room where I put all the books you intend to read and never do." She smiled tenderly at him. He was a fine man, but he wasn't without his faults.

He chuckled and pointed his fork at Luke. "My daughter keeps me in line. A good thing it is, too. Her mother was just the same. Never settle for a woman that always lets you have your way, Luke."

"I won't," Luke said quietly. His gaze was fixed on her face.

She looked away first. The sound of the buggy outside caught her attention. She glanced past her father and saw Wayne drive in. He stepped down from his

buggy, brushed off his coat and adjusted his hat before approaching the house.

Her dad glanced over his shoulder. "Well, it seems that Wayne isn't wasting any time."

"What does that mean?" Roy asked, looking perplexed.

Her father chuckled. "Nothing. I shall go see what he wants. Perhaps he can join us for our midday meal."

Emma closed her eyes and prayed that would not be the case. The thought of Luke watching Wayne court her was almost more than she could bear.

Her prayer went unanswered. Her father came in with Wayne behind him. "Set another place, Emma. Wayne will be joining us."

"This should be interesting." Luke watched her with a smirk twitching at the corner of his lips. "Wayne Hochstetler? I never would have guessed."

"Oh, be quiet and eat your turnips!" She pushed back from the table and went to fetch another plate.

There was nothing wrong with Wayne's appearance, Emma decided as he shed his coat and hat and took a seat beside Luke. The widower was a fine-looking man with thick black hair and a well-kept beard. He was tall with an athletic figure, but he didn't smile much.

Emma was hard-pressed to make the meal stretch to include another healthy appetite, but she was required by her faith to feed any person who came to her table. Luke offered Wayne some of his untouched turnips, and he accepted them with barely a nod. Emma passed the meat loaf to Wayne without taking any herself. She added a day-old roll to her plate instead. Cutting it in half, she buttered the crown. The meal progressed in si-

lence, made all the more uncomfortable by her father's contented smile. She reached for the honey.

Luke caught her eye, gave her a wink and a nod as if signaling his approval. She wanted to pour the honey over his head, but restricted herself to adding it to her day-old roll.

When the meal was done, the men retired to the living room, leaving her alone at last. She hurried through the dishes so she could join them. Thankfully, her father was hard of hearing and she had no trouble listening to the conversation taking place in the other room.

"What brings you out this way?" Zachariah asked.

"I heard about Roy falling through the ice. I came to see how he was faring after his accident. I had a cousin who perished from pneumonia after a winter dunking. I hope you have seen the error of your ways, Roy. The *Englisch* machines are dangerous and only draw us into peril."

"I did learn not to take one out on the river ice. I'll stick to the snow-covered fields in the future."

Emma flinched at Roy's flippant tone.

"You jest with me, but your accident was not a laughing matter. The bishop may well be out to speak with your father about your attitude if it does not change soon."

"I have taken my son to task. He'll not repeat his mistake. I'm sure you have work waiting for you, Roy," her father said sharply. He wasn't pleased with Roy's attitude, either.

"We do," Luke said, and rose to leave.

Emma watched Roy saunter through the kitchen. She dried her hands on a towel and beckoned him with one

finger. When he was close enough, she hissed, "Are you trying to embarrass our father?"

Roy glared over his shoulder. "What business does Wayne Hochstetler have threatening to send the bishop out here? We aren't members of his church. Why would our bishop care if I ride a snowmobile? I'm not baptized. I've done nothing wrong."

"It is the business of all good men who see others going astray to set the wrongdoer on a better path. Search your heart for *gelassenheit*, Roy."

"I don't want to be humble before Wayne."

"It's not about Wayne. *Gelassenheit* means yielding oneself to a higher authority. It means giving ourselves up to the church. Self-surrender, submission, yielding to the will of God and to others. It brings contentment and a calm spirit to our lives."

"Not to me." He shouldered past Luke, snatched his hat and coat from the pegs by the door, and stormed out.

Luke stepped close to her. "He's having a hard time about something, Emma. He'll come around."

"I hope so."

"I'll talk to him."

He was the last person she should turn to for help. "I'm more afraid of your advice than of leaving him alone."

He flinched slightly, and she was sorry she had been so abrupt. She clasped her hands in front of her and looked down. "Forgive me."

"There's nothing to forgive. Go in and enjoy your visitor."

"What makes you think Roy is having a hard time?" She glanced up to read the concern in his face.

"He mentioned a boy named Micah Yoder, a friend

of his. I got the impression they don't see each other anymore."

"Micah was a member of Wayne's church. He died almost a year ago. It will be exactly a year on Roy's birthday later this month."

"I do remember hearing about it. Some kind of farming accident, wasn't it? It must have been tough on Roy to lose a friend so young."

She gazed into his blue eyes. "It's hard to lose a friend no matter what age we are."

Luke knew Emma was referring to him. "I hurt a lot of people when I left home. I regret that, and I regret that you were one of them."

"It was a long time ago."

It felt like only yesterday. Should he try and make her understand why he left? Or was it best to leave it alone and move forward.

Her father called from the other room, "Emma, could you put on a pot of coffee?"

"Right away, *Daed*," she answered.

"Is Wayne the one?"

Luke thought she would deny it, but she didn't. "I'm considering him. He has a lot going for him."

"Such as?"

"He owns a nice farm. He has a five-year-old daughter who needs a mother. My *daed* and his are close friends. It would make my father happy."

"Will he make you happy?"

"He's reliable, Luke. That's important. He's a good man and a staunch member of the faithful."

"If he's the one, I'm glad. I want you to be happy."

She hardened her heart against his charm and the

way his soft voice pulled at her heartstrings. "I gave you the chance to make me happy once, and you threw it back in my face. You have no say in my life now."

A muscle twitched in his jaw. "You're right. It's none of my business." He walked out the door without another word.

She watched him go and wished he had been more concerned about her happiness when it *was* his business.

Chapter Six

Luke chose to walk to his destination the next morning. It was cold, but the sky was cloudless and the rising sun promised a mild day. His boots crunched through the snow as he crossed the lawn to the edge of the roadway. Yesterday's warm temperatures had caused a minor thaw, but a thick crust had frozen over again during the night. He was almost at the covered bridge when he heard a shout behind him.

"*Onkel* Luke, wait for me."

He stopped and turned around. His six-year-old niece Hannah came hurrying toward him. She was light enough that she ran over the surface of the snow without breaking through. Her ever-present shadow, a yellow Lab named Bella, trotted at her heels.

Luke waited until she was closer. "What's new, buttercup?"

Hannah took his hand and settled into a walk beside him. "We're going to practice our parts for the school Christmas pageant today. I already know my poem by heart. Do you want to hear it?"

"Sure."

Hannah stopped and folded her hands in front of her. In a loud clear voice, she recited her lines. She only stumbled once. When she was finished, she gave him a sad look. "That wasn't very good."

"It was fine. All you need is a little more practice."

"*Onkel* Timothy has been helping me. *Mamm* and *Grossmammi*, too."

Joshua had moved his wife, Mary, and her grandmother, Ada Kauffman, into a small house near the Bowman farm. "Timothy has been helping you? Is he any good at poetry?"

"I think he just comes over for *Grossmammi* Ada's gingerbread cookies."

"That sounds like Timothy."

"He's going to clean out our stable at school and help make the decorations for our program."

"Now that *doesn't* sound like Timothy." They crossed the river using the pedestrian walkway built along the side of the covered bridge. A horse and buggy trotted through on the road. Hannah waved to Jonas Beachy, the bishop, and his wife, Ellie. They both waved back.

Hannah glanced up at Luke. "Are you coming to visit our school?"

"I'm passing by, but I can't stay. I've got to see Jim Morgan and then I'm going to Zachariah Swartzentruber's place."

"I like Alvin Swartzentruber." She covered her mouth with her mittened hands and giggled.

Luke grinned. She was just too cute. "Does Alvin know that?"

She nodded, making the ties of her cap jiggle on her shoulders. "I told him."

"And does he like you?"

Her lower lip stuck out in a pout. "*Nee*, he likes Betty Lapp. She's in the seventh grade."

"I'm sorry."

She wrinkled her nose. "It's okay. Billy Lapp likes me."

"Is he related to Betty?"

"Her little brother. He's in the first grade with me. Our school is going to go caroling on second Christmas."

"Are you? That sounds like fun." Second Christmas, December 26, was a day normally devoted to visiting between Amish families and friends. Caroling was just one way they shared the joy of the season.

"We're going to a nursing home and a hospital. *Aenti* Rebecca and your *mamm* are holding a cookie exchange on December 20. I'm to invite all my friends. You can invite your friends, too. I love Christmas, don't you? Are you coming to our school pageant on Christmas Eve?"

"I wouldn't miss it for anything."

"Alvin is going to sing a solo. He has a beautiful voice, only I'm not supposed to tell him that. Teacher Lillian says he mustn't get a *gross feelich*."

A "big feeling" was another way of saying pride. "I'm sure Alvin knows his singing gift comes from God."

"He does. I'm going to be one of the angels that appear to the shepherds. Teacher Lillian has decided our program will be all about the shepherds and the good news they heard first."

"Sounds like it will be a mighty *goot* program."

"*Onkel* Timothy is coming, too. He likes my teacher." That was news, although Luke wasn't sure his source

was reliable. He'd definitely ask Timothy about it soon. "I don't remember there being so much romance at Rider Hill School when I went there."

"What's romance?"

"Something for you to ask your mother about when you're eighteen."

"Will you be a hundred then?"

He chuckled. "I'm sure it will feel that way."

"Papa Nick and *Mammi* Miriam are coming to visit us. *Mamm* has been missing them something awful on account of she gets sick every morning."

Nick and Miriam Bradley were Hannah's mother's adoptive parents. Luke knew Nick well. He was the sheriff of Holmes County.

"I'm sorry to hear your mother isn't feeling well."

"Do you know when I told *Mammi* Anna about it, she just clapped her hands and laughed. I don't think that was very nice."

"My mother gets excited when she learns…company is coming." Luke chuckled, refusing to be drawn into the conversation on what morning sickness indicated.

By this time, they had reached the one-room schoolhouse set back from the road in a clearing. A young woman was standing on the step with a bell in her hand. Lillian Keim wore the typical Amish *kapp* and a long green dress beneath her coat and apron. Around her, a dozen children of all ages were walking in quietly. Hannah darted away, but stopped and turned to wave. "Bye, *Onkel* Luke."

"Study hard, Hannah."

"I will. Come on Bella. My teacher says Bella is the best scholar she's ever had."

The child and the dog loped toward the building.

Bella would spend the day on the front steps of the school until the children came out for recess. When they went back to class, Bella would wait there until school was out and follow Hannah home. She wouldn't leave without her girl.

Hannah took Bella to her rug and stayed at her side after the others went in. The teacher went inside just as Alvin came tearing down the road. He jumped the split-rail fence at the edge of the school yard and hurried to the door. Hannah hopped up from her place beside Bella and stood squarely in front of him, blocking the doorway.

She smiled brightly. "*Guder mariye*, Alvin."

"Good morning, squirt. Morning, Bella." He stopped to pet the dog.

Hannah smiled shyly. "You sure can jump high. My aunt is having a cookie exchange party, and you're invited," she finished in a rush.

"*Danki*. We better go in. We're gonna be late." He slipped past her.

She sighed and followed him with a look of bliss on her face. Luke smiled. He would definitely have to warn Joshua that she was going to be a heartbreaker. A lot like another young woman who had attended school there. A woman he wouldn't stop thinking about even today. His heart grew light at the thought of seeing her soon, but he had something else to take care of first.

A quarter mile past the school, he turned into the snow-covered drive that led to Jim Morgan's place. Luke heard the engine of the snowmobile. He followed the sound to the pasture where Jim and Brian were unloading bales of hay from a small sled behind the machine and breaking them open for a group of hungry

steers. Luke stayed by the gate until the brothers were finished. He opened it so they could drive through and then he closed it behind them.

"Thanks, Luke." Jim stepped off his machine. Brian stayed on the seat.

Luke gestured toward the snowmobile. "I'm glad to see you got her running."

Jim smiled. "It just took a little love."

"And some new spark plugs," Brian added.

"Which is coming out of your allowance. Are we still on for Friday?" Jim pulled off his gloves.

"That's what I wanted to ask you about." On even months, Luke had to report in with his parole officer at the agency in the city. It was a two-and-a-half-hour trip by car. Too far for a horse and buggy. On odd months, Officer Merlin came to Luke's home to check on his progress.

Jim pulled the pin holding the sled to the back of his snowmobile. When he had it free, he moved the sled to the side. "You don't have to ask. You know I'll always drive you."

"It's a big imposition. I hate to take advantage of you. I can call Sheriff Bradley. He'll take me if you're busy."

"I enjoy the trip."

"Can I go with you this time? I don't have school on Friday. It's in-service day for the teachers." Brian looked hopeful.

Jim considered it and nodded. "Okay. We can get some Christmas shopping done while we're in the city. Now, get going or you'll be late for school."

"Can I take the snowmobile?"

"I guess."

"Great! Thanks, bro." Brian slipped into the driver's

seat and gunned the engine before tearing out of the yard and down the lane.

"He's growing up fast." Luke watched him until he rounded a curve and was lost from sight.

"Just as fast as we did. You're almost finished with your sentence. That has to feel good."

"It does. Two more visits with my parole officer and then I'm a free man."

"This Friday and then when is your last visit?"

"The day before Christmas."

"Is he coming here?"

Luke shook his head. "I'll have to go into the office for my final visit, too." Then the English law said his debt to society had been paid in full. Maybe when that day came, he would be free of the guilt he carried in his heart like a weighty stone.

"What will you do then?"

Luke knew what Jim was asking. Was he going to remain Amish or was he going back into the world. "I don't know. I never really fit in here."

"Yes, you did. You didn't want to believe that, but I could see it. I'm sorry I got you into so much trouble. I didn't have my head on straight after my parents were killed. Doing drugs was stupid, but I couldn't face the responsibility of raising Brian. I tried to party myself into oblivion. I didn't mean to drag you down with me. I never should have offered that stuff to you."

"I made my own choices, Jim. I didn't have my head on straight, either. I got hooked, and you got your act together."

"Do you ever think about using again?"

"Every day. Thankfully, there's not much drug traffic in Bowmans Crossing."

"Luke, if you wanted to use again, you'd find a way, even in Bowmans Crossing. You're stronger than you know."

"Am I? I'm not so sure. How do you stay clean?"

"I think about what I stand to lose. The day we got busted together was the day I saw the light, Luke."

"I remember. We were coming back from a party and we got pulled over for a busted headlight."

"With a pound of marijuana in a backpack on the backseat. Man, I was so stupid."

"We both were."

"You told the cops that the drugs were yours when they were mine so they let me go. I watched them cart you off to jail, and I knew if it had been me, there wouldn't be anyone to take care of my brother. I owe you plenty for that."

It had been Luke's first arrest. He'd spent two nights in jail before his father paid his bail. Jim had helped Luke's father hire a lawyer. The lawyer got Luke released on probation because it was his first offense, but Luke had been too ashamed to go home. Instead, he had Jim take him to the bus station.

"You've more than made up for it these past months." If Luke had someone to love and care for like Jim did with his younger brother, would he be strong enough to withstand temptation, too? Maybe.

"Hope so. I heard Zachariah Swartzentruber might be opening a hardware store. Is that true?"

"It is. I'm helping him get ready. He wants to open the Monday after Christmas."

"This area could use one that doesn't gouge prices like the one the other side of Berlin does, but I'm afraid

I can't see Zachariah successfully running a business. Now, Emma—that would be a different story."

"How so?"

"She knows how to drive a bargain. She buys a side of beef from me every year, and I end up almost giving it to her. Lots of the non-Amish I know get their eggs and vegetables from her. She's well-known for fair dealing. Her dad's well-known for collecting junk."

Luke chuckled. "That he is. Emma always had a good head on her shoulders." Except for the night she tried to run away with him. That night he had been the responsible one—for the first time in his life.

"You and Emma were an item at one time. I see that flame has been rekindled."

"*Nee*, what makes you say that?" He denied it to his friend, but he couldn't deny it to himself.

"The way your eyes light up when you say her name. You can't fool me. I see the signs. Does she feel the same?"

Luke shook his head. "She can barely stand the sight of me."

"Maybe that was the reason she was always asking about you when you were in jail."

"Emma asked about me?" Luke couldn't believe that.

"Every time I stopped in to get eggs, she wanted to know if I had heard from you. If you were doing okay. Three measly letters from you was all I had to share, but she never stopped asking until the day you got out."

"That doesn't make any sense." Why had Emma begged news from Jim and not from Luke's parents? Then the answer occurred to him. She had been ashamed of her relationship with him and didn't want

members of her church to know she had been dating a drug user.

Still, that she had asked about him at all meant she had continued to care about him. She hadn't gone on with her life and forgotten about him as he told her to do.

Did any of those feelings for him remain?

Emma discovered she didn't need to worry about Luke being under foot while he was working for her father. By his second day on the job, he had perfected the art of staying out of her way. Roy was the one who told her Luke would be bringing his lunches and not to plan on feeding him. If her unappetizing meal hadn't driven him from her table, her sharp tongue had. It should have made her happy, but it didn't.

By late afternoon, she couldn't stand it any longer. When she heard a lull in the hammering, she opened the door that led from the porch to the new store.

She paused in surprise. Luke had gotten a lot done. The walls of the store were up and insulation was pressed into the spaces between the studs. A coal stove sat glowing red in the center of the room, its chimney already in place. Sheetrock panels sat at the rear of the room waiting to go up on the ceiling. A large bay window at the front allowed in plenty of natural light and would make the perfect place to showcase the goods her father planned to sell. Maybe some of the gourd birdhouses that Luke painted could hang there. It was truly beginning to look like a store. Maybe this idea of her father's was a good one, after all.

Zachariah looked up from measuring a plank. "Emma, come see what we've gotten done. Luke is a hard taskmaster."

She glanced at Roy. He shook his head. At least her father wasn't being allowed to overdo it. He looked a bit better today. There was a sparkle in his eyes that had been missing for a while.

Luke was strapping on a pair of drywall stilts. He nodded to acknowledge her, but didn't pause. When he was ready, Roy lifted one end of the sheet and Luke grabbed the other. Using crosspieces on long poles, they wedged the sheet into position. Luke secured it with screws using a battery-operated drill. Outside, her father's gasoline generator hummed away as it supplied the electricity for a bank of lights and a battery-charging station.

"What do you think?" her father asked.

She thought Luke's muscular shoulders and arms were showing to advantage as they bulged beneath the fabric of his blue shirt, but she didn't say that. Instead, she turned to her father. "It looks like you're getting a lot done. You are taking it easy, aren't you? You know the doctor said you should."

He scowled at her. "Don't fuss. I'm fine. Luke and Roy aren't letting me lift anything heavier than a pencil."

When Luke finished fastening the sheet, he turned toward her. "Measure twice, cut once. Making sure the measurements are accurate is the most important part of the job, Zachariah. If the walls are as crooked as a dog's hind leg, it will be your fault."

She folded her arms together. "They look straight to me. Can I help?"

Luke lifted the next sheet of drywall. "We're almost done for the day."

Her father patted her shoulder. "Some *kaffi* would be *wunderbar.*"

"I can manage that easy enough." She left the room

feeling better about her father's project. Luke seemed to know what he was doing.

She returned fifteen minutes later with four mugs of coffee on a tray. The warm, pungent aroma mixed with the smell of sawdust and plaster.

"*Danki*, child." Her father took a cup and sat on a sawhorse.

Roy took his and squatted nearby. Luke accepted a cup, walked away to the other side of the room and leaned against the wall still on his stilts. He was making it clear that he could avoid her. It was what she wanted, wasn't it? So why did it hurt to be ignored?

"What's next after this?" Emma surveyed the space.

"I'm not rightly sure." Her father glanced around, seemingly at a loss.

"We'll start building the shelves," Roy said. "Luke suggested we put the counters on casters so we can move them aside and hold church services in here."

"There is plenty of space for that." More space than her living room and kitchen combined. The walls in the downstairs part of the house could be moved back to open the area for services. She usually only had to ready the place once or twice a year. The cleaning and preparation was a major undertaking. Everyone in the congregation took their turn at hosting the meeting so that no one family had the burden.

Her father rose. "Roy, where did I put that box of casters?"

"Beats me, *Daed*."

"I think I put them in the barn, or maybe on the back porch."

Roy took another sip and then put his half-empty mug on Emma's tray. "I'll help you look for them."

The two men went out, leaving Emma waiting in awkward silence for Luke to finish his drink. She wound the ribbon of her *kapp* around her finger and tried to look anywhere but at him.

"You make *goot* coffee."

"Danki." She picked up her mug to give her hands something to do.

"What's your secret?"

She scowled at him. "I don't know what you mean."

"What's your secret to such good coffee?"

Of course he wasn't talking about her father's illness. She relaxed and took a sip. "I buy the expensive brand and I only use spring water. That and I add a teaspoon of sugar to the grounds."

He sat on the sawhorse and unbuckled his stilts. "I knew something was different about yours. *Mamm* makes good coffee but yours is better. I'm not trying to give you a *gross feelich*."

"Nee, you wouldn't want to do that." He would never want to make her feel special because she wasn't special to him.

He laid the stilts aside. "I have an invitation from Hannah. Rebecca and *Mamm* are having a cookie exchange on December 20, and I was told I could invite my friends."

His words triggered a surge of warmth in her midsection. Wouldn't it be nice if they could be friends again?

"Danki, cookie exchanges are always fun. Tell, Hannah, Rebecca and your mother I can make it."

"Goot." He looked around. "What are your father's plans for this place when we get it done?"

The business was a safer subject. "I'm not sure. Will it be ready to open by the week after Christmas?"

"Even if we work night and day, I doubt we'll have it done by then."

"He has dreamed about having a hardware store for years, but until recently, he hasn't found the time to actually open it. He wants a business Roy can grow into."

"I hope it works out for him, and for you. And right on cue, here comes Wayne." He gestured toward the window and she saw Wayne getting out of his buggy. He paused and surveyed the outside of the building.

Luke came toward her and put his mug on her tray. "I'll leave you two alone. I'm sure he hasn't come to see me."

Emma realized with a start that she didn't want to be left alone with Wayne. She started to set the tray aside, but a half-empty mug tipped over and spilled on her white apron. She hissed in displeasure, whipped it off, rolled it into a bundle and tossed it onto a box on the window seat. "There's no need to run away."

Luke glanced at her sharply. "Then I'll start taping the drywall joints. The sooner we get them done, the sooner we can get some paint on the walls. Have you chosen a color?"

Wayne came through the plastic sheet that was covering the doorway. "Good day."

Emma smiled at him. "Good day, Wayne. What can I help you with?"

"I just stopped by to see the progress. After seeing the half-finished shell sitting here for years, it's quite a change to see the walls up."

"I wonder what paint color would look good. What do you think?" she asked.

Wayne glanced around. "Gray or green would look businesslike."

She nodded. "It would have to be a pale gray or a nice mint green to keep the place bright on cloudy days."

"A few well-placed ceiling lights will do that. It's a shame I don't know more about the solar panels your father has. Lighting without the cost of propane or oil would be an advantage," Luke said.

Wayne crossed his arms. "A man only needs the light of the sun to work by. God provides all we need. Such technology is not fitting for us. We must remain apart from the world."

"Using solar power is using God's power grid. Some Amish communities have already embraced it," Luke said.

Wayne scowled deeply at him. "And many have not."

The two men glared at each other. Luke glanced at her, and his face softened. "I should be getting home. It was nice chatting with you, Wayne. Get Emma to fix you a cup of coffee. You'll enjoy it. See you tomorrow, Emma."

She watched him leave and couldn't help comparing the two men. Luke was much better looking, but looks weren't everything. Hadn't she learned that lesson? A handsome face could hide an insincere heart. A steady, reliable, devout man was much more desirable in a mate. If only Wayne's smile set her pulse racing the way Luke's did.

The problem wasn't with Wayne. It was with her.

He took his hat off and swept a hand through his hair. "I hope this isn't a bad time."

"For what?" She resisted the urge to flee the room.

"Your father has made it known that I am welcome to come courting you. I would know your feelings on the subject."

How should she answer him?

Chapter Seven

Emma rearranged the mugs on her platter, playing for time to find the right answer. "Courting is a very serious undertaking, Wayne."

He nodded. "I agree. We have no need to rush into anything."

"I've not met your daughter. I feel that is important before I give you an answer. She may not like me."

"A point well taken, although the child's feelings on the subject will not sway mine."

Emma looked him full in the face. "Her feelings matter."

"Sophie is an obedient child."

Emma glanced away. "I was not suggesting otherwise."

"She will accept you."

"My cousin Rebecca Bowman is hosting a cookie exchange with her mother-in-law at Anna Bowman's home in two weeks. If you agree to it, I will take Sophie with me and we can get to know each other."

"I'm not sure that is a good idea."

That stumped her. "Why not?"

"The Bowmans are not members of my church."

"Neither am I."

"I'm sure Isaac and Anna are good people, but two of their sons have brought shame on the family."

Emma plopped her tray down and fisted her hands on her hips. "And those sons have repented and been forgiven by the family and by their church. Are you holding yourself above their bishop's ruling?"

"*Nee*, but a man must take care that his children are not exposed to worldly things. Luke Bowman is not yet baptized, nor are his brothers Noah and Timothy. I have seen Noah using a cell phone, and I have seen Luke driving a car."

The fact that Luke was still driving shocked her. She struggled not to let it show on her face. "I hope you will trust me not to let your daughter ride in a car with him."

He seemed taken aback by her displeasure. "Of course. If I did not trust you, I would not be considering courting you. You are known to all as a modest and worthy woman."

"I am happy to hear that."

"You may take Sophie to the cookie exchange if you like."

She picked up her tray again. "Please tell your daughter that I'm looking forward to meeting her. Now, I must get over to the school. I promised Lillian Keim that I would help her with the children's costumes for the Christmas play. Good day."

Luke had never been more tempted to listen at the keyhole in his entire life. He wanted to know how serious Emma was about Wayne. How serious Wayne

was about her. Did he love her? Did she love him? The thought brought a sick feeling to Luke's stomach.

Instead of eavesdropping, Luke had forced his feet to head for home. Emma's relationship with Wayne was none of his business.

Telling himself that and actually accepting the fact were two different sides of the same coin. No matter how many times he tried, he couldn't bear the idea of the two of them together. Luke knew Emma would make up her own mind and he had no say in that. Once he might have, but not anymore.

Before long, he approached the school yard. Two new snowmen stood waving their twig arms at passersby. The bright sunshine had melted the snow into perfect snowball-making conditions and it was clear the schoolchildren had taken advantage of it during their recess.

Luke scooped up a handful and packed it into a ball. He took aim at the nearest snowman, imagining it was Wayne and let fly. He missed.

He made a second snowball and tried again. He went wider this time.

Great. He couldn't best an imaginary version of Wayne. How could he hope to best the real man? Certainly not with a snowball.

"You're out of practice."

Luke looked down the road and saw Timothy approaching. Scooping up a handful of snow again, Luke grinned at his brother. "Maybe I'm better with a moving target."

He fired and the snowball splattered against Timothy's dark coat. Feeling vindicated, Luke kept walking toward his brother. He wasn't surprised when Timothy nailed him with a snowball in return. He deserved it.

Dusting the crystals from his coat, Luke waited until Timothy was beside him. His brother brushed at his own coat. "As much as I would enjoy a full-scale war with you, I'm already late for my appointment."

"Your appointment with the pretty schoolteacher?" To Luke's surprise, Timothy blushed. So he did like Teacher Lillian.

"I volunteered to help with the Christmas pageant sets and clean the stable. That's all."

Luke winked at him. "That is very community-minded of you."

"The school can use more help. What are you doing this evening?"

What was he doing? Nothing but moping over Emma's relationship with Wayne. Working with schoolkids wasn't Luke's thing, but he could happily give his brother a hand. "Unless there is work waiting for me at home, I'm free. I could help you."

"Samuel has everything in hand at home."

"*Goot.* What kind of set are we building? Hannah said the program would be about the shepherds."

"I notice you didn't volunteer for stable work."

"You're much more suited to that job. I have an artistic flair."

"I'm not sure what Lillian has planned, but whatever it is, I'll build it for her."

Timothy was the middle brother. Luke and Samuel were older. Joshua and Noah were both younger. Timothy was the easygoing one. He liked helping people. He had a knack for fixing machinery that rivaled Luke's and a winning way with customers. Luke was glad if his little brother had found a woman to make him happy.

The school doors opened and the scholars came walking out. They stayed in orderly two-by-two for-

mations until they reached the bottom of the steps. Then they rushed across the school grounds. Some headed for home on foot while others waited to be picked up by the line of buggies approaching on the roadway. Snowballs began flying almost immediately followed by shrieks and shouts.

Hannah was among the last to come out. Bella got up from her rug, raced down the steps and frolicked beside the child in the snow. A number of children stopped to give her a goodbye pat before heading off. Hannah waved to Timothy and Luke, but walked on with another girl about her own age.

Lillian Keim stood on the top step waiting as Luke and Timothy approached. She kept her gaze down as befit a demure Amish maiden. "I want to thank you again for your offer of help, Timothy. The children deeply appreciate it."

Luke couldn't detect a hint of her feelings about his brother in her manner or her words.

Timothy said, "I hope you don't mind that I have brought Luke to help."

"Not at all. Come in. A few of the eighth-grade children are staying over to help as well."

Luke followed the teacher and Timothy into the building. It was the same school all the Bowman brothers had attended. Inside, it was as if nothing had changed except for the art posters drawn by childish hands that adorned a strip of corkboard above the blackboard. Luke fondly remembered the prize he had won for the best drawing of a horse in the second grade.

The same oversize desk sat on a raised platform at the front. Even the teacher's chair was the same one Luke remembered. He had loosened the wheels on it so that when his teacher sat down it teetered precariously,

scaring the woman half to death. He'd had to write an apology one hundred times on the blackboard while the other kids were outside playing ball. As painful as that was, it paled in comparison to his father's stern punishment that night. He wondered if any of Lillian's scholars had pulled such pranks on her and decided they had. Boys were boys, after all.

The student desks were arranged from smallest to adult-size in rows either side of a wide center aisle. The plain oak planks of the floor were scuffed and scratched, but swept clean, a task assigned to the oldest girls in turn. The tall windows on each side of the single room let in plenty of light. Only the squat black coal stove was missing from its place near the front of the room. He turned to Timothy. "They got rid of that stove after I had to carry a ton of coal in when I was here?"

"The school board decided putting a new propane furnace in the basement was a better investment than buying and storing coal."

It was toasty warm in the building. "I wish they had come to that conclusion before I left school."

He saw Alvin with two other boys standing on one side of the teacher's desk while four young girls stood on the other side. The girls were busy exchanging ideas about the program. The boys were busy trying not to look bored.

Lillian addressed the group. "We are waiting on one more volunteer to get this planning meeting started. I want to thank everyone for staying after to help."

The outside door opened. Luke turned to see Emma rush in. "I'm sorry I'm late."

She came to a dead stop when she caught sight of him.

* * *

What was Luke doing here?

Emma sought Lillian's gaze and arched an eyebrow in query. Lillian shrugged, looking sorry for the situation.

She said, "You aren't late. Now that you are here, we can get started."

Emma pulled off her cape and bonnet, laying them on one of the chairs. Lillian opened a sketchbook on her desk. "We are going to tell the Christmas story from the view of the shepherds tending their flocks."

"We can glue cotton balls to Alvin and make him a sheep," Abram Shetler suggested as he nudged Alvin. He was one of her brother's friends and in the same grade.

The other boy, Jacob Weaver, laughed and said, "Baa, baa."

The girls giggled. Alvin rolled his eyes but didn't say anything.

Lillian gave them a stern look, and they fell silent.

Emma came up to the desk. Luke took a step back, placing Timothy between them. She refused to look his way. "What kind of costumes do you have in mind?"

"Four shepherds, nine angels, Mary, Joseph and the innkeeper. Is that too much?"

Emma shook her head. "I'm sure some of the mothers will help with the sewing."

"What do you want for sets?" Timothy asked.

Lillian tentatively pushed her sketchbook toward him. "I thought of having the children paint two backdrops. One depicting the hills and sheep, and the other depicting the stable and inn in Bethlehem."

He studied her drawing. "You'll need some way to

affix them to the wall and yet allow them to be changed easily." He looked at Luke. "What do you think? You're the artist in the family."

Emma had seen the brightly painted and decorated gourd birdhouses that Luke's mother sold in her gift shop. Luke did indeed have an artist's touch.

He rubbed his jaw as he studied Lillian's drawings. "I'd paint them on canvas and tack the canvas to a free-standing frame. Paper will tear too easily. Have the hills painted on one side, turn the frame around and have Bethlehem on the other side."

Lillian brightened and gave Luke a sweet smile. "That's a wonderful idea. That way, we could start the story at the inn, turn the panel and have the shepherd's part and then turn it back once more to the stable scene. How large could you make it? Could you design it so that it wouldn't tip over easily? Is it too worldly for an Amish school program?"

"I don't think so," Timothy said quickly. "Not if the children paint it. We could make it six feet high and six feet wide. Would that be large enough?"

Luke paced off the platform that held the desk and would serve as the stage for the children. "We've got fifteen feet to work with. Why not make two panels and have the backgrounds be twice as big. That way Bishop Beachy can see it without his eyeglasses."

They all chuckled. The bishop was well-known as a man who was forever leaving his glasses somewhere.

Lillian folded her sketchbook closed. "These are very good suggestions. I hope our production will be one of the best yet. The children and all their families look forward to this each year."

Emma knew that was true. It was the one time of

year when Amish children were encouraged to perform. The programs she had participated in during her school years were among her fondest memories. She glanced at Luke. Did he recall the time he had played Joseph and she had played Mary when they were in the third grade? It had been the beginning of her crush on him. One that had never faded. Even to this day.

With blinding clarity, she knew it was true. He was and always would be her first love. That would never change.

Was she foolish to consider marrying someone else when Luke still held a place in her heart? Would it be fair to ask a husband to live in the shadow of another man?

Luke said he had changed, but she wasn't a naive teenager anymore. She would have to know with absolute certainty that he would remain Amish before she would consider letting him into her heart again. If he had any interest, and she hadn't seen a clear sign of that.

"What do you think, Emma?"

Jerked back to the present by Lillian's question, Emma flushed. "I'm sorry. I was daydreaming."

"I asked if you thought the children could paint such large pictures."

"If someone were to draw the lines and lay out what colors were to be used, I'm sure the children could follow the directions. You might want to give the younger ones the simpler parts to color."

Lillian looked at her girls. "Are you prepared to take this on?"

"*Ja*, Teacher. We can do it," they agreed together.

"Emma, would you be able to supervise them?"

"I'm afraid I'm going to have my hands full with our

store and making costumes." As much as she wanted to help her friend, she knew her limits.

"I'll oversee the painting part of the project," Luke said. "Timothy and the boys can build the frames and make sure they are easy to move but hard to tip over."

Lillian pressed her lips together. Emma knew she was considering if it was proper to allow Luke, an unmarried man, to supervise the young women under her care.

Lillian looked at Emma. "If I can find someone else to make the costumes, will you help Luke and the girls with the painting?"

The young teacher's expression told Emma she was sorry for putting her in an awkward situation but she had little choice. Emma nodded in understanding. The program was important. "I can help paint."

Not only would she have to have Luke at the store every day until it was done, she'd have to see him in the evenings, too.

Lillian smiled wanly. *"Danki."*

Timothy turned to Luke. "Do you think Mary and *Mamm* would help with the costumes?"

Luke shrugged. "Mary likes to sew. We can ask. After all, Hannah told me she is going to be one of the angels, so Mary may already be expecting to make something."

Emma glanced at Luke. He was gazing at her intently. Why? What was he thinking?

"Mamm, what do you know about Wayne Hochstetler?"

Luke stayed behind in the kitchen after supper was finished that evening. His father and his brothers had

all gone into the other room to discuss what would be needed in the business while Isaac and Anna were on vacation. Luke sat staring into the half-empty glass of milk in his hand. He had been given the opportunity to spend time working with Emma. He couldn't deny he liked the idea, but was it too little too late? How could he know?

His mother dried her hands on a towel. "About Wayne Hochstetler? Not much, really. He's a widower. His wife passed away two years ago after a brief illness. He has a five-year-old daughter. His father is the bishop of their district. Why are you interested?"

"I ran into Wayne at Zachariah's again today."

"Wayne's father and Zachariah are neighbors, and they've always been close friends, although they belong to different church districts."

"I had the feeling he was there to see Emma."

"Really? I guess that's not surprising. She would make a good wife and a good mother for his daughter. She has had plenty of practice raising those brothers of hers."

"You think it would be a good match?"

"I couldn't say one way or the other. The important thing is if the *couple* believes it's a good match. It takes a lot of prayer to decide on a spouse. They must be sure it is the path chosen by God for them. Why this interest in Wayne?"

"No reason." He rolled the glass between his hands.

His mother chuckled. "Let me rephrase my question. Why this sudden interest in Emma's courtship?"

"I don't know that she is being courted." He propped his elbows on the table.

"I always thought you two would make a match of it."

He shook his head. "Emma is too good for me."

"So you are looking for a floozy."

He started laughing. "Do you even know what a floozy is?"

"A woman with a poor reputation that is well deserved. I was not born yesterday."

"And how many floozies do you know?"

"I shall leave you to wonder about that. Emma is not too good for you. You're mistaken about that. You have a kind heart, Luke, but you won't give up your crutch."

"What crutch is that?" He knew the answer but wondered if his mother did.

"Your guilt. You wield it like a club to beat away the goodness of others and to keep happiness from your door."

He thought his crutch was the drugs. He hadn't considered it was the guilt he carried. "I've done some bad things. Things I'm too ashamed to share with you or anyone."

"When you are baptized, Luke, every sin will be forgiven, even the ones I do not know about, for God *knows* all things and *forgives* all things if you allow Him. There is nothing you can keep hidden from our Lord. You would be surprised by the things you have not kept hidden from me. You cannot atone for your sins by denying yourself a chance to love and be loved by someone."

"So how do I atone for my sins?"

"Our Savior laid down His life on the cross for your sins, Luke. Why don't you think that is enough? Salvation is His gift to you. He asks only that you love Him and obey His commandments."

"How is it that I have such a wise mother?"

She smiled and winked at him. "Another gift from God. Cherish your gifts, Luke, and leave your mistakes in the past where they belong."

"I don't know if I can."

She reached out and knocked his glass over, sending milk spreading across the tabletop. "Put the milk back in your glass, Luke."

He backed away from the table to keep the milk from dripping in his lap. "*Mamm*, you know I can't do that."

She fisted her hands on her hips and glared at him. "*Nee*, you cannot. You can sit and moan about your empty glass or you can pour yourself another. What's done can't be undone, so stop complaining about it."

"Are you angry with me?"

"I am. You are wasting the gifts God has given you. Now get out of the kitchen so I can finish my dishes. If you want another glass of milk, get it yourself. If you want to go out with Emma, ask her. There's no guarantee you won't make a mess again, but at least you'll be going forward instead of sitting here crying over spilled milk."

"Asking Emma out isn't that easy."

"How do you know? Have you tried it?"

He raised both eyebrows. "Of course not. I told you I think Wayne may be courting her."

"But you don't know for sure."

The outside door opened. Samuel and Rebecca came in with their arms loaded with greenery. Rebecca's cheeks were rosy and flushed. "We've brought some pine boughs to decorate the window ledges and mantel. I love their fragrance at the holidays."

"I love the taste of sweets at the holidays." Samuel had a smug smile on his face that told Luke he'd been

kissing his wife on their outing. She gave him a saucy grin as they went into the living room.

Luke's mother folded her arms and chuckled. "What you need is a go-between to discover Emma's feelings. I know just who to ask. Shall I?"

Chapter Eight

Luke mulled over his mother's words as he finished the rest of the drywall in Zachariah's shop the next morning. Maybe *Mamm* was right. Maybe he should give his relationship with Emma another try. The trouble was, he had no idea if she was in love with Wayne or not. The last thing he wanted was to jeopardize her future happiness.

An Amish fellow could ask a girl's friends, or a family member like her brother, if she would be willing to walk out with him. Luke couldn't imagine asking Roy, but his mother's idea about asking Rebecca to be his go-between wasn't a bad idea.

He hadn't spoken to his sister-in-law when he had the chance last night. He needed to work up to that conversation. Maybe after supper tonight if he could get her aside without Samuel knowing about it. Luke didn't relish the thought of all the brotherly ribbing he would get if any of his brothers found out he was asking Rebecca to be his go-between.

"Will you be eating lunch with us today?" Emma asked from behind him. He hadn't heard her come in.

He spun around and a glop of drywall mud flew off his trowel. It landed on her black shoe. He stared at it in speechless shock.

This was not a good start.

He raised his eyes to her face. She was glaring at him, but there was a slight twitch at the corner of her mouth. "A simple no would suffice. If my cooking is that bad, just say so."

"It's not that. I'm sorry. Let me get something." He turned around looking for a rag, anything to clean her shoe. He spied a bundle of cloth on the window seat, snatched it up and began to wipe the mess off her foot. When he had most of it rubbed off, he stood with a sheepish grin. "There."

She held out her hand. "May I have my apron back now?"

"Your what?" He glanced at the gray-plaster-loaded cloth in his hand.

"My apron. I took it off in here yesterday and I was looking for it."

He held it out. "I'm sorry about that."

She took it between two fingers. "It will wash. As will my shoe. Are you eating with us today?"

"Am I restricted to bread and water?"

"If you don't make another mess, you might get a little gravy on your bread crumbs."

"*Danki.* I'll join you for the meal."

She glanced around. "*Goot.* Where is my father?"

"He's sorting through boxes in the barn, trying to see what we can sell. I think he hates to part with any of it."

"I know he wants this business for Roy. Is there any hope that it won't become a money pit?"

He shrugged. "*Daed* and Samuel have the business

sense in the family. I break things and sometimes fix things. You can ask for their suggestions."

She bristled slightly. "I'm sure we'll manage."

He gestured with his trowel. "I'm sure you will. I need to get this mud on the walls before it dries."

"Lunch will be in half an hour."

"I appreciate it, and you're a *goot* cook. Has Wayne sampled your cherry cobbler?"

"I haven't cooked anything for him."

That was promising. "Your cherry cobbler and your gooseberry tarts, those were my favorites. Along with meat loaf and boiled turnips, of course."

She flushed a dull red. "I'll have to remember that."

He chuckled as she spun around and left the room. He liked that he had flustered her. It meant she wasn't indifferent to him. He went back to work and began whistling a cheery Christmas tune. If she wasn't indifferent to him, he might have a chance. *If* he proceeded carefully.

Emma dropped her dirty apron in the sink and turned on the water to let it soak. She pulled a rag from a bottom drawer and moistened it beneath the faucet. Sitting down on a kitchen chair, she pulled off her shoe and chuckled. Luke's shocked expression was the funniest thing she had seen all week.

She sobered. He used to make her laugh all the time. His outrageous antics had horrified the elders in their church, but she knew he was just trying to get a rise out of people. Their teacher had called it attention-seeking behavior, and looking back, Emma saw the woman had been right.

But somewhere along the way, his pranks had turned

from playful to serious and ultimately ruinous for him. And for her. As much as she wanted to believe he was a changed man, she just couldn't. She finished cleaning her shoe, put it on and went back to work. Her days of mooning over Luke Bowman were long gone. She had a house to run, and soon she would have a business to run, too.

The thought brought her up short. If the business became even modestly successful, why would she have to marry to care for her brothers? Why couldn't she and Roy manage it together? She didn't know much about running a business, but she could learn. It might be a far-fetched plan considering the store wasn't even open, but it had definite appeal.

When the men came in to eat lunch, she had it all on the table for them. After silent prayer, she waited to speak until everyone had their food. "Have you enough items to get the store started, Papa, or will you need to buy more?"

"I don't know."

"Some of his things are so old, I doubt we'll be able to give them away." Roy helped himself to another biscuit.

"What kind of old things?" Emma passed him the jam she knew he liked.

"Sewing machines and old coal stoves."

"I wasn't picky about the junk I hauled home." Her father looked tired today. There was a droop to his shoulders and his cheeks were pale.

"The *Englisch* have a love of antiques. You could call it a hardware and antiques market. That might bring in more customers," Luke suggested.

"*Nee*, it will be Swartzentruber and Sons Hardware

Store. Nuts and bolts and shoes for the horses. Things my Amish neighbors can use."

Emma folded her hands and rested her elbows on the table. "I think Luke is right. I don't think you should limit yourself to just the Amish."

"We shall see how it goes. I want it to be ready by Christmas. How much still has to be done inside, Luke?"

"The mud needs to dry overnight. It really should cure for two days in this weather. After that, sanding and priming and then paint. A week should see it done. I'd say another two weeks to put in the shelves and counters and a week to stock and price things."

"That is too long. We must get it done sooner."

"Papa, what will it hurt to open a little later?" she asked gently. He was getting too upset.

Her father glared at her. "The longer it takes the less money we make."

"Have you given a thought to using solar power in your store?"

Emma gave Luke a grateful glance for his quick change of subject. "Why solar?"

Her father stroked his chin. "I've not given any thought to it. How would it benefit us?"

"I could charge my cell phone," Roy said with a grin.

Emma scowled at him and he resumed eating. "Other than the phone my brother is not supposed to have, why would we want to incur the expense of putting in solar?"

"You already own the panels. You'd only need someone to install them, so it would be almost free power for charging batteries and lighting for the store. The bishop approved the use of electricity in my father's wood-

working shop. We use a diesel generator." He began eating again.

Her father smiled. "This might be a good idea, Luke. The bishop would have to approve my use of electricity as well. Since we can't paint tomorrow, I will go see him. You must come with me. You are familiar with this technology."

Luke paused with his fork halfway to his mouth. "I can't go with you tomorrow."

Her father's scowl returned. "Why not?"

Emma saw a guarded look settle over Luke's expression. "I have another appointment."

"He has to see his parole officer," Roy said.

Luke slowly lowered his fork to his plate as a deep red flush crept up his cheeks. "That's right."

"I thought that bad business was behind you." Emma hadn't forgotten about the time he served in prison, but he had been home for over a year.

"I received an early release, but I'm on parole until I've served my entire sentence. I have to meet with my parole officer once a month until then."

"What happens if you don't?" Emma asked.

Luke stared at his plate, not meeting her gaze. "If I violate the terms of my parole, I can be sent back to prison to finish serving my time there plus whatever additional time they decide to tack on for my failure to follow the rules."

He pushed away from the table. "Zachariah, I'll start putting together some of those shelves. I can paint them while I'm waiting on the mud to dry."

He left the room with a good portion of his meal still on his plate. Emma turned to Roy. "How did you know about Luke's parole meeting?"

"Luke talked about being in prison the other day. I saw Brian Morgan yesterday, and he mentioned he was going into the city with Jim and Luke on Friday. I asked if it was for Luke's parole meeting. Brian looked surprised and said he wasn't supposed to talk about it, but I told him I already knew."

"You were gossiping about Luke? I'm ashamed of you."

"It's not gossip if it's true, and Brian already knew, anyway."

"Father, did you know about this?"

"*Nee*, I did not, but I don't see what difference it makes. The *Englisch* law is none of our business."

It shouldn't make a difference, but it did. It was a harsh reminder that Luke had been more than a wild and unreliable youth. He had fallen far from his faith and turned a deaf ear to the pleas of his family to reconcile until he had been released from prison. He claimed he had changed. It seemed as if he had, but how could she be sure?

Then she realized that she couldn't. She had to accept Luke's word.

This was a test of her faith. Could she live her beliefs?

Recalling the look of shame on Luke's face brought shame to her, too. He didn't deserve to have his past mistakes displayed before all of them. "Roy, you must never mention this again, not even to Alvin. What is forgiven is over. It should never be spoken about. Do you understand?"

"I guess." He shifted uncomfortably in his seat.

She rose from the table. "I will apologize for you.

Luke needs to know we will not hold his past against him. It is wrong to do so."

Roy held up his hands. "I don't hold it against him."

"Nor do I," her father stated.

"Then I alone have been guilty of that sin. Clear the table for me, please, Roy. I'll be back shortly."

Luke hammered in the nail with much more force than necessary. Each beat of the hammer shouted, *Fool! Fool! Fool!*

He'd seen the shock on Emma's face. Now that she knew he was still on parole, she would have even less to do with him. Like the rest of the community, she had assumed his past was behind him. Now it stood like a wall between them because he'd lacked the courage to tell her about it. He had lied by omission. Any trust that had developed between them was surely gone.

He pulled a second board in place and drove in another nail with such force that it split the wood. He pried out the nail and threw the piece aside in disgust.

"Luke, may I speak with you?"

The sound of her soft voice behind him brought him up short. He didn't look at her. "I should have told your father about my parole when he offered me the job. I'm sorry. I'll have Joshua come and help you finish."

"You've been doing a fine job for us."

"Good to know."

"Luke, I'm sorry."

He glanced at her then. "Why should you be sorry? I'm the one who made a mistake. Many mistakes."

"It was Roy who made a mistake by repeating what you had told him. In his defense, he admires you greatly

and wants to learn everything he can about you. I'm afraid he has a bad case of hero worship."

"And we both know I'm no hero, don't we?"

She didn't agree, but she was quiet for a long moment. Finally, she said, "You don't have to send Joshua to work in your place. I wouldn't be true to our faith if I turned you away because you weren't forthcoming about your parole. We forgive. We treat every man as a child of God. No man is sinless. We must not judge others lest we be judged ourselves."

A lump pushed up in his throat. "I don't deserve your kindness."

"Every man deserves kindness. I'm sorry you were embarrassed."

"I'm sorry I wasn't more honest."

"This parole thing you must do, is it the reason you have remained here?"

"*Ja.* Living at home and working in the family business is a condition of my parole. I could petition to move or get another job, but my parole officer would have to okay it."

"I see."

He picked up another board. "My sentence will be finished in a few weeks. After that, I'll be free to go anywhere, work anywhere, although jobs are scarce for ex-cons."

She folded her arms tightly across her middle. "So you will be leaving, then."

Hearing what he hoped was disappointment in her tone, he put down the board and walked up to her, stopping less than a foot away. "What would you have me do?"

She stared at her feet. "It isn't up to me."

"I know, but I'm asking. What would you like me to do? Stay, or go?"

She bit her lower lip. He wanted to kiss it. "You would make your family happy if you stayed among us."

He was putting her on the spot and that wasn't right. He stepped back and crossed to the stack of lumber to select a straight board. "*Ja*, it would make them happy if I stayed."

"That is important, but it is more important to seek God's will, Luke, not your own."

"Right. I'll tell Lillian about my situation and let her decide if she still wants me to help at the school."

"She will."

"How can you be so sure?"

"Because she is a woman of our faith. She lives it, as I try to do."

"Some of the parents may not feel the same. I wouldn't want to cause a problem for her."

It surprised and pleased Emma that he would put Lillian's concerns before his own. "If you feel you must tell her, I understand, but what you have told us doesn't need to leave this farm. I have told Roy that he is never to speak of it again."

Luke gazed at her with a soft light in his eyes. "I appreciate that, Emma. I do, but I'll tell Lillian tonight. What about you? I don't want to risk your reputation by working here."

"My father and my brothers are adequate chaperones. Don't worry about me."

He *was* worried about her—she could see it on his face—and some of the ice in her heart melted away. He must care about her a little.

Uncomfortable with the closeness that seemed to be pulling them together, she moved to where a shaft of sunlight from the open hayloft door highlighted a tarp covering something leaning against the barn wall. "What is this?"

"The solar panels I mentioned."

She lifted the tarp edge. The blue reflective surface and shiny aluminum frame glinted in the sunlight. "Will we be able to sell these if we can't use them?"

"Sure, but I'm really hoping we can use them. The English expect good lighting when they are shopping. Your father has a key cutter that could be run by solar electricity instead of your generator. You will need a cash register, too, and that takes electricity. If you have several battery-charging stations, folks could bring their car and marine batteries here, and you could expect a small fee for them to use it. Roy could recharge his cell phone at home instead of paying someone else."

Emma touched the gleaming surface and received an unpleasant jolt. The thing was dangerous. She dropped the tarp back in place and glanced at Luke sharply. "I told my brother to give his phone away."

"There's nothing wrong with him owning one."

"I hate how much he enjoys using worldly things. He wants a car. Father will never permit it."

"I had one when I wasn't much older than he is. I kept it at Jim Morgan's place so my folks wouldn't find out."

"I remember."

"You never would come for a ride with me."

"You forget, I watched you learning to drive. I saw you plow through the fence and drive across Jim's garden. It seems safer not to get in the car with you."

He laughed out loud. "That was my first day. I got better."

"You were so determined to learn."

"It was a skill I knew I would need when I left."

There it was again, the reminder that he never intended to stay in Bowmans Crossing. "Did you get your license?"

"Yup, for all the good it did me."

"What happened to your car?"

"I had Jim sell it and give the money to my parents when I was locked up. I knew they could use it."

"Someone recently saw you driving."

"I've done so once in a while. Jim Morgan has let me drive his Jeep for old times' sake. I hate to lose a skill I've learned, but it isn't something I plan to keep doing."

"Life rarely works out as we plan." She was walking proof of that. "That is why we must accept the will of God and let Him lead us."

"Why haven't you married, Emma?"

His personal question sent a rush a heat to her face. She stifled the urge to tell him it was none of his business. For some reason, she wanted him to understand. "The time never seemed right. My mother became ill and died suddenly not long after you were gone. Alvin and Roy were young and still needed me. My father was lost without *Mamm*. He needed me, too. I didn't have time for courting. After a while, the young men around here stopped asking."

"I've wondered about it. I couldn't see you spending your life alone. Not you. You are so full of life and light. My mother wrote to me every week, and I watched for news of you."

His tender words brought the sting of tears to her

eyes. At least he had spared a thought or two for her after he left. She pulled the tattered remains of her hopes and dreams around her heart to shield it from the pain of wanting him to care. She couldn't let him see the power he still held over her.

"If you thought I was pining away for you, you were sadly mistaken. The best thing you ever did for me was leave without me."

He stepped closer to gaze into her eyes. "You don't know how many nights I prayed that was true. I'm glad to know I was right."

He was telling the truth. He believed he had done the right thing. Stunned by his revelation, Emma looked away.

"I have work to do." She left the hayloft and returned to the house. She took one look at the pile of dishes in the sink and ran upstairs to her room, slammed the door, fell on to her bed and cried her eyes out with her face buried in her pillow so no one could hear.

Chapter Nine

An hour later, Emma washed the last trace of tears from her face and went downstairs. She made short work of the dishes, put a chicken in to roast for supper and changed into her good dress. She wanted to be at the school when Luke spoke with Lillian. She would be there to support him no matter how painful it was. If he was to remain in their community, he had to see he would be accepted in spite of his flawed past.

And she did want him to remain. Up until now, she wouldn't have been able to admit that. Even to herself. Luke believed he had done the right thing leaving her behind. She still didn't know why, but it hadn't been because he didn't care. All these years she thought she had failed somehow. That she wasn't good enough, pretty enough or smart enough to be loved by him. Her greatest fear had been that he never really cared about her. That leaving her had been easy.

She walked through the door into the store. Two tall shelves, painted a bright white, were lined up down the center of the room. Luke was putting away his tools. She watched him for several minutes.

He wasn't the same man who had left so long ago. He was older. His face had the start of crow's feet and brow lines that hadn't been there when she first fell in love with him. She wasn't the same, either. She was quite familiar with her appearance. The mirror didn't lie. Crow's feet touched her temples, too. Her skin wasn't as fresh. Her eyes showed her worry.

It was time to stop acting like the child she had been. It was time to stop hiding behind the hurt. "Are you ready to go to school?"

"I am." As he approached, his eyes narrowed. He studied her face. "Are you all right?"

She wasn't about to admit she had been crying over him. "I have a small headache. It's nothing. The fresh air will cure it in no time."

"Should we take your buggy so you don't have to walk so far?"

"A brisk walk is exactly what I need. We should hurry. We don't want to keep the children later than we have to."

He nodded and held open the door for her. She slipped past him and started down the lane.

Falling into step beside her, he remained silent for the first half mile. "Are you better? I can go back and get the buggy."

"Stop fussing, Luke. There are worse things in life than a little headache."

"Do you always help with the school Christmas program?"

"Every year. Lillian sometimes has trouble getting volunteers. She doesn't like to add to the workload of the children's parents, so she won't press them for additional help. I think she would find more people would

step up if she had the bishop or the school board ask for volunteers. As it is, people see that the same few folk do the work every year and they don't feel there is a real need for them to do more."

"That's just human nature, I guess."

She glanced at him. "Why did you volunteer to help?"

"Timothy asked me, and I had nothing better to do."

That wasn't the answer she was hoping for. She wanted to hear him say he was eager to help his community, or the children, or to spread Christmas cheer.

Or spend more time with me.

Had he known that she would be helping? Or was it simply a coincidence? Maybe it was something more. Maybe he was interested in impressing Lillian. Her friend was single and pretty. A tiny stab of jealousy hit Emma. She quickly subdued it. Lillian was a wonderful caring person. If she had caught Luke's eye, Emma could understand that.

She tried to gauge his interest in her friend. "Lillian is a wonderful teacher."

"Hannah likes her a lot." Luke leaned a little closer. "So does my brother Timothy."

Emma couldn't suppress the bubble of happiness that rose at his words. "I wondered about that. Timothy volunteering when he doesn't have a child in school has created some talk about the two of them."

"Is that a good thing, or a bad thing?"

"Honestly, it's just human nature."

"You know her pretty well. Do you think she would be interested in walking out with Timothy?"

Emma shot him a coy glance. "Are you his go-between?"

"Not officially. In fact, he hasn't said anything to me. Because you're her friend, I'm just trying to get a jump on the issue in case she has some objections or she is interested in someone else."

"There isn't anyone else, but you might warn Timothy that he may be facing an uphill battle."

"What makes you say that?"

"I have heard Lillian say that her desire is to remain single and to keep teaching school."

"That doesn't sound promising for my brother. I'll let him know."

She gave him a pleading look. "After Christmas?"

He chuckled. "All right. After Christmas."

Emma's heart lightened at the sound of his laughter. To her surprise, she found it made her happy to see him smiling. Perhaps they could be friends again. They weren't teenagers in the throes of first love anymore. That part of their relationship had been horribly painful, but it had been over years ago. If she truly forgave him, she had to let it go.

The school came into sight and he paused at the edge of the fence. "I want to thank you for doing this, Emma."

"For doing what?"

"For being my moral support. Maybe that wasn't your intention for coming with me, but having you here makes it easier."

"Then I'm glad I came."

"How is your headache?"

She pressed a hand to her temple. "It's completely gone."

"I reckon a walk in the fresh air was exactly what you needed, then."

He bent over, scooped up some snow and packed it into a ball. She watched in amusement as he took aim at the hapless snowman in the school yard. After a pitcher's windup, he let fly and knocked the tattered straw hat from atop his target. "Take that. Now who's going to step aside?"

Puzzled, she looked at him for an explanation. "What do you mean by that?"

"It's a little personal business between me and Frosty. Never mind. Shall we go in?"

"Only if you put the poor thing's hat back on and apologize. Violence never solves anything."

Laughing, Luke replaced the snowman's hat and brushed the loose snow off the scarf around his neck. "I'm sorry, sir, it will never happen again. You may melt into a puddle of slush at your leisure."

Emma walked past him, shaking her head. "I'm not sure that was an actual apology."

"Under the circumstances, it's all he's going to get."

Luke's good humor dried up when he walked into the building. Timothy was already building one of the frames he had promised. He and the three oldest boys had covered it with a piece of white canvas and began cutting it to size. They would staple it in place after the painting was finished. Lillian and the eighth-grade girls were testing paint colors on small strips of paper.

Luke glanced at Emma. She smiled and nodded encouragement. He walked across the room to the teacher's desk. "Lillian, I wonder if I might speak with you privately for a moment?"

Her eyebrows rose slightly. "Privately?"

Timothy scowled in his direction. Luke realized how

bad that had sounded. A single fellow asking the teacher to step out with him alone in front of her students. "I meant that Emma and I would like to speak with you privately."

Lillian relaxed and turned to the girls watching her with interest. "I think the medium brown will work best for the walls of the inn and the stable. Try mixing a little white with the green paint we have to achieve a nice grass color. I'll be back in a few minutes."

She motioned for Luke and Emma to follow her outside, stopping to grab her coat by the back door. On the small stoop at the back of the school, she crossed her arms and waited.

Luke cleared his throat. "I should have told you this before I volunteered to work on your program. I'm sure you heard that I was in prison on drug charges."

"*Ja,* I have heard this."

"Most people think because I'm at home with my folks that I served my time and I'm free. That's not true. I'm still on parole. I'm still serving my sentence, although I get to do it in this community. I have rules I must follow or I can be taken back to prison. I understand if you feel I don't belong here with the *kinder.*"

"Are you a danger to them?"

"I'm not. I promise you that. I like kids."

"I don't see that you are any different today than you were when you first offered to help us."

"Are you sure?"

"Completely."

"*Danki.*" Relief sent his breath out in a whoosh.

Lillian glanced between Luke and Emma. "Can we get back to work now, or is there something else?"

Emma smiled brightly. "Nope, that's all."

"*Goot*. We have a lot to get done and not many days left to do it. Emma, would you see if there is more paint in the back of my buggy? I'm not sure the children brought it all in."

"Of course."

The second she was out of sight, Lillian rounded on Luke. "If you hurt her again, you will regret coming back here."

He knew what she was talking about and didn't deny it. "It's not my intention to hurt Emma. Ever."

"See that you don't."

Emma reappeared a few seconds later. "There's no paint in the buggy."

Lillian's smile was only for her friend. "Then we have it all. *Danki*."

Luke followed the women inside and joined his brother. He smiled and winked at Timothy to let him know everything was okay. Timothy shrugged and went back to work.

After transferring Lillian's scene designs to the backdrops with a felt marker, Luke showed the girls how to use slightly darker or lighter shades of the same color to produce shadows and depth to their artwork. Emma had a steady hand and was able to draw the outlines of the many sheep dotting the hills.

When the girls were all busy, he left them and joined Timothy and the boys working on the second frame. Before long, he and the boys were all laughing over stories he and Timothy shared about building projects from their school days. Some of which had gone very wrong.

Lillian called a halt to the work and sent the children home before it grew dark. Timothy and Luke waited until Lillian and Emma were ready to leave, then they

followed the women outside. At the road, the women walked up the road together. Luke waited and was rewarded with the sight of Emma looking back at him. He raised a hand, but she didn't wave. Still, he knew their relationship had taken a new turn.

"What are you grinning about?" Timothy asked and started walking toward home.

"Nothing." Luke pushed his hands in the pockets of his coat. The sun was just touching the horizon. Bands of low clouds were glowing with gold and pink colors that reflected off the snow in the fields, giving them pink hues as well.

"So what was your short personal conversation with Lillian about? I hope you didn't mention my name."

"Roy spilled the beans about my parole to Emma and her father. They were shocked, but Emma said it didn't matter. I was afraid it might matter to Lillian so I offered to step aside and let someone else help with the Christmas program."

"What did she say?"

"That I was the same person who offered to help. My situation didn't matter."

"I thought that's what she would say."

Luke glanced at him. "You like her a lot, don't you?"

Timothy's expression softened. "I do."

Luke didn't want to destroy his brother's hopes, but he felt he had to warn him not to get them too high. "Lillian likes being a teacher. If she were to wed, she would have to give that up."

"I'm not in a hurry to change things for her. We're friends. I just like being around her. Time will tell if we are meant to be together."

"I know what you mean," Luke said, thinking of

Emma. He liked being near her, too. It was enough for now. He wouldn't push for more. Not yet.

"You mentioned Zachariah has some solar panels he might use or sell. I spoke with a friend from over near Berlin. His father makes furniture, but he also has a booming solar business sideline. I thought Zachariah might want to talk to him about it. Solar is gaining popularity, and a lot of Amish businesses are going to it because the lighting is safer than gas or kerosene and it's sure cheaper than running a diesel generator all day."

Luke looked at his younger brother with a newfound respect. "*Danki.* I'll tell him that. I didn't know you were interested in new technology."

"I'm not looking to run a television or a game console, but whatever we can do to make our business more profitable interests me. We employ six young men from the area now. Each one we hire means one less family has to move away to find work."

"You sound like Samuel."

"That's a nice compliment."

"How have you learned so much?"

"I like to read. If Zachariah decides he wants to use solar in his hardware store, he's going to have to get permission from the bishop first. I don't imagine everyone will be in favor of it. He should talk to the bishop on Sunday after the church service."

Luke sent Timothy a sidelong glance. "Doesn't it annoy you that we have to ask permission before making a change to our businesses?"

"*Nee.* Well, maybe just a little. But our ministers know that they must consider more than what benefits one family. Will this technology maintain our separation from the world? What impact will it have on our

entire community? I tend to see the small picture. I'm glad there are prudent men who look at the big picture."

When had his younger brother developed into such a smart fellow? Luke admitted he was guilty of looking at the smallest picture. The one with only himself in the center. Maybe helping Emma and Zachariah with their business and the school with the Christmas program was letting him expand his view.

If Emma saw he wasn't the selfish fellow he'd once been, would it improve his chances with her, or would she still see Wayne as the better man?

She hated to admit it, but Emma missed having Luke around on Friday. Her father couldn't seem to settle on any task and very little got done in the store. It was only thanks to her nagging that she managed to get Roy to finish sanding one wall. The cans of primer and paint were never opened.

She was frosting a cake for supper when Alvin came in with the mail. "That looks yummy, Emma. I don't reckon I could have a slice now, could I? I'm mighty hungry."

She handed him the spatula loaded with frosting. "See if this will take the edge off your appetite. Does Lillian need me to come to the school this evening?"

He laid the mail aside and took the spatula from her, cleaning it with two licks. "*Nee*, tonight is the school board meeting so she wanted me to tell you to stay home."

"I expected as much. Go find your father and your brother, and tell them supper will be ready in five minutes."

"Is Luke here? Can he stay for supper?"

She shook her head. "He didn't come today."

"Is he coming tomorrow? I haven't had a chance to work with him here yet. He's loads of fun. He can sure tell some funny stories. Did you know that he and his brother Timothy nailed their teacher shut in the outhouse?"

Emma chuckled. "I remember that day very well. Luke was always getting into trouble." Sadly, while Luke was the instigator of some funny pranks, he often got his hapless followers in trouble, too.

After supper was finished and the dishes were done, Emma sat down in her chair in the living room to read the circle letter she had received from her mother's cousins in Pennsylvania. It was always fun to see what their faraway family was up to. She took out her old letter to them and set it aside. She would add her news and send the letters on to the next cousin until they got all the way around the family and back to the start. She read a particularly cute story about her cousin Millie's new baby and looked up to share it with her father. He was sitting in his recliner with a grim look on his face as he read his mail. "*Daed*, what's wrong?"

"It's a letter from my brother William. His wife passed away."

"*Aenti* Laura? How awful. Was she sick? They never mentioned as much."

"She had a stroke and died the next day. Her funeral will be on Tuesday."

"Are you going?"

"I don't see how I can. We don't have the money for that."

"You have been wanting to see your siblings. The boys and I can manage here."

"We can," Roy assured him.

She watched her father struggle with his decision. "I do want to see my brothers and my sister before…"

He didn't say *before it was too late*, but she knew that was what he meant. "Then go. Take our prayers with you and spend some time in Missouri."

She rose from her chair. "I'm going to go to the phone shack and make arrangements for a driver for you."

He laid the letter aside. "We can't afford to pay a driver for that long of a trip."

"We have enough money in the bank to cover this."

"As much as I want to go, I don't think I should. That money is for your dowry."

"Arthur Yoder came by the other day and asked if he could buy the old corn binder. You weren't here so I told him to come back later. He offered a good price. That will cover the cost of the trip, and I'll put the money back in the bank as soon as he pays me."

"*Nee*, the money from the farm equipment will go for your dowry. We decided this."

"I insist, Papa. You know you need to do this. I'll go make the call. You start packing."

"How will we get the store finished if I leave?"

She sighed in exasperation. "It can wait." Why was he being so stubborn?

"It can't. I have sent notices to the papers telling folks we'll be open for business the Monday after Christmas."

"Papa, why would you do that? We aren't ready." He could be the most irritating man.

"Because I wanted us to be ready."

Roy laid aside his magazine and came to stand at his father's side. "Luke and I can get it done. Don't worry."

In order to do that, Luke would have to come over

more than a couple of days a week. Would he do it if she asked?

"Roy is right," Emma agreed. Luke and Roy would get more done without her father underfoot. She would help, too. She knew how to wield a paintbrush and she could learn to price merchandise on shelves.

"Very well. You are right, Emma. I do need to go. This could well be my last chance to see them."

Alvin, sitting across the room, cocked his head to the side. "Why would it be your last chance, *Daed*?"

Her father cast a stricken glance in her direction. She forced a stiff smile to her lips and looked at her baby brother. "You father's brothers and sister are all older than he is. Who knows how long they will be with us."

"*Ja*, that is right." Her father nodded vigorously. "Roy, Alvin, your sister will be in charge. You must do as she says."

"But I'm the man of the house when you're gone. I should be in charge. I'm not in school anymore." Roy's eyes held a mutinous gleam.

"I'm older than you, so don't argue with your father about this." She brushed aside his hurt pride. She would deal with it later. For now, she had to get her dying father to his family in Jamesport, Missouri, as quickly and easily as possible and without alerting her brothers to what was wrong with their father.

Chapter Ten

Saturday morning dawned bitterly cold. Fresh snow was falling as Luke drove his buggy into Zachariah's yard. A white car sat in the driveway with the motor running. As he got down from his buggy, Luke saw the door to the house open. Zachariah and an English fellow Luke didn't know came out carrying a set of luggage. The driver put them in the trunk and opened the car door.

Zachariah spoke to him briefly and then approached Luke. "I was hoping to see you before I left."

"Where are you off to?"

"My sister-in-law has passed away. I'm going to her funeral in Missouri."

"I'm so sorry to hear this. You have my condolences." Luke looked over Zachariah's shoulder. "Are your children going with you?"

Zachariah shook his head. "I am going alone. Emma and Roy are needed here to get the store open on time. I know I asked you to come here three days a week, but would you be able to come more? I don't think my children can do it all by themselves."

"That won't be a problem. I'll be here as often and for as long as they need me. Don't worry. I'll watch over them." It wasn't officially a new job, so it shouldn't matter to his parole officer, but he would send the man a note about it, anyway.

"*Danki*. I will let Wayne know that Emma is here with just the boys. I know he will want to stop in and check on her…on them as well."

"Of course."

"I must go. I appreciate your help, Luke. May God bless and keep you."

"And you as well. Safe travels." Luke watched Zachariah get in the car. A moment later, it drove away.

Luke walked up to the house and entered the kitchen. The Swartzentruber children were all sitting at the kitchen table with long faces. He pulled off his hat. "I'm sorry to hear of your loss."

Emma sat up straight. "It was God's will. Our aunt is with Him in Heaven now. There is no more pain and suffering for her. Roy, I want you to gather the eggs and feed the chickens and the horses. Alvin, I need you to milk the cow and feed the hogs."

Roy folded his arms across his chest and glared at her. "The chickens are your chores, Emma."

"I have other things I must do. Luke and I need to discuss what is needed to get the business open."

"I should be in on this discussion. It's going to be my business someday."

"Don't argue with me. Just go."

Roy shoved away from the table and stormed outside. Alvin got up, too. "Hi, Luke. I'm glad you're helping out. We're going to need somebody in charge."

"I am in charge, Alvin," Emma said. "You heard

your father say that. Now get your chores done so you can help Luke finish painting the store."

Alvin had his back to his sister so she didn't see him roll his eyes. Luke smothered a smile as the boy walked past.

Luke twirled his hat in his hands. "Mutiny in your crew already?"

"Roy thinks he should be the one who was left in charge. I have been telling him what to do since he was a toddler. I don't see what difference it makes if *Daed* is here or not."

"Roy is almost an adult. You shouldn't treat him like a little child."

"As long as he is acting that way, that's how I will treat him. I need your support, Luke, not your criticism."

"I didn't mean to criticize, and you do have my support, Emma." He would do whatever he could for her and her family.

"Have a seat, Luke. Would you like some *kaffi*?"

"Your good coffee? Sure." He hung his hat on a peg by the door and returned to take a seat at the table. Emma filled a cup for him and then sat down across from him.

He took a sip. "Sure *goot*. As always."

"How did your parole meeting go, or would you rather not talk about it?"

"I don't mind." To his surprise, he didn't. "I met with Officer Merlin. We went over the paperwork that needs to be done for my release on December 24. He talked a lot about the reasons people like me end up in jail again. He wants to make sure that doesn't happen."

"People like you? Amish?"

"Drug users." He watched closely for her reaction. She flinched and he knew it was hard for her to accept, but he had to be brutally honest with himself.

"What reasons did Officer Merlin give?"

"A lack of support from families. Loneliness, feelings of isolation, inabilities to get and keep a job."

"You don't have those problems. Your family has supported you. You have a job."

"I have it better than a lot of people." He didn't tell her how isolated and alone he felt at times. He didn't know anyone but Jim Morgan who had given up drugs and been able to stay clean. It was frightening how many of the people he knew had tried and failed.

He decided to change the subject. "Your father asked me to help get the store ready until he returns. I would've thought a funeral would be reason enough to stop work on it for a few days."

She swept a stray strand of hair back from her temple. "Father put notices in all the local papers announcing that we would be open on December 27."

"That's less than three weeks away. It won't be ready."

"The interior of the building is almost finished. What else do we need to do?"

"There's a lot of interior work to be done yet. The floor has to be laid. The walls and ceilings need sanding and priming before we can paint. More shelves have to be built. You'll need to stock the shelves, arrange and price your items. And decide on what kind of items you want to sell. You can't just offer boxes of random stuff that your father has stashed in his sheds and barns."

"What kind of things do you think we should offer?"

"All the things that people go to a hardware store

to buy. Batteries, muckrakes, clotheslines, gas lamps, cooking utensils. You will need to find suppliers to sell to you on a regular basis."

"I'll have to start a list. This is overwhelming."

He reached across the table and covered her hand with his own. "It won't be easy, but if anyone can do it, I believe you can."

Her lips trembled as she smiled. "I will hold those words in my heart."

He couldn't ask for anything more. He squeezed her fingers. "You don't have to have everything done before you open your doors. If you offer the basics at a good price, people will be back and your father can gradually expand."

She pulled her hand away and looked down. Why did she suddenly look sad? "Emma, what's wrong? Don't tell me nothing. I can see something is troubling you."

"I am troubled, but there is nothing you can do to help me. I wish I could tell you about it, but I can't, so please don't ask again."

"All right. But if you find you want to talk, I can listen."

"Let's go take stock of what needs to be done. The time will go faster if I stay busy, and my father will be home before I know it."

He got up from the table and together they went to tour the building. Emma produced a notepad and jotted down the things they needed. After they were done, he could see that she felt even more overwhelmed. He didn't have a head for business, but she seemed to value his input. He hoped that he wasn't steering her wrong.

With the help of the boys, they soon had another set

of shelves put together. By the end of the day, four new freshly painted shelves lined all the walls.

Emma looked around. "I think we should put a counter beside the front door where customers can pay for their purchases."

Luke nodded. They had accomplished a lot, but Emma still had a sad, worried look in her eyes when she thought he wasn't looking. When the boys were with them, she wore a stern, no-nonsense expression. Her curt comments annoyed Roy, but she didn't seem to notice, and Luke held his tongue.

After the evening meal was finished, Luke followed his father into the living room where a partially finished game of checkers sat waiting for them. Luke took his usual chair, and made the first move.

"Do you have any words of wisdom for me on how to help make Zachariah's business a success?"

His father frowned deeply. "*Nee*, I have no words of wisdom."

Luke realized his mistake at once. No Amish man would claim to have wisdom. Wisdom belonged to God and God alone. "I meant do you have some suggestions for me? You started our woodworking business from scratch. I value your advice."

Mollified, his father made his move. "When you go out to plant corn, do you plant it in winter?"

At one time, Luke would have been impatient with his father's roundabout way of answering a question, but he had learned to appreciate his father's methods. "I would plant corn in the spring when the earth begins to warm."

"Would you scatter the seeds on the ground?"

"Corn seed has to be planted one and a half to two inches into the soil."

"*Goot.* What comes next?"

"It must be cultivated to keep the weeds out."

"And when would you harvest it?"

"In the fall when the corn kernels are dry so they don't rot in the cribs."

His father nodded and jumped one of Luke's men. "That would be the best plan for corn."

"What would be the best plan for a hardware store?" Only after he made another move did Luke see his mistake.

"Now you are asking the right question." His father jumped two more men. "Crown me."

Luke complied. "Without a plan, I'm afraid Zachariah and Emma aren't going to know what to do next."

"If a farmer can teach you to grow corn…"

Luke sat up straighter. "Then a hardware-store owner can teach me about the hardware trade."

His father smiled. "A man has only one reason to invest his time and talent into a business. To provide for his family. I knew with five sons there wouldn't be enough farmland to support all of you. My goal was to grow a business where my sons and grandsons could work beside me and support their families. It was never about making money so that I could buy fancy things. It is, and always was, about keeping those I love near me."

Luke nodded. "That is Zachariah's aim as well, I think."

"Then it is likely that his efforts will prosper, too. Your mother has a cousin who owns a hardware store over by Mount Hope. He's a good fellow. I'm sure he'll be happy to show you and Zachariah the ropes." He

took Luke's last checker from the board. "I win. Noah, are you up for a game?"

"Sure. I haven't had a sound beating in a week or more." He sank into a chair and redistributed the checkers.

Samuel, who had been working on the books in the corner of the room, got up and handed Luke a stack of magazines and books. Luke raised one eyebrow. "What's all this?"

"Information about operating a business, about marketing, about taxes and hiring laws. A smart businessman never stops learning."

"I appreciate it, although I'm not sure when I'm going to have a chance to read all this."

"Anytime after you get our planer running again. It's stalled."

"The problem is that you don't love it enough, Samuel. Machines know who likes them and who doesn't."

A grunt was Samuel's only answer as he left the room.

Tomorrow was Sunday, and Luke wouldn't be able to work on the broken machine until Monday. Or he could do it tonight. Luke noticed his mother and Rebecca standing silently by the stove. His mother had a knowing smile on her face.

"What?" he asked, wondering why she looked so pleased.

"I was just giving thanks for answered prayers. Seeing my sons helping others and one another does my old heart good."

"I'm not sure how much help I'm giving Emma with Zachariah gone. I feel like I know less than she does. I'm afraid I may steer her wrong." And drain away Em-

ma's dowry instead of increasing it. Not that he cared about the money.

With a start, he realized he was thinking about marriage. To Emma.

He glanced over his shoulder. All his brothers were occupied. He chewed on his lower lip for a second as he stared at Rebecca.

His mother elbowed her. "He's getting up his courage."

Rebecca folded her hands in front of her. "He's pretty slow about it."

"He takes after his father."

Luke scowled at them. "This is serious."

Rebecca smiled. "I will happily be your go-between with my cousin Emma."

"What makes you think I was going to ask you that?" He didn't like the idea that the women in the house were one step ahead of him.

Rebecca and his mother exchanged glances and laughed. Between chuckles, his mother said, "We have been waiting for you to realize what it is that you want. All this talk of helping her make her business a success shows you've made up your mind."

He looked down at the book he held. "I guess maybe I have." Saying it meant he would stay in Bowmans Crossing, join the church, settle down and hopefully marry one day. Once he was a free man.

Rebecca gave him a sympathetic look. "We are all going to the cookie exchange. I'll find a time to speak to her alone then. You'll have your answer by Wednesday of next week."

Could it really be that easy?

Only if the answer was yes. If it was no, how did he deal with that?

Rebecca left the room and his mother came to his side. She pointed to the books he held. "In all your reading, I want you to remember one thing. Business is about relationships. Treat a customer right—he comes back. Treat him right again and he'll send his friend. It's not about what you can sell him today. It's about what he'll buy from you in his lifetime. Tell Emma she must not work in fear of failure. That is shortsighted. She should work as if she knows God will take care of it all. Because He will."

"I'll share that with her."

"It is a lesson you should learn, too, my son."

"What do you mean?"

"If you live in fear of failure, you doubt God's goodness and mercy. Fear steals your strength."

He did live in fear. Fear of failure, fear of returning to drugs. Could he find the faith, the strength, to believe God would not let that happen to him again? He had to or he couldn't ask Emma to consider him. He had to be sure, for her sake as well as his own.

Emma sat beside Roy as he turned in at the Aaron Miller farm. Dozens of buggies were already lined up on the hillside west of the barn. The horses, still wearing their harnesses, were tied up along the fence. Most stood dozing in the sun while others were content to munch on the hay spread in front of them until they were needed to return home.

The bulk of the morning's activity was focused around the barn. Aaron Miller's home was too small

to accommodate all the church's family members. The service would be held in his barn.

The men of the community were busy unloading backless seats from the large gray boxlike bench wagon that was used to transport the benches from home to home for the services held every other Sunday. Bishop Beachy was supervising the unloading. When the wagon was empty, he joined his two ministers, and they all approached the house.

Emma entered the farmhouse ahead of them. Inside, it was a beehive of activity as the women and young girls arranged food on counters and tables. The smaller children were being watched over by elder sisters or cousins. She knew Alvin would be outside with the young boys, playing a game of tag. Roy would find his friends to gossip with and watch the girls bringing food inside.

Catching sight of her Aunt Ina visiting with Rebecca, Emma crossed the room toward them and handed over her basket of food. *"Guder mariye."*

"Good morning," Rebecca replied, taking the basket from her. "Isn't this weather nice? I hope it lasts."

Emma said, "I see the bishop and the ministers coming already. We should hurry." Bishop Beachy and his two ministers entered the house and went upstairs to one of the bedrooms. There they would discuss the preaching for the day. Nothing would be written down.

The service would last for approximately three hours and all the preaching would be done from memory alone. Amish ministers had no formal training. They spoke from the heart, as they believed God inspired them.

When Emma reached the barn with her aunt and

cousin, she saw it was already filled with people sitting quietly on rows of backless wooden benches. The women sat on one side of the aisle and men on the other side. Tarps and blankets had been hung over ropes stretched between upright timbers to cordon off an area for the service. The sounds of cattle and horses could be heard from the nearby stalls.

Rebecca and Ina took their places among the married women. Emma spied Lillian among the unmarried women and went to join her. She looked about for her brothers and saw them sitting in the back row on the men's side as close to the open door as they could get. The moment the service was finished, they would rush out.

From the men's side of the aisle, the *Volsinger* or song leader announced the first hymn. There was a wave of rustling and activity as people opened their thick songbooks. The *Ausbund* contained the words of all the hymns the Amish used, but no musical scores. The songs were sung from memory, passed down through countless generations. They were sung slowly and in unison by people opening their hearts and minds to receive God's presence without the distraction of musical instruments. The elderly man started the hymn in a clear, sweet voice that reminded Emma of Alvin's voice. The rest of the congregation joined in, and she could hear Alvin singing loud and strong behind her. She couldn't pick out Roy's voice and knew he was mumbling his way through. He hated singing. She tried to pick out Luke's voice, but couldn't.

At the end of the first hymn, Emma took a moment to glance toward the men's side. She spotted Luke sitting just behind the married men. His unmarried brothers sat near the back while Joshua and Samuel sat beside

their father. Luke glanced in her direction, and she smiled at him. He smiled back and then focused on his songbook. The song leader announced the second hymn: *"O Gott Vater, wir Loben dich* (O God the Father, We Praise You).*"* It was always the second hymn of an Amish service.

Emma forgot about Luke and her brothers as she joined the entire congregation in singing God's praise, asking that He allow the ministers to speak true to His teachings, and praying that the people present would receive His words and take them into their hearts.

At the end of the second hymn, the ministers and Bishop Beachy came in. They hung their black hats on pegs set in the wall for that purpose. It was the signal that the preaching was about to begin. Nearby, a young child began to fuss. His mother slipped a string of beads and buttons from her purse and gave them to her little one. He quieted and played with his toy, chewing on it and shaking it while his mother focused on the preachers.

Emma tried to listen closely to what was being said, but she found her mind wandering. She thought of her father and prayed for his healing. She asked God to grant her patience to deal with Roy and she prayed for Luke, that he would find peace and acceptance within the community. Finally, she prayed to accept God's will if it was His desire that she marry as her father wished. Wayne was a good man and he would make a good husband. It wasn't his fault that he didn't make her heart race. Marriage had to be about more than simple physical attraction. It was about hard work, respect. and duty to God and church.

When the service was finally over, Emma joined

the women in the house as they prepared a luncheon. The men stacked the backless benches to make tables and the food was laid out for people to help themselves. The ministers and elders were served first. The youngsters played games outside until it was their turn to eat.

Luke came inside with Noah and Timothy when it was their turn. Emma was filling glasses with lemonade and cups with black coffee for those who wished it. Luke took a glass of lemonade from her. "I would like to speak to you when you're done here."

She looked around. "I think they can spare me for a few minutes."

He looked pleased. "Why don't we step outside?"

Her heart started hammering wildly. Was he about to ask her to ride home with him? Would she accept? "Let me get my cloak."

He walked out but before she could follow, Lillian caught her by the arm. "Emma, what are you doing?"

"Luke wants to have a word with me."

"If he asks to drive you home and you let him, you are a bigger fool than I would have believed possible."

"I know you think he treated me badly in the past."

"I don't *think* it. I saw it. You cried on my shoulder for hours that night."

"The other day you didn't have any objections to him working with the children."

"I don't object to him helping his community. I do have an objection to him breaking your heart again. He's not worth it, Emma. You can do better."

She glanced out the window where Luke was waiting on the porch. "What if I don't want to do better?"

What if Luke was the man she wanted? How could she know if he was the man God had chosen for her?

Chapter Eleven

Luke waited for Emma to come outside. He was already more nervous than he had been since the first time he asked the girl if he could drive her home after a Sunday-evening singing. That girl had been Emma and he had been a nervous sixteen-year-old. Why couldn't Rebecca find a way to speak to her today? Why did he have to wait? He wasn't good at waiting.

What answer would Emma give Rebecca? Would she be willing to go out with him or would he find out that Wayne was her choice. He tried to prepare himself to hear that answer.

He looked through the window and saw her talking to Lillian. Both women wore serious expressions. Lillian stood with her arms crossed and a scowl on her face. It deepened when she caught sight of him. There was more than a friendly conversation going on. His hopes took a nosedive. Lillian might think it was all right for him to make Christmas decorations for the school, but he knew dating Emma would be a different story. Was she telling Emma as much?

"Luke, it's good to see you this holy day. How have you been?"

He turned to see Bishop Beachy approaching. "I've been well and hoping to speak to you."

"I just heard from Roy that you are helping to finish Zachariah's store while he has traveled to his sister-in-law's funeral in Missouri. I will spread the word so that others may offer their condolences. Do his children need anything?"

"A few extra hands to help finish the store before he returns would be wonderful."

"I and my boys will come by this week. I'm sure I can find a few more volunteers, too."

"That would be a blessing. Speaking of volunteers, I believe Lillian Keim could use a few extra hands getting the school ready for the Christmas program."

"Really? She hasn't mentioned this to me."

"My brother Timothy and I built part of her set, but I overheard her say she could use more help making the costumes."

The door to the house opened. Emma came outside with Lillian right behind her. The bishop turned to address them. "My condolences on your loss, Emma. With your father gone, you can depend on our community for any help."

"Danki."

"You will find many willing hands at your door this week to finish Zachariah's store. Teacher Lillian, Luke tells me that you require more help with the costumes for the Christmas play. My wife and my daughters-in-law will be happy to assist, as will other women. You must not think you need to do all the work yourself.

You must allow others the joy of making our Christmas program a success, too."

Luke caught the look of surprise Lillian cast in his direction. She blushed slightly and dropped her gaze to her clasped hands. "I know the women of our community are especially busy this time of year getting ready for Christmas, Bishop. Many are cleaning to make ready for out-of-town visitors, baking for their families and for others. I hate to take them away from their tasks."

"Those who cannot spare the time are excused, but those who do have a few extra moments on their hands will be glad to do something to benefit our *kinder*. I will spread the word. When should they meet with you?"

Lillian nodded once. "*Danki*, Bishop Beachy. Anyone who can help should come to the school on Tuesday at one o'clock."

"I'll pass on the message. Now I must see Aaron Miller and congratulate him. I hear he had a new grandson in Illinois."

Luke spoke quickly. "Before you go, sir, Emma and I have one more concern."

"What is it?"

Luke waited for Emma to speak; when she didn't he charged ahead. "Zachariah has a number of solar panels that he has collected."

The bishop laughed. "That doesn't surprise me."

Luke grinned, too. "They would provide electricity for the store if you were to approve their use."

Slipping his thumbs beneath his suspenders, the bishop slid them up and down. "I have heard from other bishops that there is a great deal of interest in this new technology. Some communities have already embraced

it. I'm afraid I can't give you permission to use it without further study. This year's regional bishops' meeting is being held next week. I will seek the counsel of others on this matter and render a decision after that."

"It uses God's sunlight. It doesn't connect us to the outside world," Luke said, hoping to sway him to their side.

Smiling gently, the bishop nodded. "As you know, we Amish sometimes embrace a new invention only to find it does not promote our way of life. When I was a small boy, our community allowed the new telephones into our homes. It appeared on the surface to be a *goot* thing. A way to keep in touch with our families and to summon help in an emergency. For a while, it worked, but many soon began to notice people were spending too much time talking with others, not about business, but in gossip and other ways that were not beneficial to our people. The bishops met and agreed having a phone for emergencies was essential, but not in every home. My mother cried when my father took our phone out. We only have a community phone booth now. As others use solar power, they will gain a better understanding of its benefits and problems, and they will share what they have learned at the bishops' meeting."

"Thank you for considering it," Emma said.

The bishop turned to Lillian. "Come with me and speak with my wife about what is needed for the school."

When they were out of earshot, Emma smiled at him. "That was very kind of you to think of getting more help for Lillian."

"I didn't want you to worry about her since you aren't able to help as much now that your father is gone."

"I appreciate that, Luke. What did you want to speak to me about?"

He glanced around and noticed they were getting a few stares and frowns from some of the older members and his courage failed him. "I wanted to ask if you'd like to check out the hardware store over by Mount Hope. The owner is my mother's second cousin. My father says he'll be happy to show us how to run a hardware business."

"Sure. When?"

She smiled shyly at him and his hopes soared high once more. A long buggy ride without prying eyes on them was a better place to speak of courting than this. "The sooner the better. I'll be at your place bright and early tomorrow."

"I'll see you then."

She had to like him. But did she like him enough to agree he could come courting?

"Emma, get your coat."

She looked up in surprise when Luke came rushing into the house on Monday morning. "My coat? Why?"

"Because we are going shopping."

"For what?"

"Experience and information. Hurry, it's a long drive and it looks like it could snow." He rushed out the door.

She got her coat and followed him, but she didn't get in the buggy. "I still don't understand what we are doing. We need to be here to direct the men working inside."

"There were already five men working with Roy in the store. Roy knows what needs to be done. Get in."

Exasperated, she climbed in the buggy and shut the

door. A basket with warm bricks at her feet kept the chill away. "At least tell me where we're going."

Luke slapped the reins against the horse's rump. "I already told you. The hardware store in Mount Hope."

"I didn't think you meant we'd go rushing off first thing this morning."

"My father said if I wanted to grow corn, I should talk to a farmer, and if I wanted to run a business, I should talk to someone in the business."

He seemed so pleased with himself that she couldn't help but smile. "Let's hope your mother's cousin is a good businessman."

"Amen to that."

They rode in silence for a while with the steady clip-clop of the horse's hooves and the hum of the tires on the road the only sounds to fill the void. She had so many questions that she wanted to ask him, yet she didn't know how to start. Why had he left her behind? Why wasn't her love good enough for him? Had there been someone else? An English girl?

As often as she told herself the past no longer mattered, the same questions came back to nag her.

"How is Roy doing with your father gone?" Luke glanced at her.

Her family was a safer subject than her past hurts. "He hasn't been an easy person to have around. He resents every task I give him."

"What does he want to do?"

"I don't know."

"Maybe you should ask him."

She scowled at him. "He wants to be in charge."

"Maybe you should let him."

"He's only a boy. I'm overwhelmed with all that

needs to be done. How can he possibly hope to know what is needed?"

"Roy has spent a lot of time with your father. He knows what Zachariah has in the sheds. If you ask him he can tell you what is broken and what just needs a little work."

"If you have so much faith in him, why didn't you bring him instead of me?"

"He wanted to get started on the floors."

"I will admit he had done a lot of work already. I know the business will be his one day, but will he be an Amish or an *Englisch* businessman when that day comes?"

"Only your brother can make that decision. You can't make it for him."

Emma bit back a retort, knowing he was right. She stared at the window at the passing scenery. Snow covered the shocks of corn stacked in the fields. It clung to the backs of horses and cattle grazing by the fences. "I know it seems like I nag, but I can't help it. I want so much for him to be happy with our simple ways."

"I can understand that."

She glanced at him. "Are you happy with your Amish life now or do you long to return to the world?"

"I'm finding…contentment." He looked at her and smiled, but something in the way he said it made her doubt him.

"Is that enough?"

"I pray it will be."

She fell silent, not knowing what else to say. It wasn't too much later that they pulled into the parking lot of the Big River hardware store.

There were three hitching posts out front for bug-

gies as well as parking spaces for cars. Two buggies and three cars occupied spaces. "I wish I'd brought my notebook."

"One like this?" Luke pulled a notepad from his pocket and handed it to her along with a pencil. She smiled her thanks. "You've thought of everything."

Flipping it open, she wrote *hitching rails* and *parking spaces.*

Luke got out and came around to open the door for her. She grasped his hand to get down, and even with gloves on she could feel the energy that seemed to arc between them. Almost like the jolt she had received from the solar panel. After that, she made a point to avoid touching him. It was already hard to concentrate when he was near.

Inside the building, she met his mother's cousin and they were soon being treated like honored guests. Albert Chupp and his wife, Esta, answered Emma and Luke's questions, showed them how they kept track of inventory and wrote down the names of the suppliers they used. Emma had already thought of stocking lamps and lampshades, but she hadn't considered the need for yards of cotton wick material or the replacement wheels that fed the wicks into the lamp. Nor did she have any idea that there were so many sizes of screws and bolts to be had.

By the time they left, she had pages and pages of her notebook full of simple items they could carry and tips for displaying merchandise. As she climbed back into the buggy, she sighed heavily. "There's no way we can have a place like this."

Luke got in and picked up the reins. "Don't work in

fear. Work as if God has everything under control because He does."

She studied the building in front of her. "I reckon I'll have to try. How am I going to make the outside of our store as inviting as theirs?" Patio furniture was grouped to one side while birdbaths and stacks of garden pottery lined the other side of the building. Her father's store was much smaller. They wouldn't have room for such big items.

"A little more color will help. Some of your colored lamps in the window along with pretty shades."

"You're right. Something bright. It will come to me."

"Of course it will. You're one of the smartest women I know."

Her mouth dropped open at his compliment, but she quickly snapped it shut. He thought she was smart. Was she, or was she being foolish to hope he cared for her? He was being helpful—there was no denying that—but why? Was it because he cared about her?

Luke hoped he had done the right thing by bringing Emma with him. He didn't want to discourage her, but she had to know what was involved in running a business like the one Zachariah was intent on starting. He regretted his decision to let Roy remain at home, but Luke was still working up the courage to ask Emma out. He didn't want her brother in on that conversation. Next time, he would take the boy with him and let him see what kind of business his father was getting into, too.

Emma was quiet on the way home. She sat reading and rereading her notes. He glanced at her often, happy to simply be traveling with her. It amazed him that she

didn't have to do anything or say anything and he still enjoyed being near her.

Isn't that what love is?

He listened to the small voice in his heart, knowing he was truly falling in love with Emma. It wasn't the mad passion they had shared as teens. That passion was still there—he felt it whenever he looked at her or thought of her—but this new gentleness carried with it much richer emotions. Even so, he couldn't act on those feelings until he was certain he belonged among the Amish. He had to know staying was God's will for him. And he needed to know Emma's feelings about Wayne.

He sighed deeply as he realized he couldn't ask her out until he had those answers.

"Can we see some solar panels while we are out?" she asked.

"Sure. Timothy said he knows a man near Berlin that sells them. It's not too far out of our way."

"I think one of those we have is defective."

"Why do you say that?"

"Because it shocked me just as hard as Jim Morgan's electric fence."

"Was the sun shining on it at the time? They produce electric power even in dim light."

"Now you tell me. Are they dangerous? Can they start fires?"

"I don't know."

"These are things we must investigate before we install them for our new business."

"I agree."

"Goot."

"You're getting kind of bossy, aren't you?" There was a hint of challenge in his tone.

She gaped at him. "I am not."

"My mistake. I've been listening to Roy too much."

"Roy says that I'm bossy?"

"He says you are always coming down hard on him."

"The boy knows how to make me angry. I can't seem to stop harping at him. I know I'm doing it, but he pushes until he gets that reaction from me."

Luke tried to draw on some of his feelings and mistakes as a kid. "Give him more responsibility. Let him fail if he doesn't get it right. He'll learn more that way than you telling him he's wrong."

"I wish my father were here."

"You're doing a fine job. Just lighten up on Roy."

Emma gritted her teeth to keep from replying to his suggestion. He didn't have to deal with an unruly teenager day in and day out. He had been the unruly teenager.

Her fair-mindedness asserted itself. Maybe he did have a special understanding that she lacked because of his own teenage years. She would follow his suggestion and see if it made a difference. She wasn't getting anywhere with Roy by doing it her way.

It didn't take long to reach their second destination of the day. The furniture maker with a solar sideline turned out to be a jovial Amish fellow by the name of Reuben Kaufman. Emma discovered he sold all the usual Amish-made furniture along with solar-powered garden lights, solar panel kits and fence chargers.

"A while back Amish people frowned at solar power. But now they see all the good it can do. I've run my cash register and key-cutting machine for ten years on solar alone. This summer I'm going to upgrade from

my four small panels to eight larger panels. I've got this paint-mixing machine that takes a lot of energy. Gets expensive running my diesel generator all day."

Luke asked a question about fuses, voltage and amps that left Emma completely in the dark. After that, the conversation turned technical. She had very little idea what they were discussing. Luke, on the other hand, appeared to be thoroughly enjoying himself. She was astonished and a little bit uneasy at how well he understood the workings of the solar panels. He seemed more *Englisch* than Amish when he talked about the potential of solar energy. He was eager to learn everything he could. When Reuben mentioned there was a school to teach installation, Luke took particular note, jotting down the address and the phone number.

On their way home, she questioned his interest in the school. "Are you going to become a solar installer?"

"There's no sense in selling something people can't use. I was thinking it might be something that would interest Roy. He likes gadgets. With a certified installer, you could sell and install small panels for things like battery-powered fence chargers to keep cattle in. With a large enough array, a fellow could run a sewing machine, a vacuum, or a water pump and still have enough juice left over to charge the batteries for his buggy lamps. Imagine while you are working in the sun, the sun is working for you by charging your batteries so you would never have to buy gas or diesel to run a generator."

"This all seems much too fancy."

"Now you sound like Wayne. Very old-fashioned."

"There's nothing wrong with Wayne's opinions. They are shared by many others."

"By you?"

"In some cases." She closed her mouth, refusing to argue with him.

"Then you should make a good pair."

"I have told you nothing is decided between us."

"But you are still considering him."

"Because father wishes it."

"Right." He clicked his tongue and put the tired horse into a trot. Emma didn't object. She was every bit as eager to get home as he was. And why wouldn't he be? He thought she was bossy and old-fashioned and all but married to Wayne Hochstetler.

Luke Bowman didn't know her well at all. And she barely knew him anymore. Could that change or would they always be on edge with each other?

Chapter Twelve

With the help of the bishop, his sons and several other men from the church district, the inside of her father's shop was completed within a week. Late one morning, Emma left the last batch of chocolate-mint cookies she had baked for the cookie exchange cooling on the counter and walked through the store in amazement.

The ceiling was painted a bright white. Two skylights kept the interior from being dark. The walls were painted a soft mint green that made her think of summer and green apples. Two dozen shelves stood in rows waiting for merchandise. The wide-plank pine floors gleamed with wax. She would put a pen to paper tonight and describe for her father all that had been accomplished. The next step was filling the shelves. She pulled out her notebook and began to make notes about where things should go.

Shouting from outside drew her attention sometime later. She walked to the bay window and looked out but didn't see anything. Pulling on her coat, she went outside and followed the noise to the west side of the house. Roy and Alvin were engaged in a running snow-

ball battle around the henhouse. Luke stood a few feet in front of her, laughing at their antics. She had a perfect view of his broad back.

Opening her mouth to scold her brothers for playing when they should be working, she held her tongue instead. Luke's advice to stop being so hard on Roy kept her silent. Everyone had been working hard. Maybe it was time for a little fun.

She glanced down at the sparkling snow by her boots and scooped up a handful. It was perfect for making snowballs. The sun had melted it just enough so that it packed together nicely. Quietly, she added another handful, making the ball she held almost the size of a softball. Hefting it from hand to hand, she stared at Luke's back. It would be an easy shot.

"Don't even think about it." He hadn't turned around. How did he know?

"Don't think about what?" She feigned innocence and hid the ball behind her back.

He glanced over his shoulder. "You'll be sorry."

"Not as sorry as you'll be." She threw the snowball. It struck his shoulder, sending an explosion of icy crystals into his neck and face.

"That wasn't nice, Emma Mae."

A giggle escaped her. "Maybe not, but it was remarkably satisfying."

Slowly, he brushed the snow away. "You know what has to happen now."

"You must turn the other cheek." She scooped a handful at him and bolted toward the house.

She didn't make it five feet before he retaliated with a hit to the back of her head. She scrunched her neck

against the cold sensation of snow sliding down beneath her collar. "Argh."

"Told you that you'd be sorry."

Glaring at him, she turned around. "This means war."

He held up both hands. "Turn the other cheek, Emma. You'll feel terrible if you don't."

Roy and Alvin had stopped and were watching. She hefted a new snowball and motioned slightly with her head. Roy nodded and grinned. He and Alvin left the henhouse and advanced quietly from the rear with a snowball in each hand.

To keep Luke's attention. She planted one hand on her hip and held her snowball aloft like a shot put. "I will consider turning the other cheek after I hear an apology."

"I'm sorry you hit me with a snowball first."

"Not good enough."

"I'm sorry you can't throw very well."

"I hit what I was aiming at."

"I think you wanted my face but got my shoulder." He took a step toward her.

Hopping back, she shook her head. "No, you don't. You aren't going to stuff snow down my back."

"The idea never crossed my mind. Until you mentioned it." He gave a deep laugh and advanced steadily.

She turned as if to flee, but spun back quickly enough to slap the snow in his face as he ran at her. He stopped and shook like a dog. "You are going down, and you are going to eat snow, girl."

Giggling, she hopped from side to side, daring him to catch him. In a singsong voice, she chanted, "I have

something you don't have. I have something you don't have."

"And what would that be?"

"My brothers behind you."

He spun around and ducked as Roy and Alvin threw with both hands. The snow hit Emma in the face and chest. She stood in openmouthed shock at the cold.

Luke and her brothers were laughing so hard they couldn't stand up. Luke was rolling with mirth. Turning slowly around, Emma walked back to the store and lifted one of her father's grain shovels from the rack. She walked outside, scooped up a shovelful, rounded the corner and dumped it on Luke. Her brothers scrambled to their feet, but she already had a second scoop loaded and she flung it toward them, showering them with white powder.

"I give up." Luke was still laughing as he pulled his coat off to shake the snow out.

Her brothers took off firing at each other again.

Luke came toward her with his hands up. Something in his eyes alerted her to his intentions, but it was too late. He dove at her, carrying her into a nearby snowdrift. His fingers around her wrists prevented any retaliation. She was forced to lie in the cold snow until he released her.

The playful gleam in his eyes slowly vanished. His pupils darkened. "I think we should kiss and make up, don't you?"

Slowly, he leaned down.

Emma knew he was going to kiss her. If she turned her head to the side, it would be a simple peck on the cheek, part of the game, but she didn't turn her face.

She licked her lips, tasting the cold snow, and closed her eyes.

She could feel his warm breath on her lips, but he didn't touch them. She lifted her face ever so slightly in invitation. He groaned and rolled away from her. Disappointment stabbed through her, followed by shame.

Sitting up, she pulled her coat tight at her throat. He lay on his back looking up at the sky. "I'm sorry."

"For what? Nothing happened. It was a silly game that got out of hand."

He raised his head to look at her. "I wanted it to get out of hand."

So had she, but she didn't admit it. Wasn't she pretty enough? Wasn't she tempting enough? Why was she forever wanting him and he was forever turning away? It was cruel.

He rose to his feet and held out his hand. "Truce?"

She knocked his hand aside, pleased by the look of shock on his face. Rising to her feet, she stomped toward the house to change. He caught her by the arm. "Emma, wait."

"Let me go." She tried to jerk away, but he held her fast.

"I'm not sure what I did wrong." He sounded so pathetic that she almost felt sorry for him. Almost.

"You didn't do anything wrong. Now, let go of me."

"I did something to upset you. I'm sorry. Emma, I respect you. I would never dally with your affections."

"You don't want to kiss me, that's fine. Don't make a big deal out of it."

He tipped his head slightly. "Wait, you're mad because I didn't kiss you?"

"Let it go."

"*Nee*, not till I've righted a wrong." He pulled her into his arms and kissed her soundly. His lips moved over hers with a skill that left her breathless. He tasted of mint and chocolate. When her knees grew weak, he pulled away as breathless as she was.

"Was that better?"

She touched her tingling lips with her fingertips. "You've been snitching cookies."

He threw up his hands. "Busted. Haul me away. Your brothers gave me some."

She smoothed her dress and straightened her *kapp*. "Stay out of my kitchen. In fact, go home. We're done for the day."

"Okay." He took a step back, stumbled and sat in the snow.

She marched into the house, went up the stairs and straight to her room. After closing the door, she lay down on the bed and pressed her fingers to her lips again. That had been a very fine kiss.

Luke got up, dusted off his pride and began walking home. He was almost to the covered bridge when Joshua and Mary drove past in their buggy. Joshua drew the horse to a stop. "Need a ride?"

Luke shook his head. "I need to walk."

"What's wrong?"

"Women. When someone understands them, let me know. No offense, Mary."

"None taken. Joshua, I'll drive on to school and get Hannah. Why don't you walk your brother home? He looks like he can use some company."

Joshua handed the reins to his wife and got out. She drove away and he turned to Luke. "Women troubles?"

"Woman. One woman. Emma."

"Let's hear your side of the story before Mary gets it out of Emma."

"It all started so innocently."

"It always does."

"One minute I was chucking snowballs at an old friend. The next minute, I was lying next to her in the snow acting like a scoundrel. I got up before anything happened, and she got mad."

"Most women don't like a man to act like a scoundrel."

"That's not it. She was mad because I didn't kiss her."

"Odd."

"You're telling me."

"What did you do?"

"I kissed her."

"Luke, I have to tell you that might have been the wrong move. Did she slap you?"

He shook his head. "She accused me of swiping cookies and told me to go home."

"That's it?"

Nodding, Luke pulled off his hat. "That's it. It was like I was five again." He raked his fingers through his hair.

"You got off easy, *brudder*."

"Joshua, give me a reason for her actions that I can wrap my brain around."

"I'm no romance expert."

"Are all women as confusing as Emma is?"

"I have no idea. If I were you, I'd pretend it didn't happen."

"I can try that." But he knew that it wouldn't work.

He was never going to forget the feel of her soft lips against his.

What do you want me to do, Lord? Is she the one, or am I kidding myself? I need Your help, Heavenly Father. Show me what You desire for me.

The two men walked in the back door of their father's house and were immediately surrounded by the aroma of gingersnaps, snickerdoodles, chocolate-chip cookies and oatmeal-raisin bars.

They looked at each other and smiled. "Cookie exchange."

Joshua peeked around the corner of the kitchen. "I'll distract *Mamm*, you grab as many cookies as you can and I'll meet you in the barn. Deal?"

Before they could make a move, their father bolted out of the kitchen with his hand covering his head. "I only took one."

"And that is the last one you will see until next Christmas." Their mother stopped in the doorway with a rolling pin in her hand. "What are you boys doing here?"

Joshua being closest took a step back. "Nothing, *Mamm*. We're—nothing, *Mamm*."

"Go make yourselves useful. The buggy needs to be washed."

"On it," Luke assured her.

"Hmmph!" She raised one eyebrow, spun on her heels and went back to the kitchen.

Joshua tried to see the top of his father's head. "Did she get you?"

"Missed me by a hair. This hair." He pulled a silver strand straight up.

Luke looked toward the kitchen and then gathered

the others into a huddle. "She can't get all of us. If we rush her, we can snag a bunch of those awesome ginger-snaps and get out before she knows who to swing at."

"Sounds like a plan. Which side of the table shall I take?" Joshua asked.

"What are you guys up to?" Timothy came strolling in from the kitchen with a cookie in each hand.

"How did you get those?" his father demanded.

"These?" He held out his cookies. "I asked *Mamm* if I could have one. She gave me two."

Luke's father turned and looked at each of his sons in turn. "He asked."

"I still say we rush her." Joshua rubbed his hands together.

"Shall I go get some for you?" Timothy offered.

"She won't let you have them. They're for the cookie exchange."

"Sure she will." Timothy handed his uneaten cookie to his father and went back to the kitchen. He came out a few minutes later with a plate of assorted cookies. "You just have to ask nicely, guys."

Luke took one from the plate. "Stealing them is more fun." It was the same with kisses, too, but how much better would it be to have Emma give them freely? He had to know how she felt about him.

Emma waited impatiently in the kitchen for Wayne to arrive with his daughter on the evening of the cookie exchange. Maybe some time with Wayne's daughter would get the memory of Luke's kiss out of her mind. It was all she could think about. What had it meant to him? Had it meant anything? She touched her lips

again. Had he felt the same thrill that raced through her nerve endings?

Would Wayne's kiss thrill her in the same way? Wayne was everything that Luke was not. Steady, dependable, grounded in the Amish life and faith. He would make any woman a good husband. If she wasn't so foolish, she would encourage Wayne's attention.

But the only man whose attention she wanted was Luke. Not dependable. Not a member of her faith. Not good husband material. Why couldn't she get over him?

Now that the store was finished, she wouldn't see him as much. That was for the best. She needed to concentrate on helping her father and her brothers in the coming months.

Roy came through the room with a rolled up magazine under his arm. "What's for supper?"

"I've got ham and beans on the stove. You and Alvin can just help yourselves when you're ready. What are you reading?"

He pulled the periodical out and held it up for her inspection. "It's a magazine that tells you how to set up solar arrays, how to install them and how to wire them. Luke gave it to me. It's really cool. He said I might be able to go to school to learn this."

"Luke shouldn't promise things he can't control. Your father and the bishop will have to decide if it is acceptable. What if we can't afford it?"

"Luke didn't promise anything. We just talked about it. Don't forget to bring back lots of cookies." He tucked the magazine under his arm and went outside.

Emma heard a buggy arrive a few minutes before five. Wayne was prompt. Another point in his favor. Going to the door, she held it open. He stepped down

from the buggy and lifted out his child. She held a small white plastic pail to fill with cookies.

Wayne walked to the door. "Emma Swartzentruber, this is my daughter, Sophie. Sophie, this is my friend Emma. She is taking you to the cookie exchange tonight."

Emma knelt to put herself at the child's level. "Hello, Sophie. I'm pleased to meet you. We're going to have so much fun. There will be lots of *kinder* there for you to play with and good things to eat."

Blond with pale blue eyes, Sophie held on to her father's leg and looked painfully shy.

"I have to take some cookies home for *Daed.*"

"I will remind you." Emma rose to her feet. "Wayne, I want to thank you for this chance to get to know Sophie. I shall take good care of her. I'll bring her home about seven. Is that acceptable?"

"I reckon." He tipped his hat and left.

Sophie went to a kitchen chair and sat down. She turned her pail first one way and then the other.

"Shall we go to the party?" Emma tried to put some eagerness in her voice.

"Okay." Sophie followed her outside but balked at getting in Emma's buggy.

"What's wrong?" Emma bent to her level.

"It's fancy. I can't ride in a fancy buggy. It has the orange sign on the back."

"It is okay for you to ride in my buggy. My church wants us to use the slow-moving-vehicle sign."

Sophie shook her head. "Nope."

It was too cold for Emma and the child to walk all that way. Emma went to the house and searched for a dark piece of cloth to cover the sign. She found one that

worked. Sophie studied it for a few seconds and nodded. "Okay, but you can't turn the lights on."

"I won't."

"My *mamm* died last year. *Daed* doesn't like me to talk about her."

"I'm sorry."

"*Daed* says he might marry you. I don't like that."

"If you don't like it, I for sure won't marry him, but you might like me when you get to know me."

"Maybe. Can we go to the party now?"

"Yes, we can and we are going to have a wonderful time."

Luke stood in the corner of the living room, waiting and watching for Emma. Rebecca stopped beside him. "She'll be here."

"Who?" he asked with indifference.

"Emma. You aren't fooling anyone. It's easy to see how you feel about her."

He gathered his nerve. "I do care for Emma but I don't know how she feels about me or about Wayne. Do you?"

"I can ask her."

"I was hoping you'd say that."

She just chuckled as she walked away.

People from his church group and others mingled throughout the house. Children had been relegated to the basement. The downstairs room ran the entire length of the house and was used mainly for parties and singings for the teenagers.

Long tables held goodies in every shape and form from brownies to cookies to cake and pie. People were required to bring a large pail of treats, set them out

and then fill up their pail with treats made by someone else. There were several group games in progress downstairs and the noise level was high. Older people sought the comfort of his mother's plush sofa and chairs in the living room. Not caring for crowds, Luke picked a spot where he could watch for Emma without having to visit with people.

He spied her the minute she walked in, but he didn't know the child with her. Was it Wayne's daughter? Or some other relative of Emma's that he didn't know about? He gathered his courage and made his way across the room. He'd soon know if she was still angry with him, but for the moment he was going to take Joshua's advice and act like the kiss hadn't happened. "Evening, Emma. Who have you got with you?"

Her smile looked strained. "This is Sophie Hochstetler. Wayne's daughter. She and I are getting to know each other. Sophie, say hello to Luke."

Sophie buried her face in Emma's skirt. "I can't talk to strangers. They might be shunned."

Emma lifted the child's face. "I know for a fact that Luke is not shunned."

"I don't like him."

"Not many people do," Luke said with a smile, hoping to tease her out of her sour mood. If Emma was getting to know Wayne's daughter, it must be serious between them.

Sophie scowled at him. He smiled at Emma. "This may be a job for Hannah and Bella."

"That's just who I was going to find." Emma looked around the room.

"Basement." He nodded toward the steps.

"Danki." She went downstairs with the child and he didn't see either of them again for over an hour.

Emma finally managed to get Sophie to play with some of the other children. Rather they were playing and Sophie was watching them, but at least she wasn't clinging to Emma's hand.

Rebecca stopped beside her. "How is it going with Sophie?"

"Not great."

"How are things going with Wayne?"

Emma knew she could tell Rebecca the truth. "Not great, either."

"What seems to be the problem?"

"Me."

Rebecca leaned closer. "Care to elaborate on that?"

"When did you know Samuel was the one for you?"

"I realized it when I couldn't fall asleep at night without thinking about him. Who do you fall asleep thinking about?"

Not Wayne. "I don't care to say."

"Someone has asked me to be their go-between."

Emma's pulse jumped up a notch. Was it Luke? "Who asked you?"

"I think you know." Rebecca leaned away with a decided twinkle in her eyes.

"Luke." Emma's excitement dimmed. A growing sense of annoyance settled in her chest. He could have asked her anytime they were together in the store or on the buggy ride to the hardware store or after he'd kissed her in the snow. Why did he feel the need to send a go-between?

Was she that hard to speak with? Did he expect her

to reject him? Scold him? He could kiss her, but he couldn't ask her a simple question.

Emma folded her arms. It wasn't a simple question or she would have an answer for Rebecca at this very moment and she didn't.

"Well?" Rebecca prompted. "What shall I tell him?"

The party was winding down when Luke finally met up with Rebecca. "Have you had a chance to get Emma alone?"

Her smile was forced. "I did."

"She doesn't want to go out with me." His hopes withered on the vine.

"That isn't exactly what she said."

"What did she say?"

"That you're a big boy now and you can ask her yourself."

"That's not bad, is it?"

"It was more in the way she said it."

"I see." So it wasn't good.

"If God wants you to be together, Luke, you will overcome every obstacle. Samuel and I are proof of that."

"At least I didn't get shut down."

Rebecca nodded and walked away. Luke considered his next move. Emma hadn't said no. Was she waiting to say that to his face? He could see her doing that.

He started down the steps to the basement to locate her. She was easy to spot. He never had trouble picking her out in a crowd. There was just something special about her.

Standing by Mary and Joshua, Emma was encouraging Sophie to pet Bella. It wasn't working. Sophie was

afraid of the dog and batted at her if she ventured too close. Hannah came to stand beside him. "I don't like her. She said my dress was too fancy. It's not. *Mammi* Ada made it for me. She doesn't like Bella, either."

"Maybe she's never had a dog."

"That would be sad," Hannah said with a quivering lip.

It would be sad for the motherless child to be fearful of everything including the most lovable mutt in the world. She was blessed to have Emma watching over her. He might selfishly want Emma to choose him over Wayne, but there was more than his feelings at stake. He walked up to Sophie. "Hi, remember me? I'm not shunned."

"Can we go now?"

"How would you like to go down to the river? Have you seen it at night? It's very pretty."

"That's a *goot* idea. I'll get our coats." Emma cast a relieved smile his way, and he knew he'd made the right decision.

When she had the child bundled up, Luke opened the back door, and they walked out to find a young couple smooching on the garden bench. He cleared his throat and the couple sprang apart. It was Noah and their neighbor's daughter, Fannie Erb.

Luke walked past and whispered, "Carry on, bro."

"Will do."

Luke and Emma continued down to the water's edge with the child. Away from the noise and the crush of people, Sophie slowly relaxed. After a few minutes, she looked at Luke. "Can I throw a rock in the water?"

Emma crouched beside her. "You can throw every

rock you find in the river. Just don't get too close to the water."

"Danki." She picked up a pebble from a spot free of snow and chucked it in. The ripples spread out, sparkling in the moonlight.

She spun to Emma. "Did you see that?"

"I did. Try throwing two rocks together," Emma suggested.

Sophie became more animated as she tossed stones and ran along the riverbank.

"How did you know she would do better outside?" Emma was looking at him with curiosity.

"You could pick them out in prison, the ones who couldn't tolerate being closed in. She had that look of panic on her face."

"I'm glad you saw it. I was at my wit's end." Her eyes held a softness he hadn't seen before. Not when she was looking at him. Could he kiss her again? Would she let him? The thought had barely formed when a shriek split the night.

Chapter Thirteen

Emma dashed away from Luke and ran to the water's edge. Sophie, cowering and crying, was backed up against a tree as Bella tried to interest her in a stick. She laid it at the girl's feet and pushed it closer.

Emma picked Sophie up. "It's all right. She won't hurt you. Go away now, Bella."

The dog walked off with her head down. Sophie kept her arms locked around Emma's neck. "I don't like her."

"I'm sorry she scared you." Emma turned to Luke. "I need to take her home."

"I'll drive you." He hurried away to get her horse and buggy hitched.

She walked up the hill with Sophie in her arms. Several people had come out, Isaac and Anna among them. "What happened?" Anna asked.

"Bella scared her."

"Poor Bella wouldn't hurt a fly. What did she do, child?" Anna stroked the girl's cheek.

"She hit me with a stick."

Emma explained. "Bella was trying to give it to her so she would throw it in the water."

Isaac patted his wife's arm. "The dog will fetch right through the ice if she has to. She doesn't care how cold the water is."

Pressing her way through the crowd, Emma murmured her excuses and carried Sophie to the door. She only had to wait for a minute before Luke drove up. Sophie scrambled from her arms into the front seat. She glared at Luke. "I don't want him to come along."

Emma said, "I'll drive, Luke. Thanks for the offer."

"Are you sure?"

"We'll be fine, won't we, Sophie?"

"I want to go home now."

Luke handed Emma up into the driver's seat. She grasped his hand. "*Danki.* I appreciate all your help."

"Anytime."

Hannah came running out with Sophie's pail. It was filled with cookies. "Don't forget this. I'm sorry you didn't like my dog."

Sophie didn't answer. Emma set her horse in motion and drove Sophie to her father's farm. Wayne came out when they pulled up. "How was the party?"

"I didn't like it. They had a dog that scared me, but Emma chased it away. She's nice. I brought you some cookies." He lifted her out of the buggy.

Emma gave him a sympathetic smile. "I'm sorry she didn't have a good time. She was frightened by Hannah's dog, but no harm was done."

"Will I see you again?" he asked.

"I'm usually at home." She couldn't in good conscience invite him for a visit, but she hated to disappoint him after her disastrous evening with his daughter.

"I'll stop in one of these days."

"Can I come, too?" Sophie asked.

Emma nodded and turned her horse toward home.

* * *

On the Sunday before Christmas, Luke made up his mind to ask Emma if he could court her. He decided to get it over with after church and kill the butterflies in his stomach. Once she said no, he was free to look elsewhere. Not that he would.

If she agreed, it would mean he would have to join the faith. Was he ready for that? He had to be. It was the only way they could be together. This had to be what God wanted for him.

When the long service was over, he stood beside her buggy, waiting for her to come out of the house after the meal had been served. She came up the hill toward him with a basket over her arm. "Hello, Luke."

"Emma, would you like to ride home with me?"

She raised her chin a notch, and he prepared himself for her rejection. She nodded once. "I would."

Had he heard her correctly? "You would?"

"Are you ready to leave now?"

"*Ja. Ja*, we can leave now. Let me get my horse hitched up and tell your brothers you won't be going home with them."

"All right. I'll wait here."

He tripped getting down the hill but recovered without falling. He looked to see if she was watching. She was. She pressed her hand to her lips to hide her smile, but he could see the humor in her eyes.

Hurrying across to the corral, he located his mare and soon had her harnessed to his open cart. He gave thanks for the mild weather as the sunshine warmed his face. Emma wouldn't be uncomfortable riding with him.

She had agreed so readily. He was still amazed. Locating Roy and Alvin in the barn with other boys their age, Luke told the pair he was taking their sister home.

Roy never even glanced up from the phone in his hand. "Okay, fine."

So much for opposition from her family. Luke hurried back outside and skidded to a stop when he saw Emma wasn't by her buggy. Had she changed her mind?

Glancing around, he saw she was standing on the other side of his cart. When his heart started beating again, he walked calmly in her direction. "Are you ready?"

"I am."

Taking the basket from her, he placed it behind the seat, and held out his hand so she could steady herself while getting in. After a second of hesitation, she laid her hand in his. A jolt of pleasure raced up his arm and spread throughout his body. Her cheeks turned pink. Did she feel it, too? He wanted to say something, but nothing came to mind so he walked around the cart and got in.

When he was seated, he glanced her way. "Are you worried about people seeing us together?"

"*Nee*, why should I be?"

"I don't have a spotless reputation."

She fixed her gaze on his. "I'm not concerned about what you did in the past. It's your action now and in the future that truly matters to me."

"Then I'll behave myself."

Arching one eyebrow, she snapped back, "See that you do."

He laughed as he turned the horse and started down the lane. At the highway, he paused. "Shall I take you directly home, or would you like to take the long way there?"

"The long way should be a very pretty drive today."

Happiness surged through his blood. "The long way it is."

A secondary road split off from the highway a few hundred yards from the lane that followed the curve of the river between the low hills. Luke turned into it, noticing several other sets of tracks in the fresh snow. It was a popular drive for young couples with several secluded places they could turn off and enjoy some privacy. The first two such places already had buggies parked in them, so Luke drove on. He wanted to say something, but Emma's silence had stifled his tongue. She sat beside him, seemingly enjoying the ride. He didn't want to spoil it for her.

He relaxed and began to enjoy the view, too. Snow covered the hillsides in a thick white blanket that sparkled everywhere the sunlight touched it. The trees had long since lost their leaves and their stark branches reached toward the blue sky while their identical shadows intertwined with their neighbors on the snow-covered ground. The river, nearly a solid sheet of ice, gurgled up in open spots before disappearing under the ice again. A dozen Canada geese occupied one section of open water. He gestured toward them with his head. "Think one of them will become someone's Christmas goose?"

"I hope not. They're so pretty. I love to see the flocks in huge Vs traveling across the sky. Sometimes I hear them at night and wonder why they travel in the darkness."

"I reckon because they can tell where they are by the stars or by the rivers heading south below them."

She gazed upward. "It must be a wonderful thing to see the world from so high in the air."

"True, but I think a snug house and a warm fire must beat the view when the weather turns nasty. I'm glad I'm not a goose."

Chuckling, she glanced his way. "So true." She paused. "Father will be so happy that the store can open when he returns."

"He's been really pressing to get it done. Why the rush?"

He glanced at Emma in time to see a look of pain flash across her face before she schooled her features into a calm expression. "He has his reasons."

Luke knew something wasn't right. He pulled the horse to a stop. "Emma, what's wrong? Tell me."

"Nothing. It's nothing."

"It is. I can see you're worried."

"It's nothing that concerns you."

She didn't want to discuss it. Not with him. It wasn't his concern. His happiness at the day faded. If she couldn't confide in him, then what hope was there for something more between them?

Emma wished with all her heart that she could tell Luke about her father's illness. She needed to talk to someone about it, but her promise to her father kept her silent. She shivered and pulled her cloak tightly across her chest.

"I should get you home. It's too cold for an open buggy ride."

"I'm fine."

"You always say that. Even when you aren't fine. I'm taking you home." He set the horse in motion.

He looked so serious. Had she upset him? It wasn't her intention. She had been thrilled when he asked her

to ride home with him. Did he know that? Should she say something? She didn't want to appear forward.

An awkwardness appeared between them and she didn't know how to combat it. She sat in silence until they had almost reached her house. She gave one last try to lighten the mood. "Would you like to come in for some apple cake and coffee?"

He pulled his horse to a stop. A hint of a smile lifted the corner of his mouth. "Apple cake isn't cherry cobbler, but it will do."

She saw her brothers coming out of the barn. They had reached home before her. She had been hoping for some more time alone with Luke. Her spirits plunged lower when she saw Wayne Hochstetler was with them. She wasn't up to a visit with him, but she could hardly send him home.

"Have I come at a bad time?" Wayne eyed her closely. It must look as if she had accepted a ride home from church with Luke, because she had. From the look on Wayne's face, she knew he thought she was behaving poorly by stepping out with Luke, too, but she wasn't dating Wayne. Not yet.

Wayne was her father's choice. She couldn't turn him away. She had promised to consider him and, so far, she had barely given him a chance. He wasn't as fun-loving as Luke, but he was firmly rooted in their community and their church. Something Luke couldn't say.

She forced a cheerful smile for Wayne's benefit. "It's not a bad time at all. I was just offering Luke some apple cake. Would you care for some?"

He smiled for the first time since he had been coming by. "It's a favorite dessert of mine."

"How is your daughter?"

"Fine. She talks about you all the time. About how you and she threw stones in the river, and how you comforted her when the dog scared her. She likes you a great deal and hopes to see you again soon so she can learn how to make cookies and cakes for me. I didn't realize how much she missed having a woman's company."

"I'm glad I could help. She's a sweet child. Let us go inside."

Roy took hold of Luke's reins. "Do you want me to put her in the barn for you?" he asked hopefully.

Luke shook his head. "I won't be staying that long."

"But you just got here." Roy gave Wayne a sour look.

It didn't faze Wayne. He held out his hand to help Emma down from the open carriage. "You must be cold after riding in this. Luke should have more sense."

Luke's eyes narrowed. Emma spoke quickly. "I'm not cold at all. A ride in the open was very refreshing. *Danki*, Luke, for obliging me."

If that gave Wayne the impression the buggy ride had been her idea, that was fine. She allowed him to help her down. Pulling off her gloves, she stuffed them into the pocket of her cloak. "Come inside."

The glare the two men shared would have been funny if she hadn't been the cause. Feeling like a mouse caught between two tomcats, she strode into the house and took off her cloak and bonnet.

Her brothers, Luke and Wayne came in and hung up their hats and coats.

"Have a seat in the living room, all of you. It will take me a few minutes to get things ready."

They all trouped into the other room. Instead of friendly chatter, Emma heard only silence. That did not bode well for a congenial visit. After making cof-

fee and handing out slices of cake, Emma took a seat in her chair. Everyone ate without speaking.

The minute he had finished his cake, Luke rose. "I have to be going."

"Already?" Yes, Wayne was her father's choice, but Emma was loath to spend an afternoon with him. She was afraid the silence would continue.

Luke turned to Wayne. "It was good to see you again."

Wayne nodded, but he didn't say anything.

Roy rose to his feet quickly. "I'll see you out, Luke." They both left.

The silence was broken by Alvin jumping up. "I'll go see him out, too," he said, and left the room.

Wayne scowled after Alvin. "How many people does it take to show Luke Bowman the door?"

"Apparently, all of us. Excuse me. I forgot to tell him something. I'll be back in a moment."

Emma told herself she wanted to know if Luke would be over the next day, but it was just an excuse to see him again. She opened the door and stepped outside. Luke stood beside his horse, adjusting the headband. "The man has a personality of a toad. An old thick toad."

"Not even a toad. A rock," Roy added.

Alvin punched his brother's shoulder. "More like a stick of wood. Or a thick block of wood between his ears."

Her brothers and Luke all laughed.

Emma marched down the steps. "How dare you make fun of a guest in this house! Alvin, Roy, I'm ashamed of you. And of you, too, Luke Bowman."

She glanced at the house to make sure Wayne hadn't followed her. "It's one thing to have a poor opinion

about someone, but don't lead my brothers astray by voicing it in front of them."

Luke flushed a dull red. "I'm sorry, but you have to admit that Wayne doesn't have much of a personality. Come on. Anyone can see that."

"And everyone can see how immature you are when you hold him up to ridicule. You need to grow up, Luke."

"Why does Wayne keep coming over, anyway?" Roy asked.

Emma pressed her lips tightly together. "Your father asked him to look in on us."

"He wants to marry your sister." Luke climbed into his buggy and picked up the reins.

Roy turned stricken eyes to her. "You aren't considering him, are you?"

"He's a stalwart member of our faith. I am considering him," she said loudly, wanting Luke to hear.

He did. His face went blank. "I pray you'll be happy."

Why won't you speak up and tell me how you feel, Luke? You have to know I still care. I let you kiss me. Tell me you're going to stay, join the faith and be happy among us. Don't make me watch you leave again.

Roy took a step away from her. "Even if you marry him, I'm not going to let that toad boss me around."

She whirled to face her brother. "Wayne is not a toad. He's a God-fearing man who has suffered the tragic loss of his wife. He has a daughter who has lost her mother. We know what that feels like, don't we? Where is your sympathy, Roy?"

His expression grew mulish, then the cell phone in his boot rang. He pulled it out. Emma snatched it from his hand and threw it away. "I told you to get rid of that."

Roy raced to pick it up. "I hate you and this whole backward place."

He took off toward the barn with Alvin following him and begging him to wait.

"Emma, that was uncalled for," Luke said quietly.

Everything was so wrong. Her father was dying. Her brother hated her. Luke didn't love her. She couldn't carry it all alone. Her self-control fell into tatters.

"You don't get to tell me what to do, Luke Bowman. You don't have that right."

"Emma, please, I don't want to fight."

"Then you should leave. I don't need you anymore. We can handle things ourselves and I sure don't need you encouraging my brothers to make fun of Wayne or filling Roy's head with ideas about going away to school and working on solar cells. We were better off before you started interfering."

"Don't worry. It'll never happen again." Luke turned his horse and drove out of the yard without another word.

She watched him leave and pressed a hand to her forehead. "Oh, what have I done?"

Luke rode home in a daze with Emma's words echoing in his mind. *I don't need you anymore.*

Hearing them hurt more than he had imagined any words could hurt. Now he knew how badly he must have wounded Emma in the past and he grew sick to his stomach. She had needed him then, and he turned away from her out of shame.

He had been wrong to make fun of Wayne, that was true, but Emma's anger was about more than that. She didn't trust him enough to share her troubles. Without

trust, there wasn't anything to build a foundation on. He'd been foolish to dream things might change between them.

It didn't take him long to reach home. He was rubbing down his horse when his father walked into the barn. "Luke, I'm surprised to see you home so soon. Rebecca said you'd be visiting until late today."

"That was the plan. It didn't work out that way."

"Care to talk about what's wrong?"

Luke almost said no, but then stopped himself. It wasn't fair to expect Emma to share her troubles if he was too proud to share his own with his father.

He took a deep breath. "I'm in love with Emma, but she doesn't love me." It was a deeply humbling experience to say it aloud.

"I see." His father came to the stall door and leaned on it. "I'm sorry. You told her how you feel and she told you she didn't feel the same?"

"It wasn't hard to figure out. I don't know why I thought she might care for me."

"The heart is a fierce thing. It will hold on to hope in the face of all evidence to the contrary. It is our mind that tricks us into giving up."

"Or it's our mind that lets us see the truth our hearts don't want to accept."

"I would rather believe my heart. It has stood me in good stead these many years. My mind said you were lost to me forever not so long ago, but my heart never gave up on you."

Luke blinked back the sting of his tears. "I'm sorry for all the pain I caused you and *Mamm*."

"And I am grateful to *Gott* that He brought you back

to us. Maybe you should tell Emma what is in your heart and not let your brain have the final say."

"It's too late for that."

"As you will. Seek the council of our Heavenly Father in this matter. He knows the secrets of every heart."

Luke nodded but didn't speak. His head and his heart were telling him it was over with Emma.

Could he stay in Bowmans Crossing if she married someone else?

No, he couldn't bear to see her with another. He couldn't live with that kind of torture.

At last he had the answer to his question. When he was free, he would go. He couldn't stay. He wasn't strong enough.

"I may have overreacted." Emma sat across from Rebecca in her living room two days after her disastrous afternoon with Luke. Rebecca had stopped by with a coffee cake and the two were enjoying a late breakfast. At least Rebecca was enjoying it. Emma couldn't swallow a bite.

"In what way?" Rebecca took a sip of coffee.

"I accused Luke of encouraging Roy to poke fun at Wayne. I felt so sorry for Wayne and his daughter. Roy looks up to Luke. Anything Luke says, Roy takes to heart. I yelled at Roy and I threw his phone down and broke it. I yelled at Luke, too. I wasn't a nice person." She needed to apologize to him soon.

"Why do you keep pushing Luke away, when you are clearly in love with him, Emma? It's as plain as the nose on your face. You've loved him for years."

Emma wanted to deny it but she couldn't. She was in love with Luke. "What am I going to do?"

"You know you can't keep stringing Wayne along. You have to tell him how you feel about someone else. You don't have to say it's Luke."

"I don't want to hurt Wayne."

"You could marry Wayne and be miserable for the rest of your life."

"Not such a good option when you put it that way. Do you really think Luke is in love with me? I'm not convinced. He hasn't spoken of it. He hasn't made a move to join the church. What if he intends to leave again?" How could she bear that?

Rebecca finished her coffee and stood. "I've got to get going. Luke will convince you in his own time. Give him some encouragement. Give him a chance."

"How many does he deserve?"

"As many as God gives all of us. When will your father be home?"

"Tomorrow."

"In time to see Alvin in the school Christmas program?"

"Of course."

"Then I shall see him there. Be of good cheer, Emma. It will all work out as God wills. I've got to run the rest of the costumes up to the school and get busy baking. I can't believe Christmas is almost here."

After saying goodbye to Rebecca, Emma went out to the new hardware store half-filled with items waiting to be sold. Alvin was stocking the shelves from his boxes. At least this project had gone right.

She looked around for Roy. "Alvin, where is your brother?"

"I haven't seen him. I think he's still in his room. Do you realize we missed his birthday yesterday?"

Emma slapped her hands to her cheeks. "I forgot. How could I forget? No wonder he is staying out of sight. I'll go up and apologize."

She climbed the stairs and knocked on his door. There was no answer. She opened it and stopped in the doorway. The room was empty. The bed neatly made. His clothes were gone from the pegs on his wall. His dresser drawers were open and empty as well. Checking under the bed confirmed her worst fears. His suitcase was missing. She turned and raced downstairs.

Luke was almost done packing when there was a knock at his door. He hesitated to speak to anyone, but he said, "Come in."

Samuel looked in. "We missed you at breakfast. Are you sick?"

"I'm fine."

"Tomorrow is the big day. Last parole visit. You'll be a free man."

"Yup."

"So why are you packing now? And why are you packing so much?"

"Jim and I are going to Cincinnati a day early."

"You've got more than two days' worth of clothes in that bag."

Luke stopped what he was doing. This was so hard. "That's because I'm not coming back."

"That was my next guess. Are you sure about this?"

Emma was considering marrying a man with a daughter who needed her. Luke couldn't compete with that. He was nothing but an ex-con and an ex-junkie. "I'm sure. I'll write this time."

"Can't you wait until after Christmas to leave? For the family?"

A honk outside told him Jim was waiting. "Nobody is going to be shocked by this." He zipped his bag shut and headed for the door.

"You're wrong about that. We all thought you would stay."

"Sorry to disappoint you again. Goodbye."

Chapter Fourteen

"What do you mean our brother is missing?" Alvin frowned at Emma.

"Missing. As in not here. His clothes are gone along with the money I know he keeps in an envelope taped under his bedside table."

Emma was already moving toward the kitchen as a sickening sensation churned in her midsection.

Alvin grabbed her arm. "He wouldn't do this."

Shouting for Roy, Alvin charged up the steps. There was no answer.

Emma folded her arms tightly across her middle. How could he do this when she needed his support more than ever?

Unable to accept that his headstrong brother had abandoned them, Alvin flew down the stairs and raced out the front door. Standing on the front porch, he shouted Roy's name into the whirling snow and then raced to the barn.

Emma sat at the table with her head in her hands. After a few minutes, she felt Alvin's hand on her arm.

"He wants to live *Englisch*. I reckon he decided it was time."

"Not now. Not at Christmas. Not with our father ill. How could Roy do this to us?" Emma realized she was wringing her hands. She crossed her arms and tucked her cold fingers beneath her armpits.

"I thought *Daed* was better."

She stared into Alvin's worry-filled eyes. This wasn't the time to share what she knew about their father's condition. "He doesn't want us fretting about him, you know that. He is in God's hands, and *Gott es goot. Ja?*"

"*Ja.* Do you think God will bring Roy back? I mean, Luke came back."

"Roy will come to his senses. I'm sure of it." Only she wasn't. If only she could talk to Roy and make him understand how much she needed him, how sorry she was.

Was Luke right? In her struggle to manage the business and the home, had she pushed Roy aside, making him feel like a troublesome child instead of the man of the family?

Alvin turned back toward the front door. "Luke will be here soon. He'll know what we should do."

Her heart sank. "I'm afraid Luke isn't coming today."

Alvin scowled at her. "Why not?"

Emma walked to the kitchen window and looked out. "We had a disagreement. I told him we didn't need him anymore. We don't. We'll be fine."

"Are you crazy? How could you tell him we didn't need him? We do. We've only got half the inventory priced and on the shelves."

"He's not dependable."

"I love you, sister, but you can be every bit as willful and stubborn as Roy. This isn't the time to be prideful."

"I'm not prideful."

"You're not forgiving, either. We need Luke."

"Let's worry about your brother. Where do you think he would go?"

"To the city."

Tears filled her eyes. She threw her arms around Alvin and pulled him close. "*Nee*, he wouldn't do that. Not now."

Alvin pulled away. "I hear a buggy. Maybe it's Luke." He shot out the front door.

Maybe it was Roy returning. Had he taken the buggy? She hadn't checked. She snatched her coat from the peg and ran out after Alvin.

It wasn't Luke or Roy. Wayne stepped down from his buggy. She rushed to his side. "Wayne, I'm so glad to see you. Roy has run away. What should I do?"

"Are you certain? Maybe he is staying with one of his friends."

"He's taken all his clothes. Can you take me to the bus station? I'm not sure when the next bus leaves. He might still be there."

"*Nee*, Emma. You must not seek him out. If he has left the faith, then you must shun him until he repents and returns of his own accord."

"He's only a boy, Wayne. He's not been baptized."

"Then according to your ways, he is free to go. Our Creator endowed all men with free will."

"Yes, he's free to go, but he has no idea what is waiting for him out there."

"I will pray that he learns the error of his ways and

comes home a humbled man. I need two number-0 horseshoes. Do you carry them?"

"You can ask me about horseshoes when my brother is missing?" She stared at him in horror.

"Emma, your brother made his choice."

"And I have made mine. We will not suit. I will not go out with you. I wish you well."

"I'm sorry to have wasted my time."

"As am I. You will find horse supplies in the back of the store. Take what you need and leave the money under the counter. Alvin, get a horse hitched. We'll go after Roy ourselves."

He ran to do as she asked. She jumped in when he came out of the barn, took the reins and put her horse into a fast trot. Twenty minutes later, she pulled her tired horse to a stop beside the filling station that doubled as a bus stop. She handed the reins to Alvin. "Walk him to cool him down and keep an eye out for Roy. I'll check the bus schedule."

Hopping down from the buggy, she hurried inside. The man behind the counter was helpful and used to seeing Amish kids heading off on their own.

"I knew as soon as I saw him he was a runaway. They have that look about them. Scared and trying to look bold at the same time. Your brother, you say?" He leafed through his ticket book.

"He's only seventeen." Just a baby. She bit her lip to keep from crying.

"Here it is."

"I'll take a ticket for one to wherever he went."

"He purchased a ticket to Columbus with a transfer to Cincinnati at four-thirty last evening. The line makes

a lot of stops. If he stayed on the bus, he would have arrived in Cincinnati by one in the morning."

"Cincinnati? Oh, Roy, what have you done?" Her plan to follow him vanished like her breath on a cold windy day. Even if she followed him, how would she find him among the thousands of people there?

"Do you still want a ticket? The next bus taking the same route doesn't leave until four-thirty in the afternoon on Christmas Eve."

She shook her head. "*Nee*, but thank you."

Roy was gone. Would she ever see him again? She walked slowly outside.

Alvin drew the buggy to a stop beside her. "I didn't see him. Did you find out if he's left?"

"He has gone to Cincinnati."

Worry filled Alvin's eyes. "What does that mean?"

"It means your brother is *Englisch* now."

"But he'll come home, right? Emma, he'll be home soon."

"I don't know."

"We should talk to Luke. He'll know what to do."

It was so tempting, but no. She hardened her heart. "*Nee*, this is our business and none of his."

"Roy wouldn't miss Christmas with us. He'll be back for Christmas. I know it."

She prayed Alvin was right. "Let's go home. You must get to school. God will deliver Roy to us. We will pray and we will have faith."

Emma drove Alvin to school in a state of shock. Her mind had stopped functioning. After dropping her brother at school, she drove home. Only the echoes of the empty house greeted her when she walked in. How could Roy do this? If she had told him about his father,

would it have made a difference? There was no way to know. She was simply second-guessing herself now.

Her father's letter said he would be home about noon tomorrow. More than anything, she dreaded giving him this news.

Did Luke know? Had he helped Roy escape a life he didn't want? Luke knew how to do it. She longed to throw herself in Luke's arms and beg his forgiveness. She needed his strength and comfort. Tears slipped down her cheeks. She had driven Luke and Roy away. Her pride was cold comfort now.

That night she didn't sleep at all. Instead, she paced her bedroom floor, stopping every few minutes to look out into the night. Hoping and praying her brother would return. She saw only darkness beyond her windowpane. When the sky grew light again just before dawn, Emma fell to her knees at the window. It was Christmas Eve morning.

"Please, God, show me what to do. Keep Roy safe. That's all I ask."

She closed her eyes in prayer and Luke's face appeared to her, his eyes full of pain at her cruel words. Her fear of being abandoned again had caused her to push away the man she loved. The one man who could help her now.

She needed Luke, not just to help find Roy but to make her life complete. She had to tell him. She wouldn't let one more chance pass her by.

When Alvin came down to breakfast, she could tell he hadn't slept, either. "I don't want to go to school."

"I know, but your classmates and Teacher Lillian are depending on you. There is so much that still needs to be done."

"How can I sing with Roy gone? I don't want to."

"*Daed* will be home today. You want him to hear you sing, don't you?"

"Knowing Roy is gone will break his heart."

That was what she feared, too. "Your songs will give him comfort, Alvin. I think you should go to school."

"What are you going to do?"

"I'm going to ask Luke to help us. I'm praying he knows where Roy might have gone."

Alvin threw his arms around her. "*Danki*. He'll know how to get Roy back. You'll see."

She patted her brother's back. "I know he will. The bus leaves this afternoon, so I won't get to see your program tonight."

"That's okay. Roy is more important. What do we tell *Daed*?"

"The truth. He'll be home around noon. I'll go to see Luke as soon as I've explained things to *Daed*."

Alvin reluctantly left for school. Emma worked in the shop until she heard a car pull in a little after nine. She walked slowly to the door, dreading the coming reunion.

Luke walked out the door of the parole office and stopped in the bright winter sunshine. The early-morning air was cold and tainted with the smell of car exhaust, but he breathed in deeply.

I'm free. It's over.

"What now?" Jim stood waiting for him at the bottom of the steps. He glanced at his watch. "It's half past nine. Want to get in a little shopping before we head home?"

"Take me to the bus station."

Jim's smile faded. "Let me drive you home, Luke. That's where you belong."

What was the point of going back? Emma would never be his. He didn't deserve her, anyway. He'd done his time. He was a free man. Free to go anywhere and do anything except the one thing he wanted to do more than he wanted to draw his next breath. To tell Emma he loved her. To hold her in his arms and never let her go. But it would be another man who held her. Another man would care for her, give her children and grow old beside her.

A black hole of despair opened in front of him. Facing a life without her was impossible. He wanted to forget his burning need for her. He needed to forget. And he knew exactly how he could make that happen.

"There is a motel called the Gray Cat a few blocks from the bus depot. If you can drop me there, that's all I need. That and some time to think things over."

"I wish you'd change your mind."

Luke shook his head. Jim walked ahead of him to the car and drove him to his destination without another word until he pulled into the parking lot of the motel. He turned in his seat to look at Luke. "Don't do something stupid."

"I won't." He smiled at his friend. Something stupid had been thinking that he could have a life with Emma. She had been the smart one this time.

He got out of the car and went to check in. The three-story building was old and smelled of the unwashed occupants that frequented it. It was cheap, and the owner had friends in low places. He was the man Luke needed to see. He stopped in front of the desk. Behind the wire

mesh, a woman in a tight minidress with pale purple hair was filing her nails.

"Can I get a room?"

She looked up and her eyes widened. "Luke Bowman, is that you?"

It took him a second to realize he was facing the woman who had testified against him and wrongfully imprisoned his brother Joshua. Time had not been kind to her. She looked ten years older instead of three. "Hello, Maggie."

"I sure never thought I'd see you again. So you got out."

"No thanks to you."

Her eyes hardened. "A girl has to do what a girl has to do. I was looking at a long stretch. It was my third arrest. The DA offered me a deal if I rolled on you and your brother. What choice did I have?"

"You had a choice. You could've told the truth. My brother had nothing to do with the drugs I was moving for you."

"Don't be like that. He got out early, didn't he? I'm sure he's back on the farm, milking cows and growing corn. You Amish boys are a funny bunch. You race here to live it up and go crying home when life gets hard. I had another one come in yesterday. What a dope. He thinks I'm the hottest thing since horseshoes."

"I hope he comes to his senses long before I did."

She moved to the door at the side of her desk, unlocked it and came out to stand beside Luke. "We can let bygones be bygones, can't we, Luke? You kept your mouth shut about my operation, and I appreciated that. I always liked you."

She placed her fingers on his arm, walked them up to

his shoulder and slipped them into his hair at the nape of his neck. "I've got some good stuff at my place. I'll share. It won't even cost you."

It was what he wanted, wasn't it? This was why he'd come here. To forget. To close his eyes and slip into that sweet stupor that made everything tolerable. His body trembled at the thought of it.

God help me. What am I doing?

Emma's face appeared before his mind's eye, followed by his mother and father. He was free now. Free to go where he wanted. Free to live a worthy and decent life.

Forgetting Emma was impossible. It would be hard to see her married to another if she chose that path, but it would be harder still to have her know he had fallen so low again. Seeing her happy would be enough for him.

Newfound warmth spread through his body. He didn't have to do this alone. God was standing beside him, offering His comfort and His strength when Luke's failed.

He lifted Maggie's arms from his neck. "I've changed my mind about a room."

"You're welcome to stay with me. I'm on my own at the moment."

"None of us are really alone, Maggie. God is with us always. I forgive you for the lies you told about me and my brother. I pray you find the peace that I have now."

"Well, la-di-da. You got religion, did you? Take it someplace else. My clientele won't appreciate it." She turned her back on him and reentered her cage, snapping the door shut behind her.

He left the building and walked outside with a light heart. He didn't have to be a slave to drugs. He was free.

It would always be a struggle, but for the first time he believed it was a battle he could win with God's help.

He didn't have to return to Bowman's Crossing. It might be easier for Emma if he didn't, but he would visit his family often. The solar installation school he had read about was here in the city. Maybe he should start there.

After he got a letter off to his family letting them know his plans.

To Luke's surprise, Jim Morgan was still sitting in his car at the curb. His face lit up in a bright smile when he caught sight of Luke. With a casualness that belied his racing heart, Luke opened the passenger's side door and slid in the front seat.

Jim pounded Luke's shoulder with his fist. "I knew you didn't belong here. Thank God you realized it. It's really a merry Christmas Eve now. Buckle up. I know exactly where to go to celebrate."

Emma's father sat at the kitchen table nursing a cup of coffee. Emma sat across from him waiting for him to speak.

He looked up with bloodshot eyes. There were still traces of tears on his cheeks. He'd lost more weight while he was gone. Her heart ached for him.

He pushed his coffee aside. "Wayne is right. We'll have to pray Roy comes home. That's all we can do. He has to come home on his own."

"I'll pray but I'll look, too. I have to try."

"It should be me going to Luke."

"You're tired. You've had a long journey. You need to rest up. Alvin is looking forward to you watching his school program and hearing him sing. It's all he has

talked about since you've been gone. You can't disappoint him."

"You should be there, too."

"I will be. In spirit. Lie down for a little while." She glanced at the clock. It was almost eleven. She helped her father to his room, saw him settled and then raced out the door on foot. Her father would need their buggy later.

It took her twenty minutes to reach the river. She was out of breath but once she entered the covered bridge, she got her second wind and ran all the way to the Bowmans' front door. Breathing heavily and worried about what Luke would say to her, she knocked on the door, then pressed a hand to her pounding heart.

She looked up when the door opened, but it was Samuel. "Emma, what's wrong?"

"I must speak to Luke. It's terribly important."

"I'm afraid Luke is gone."

She closed her eyes. "I forgot about his parole meeting. When will he be back?"

"He's not coming back."

Her eyes flew open and she saw the sadness etched on Samuel's face. Her blood turned cold and stopped flowing. "I don't understand."

"Luke has gone back to his *Englisch* life in the city."

"He can't be gone. I need him." A loud buzzing filled her brain. She watched in stunned surprise as the ground rushed toward her face.

Emma, Emma, Emma. The tires on the road hummed her name as Jim's car flew along. Luke's friend hadn't stopped for the past two hours. It turned out the place Jim decided Luke should celebrate Christmas Eve was

in Bowmans Crossing. Luke hadn't protested once since he figured out what Jim was up to. Home was where he wanted to be on his first night as a truly free man. A move and a new career could wait until after the holidays.

Leaning back in the seat, he drummed his fingers on the armrest in time with the tires.

"Are you thinking about Emma?" Jim glanced toward Luke.

"All the time, it seems."

"What's going to happen with the two of you?"

"Nothing. If she is happy, that's all I need. I wish I were the man who could make her happy, but it wasn't meant to be. It seems God has other plans for my life and for hers."

"You'll see her tonight. She's not going to miss the school program and neither should you."

"I'm going. I promised Hannah I would be there. Thanks for making me keep that promise. You are welcome to join us."

"Thanks, but no thanks. I've got an aunt in Millersburg who is expecting us for dinner. As soon as I drop you off, I'm collecting Brian and we are on our way."

"It's good to have family close, isn't it?"

"You've never met my aunt or tasted her cooking. We're grabbing a bucket of fried chicken on the way."

As Jim sped on toward Bowmans Crossing, Luke couldn't get his mind off Emma. He realized he wouldn't be able to do that until he had the chance to tell her exactly how he felt about her.

He loved her. He always had and always would.

If she didn't want him, he would bow out of the way. He'd go to school and afterwards he would return to

work with his family and try to live a good Amish life. One centered around his faith and his family. It was amazing how those simple words filled his heart and his mind. Once the plain way of life had seemed like a trap. Now it felt safe and welcoming.

It was almost noon by the time Jim dropped Luke at his own front door. He stood outside looking at his home and tried to imagine the shock on Samuel's face and the joy on his mother's when they saw him. He had a lot of apologizing to do.

He pushed open the door and saw the kitchen was empty. He heard the sound of voices and followed them to the living room. Stepping inside, he realized his entire family was gathered there. Samuel saw him first. His eyes widened in astonishment. "Luke, you're back."

"Bad pennies always do that, right?" He set his suitcase down.

His mother gave a glad cry and rushed to throw her arms around him. He held her tight, savoring the smell of cookies that clung to her. "I'm so sorry for the hurt I caused you. I'm home for good, *mudder*," he told her softly. "I will take my vows as soon as possible. I have found forgiveness in God's grace."

She drew back and cupped his face with her hands. "I see that in your eyes. Welcome home. Emma arrived a short time ago. She needs you."

Rebecca and Mary stepped aside and he saw Emma lying on the sofa. He rushed to her and dropped to his knees, taking her cold hand between his own. There were tears on her face. "Darling, what's wrong?"

"Oh, Luke, Roy has run away. Can you find him? Do you know where he's gone?"

Chapter Fifteen

Luke was here. God be praised. Emma held her breath as she waited for him to answer her question. He shook his head. "I don't have any idea where Roy could be. He didn't confide in me."

She closed her eyes against her pain and disappointment. "When I heard you were gone, too, I thought maybe he was with you."

"How long has he been missing?"

"Since the night before last. Help me sit up."

He did, his face a mask of worry. "Are you ill?"

She shook her head. "I was so worried I forgot to eat and the shock of hearing you were gone, too... I guess I fainted."

"You scared me out of a year's growth," Samuel said without malice.

She tried to smile, but failed. "I'm sorry."

"Don't be," Luke said, slipping his arm around her as he sat beside her.

She looked into his beautiful eyes. "Did I hear correctly? Did you say you plan to take your vows?"

"I did."

"You called me darling."

"You had better get used to it. Unless you don't welcome my attention. If that is the case, I apologize."

She cupped his cheek. "I find I do welcome your attention."

"That's the sweetest thing you have ever said to me."

There were a hundred sweet things she wanted to say to him, but all she could think about was her brother. "Have you any idea where Roy might go?"

"None. Do you think he might have hitched a ride out of town?"

"He took the bus. He purchased a ticket to Columbus and then on to Cincinnati. Does that help?"

"It helps a great deal. At least I know where to start looking. Noah, can I use your phone? I need to hire a car to take me to Cincinnati."

"I'm coming with you." She wasn't going to wait at home. She couldn't.

Luke looked as if he would object, but then he slowly nodded. "If you feel well enough."

She turned to Luke's mother. "Anna, if I could have a cup of tea, I would be very grateful."

For the next half hour, Emma sipped her tea and ate a thick ham sandwich while Luke tried to find someone to drive them to the city. He drew a blank on every person the family knew who provided rides for the Amish. Timothy had gone to her father and filled him in on what was happening.

"We can try Nick," Mary suggested. "I know he'll do it for me."

"Might as well try." Luke dialed the number of the sheriff's office and spoke briefly with someone on the

other end. He hung up and looked at Emma. "Nick is tied up at an injury traffic accident. He can't get away."

"What about Jim?" Emma asked.

"He's on his way to Millersburg. But…"

"But what?" she demanded.

He tipped his head to the side. "I know where he keeps the spare keys to his old Jeep. Are you still afraid to ride with me?"

"*Ja*, but I'm coming, anyway."

He smiled and her heart grew light. "That's my girl."

If only she could be.

"I'd better call Jim and tell him my plan." He started to dial the number, but ended up shaking the phone. "Noah, your battery is dead."

Noah took his phone back. "I meant to charge it last night and forgot. I'll hitch up the buggy and drive you to the Morgan place. I can use the phone at the booth to contact Jim after I drop you off."

It only took a few minutes for Noah to bring the buggy around. Luke's father, who had remained quietly beside his wife, spoke up as Emma and Luke got in. "Be careful, *sohn*. Are you breaking the law by doing this?"

Luke gave him a thin smile. "I have a driver's license somewhere. I'm pretty sure Jim will say it's okay for me to borrow the car, so it isn't stealing. If I get pulled over, I'll have a lot of explaining to do, but I don't think I'll go back to jail."

How could she ask Luke to jeopardize his freedom? Emma bit her lower lip. "Is it worth the risk?"

Luke squeezed her hand. "For Roy, *ja*, it is."

Noah drove them to Jim's place. Luke found the key and the old green Jeep roared to life. Emma got in the front seat.

Noah opened Luke's door and took Luke's straw hat, replacing it with his ball cap. "You'll be less likely to get stopped if you don't look like an Amish dude driving a stolen car."

"Danki."

Within a few minutes, they were driving down the highway. Emma watched the scenery flying past. "Do you think we can find him?"

"Maybe. It's a big city, and it's easy to simply disappear. I did for a while."

Emma looked toward him. She had to know why he'd left. "Did you ever think about me after you were gone?"

Luke's stomach lurched. How could he explain? That episode of his life contained all the shameful things that he had done. More than she knew. How could he make her understand that she—that her memory—had saved him?

"Did I think about you? Only every day."

He glanced her way, but she kept her eyes down, refusing to look at him. "How can I believe that? You never wrote. Not once."

"I wanted you to forget me. I thought it was easier that way."

Her gaze shot to his. "Forget you? You wanted me to forget you? Luke, I fell in love with you when I was twelve. I had been in love with you for years. I was just waiting to grow up so we could marry. And you thought I could forget about you? Why? Because my love couldn't have been real? No, you made it clear how much you cared about me. I was nothing to you. The

big wild world beyond Bowmans Crossing was what you loved."

"You're wrong, Emma. I did love you."

"You had a dreadful way of showing it." Her voice was ice-cold.

He gripped the steering wheel even harder. "Don't you see? I did it for you. You belonged in Bowmans Crossing. I never did."

"I belonged with you. Or at least that was what I believed when I was young and foolish. I cried myself to sleep every night for a year. I prayed every night that you would come back. Then I heard you were in prison. I prayed for a letter, a word, anything. Why would a person do that to someone they love? Then I realized I knew the answer. You never loved me. I was a fool."

"Emma, I'm sorry."

She wrapped her arms around herself. "Then don't tell me you thought of me every day."

He wanted to take her in his arms. "I did think of you. I believed that leaving you behind was the only unselfish, honorable thing I ever did in my life. Will you listen to me? Will you hear my story?"

"What can you say that will undo all my pain?"

"Nothing. I hurt you and I'm so, so sorry."

"Was there someone else?"

"*Nee.* There was never anyone but you. But from the time I was little, I knew I didn't belong. I didn't fit in. Samuel was the best possible son. I was the worst possible son. Samuel could do no wrong, and I could do no right. Even when my other brothers came along, that didn't change. I think I hated Samuel as much as I loved him."

"Siblings don't always get along," she said quietly, and he knew she was thinking about Roy.

"Most of the tension was my fault. I couldn't get *Daed*'s attention by being better at anything, so I got his attention by being a problem. Samuel never wanted anything but to work beside our father and take care of the family. I didn't have the gift for woodworking that they shared. I wanted to know how things worked. I wanted to see what made a machine work. I wanted to understand how men used machines to alter the world. I knew I was going to leave the Amish as soon as I was old enough, but then I noticed you."

She looked out the window. "We've known each other since we were toddlers. We went to the same school for eight years. What do you mean you noticed me?"

He chuckled. "It was during the Christmas play our last year at school. Do you remember it?"

"Of course. It was the highlight of my eighth-grade year. You played a miser without family or friends and I was a poor widow begging shelter on Christmas night."

"I don't remember your lines, only the way you looked at me when you begged me to let you come in out of the storm."

"'Kind sir, you know me not, but I am a cold and hungry widow. Can you not spare a crumb of bread on this feast day?'"

"That was it. I turned you away, but the look in your eyes stayed with me long after the play was done."

"I must have played the part of a cold, hungry widow very well."

He laughed. "Your eyes were green daggers of loathing."

"For your character's actions, not for you."

"So you say now."

"All right, maybe I was upset with you."

"I've always wondered why."

"Because you had asked Mae Beth Shetler if you could walk her home after the singing the week before."

"She turned me down."

"Because she knew I liked you."

"I did ask to drive you home at the next singing."

"It was about time. But I couldn't make you stay when it mattered, could I?" She turned her gaze on him again.

"None of what happened was your fault. Samuel and I had one of our big rows."

"You told me about it when you came over that night. You said you had decided to leave for good."

"And you surprised the life out of me when you said you wanted to come with me."

"I thought you were happy about it."

"I was."

She stared at her clasped hands. "But several nights later you had changed your mind. You didn't want me."

"I wanted you more than ever, but I truly believed I was doing the right thing by sending you home. Samuel caught me as I was sneaking out one night. We had another argument, but I never told you the whole truth about that night. I threw it in Samuel's face that you were going with me. I didn't know it for sure, but I hoped it was true. I just wanted to impress him, to prove someone loved me for who I was. He said my going was the best thing that could happen to our family, but I was ruining your life by taking you with me. He told me your mother was ill. He knew your family was going to need you."

Her head snapped up. "He knew? How did he know? I didn't learn of it until weeks later."

"Your mother came into the shop to ask about having a casket made. She didn't want your father to be burdened with the details."

"That is so like her. She was always looking out for him."

"I was arrested for the first time shortly after that. When I got probation I was too ashamed to go home. Jim took me to the bus station and you know the rest. That was why I left without you. Because Samuel was right. Your family needed you."

"My father is ill. Samuel will be making his casket in a year or two."

"Oh, Emma. I'm so sorry. I didn't know."

"He didn't want the boys to learn of it until after Christmas. You've seen how excited Alvin is about his school pageant and his solo. *Daed* didn't want to spoil it for him."

"I can understand that."

"Why didn't you write if you cared for me?"

"I wrote you a hundred letters, but I never mailed them. I thought I was ready for the *Englisch* world. I was a naive fool. I couldn't get a job. I didn't have a social security number or a birth certificate. I was too proud to go home. I met someone, a woman. Her name was Maggie."

"Did you love her?"

"It wasn't like that. She said she could help me. I only had to deliver packages for her. I didn't know it was drugs until later. When I found out, she told me it was the only way she could earn enough money to pay for her baby's medical care. She told me he was in the

hospital and needed surgery. I believed her and I delivered the packages. She invited me to a party afterward and paid me handsomely. It was easy money and I discovered that drugs made a lonely, scared country boy feel as if he owned the world."

"That still doesn't explain why you didn't write to me. You knew my mother was dying. You knew I would need someone to talk to."

"I'm not making any excuses for what I did. God gave me several chances to turn myself around, but I didn't. It wasn't something I wanted to put on a postcard and mail home. How could I admit what a failure I was? You know the rest of the story. Joshua came to try and talk some sense into me. He was caught up in a drug raid. Maggie told them that he and I had been making and delivering drugs for months."

"Why did she lie about Joshua's involvement?"

He shrugged. "To save her own hide. She cut a deal for a lesser sentence. Turns out she didn't have a kid. It was all a lie."

"Thank you for telling me this." Emma turned her face to the window again, and he wondered if he had lost her forever by telling the truth.

Emma jolted upright when the car came to a stop. She blinked and rubbed her eyes. "Did I fall asleep?"

"I think so. We're in the outskirts of the city."

There were houses as far as she could see. Soon, the buildings towered over them as they drove along. People streamed along the sidewalk, and cars clogged the road. Hope dwindled in her heart. "How will we ever find him?"

"Don't give up now. I told Roy about a place where I stayed when I first came here."

"You think Roy would go there?"

He turned onto a quieter side street. "Maybe. It's a cheap motel not far from the bus station. I mentioned that a number of runaway Amish kids end up living there. It's a very bad neighborhood. I tried to get that across to Roy, but I'm not sure it sank in."

She stretched her stiff muscles. The houses had given way to high-rises and now the high-rises gave way to brick buildings with boarded-over windows. The people here weren't hurrying along. They sat on stoops and lounged on car hoods.

"That's it up ahead." Luke pulled the car to a stop. "I want you to wait here, Emma. You will attract too much attention in that garb."

"I am who I am. I won't hide or pretend otherwise. I'm coming with you."

"Then stay close to me."

She didn't argue with that suggestion. Together, they walked along the cracked sidewalk until they reached the parking lot of the motel. Emma heard the sound of a basketball being dribbled in the alley. Roy loved basketball. She caught Luke's sleeve.

He nodded. "We can check it out."

They followed the narrow walkway until it widened into a flat semicircle between three buildings. Someone had put up a makeshift goal. Roy and three other boys were shooting hoops. A woman with purple hair lounged on a chair that held open the back door of the motel. She cheered the boys on.

She caught sight of Luke and frowned. "What are you doing here?"

"Just looking for a friend, Maggie. Roy, can we speak to you?"

Maggie rose to her feet. "He's working for me now, Luke. You should move along before I make trouble."

"Maggie, I know a few good cops these days. My brother married the daughter of a sheriff, did you know that? If I were to tell him where you keep your good stuff stashed and maybe name some of your contacts, like your supplier, how long do you think you'd get this time?"

Her eyes narrowed. "You wouldn't. The Amish don't do things that way."

He simply smiled. "Roy is coming with us."

Emma ignored them. She couldn't take her eyes off Roy. He was all right. Luke had found him.

Roy bounced the ball to one of the other boys and came toward Emma. "I'm not going back. You can't make me."

She pressed a hand to her mouth, then said, "What if I ask nicely?"

Luke laid a hand on Roy's shoulder. "Roy, your sister needs you."

"Emma doesn't need anyone."

She came to stand beside him. "That's where you're wrong, *brudder*. I may act as if I don't need anyone, but that's all it is—an act."

She gazed at Luke, willing him to understand that she was speaking to him as well as Roy. "I know now that I can't do it alone. I need my family. I need my friends, my dearest friends, to understand how frightened I am every single day."

Roy half turned toward her. "Why are you scared?"

She reached out to stroke his hair. "I'm afraid I will

do the wrong thing or say the wrong thing and I'll lose what is most precious to me."

Tears blurred her vision, but she saw Luke watching her. What she had to say was for him, too. "A long time ago, I was very much in love with a young man. He left our community, and I thought it was my fault. I mistakenly believed he saw my love as a weakness, as a chain that would bind him when he wanted his freedom. He broke my heart. Afterward, I grew determined to never show that weakness again."

"Love isn't weakness, Emma. Your young man was a fool." Luke walked back to the car, leaving Emma alone with her brother.

"It was Luke, wasn't it?" Roy asked with more perception that she gave him credit for.

"*Ja*, it was Luke, but that is all in the past. Now it's about you. I understand your desire for freedom, Roy. I do. I want you to come home, but if you can't, I will accept that. All I ask is that you forgive me."

"For what?"

"For failing to see what a fine young man you have become. I was afraid of losing my little brother, the one with the runny nose and skinned knees who came crying to me when he got hurt. I wanted to be needed by you, but I could see that you were outgrowing me. I couldn't accept that, so I tried to keep you little. I treated you as the child I wanted you to be. I should have treated you like a man. Can you forgive me?"

"I never really wanted to leave."

"You didn't?" She wanted to hold him close.

"I only did it for Micah."

Puzzled, she shook her head. "I don't understand.

I thought it was because you didn't want me to marry Wayne."

"I don't like Wayne, but he wasn't the real reason I left. Micah was the one who wanted to get away. He hated being Amish. He couldn't wait to leave. We talked about it all the time. He had all these big plans. He made me promise to go with him. We were going to go the day after my seventeenth birthday. When he died, I knew I had to follow through on my part. To honor him and what he wanted. What we had planned to do together."

"I can't believe Micah would want you to do this by yourself."

"I miss him so much."

Emma's heart ached for his pain. "I know you do. If you weren't all grown up, I would give you a hug."

"Maybe I'm not that grown up."

She cupped his face with her hands. "You are, but I won't tell anyone if you don't."

"Okay."

She pulled him close and held on to him as he cried for his friend.

Luke gave them a few minutes together before he approached again. "If we leave now, we can make it back in time to see Alvin's school pageant."

Emma drew away from Roy and smoothed his jacket with her hands. "Will you be okay? Will you write? I'll be mad if you don't. I will send you money if you need it."

"Alvin's gonna be pretty upset with me if I miss his solo."

Luke smiled, knowing one innocent lamb was about

to return to the fold. "He will. He's been practicing for weeks."

Roy rubbed his face on his sleeve. "You don't know the half of it. He sings in his sleep."

"If you want to ride along, that's fine with me, but I won't be able to bring you back here. I borrowed the car, and I have to return it."

Roy glanced around at the gray, dingy walls. "I reckon I'd rather spend Christmas at home than in this place."

The wail of a siren grew louder and then passed by. Luke looked at Roy. "Won't you miss all the lights and the excitement of the holidays?"

"The lights are mighty pretty, but I've noticed one thing about them."

"What's that?"

Luke looked up. "You can't see the stars at night because the light hides them. You may not be able to see them, but the stars are like God's love for us. Always there no matter what."

Emma laid a hand on Roy's shoulder. "Even when we aren't looking for it. His love is there. We'll wait while you pack."

A short five minutes later, he returned with a duffel bag over his shoulder. "I reckon I've got everything I need."

Emma had her brother back and she was grateful. All she needed now was to win Luke back. So where did she start?

Chapter Sixteen

Luke held his speed to just under the posted limit all the way back. It would be the last time he ever drove a car. To his surprise, he didn't mind the thought. A horse and buggy wouldn't carry him very fast, but it wouldn't carry him very far, either. From now on, he would be sticking close to home. He glanced in the rearview mirror. Close to Emma if she allowed it. He still wasn't sure how she felt about him.

Emma and Roy shared the backseat as Roy recounted his adventures. It was a healing time for them and Luke hated to see it end, but Zachariah's mailbox had come into view. Luke slowed and turned into the lane. As he pulled to a stop, the front door opened. Zachariah and Alvin stepped out onto the porch. No doubt they were wondering who was arriving in an English car.

When Roy and Emma got out of the backseat, Alvin gave a whoop of happiness and rushed toward them. Zachariah followed more slowly, but his grin was every bit as wide. Luke got out of the car and stood waiting for the reunion to end.

Emma, her face glistening with tears of joy, came to

his side. "Come inside, Luke. I know Father will want to thank you for all you've done."

"I'd love to stay, but I have to get going. I need to return the car and make it to the school play on time. Hannah will never speak to me again if I'm late."

"We have to get ready as well. I reckon we'll see you there."

"I reckon."

As goodbyes went, it wasn't much. He wanted to get Emma alone and tell her that he loved her and that he couldn't live without her. But those words would have to wait for another day. "*Frehlicher Grischtdaag*, Emma."

"Merry Christmas to you, too, Luke." Her soft smile warmed his heart and gave him hope.

Emma and her family took their seats in the school-room that was quickly filling with family and friends of the children. Soon, all the lanterns in the room were turned down except one. Alvin walked out on the stage and into the circle of light, silhouetted against the back-drop painted to resemble the village of Bethlehem. After a hush fell over the room, Alvin's voice rang out pure and sweet, each note a living thing of splendor as he sang "While Shepherds Watched Their Flocks." Only the multitude of the heavenly hosts praising God on that first Christmas night could have sounded more beautiful. For the first time, she didn't see her brother—she saw a messenger of God bearing tidings of great joy. When his song was done, the shepherds entered the stage and the play began.

Tears filled Emma's eyes. She slipped her fingers into her father's hand, and he squeezed them gently. There were tears in his eyes, too. Emma listened, en-

tranced by the age-old story and the peace that settled over her.

After one angel lost her wing and had to run back for it, the stage cleared again and Alvin walked to the center once more and began "The First Noel." No one moved. Even after the last clear note died away, a hush remained. It was as if no one wanted to mar the holiness filling the room.

Lillian walked to Alvin's side, touched his arm gently and turned to the audience. "That concludes our program tonight. There are refreshments at the back. Our scholars are so pleased that you could join us and we want to wish all of you a very Merry Christmas. *Frehlicher Grischtdaag.*"

Her father leaned over. "I think he will be the *Volsinger* one day."

"I think you are right." The *Volsinger* was the man who began each hymn during the Amish church service. It was a solemn responsibility to lead the congregation in songs handed down through the generations.

The lights were turned up again, and the audience rose to enfold the excited children and move en masse toward the tables bearing goodies. Emma visited with her neighbors and friends, but she kept one eye on Luke where he stood with his family. Hannah was imploring her mother to fix her wing. As the crowd thinned out and began to go home, Emma made her way to her father's side. He sighed deeply and said, "Are you ready to go home?"

"You and the boys go on without me."

"Are you sure?"

"There's something I need to take care of, and you have a lot to discuss with your sons."

"I do. We'll see you later. *Guten nacht.*"

"Good night, *Daed.*"

As soon as her family went out, she fixed her gaze on Luke. What if she was wrong and he didn't feel the same about her? There was only one way to find out. He was getting his hat when she caught up with him. "It has been a remarkable night, thanks in large part to you, Luke."

He shook his head. "I didn't repeat a single poem or sing a note. The children made it special."

"I wasn't talking about the program."

His eyes searched her face. "I'm happy I was able to help."

She gathered her courage. "There is something else I'd like you to do for me tonight."

"Anything. What is it?"

"Would you walk me home?"

Luke's heart jumped into his throat. Had he heard her correctly? "I'm sure my family has room for you in the sleigh."

She looked down at her hands clasped in front of her. "It's not terribly cold. I thought a walk might be nice."

Happiness made him giddy. "It sounds *wunderbar.*"

She looked up and met his gaze. "It does, doesn't it? It will only take me a minute to get my bonnet and coat."

Was she giving him another chance, or was this her way of saying a permanent goodbye? He closed his eyes and breathed a silent prayer, begging God for one more chance with the woman he loved. When he opened them, she was standing in front of him looking lovelier than ever.

"I'm ready."

That meant he had to be, too. *"Goot."*

They reached the road and he turned toward her home, but she stopped. "Would you mind if we went to the river?"

"I don't mind at all." She began walking, and he fell into step beside her.

A few straggling families from the school passed them. He politely turned aside several offers of a ride. Before long, the road was empty and they walked in silence. The crunch of snow under their feet was the only sound.

She looked up into the night sky. "How do the people in cities live without this beauty?"

"They have learned not to look. They pretend there is nothing above them." He wanted to hold her hand. Would she let him? He balled his fingers tight inside his coat pockets.

"How sad."

"It is a little, but people survive and thrive."

"The good Lord made us a resilient species."

"He did. Emma, can I ask you a question?"

"Certainly." She glanced at him shyly.

"Are you serious about Wayne?"

"Serious in what way?"

He stopped walking. "You know what I mean."

She hooked her arm through his. Astonished by the move, he let her pull him along. "I am no longer seriously considering Wayne as a suitor. Does that answer your question?"

"Is there anyone else?"

"Ja, there is."

His heart plunged to his boots. "Oh."

They reached the covered bridge and walked into the shadowy interior of the walkway. She shot him a sidelong glance. "Aren't you going to ask me who it is?"

He wasn't sure he wanted to know. So this was good-bye, then. "Whoever he is, he is a fortunate man."

"I'm glad you think so."

She stopped walking and turned to look out over the river. Luke leaned on the railing. Snow-covered trees lined the riverbanks. Overhead, the moon shone down, making it almost as bright as day. The dark water below them hissed and gurgled as it rushed around the pylons. Moonlight glinted in the ripples.

Emma looked at Luke. "Can I ask you a question?"

"Sure."

"Have you ever told a woman that you love her?"

"Never. I did tell a girl once when I was a foolish kid, but I didn't really know what those words meant. I've been wanting to say those words to one special woman. They burn in my heart."

"Why haven't you spoken of this?"

"Because I wasn't sure my feelings were returned. I couldn't imagine how they could be. The one I love deserves a much better man than I will ever be."

"You're not so bad. You have potential."

He grinned. "I do?"

"This woman you admire, she has faults, too. I'm sure of it."

"Only small ones."

"She not very humble. She is bossy and prideful."

"She is perfect because I only see her through the eyes of love. Don't tease me anymore, Emma. I love you with my whole heart and with my soul. I will love you forever if you give me the chance."

"That's a lot of love."

"Yes, it is." He pulled her into his arms. "Tell me that you love me, too."

Emma's heart swelled with joy. She had wanted to be in his arms for so long that it was hard to believe it was really happening. The words she had kept inside for years slipped effortlessly from her lips on a soft breath. "I love you, Luke Bowman. I always have. I always will."

"I don't deserve your love, Emma, but I will do everything within my power to be worthy of it until the day I die." He gently covered her lips with his own and Emma was swept away by the wonder of it.

Soft yet firm, the touch of his warm mouth against hers sent her mind reeling. The same wonderful feelings she remembered from her youth exploded in her chest, tempered by loss and honed by pain into an exquisite ache that made her press closer to him. All she wanted was to keep on kissing him. Her arms crept around his neck and he pulled her closer still.

He was the first to break away, drawing a deep unsteady breath that made her smile. He tucked her head beneath his chin. "I hate to be the practical one, but we should find somewhere warmer to continue this."

In the shadow of the covered bridge with the cold, bright moonlight sparkling on the icy waters below, Emma had never been warmer in her life. "I'm fine."

"I'm happy for you, but my toes are freezing."

She laughed. He could always make her laugh, and she loved that about him along with everything else, even his past. "Let's go to your house—it's closer."

He pulled her close again and kissed her. She didn't

resist. When he drew back, he cupped her cheek with his hand. "I don't know why God chose to send us on such a roundabout journey to this moment."

"To make it that much sweeter for us. So that we'll never take our feelings for granted."

"That's what I think, too." He bent and kissed her again.

She threaded her fingers through his hair and kept him close when he would have pulled away. "Your toes will thaw. We might not find this much time alone together for ages."

"That is why I want you to marry me. I plan to spend a lot of time kissing you. Will you marry me, Emma?"

"Gladly. And I plan to spend a great deal of time kissing you back." She smiled and did just that.

Epilogue

Alvin rushed into the kitchen. "I see them coming up the lane. They're almost here."

"Calm down." Emma smiled as she pulled on her coat. "You act as if you have never gone caroling before."

"I just want the people to like our songs and feel the happiness of the season."

Roy strolled into the room. "I remember the time you were so nervous to sing in front of people that you threw up on *Daed*'s shoes."

"I didn't."

"I believe that was you, Roy," Emma teased. She was secretly as excited as Alvin at the prospect of traveling to the community of Litchfield. Ten of the *kinder* from Alvin's school had been invited to sing at the nursing home there. Isaac Bowman was collecting some of the children and parents in his bobsled. They would meet up with the others at the retirement center and carol to various neighbors as they traveled home. And Luke would be with them. She couldn't imagine being happier.

Emma hustled her brothers outside. Her father waved

to them from the door. His store was ready to open the next morning but he didn't want to leave it. Emma had seen him walking up and down the aisles, touching some of the items, straightening them and dusting others. He was as happy as he could be among his things displayed for everyone to see. She prayed he would enjoy his store for many years before the Lord called him home.

The gray draft horses and large sled stopped in front of the house. Isaac had outfitted his sled with wagon sides and filled the interior with benches. There were already a dozen people aboard. The men and boys in dark coats and black hats marked the riders as members of the Amish faith. The women and girls wore dark coats and black bonnets with bright quilts spread over their laps.

Emma put out her arms to stop the boys from rushing down the steps. "Remember that you have been invited to share the joy of this season with people who may not have families to care for them or who may be too ill to be in their own homes. No rowdy behavior."

"*Ja,* sister," they said in unison.

With that, she stepped aside and watched them rush out. She settled her black traveling bonnet over her *kapp* and followed them. Luke was sitting in the driver's seat. Her pulse jumped a notch higher.

He tipped his hat to her. "My father has a head cold and has chosen to stay home. I hope you don't mind that I'm taking his place."

"Of course not." Spending an entire evening in Luke's company was exactly what she wanted to do. She climbed up and took a seat beside him.

Hannah leaned in between them. Her bright eyes

sparkled as she clapped her hands together. "I have new mittens. See?"

Emma dutifully inspected them. "They are very nice mittens."

"*Onkel* Luke bought them for me for Christmas 'cause I lost my others."

Emma smiled at him. "That was very nice of your *onkel*. You must be extra careful with them."

"I will. Did you get something for Christmas?"

"I did. My brothers bought me material for a new dress. Isn't that funny? Who would think of boys shopping for dress material? My father gave me a new set of dishes. They aren't exactly new, but they are new to me. They have pretty pink flowers on them."

"I like pink flowers."

"You should sit down, Hannah," Luke said. "The road is rough here and I don't want you to fall."

"Okay." She returned to her mother's side.

Emma shot him a sidelong glance. "The road is just as smooth here as anywhere else."

"I see that now, but I was sure it would be bumpy. Besides, I wanted you all to myself."

"I'd hardly think we can be alone with a sled full of people."

He leaned toward her. "Maybe not, but I can pretend when you're sitting beside me that we are the only two people in the world."

His soft whisper sent shivers down her spine. "I like that. I shall pretend the same." She inched a bit closer and settled in to enjoy the ride.

"God willing, we will ride many miles seated beside each other," he said with a wink.

"God willing we will have a daughter like Hannah to occasionally come between us."

"I think we will have boys. There are only sons in my family, after all. Eight sons, that's what I predict."

"Well, then, I shall predict eight girls to liven our lives."

Hannah popped up between them again. "*Mamm* says everyone can hear you."

Luke turned in his seat. "If everyone can hear me, I'd like to tell you that Emma has agreed to be my wife."

A cheer rose from his brothers. So much for secrecy. She yanked on his coat to turn him back around, then she scooted to the end of the wagon seat, leaving plenty of room between them.

"We should warm up our voices before we get there," Alvin suggested, and the others agreed. He led them in the scales and then started "O Little Town of Bethlehem." Everyone joined in. The horses picked up the pace and their bells jingled merrily. Luke grinned at her, reached out and pulled her close.

She settled happily beside him.

"What song next?" someone asked.

Hannah spoke up. "Alvin, will you sing 'The First Noel'?"

As her brother's beautiful voice rang out across the fields, Emma whispered to Luke, "What was Christmas like in the *Englisch* world?"

"Light, parties, they sing the same song and other silly ones. A plump fellow with a white beard gets all the credit for the holiday. I think there are people who truly don't know the meaning of the day. They don't know that God sent us the greatest gift in His only Son."

"How sad. They need to experience an Amish Noel."

Hannah leaned in between them again. "If all the *Englisch* came with us, this sled would be very crowded."

Luke gently pushed her back with a hand on her head. "It already is."

Hannah giggled and Emma scooted over to make room for her. Lifting the child to the front seat, Emma endured Luke's scowl. She knew it was faked. "Christmas is about sharing our joy. There is no better messenger than a child to show us the way."

Hannah looked at her. "I wasn't the messenger. I was an angel."

Luke hugged her and winked at Emma. "How right you are. Merry Christmas."

* * * * *

WE HOPE YOU
ENJOYED THIS

LOVE
INSPIRED®
BOOK.

If you were **inspired** by this

uplifting, **heartwarming** romance,

be sure to look for all six Love

Inspired® books every month.

Love Inspired®

www.LoveInspired.com

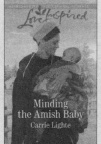

Love Inspired®

Save $1.00
on the purchase of ANY
Love Inspired® book.

Available wherever books are sold,
including most bookstores, supermarkets,
drugstores and discount stores.

Save $1.00
on the purchase of ANY Love Inspired® book.

Coupon valid until March 1, 2019.
Redeemable at participating retail outlets in the U.S. and Canada only.
Limit one coupon per customer.

52616235

5 65373 00076 2 (8100)0 12409

SPECIAL EXCERPT FROM

Love Inspired®

After returning to his Amish community after losing his job in the Englisch world, Aaron King isn't sure if he wants to stay. But the more time he spends training a horse with childhood friend Sally Stoltzfus, the more he begins to believe this is exactly where he belongs.

Read on for a sneak preview of
The Promised Amish Bride *by Marta Perry,*
available February 2019 from Love Inspired!

"Komm now, Aaron. I thought you might be ready to keep your promise to me."

"Promise?" He looked at her blankly.

"You can't have forgotten. You promised you'd wait until I grew up and then you'd marry me."

He stared at her, appalled for what seemed like forever until he saw the laughter in her eyes. "Sally Stoltzfus, you've turned into a threat to my sanity. What are you trying to do, scare me to death?"

She gave a gurgle of laughter. "You looked a little bored with the picnic. I thought I'd wake you up."

"Not bored," he said quickly. "Just…trying to find my way. So you don't expect me to marry you. Anything else I can do that's not so permanent?"

"As a matter of fact, there is. I want you to help me train Star."

So that was it. He frowned, trying to think of a way to refuse that wouldn't hurt her feelings.

"You saw what Star is like," she went on without waiting for an answer. "I've got to get him trained, and soon. And everyone knows that you're the best there is with horses."

"I don't think everyone believes any such thing," he retorted. "They don't know me well enough anymore."

She waved that away. "You've been working with horses

while you were gone. And Zeb always says you were born with the gift."

"Onkel Zeb might be a little bit prejudiced," he said, trying to organize his thoughts. There was no real reason he couldn't help her out, except that it seemed like a commitment, and he didn't intend to tie himself anywhere, not now.

"You can't deny that Star needs help, can you?" Her laughing gaze invited him to share her memory of the previous day.

"He needs help all right, but I don't quite see the point. Can't you use the family buggy when you need it?" He suspected that if he didn't come up with a good reason, he'd find himself working with that flighty gelding.

Her face grew serious suddenly. "As long as I do that, I'm depending on someone else. I want to make my own decisions about when and where I'm going. I'd like to be a bit independent, at least in that. I thought you were the one person who might understand."

That hit him right where he lived. He did understand— that was the trouble. He understood too well, and it made him vulnerable where Sally was concerned. He fumbled for words. "I'd like to help. But I don't know how long I'll be here and—"

"That doesn't matter." Seeing her face change was like watching the sun come out. "I'll take whatever time you can spare. Denke, Aaron. I'm wonderful glad."

He started to say that his words hadn't been a yes, but before he could, Sally had grabbed his hand and every thought flew right out of his head.

It was just like her catching hold of Onkel Zeb's arm, he tried to tell himself. But it didn't work. When she touched him, something seemed to light between them like a spark arcing from one terminal to another. He felt it right down to his toes, and he knew in that instant that he was in trouble.

Don't miss
The Promised Amish Bride *by Marta Perry,*
available February 2019 wherever
Love Inspired® *books and ebooks are sold.*